"Deana?"

Something popped, dim and dull. Bren heard the phone fall, he heard Deana's voice, muffled—he had the presence of mind to push Record—and to leave the phone open as he ran out into the hall. "Algini!" he yelled, and ran as far as the center hall, with servants staring in shock.

"Nand' paidhi!" Algini met him halfway to the foyer, gun in hand, servants gathering all around. "What's happened?"

"Hanks-paidhi's in trouble. Something's happened. Get security down there. I think it was gunfire. I was on the phone with her. Hurry!"

He wanted to go back to the phone again and hear what he could—but there was no assurance where the attack was aimed or where it might aim; he ducked into his bedroom, flung open dresser drawers, one after another, desperately searching beneath stacks of clothes for the gun Banichi had told him was there.

Sixth drawer on the left. He pulled it out from under sweaters, checked the clip as Tabini had shown him, his hands starting to shake as he shoved the clip back in. He stood up, tucked it in his coat under the bad arm, and exited his bedroom, headed down the hall to the private rooms, where he'd left the phone open to Hank's apartment.

The line sounded dead, now. He couldn't tell. He laid down the phone, left the recorder going.

He went back out into the hall, light to his left, darkness to his right—covering darkness, darkness that didn't cast a shadow.

He walked briskly down the hall—found the breakfast room all dark, the white gauze curtains resting still, in moonlight. He moved them aside, assured of his invisibility there.

Then he felt a draft—saw the curtains move, and realized to his dismay the farther door was open.

He moved to shut it and felt a faint presence on his side of the room—he couldn't see it, he couldn't identify it . . . he couldn't swear it was there. Panic sweated his palms.

The glass doors near him burst in gunfire, curtains billowed, glass fell in shards, and the presence he'd felt hurtled out of the dark, knocked him stunned to the floor. . . .

Coming in hardcover in April, 1996

C.J. CHERRYH
INVADER

DAW BOOKS, INC.

DONALD A. WOLLHEIM, FOUNDER

375 Hudson Street, New York, NY 10014

ELIZABETH R. WOLLHEIM
SHEILA E. GILBERT
PUBLISHERS

DAW Books are distributed by Penguin U.S.A.

First Paperback Printing, February 1996

1 2 3 4 5 6 7 8 9

DAW TRADEMARK REGISTERED
U.S. PAT OFF. AND FOREIGN COUNTRIES
—MARCA REGISTRADA.
HECHO EN U.S.A.

PRINTED IN THE U.S.A.

For Jane

1

The plane had entered the steep bank and descent that heralded a landing at Shejidan. Bren Cameron knew that approach for the north runway in his sleep and with his eyes shut.

Which had been the case. The painkillers had kicked in with a vengeance. He'd been watching the clouds over Mospheira Strait, the last he knew, and the attendants must have rescued his drink, because the glass was gone from the napkin-covered tray.

One arm in a sling and multiple contusions. Surgery.

This morning—he was sure it had been this morning, if he retained any real grasp of time—he'd waked with a Foreign Office staffer, not his mother, not Barb, leaning over his bed and telling him . . . God, he'd lost half of it, something about an urgent meeting, the aiji demanding his immediate presence, a governmental set-to that didn't wait for him to convalesce from the last one, that he thought he'd settled at least enough to wait a few days. Tabini had given him leave, told him go—consult his own doctors.

But the crisis over their heads wouldn't wait, evidently: he'd had no precise details from the staffer regarding the situation on the mainland—not in itself surprising, since the human government on Mospheira and the aiji's association centered at Shejidan didn't talk to each other with that level of frankness regarding internal affairs.

The two governments didn't, as a matter of fact, talk at all without him to translate and mediate. He wasn't sure just how Shejidan had made the request for his presence without him to translate it, but whoever had made the call had evidently made Mospheira believe it was a life-and-death urgency.

"Mr. Cameron, let me put the tray up."

"Thanks." The sling was a first for him. He skied, aggressively, when he got the chance; in his twenty-seven years he'd spent two sessions on crutches. But an arm out of commission was a new experience, and a real inconvenience, he'd already discovered, to anything clerical he needed to do.

The tray went up and locked. The attendant helped him with the seat back, extracted the ends of the safety belt from his seat—and would have snapped it for him: being casted from his collarbone to his knuckles and taped about the chest didn't make bending or reaching easier. But at least the cast had left his fingers free, just enough to hold on to things. He managed to take the belt in his own fingers, pull the belt sideways and forward and fasten the buckle himself, before he let it snap back against his chest, small triumph in a day of drugged, dim-witted frustrations.

He wished he hadn't taken the painkiller. He'd had no idea it was as strong as it was. They'd said, if you need it, and he'd thought, after the scramble to get his affairs in the office in order and then to get to the airport, that he'd needed it to take the edge off the pain.

And woke up an hour later in descent over the capital.

He hoped Shejidan had gotten its signals straight, and that somebody besides the airport officials knew what time he was coming in. Flights between Mospheira and the mainland, several a day, only carried freight on their regular schedule. This small, forward, windowed compartment, which most times served for fragile medical freight, acquired, on any flight he was aboard, two part-time flight attendants, two seats, a wine list and a microwave. It constituted the only passenger service between Mospheira and the mainland for the only passenger who regularly made trips between Mospheira and the mainland: himself, Bren Cameron, the paidhi-aiji.

The very closely guarded paidhi-aiji, not only the official translator, but the arbiter of technological research and development; and the mediator, regularly, between the atevi capital at Shejidan and the island enclave of human colonists on Mospheira.

Wheels down.

The clouds that had made a smooth gray carpet outside the window became a total, blind environment as the plane glided into the cloud deck.

Water spattered the window. The plane bounced in mild buffeting.

Unexpectedly rotten weather. Lightning whitened the wing. The attendants had mentioned rain moving in at Shejidan. But they hadn't said thunderstorm. He hoped the aiji had a car waiting for him. He hoped there wouldn't be a hike of any distance.

Rain streaked the windows, a heavy gray moil of cloud cutting off all view. He'd arrived in Malguri, far across the continent, on a day like this—what? a week or so ago. It seemed an incredibly long time. The whole world had changed in that week.

Changed in the whole balance of atevi power and threat—by the appearance of a single human ship that was now orbiting the planet. Atevi might reasonably suspect that this human ship came welcome. Atevi might easily have that misapprehension—after a hundred and seventy-eight years of silence from the heavens.

It had also been a hundred seventy-eight years of stranded, ground-bound humans on Mospheira making their own decisions and arranging their own accommodations with the earth of the atevi. Humans had been well satisfied—until this ship appeared, not only confounding individual humans whose lives had been calm, predictable, and prosperous in their isolation—but suddenly giving atevi *two* human presences to deal with, when they'd only in the most recent years reached a thoroughly peaceful accommodation with the humans on the island off their shores.

So, one could imagine that the aiji in Shejidan, lord of the Western Association, quite reasonably wanted to know what was in those transmissions that now flowed between that ship and the earth station on Mospheira.

The paidhi wanted to know that answer himself. Something in the last twenty-four hours had changed in the urgency of his presence here—but he had no special brief from the President or State Department to provide those answers, not one damned bit of instruction at least that he'd been conscious enough to remember. He did have a firsthand and still fresh understanding that if things went badly and relations between humans and atevi blew up, this side of the strait would not be a safe place for a human to be: humans and atevi had already fought one bloody war over mistaken intentions. He didn't know if he could single-handedly prevent another; but there was always, constantly inherent in the paidhi's job, the knowledge that if the future of humankind on Mospheira and in this end of the universe wasn't in his power to direct—it was damned sure within his power to screw up.

One fracture in the essential Western Association—one essential leader like the aiji of Shejidan losing position.

One damned fool human with a radio transmitter or one atevi hothead with a hunting rifle—and of the latter, there were entirely too many available on the mainland for his own peace of mind: guns meant food on the table out in the countryside. Atevi youngsters learned to shoot when human kids were learning to ride bikes—and some atevi got damned good at it. Some atevi became licensed professionals, in a society where assassination was a regular legal recourse.

And if Tabini-aiji lost his grip on the Western Association, and if that started fragmenting, everything came undone. Atevi had provinces, but they didn't have borders. Atevi couldn't understand lines on maps by anything logical or reasonable except an approximation of where the householders on that line happened to side on various and reasonable grounds affecting their area, their culture, their scattered loyalties to other associations with nothing in the world to *do* with geography.

In more than that respect, it wasn't a human society in the world beyond the island of Mospheira, and if the established atevi authority went down, after nearly two hundred years of building an industrial complex and an interlinked power structure uniting hundreds of small atevi associations—

—it would be his personal fault.

The plane broke through the cloud deck, rain making trails on the window, crooked patterns that fractured the outward view of a city skyline with no tall buildings, a few smokestacks. Tiled roofs, organized by auspicious geometries atevi eyes understood, marched up and down the rain-veiled hills.

The wing dipped, the slats extended as they passed near the vast governmental complex that was his destination: the Bu-javid, the aiji's residence, dominating the highest hill on the edge of Shejidan, a hill footed by hotels and hostels of every class, a little glimmer of— God—audacious neon in the gray haze.

Witness atevi democracy in plain evidence, in those hotels. In the regular audiences and in emergency matters, petitioners lodged there, ordinary people seeking personal audience with the ruler of the greatest association in the world.

In their seasons of legislative duty, lawmakers of the elected hasdrawad occupied the same hotel rooms, with their security and their staffs. Even a handful of the tashrid, those newly ennobled who lacked ancestral arrangements within the Bu-javid itself, found lodging for themselves and their staffs in those pay-by-the-night rooms at the foot of the hill, shoulder to shoulder with shopkeepers, bricklayers, numerologists and television news crews.

With the long-absent emergency hanging literally over the world, the hotels down there were crammed right now and service in the restaurants was, bet on it, in collapse. The legislative committees would all be in session. The hasdrawad and the tashrid would be in full cry. Unseasonal petitioners would batter the doors of the aiji's numerous secretaries, seeking exception for immediate audience for whatever special, threatened interests they represented. Technical experts, fanatic number-counters and crackpot theorists would be jostling each other in the halls of the Bu-javid—because in atevi thinking, all the

universe was describable in numbers; numbers were felicitous or not felicitous: numbers blessed or doomed a project, and there were a thousand different systems for
reckoning the significant numbers in a matter—all of
them backed by absolute, wild-eyed believers.

God help the process of intelligent decisions.

The runway was close now. He watched the ware-
houses and factories of Shejidan glide under the wing:
factory-tops, at the last, rain-pocked puddles on their as-
phalt and gravel, a drowned view of ventilation fans and
a company logo outlined in gravel. He'd never seen
Aqidan Pipe & Fittings from the ground. But it, along
with the spire of Western Mining and Industry and the
roof of Patanandi Aerospace, was the reassuring landmark
of all his homecomings to this side of the strait.

Curious notion, that Shejidan had become a refuge.

He hadn't even seen his mother this trip to Mospheira.
She hadn't come to the hospital. He'd phoned her when
he'd gotten in—he'd gotten time for three phone calls in
his hospital room before they knocked him halfway out
with painkillers and ran him off for tests. He distinctly remembered he'd phoned her, spoken with her, told her
where he was, said he'd be in surgery in the morning.
He'd told her, playing down the matter, that she didn't
need to come, she could call the hospital for a report
when he came to. But he'd honestly and secretly hoped
she'd come, maybe show a little maternal concern.

He'd phoned his brother Toby, too, long distance to the
northern seacoast where Toby and his wife lived. Toby
had said he was sure he was all right, he was very glad
he'd turned up back on the job under the present
conditions—which the paidhi couldn't, of course, discuss
with his family, so they didn't discuss it; and that had
been that.

He'd called Barb last: he'd known beyond any doubt
that Barb would come to the hospital, but Barb hadn't answered her phone. He'd left a message on the system: Hi,
Barb, don't believe the news reports, I'm all right. Hope
to see you while I'm here.

But it had been just a Departmental staffer leaning over

his bed when he woke, saying, How are you feeling, Mr. Cameron?

And: We really hope you're up to this. . . .

Thanks, he'd said.

What else could you say? Thanks for the flowers?

Wheels touched, squeaked on wet pavement. He stared out through water-streaked windows at an ash-colored sky, a rainy concrete vista of taxiways, terminal, a functional, blockish architecture, that could, if he didn't know better, be the corresponding international airport on Mospheira.

A team from National Security had taken charge of his computer while he was down-timed on a hospital gurney; State Department experts and the NSA had probably walked all through his files, from his personal letters to his notes for his speeches and his dictionary notes, but they'd had to rush. He'd expected, even knowing his recall would be soon, at least one day to lie in the sun.

But something having hit crisis level, when the security team had picked him up at the hospital emergency desk to take him to his office, they'd handed his computer back to him and given him thirty minutes in his office on the way to the airport—thirty whole minutes, on the systemic remnant of anesthetic and painkillers, to access the files he expected to need, load in the new security overlay codes, and dispose of a request from the President's secretary for a briefing the President apparently wasn't going to get. Meanwhile he'd sent his personal Seeker through the system with all flags flying, to get what it could—whatever his staff, the Foreign Office, the State Department and his various correspondents had sent to him.

In the rush, he didn't even know what files he'd actually gotten, what he might have gotten if he'd argued vigorously with the State Department censors, or what in the main DB might have changed. They'd had an uncommonly narrow window of authorization for their plane to enter atevi airspace, itself an indicator of increased tensions: they'd driven like hell getting to the airport, bumped all Mospheiran local aircraft out of schedule, as it was, and when he'd just gotten served a fruit juice and they'd reached altitude, where he planned to work for his hour in the air, he'd dropped off to sleep watching the clouds.

He'd thought—just rest his eyes. Just shut out the sunlight, such a fierce lot of sunlight, above the clouds. He wasn't sure even now the damned painkiller was out of his system. Things floated. His thoughts skittered about at random, no idea what he was facing, no solid memory what the man from the Department had told him.

The plane made the relatively short taxi not to the regular debarkation point but to the blind, windowless end of the passenger terminal. He managed to get unbelted, and as the plane shut down its engines, cast an expectant look at the attendants for help with his stowed luggage, and gathered himself up carefully out of the seat.

One attendant pulled his luggage from the stowage by the galley. He defended his computer as his own problem, despite the other attendant's reach to help him with that. "The coat, please," he said, and turned his back for help to get it on—one slightly edge-of-season coat he'd had in reserve in Mospheira, atevi-style, many-buttoned and knee-length. He got the one arm in the sleeve, accepted the other onto his immobile shoulder—the damned coat tended to slide, and if it were Mospheira, in summer, he wouldn't bother; but this was Shejidan and a gentleman absolutely wore a coat in public.

A gentleman absolutely took care to have his braid neatly done, too, with the included ribbons indicative of his status and his lineage; but the atevi public would have to forgive him: he'd had no one but the orderly at the hospital to put his hair in the requisite braid. He'd intended to protect it from the seat-rest during the flight, but after his unintended nap, he didn't know what condition it was in. He bowed his head now and managed one-handed to pull it from under the coat collar without losing the coat off his shoulder, felt an unwelcome wisp of flyaway by his cheek and tried to tuck it in.

Then he picked up his computer, eased the strap onto his good shoulder and made his unhurried way forward, an embarrassingly disreputable figure, he feared, by court standards.

But he'd gotten here, he hoped *with* the files he needed to work with, and he hoped to get to the Bu-javid without undue delay and without public notice. If everyone who was supposed to communicate had communicated and if the aiji hadn't been in nonstop meetings, he should have a car waiting as soon as they moved the ladder up. It thundered, sounding right overhead, and the paidhi prayed that he at least had a car waiting.

He had to remember, too, that he was now leaving the venue where seats and tables and doorways fit people his size: the stairs out there had a higher rise, and he was, lacking the use of one hand, feeling chill and rather petulantly fragile at the moment.

"Thank you," he said to the attendants who opened the aircraft door. The staircase was moving up—*not* the canopied portable, much less the covered walk: it bumped into contact, rocking the plane, and one attendant set his luggage out on the rainy landing at the top of a shaky, rain-wet, metal ladder.

No car. It wasn't going well. Everything had the feeling of haste exceeding planning. Wind-driven mist whipped through the open doorway, and he was ready to go back where it was dry, when a van with the airport security logo whisked from around the nose and braked just short of an epic puddle, so abrupt an arrival his security-conscious nerves had twitched, his whole body poised to fling himself backward.

"Take care, sir. The steps are higher."

"I know. I know, thank you, though. Good flight. Thank you so much. Thank the crew." He raised a shoulder to keep the computer strap in place and felt a sudden, perilous challenge of balance as he ventured out onto the stairs into the wind-borne spatter of rain. He grabbed the rail, shoulder still canted, struggling not to let the computer strap slip off.

The van's side door opened. An armed atevi, a brisk dark giant in the silver-studded black of Bu-javid security and the aiji's personal guard, exited the van and raced up the steps, making the stairs rattle and shake under atevi muscle.

"Nadi Bren!" a woman's voice hailed him, and a bleak day brightened.

"Jago!"

"I'll take that, nadi Bren. Give me your hand." Two steps below him, Jago stood eye to eye with him. She seized the computer strap on his shoulder, took it from him in relentless courtesy and captured his chilled white hand in her large black one, competency, solidity in a thunderous, wind-blown world. He had no doubt at all Jago could catch him if he slipped—no doubt that she could carry him down the steps in one arm if she had to.

And on his tottery, rain-blasted way down the ladder, he was not at all surprised, having encountered Jago, to see Banichi exit the van more slowly to welcome them.

He was glad it was them. God, he was relieved—

He was so relieved he had a dizzy spell, forgot the scale of the next step, and if Jago hadn't had an instant and solid grip under his good arm he'd have gone down for sure.

"Careful," she said, hauling him back to balance. "Careful, Bren-ji, the steps are slick."

Slick. Lightning flashed overhead, whiting out detail, glancing off the puddle. He reached the bottom rubber-legged as Banichi stepped out of the way for him and for Jago, who helped him into the van and climbed in after.

Banichi brought up the rear, swung up and in and slammed the door, sealing out the rain and the thunder. Like Jago, black leather and silver studs, black skin, black hair, gold eyes, Banichi fell into the available door-side seat, saving his leg from flexing, Bren didn't fail to note, as he settled next to the far window.

"Go," Jago said to the driver.

"My luggage," Bren protested as the van jerked into motion.

"Tano will bring it. There's a second van."

Tano was another familiar name, a man he was exceedingly glad to know was alive.

"Algini?" he asked, meaning Tano's partner.

"Malguri Hospital," Banichi said. "How *are* you, Bren-ji?"

Far better than he'd thought. People were alive that he'd feared dead.

But other people, good people, had died for mistaken, stupid reasons.

"Is there word—" His voice cracked as he leaned back against the seat. "Is there word from Malguri? From Djinana? Are they all right?"

"One can inquire," Jago said.

He hadn't remotely realized he was so shaky. Maybe it was the sudden feeling of safety. Maybe it was the haste he'd been in back on Mospheira to gather everything he needed. His mind wandered back into the web of atevi proprieties, lost in the mindset that didn't allow Banichi or Jago the simple opportunity to inquire about—

Atevi didn't have friends. God, God, wipe the word from his mind. Twenty-four hours across the strait and he was thinking in Mosphei', making psychological slips like that, a dim-witted slide toward what was human, when he was no longer in human territory.

The van swerved around a corner, and they all leaned. It was summer in Shejidan, but they seemed to have the heater on, all the same, because the clammy chill was gone. He leaned his head back on the seat, blinked his stinging eyes and asked, as the straightening of the course rolled his head toward Banichi, "Are we taking the subway out, or what?"

"Yes," Banichi told him.

Banichi hadn't come up the ramp after him.

"The leg, Banichi?"

"No detriment, nand' paidhi. I assure you."

To his efficiency, Banichi meant. Back on mainland soil and he'd assigned Jago a diplomatically touchy inter-staff inquiry and insulted Banichi's judgment and competency. He didn't know how he could improve on it.

"Ignore my stupid questions," he said. "Drugs. Just got out of hospital. I took a painkiller. I shouldn't have."

"How did the surgery go?" Jago asked.

He tried to remember. "I forgot to ask," he admitted,

and didn't know why he hadn't, except that in some con-
voluted, drug-hazed fashion he'd taken for granted he was
going to have a shoulder that worked. He hoped so.

Hell, it felt as if he'd picked up where he'd left his life
yesterday—was it yesterday?—and everything about
Mospheira was a passing dream. It felt good, it felt *safe*
to be back with these two. He wasn't tracking outstand-
ingly well on anything at the moment, except that between these two individuals he felt he could handle
anything.

If these two were here, he knew that Tabini, none other,
had sent them.

The van's tires made a wet sound on the airport pavement. He let his eyes shut. He could let down his propriety with these two, who'd lived intimately with him,
who'd cared for him when he was far less than self-
possessed—and he'd know even blind that he was in
Shejidan, not Mospheira. He knew by the smells of rain-
wet leather and the warmth of atevi bodies, the slight
scent that attended them, which might be perfume, or
might be natural—it was an odd thing that he'd never
quite questioned it, but it was pleasant and familiar, in the
way old rooms and accustomed places were comfortable
to find.

The van nosed down an incline, and he blinked a look
at his surroundings, knowing where they were before he
used his eyes: the ramp down into the utilitarian concrete
of the restricted underground terminal. The aiji used it—
the aiji and others whose safety and privacy the government wanted to guarantee.

He'd discovered a comfortable position in which to sit,
good shoulder against the van wall. He truly, truly didn't
want to move right now.

"I trust," he said, shutting his eyes again, "that there'll
be a chance for me to rest, nadiin. I really, really hope to
rest a while before I have to think or do anything truly
critical."

Jago's fingers brushed his shoulder. "Bren-ji, we can
carry you to the car if you wish."

The van braked to a halt. "No," he said, and remembering that these two afforded themselves no weakness and rarely a sign of pain, he opened his eyes and tried to drag himself back to the gray concrete and echoing world. "I'll manage, thank you, nadiin, but, please, let's just wait for my luggage. I have every confidence in Tano. But it's only a single case. It has my medical records."

"We've orders, nadi," Banichi said.

Tabini's orders. No question. No dawdling even in a secure area. Possibly there had been some filing of Intent against his life, but most likely it was simply Tabini's desire to have the paidhi in place, under a guard he trusted, and to have one more ragged-edged problem off his mind.

Banichi opened the door and stepped down to the pavement, Jago got out after, taking the computer, and Bren edged across the seat and stepped down with less assurance, into their competent and watchful care.

The subway had its own peculiar atmosphere: oil, cold concrete and echoes of machinery and voices—like any station in the city system, like any in the continent-spanning rail that linked to the city subway; a connection which argued there could be a small risk of some security breach, he supposed, but no one came into this station without a security clearance, not the baggage handlers, not the workmen: cars didn't stop here.

Which meant there was no burning reason now, in his unregarded and probably uninformed opinion, that the paidhi couldn't stand about for half a minute and wait for his luggage—but considering the wobble in his knees and the disorientation that came buzzing through his brain with the white noise of the echoing space, he let himself be moved along the trackside at Banichi's best limping pace.

A pair of Bu-javid guards, standing outside on the platform, opened the door of the car—seemingly a freight-carrier—that waited for them. They were guards he didn't know, but clearly Banichi did, sufficiently that Banichi sent Jago into the car for no more than a cursory look before letting Bren inside.

It was residential-style furnishing inside the car, false windows inside curtained in red velvet. It was the aiji's own traveling salon, plush appointments, the whole affair in muted reds and beige, a complete galley, soft chairs— Bren let himself down in one that wouldn't swallow him in its cushions, and Jago, setting the computer down, went immediately to open the galley, asking him did he want fruit juice?

"Tea, nadi, if you please." He still felt chilled, and his ears had felt stuffed with wool since the change in altitude. Tea sounded good. Alkaloids that atevi metabolisms didn't mind at all in ordinary doses were especially common in herbal teas and concentrated in some atevi liquor, a fact he'd proved the hard way: but Banichi's junior partner wouldn't make mistakes like that with her charge. He shut his eyes in complete confidence and only opened them when Jago gently announced the tea was ready, the train was about to couple the car on, and would he care for a cup now?

He would. He took the offered cup in his hand, as Banichi, having made it aboard, shut the outside door and went on talking to someone, doubtless official, on his pocket-com.

Jago cradled her cup against the gentle bump as the coupling engaged. "We're a three-car train," Jago said, settling opposite him.

"Tano's made it on," Banichi said as he came up and joined them. "Station security wouldn't let him in this car. I did point out he's in the same service, little that penetrates the minds in charge."

Bren didn't worry that much about his luggage at the moment. Climbing up the high step to the car had waked up the pain in his shoulder.

But after half a cup of tea, and with the train approaching the terminal in the Bu-javid's lower levels, he recovered a wistful hope of homecoming, his own bed—if security afforded him that favor.

"Do you think, nadiin, that I'll possibly have my garden apartment back?"

"No," Banichi said. "I fear not. I'll inquire. But it's a fine view of the mountains, where you're going."

"The mountains." He was dismayed. "The upper floor? —Or a hotel?"

"A very fine accommodation. A staunch partisan has made you her personal guest, openly preferring the aiji's apartment for the session."

A staunch partisan. Tabini-aiji's staunch partisan. Tabini's apartment.

The train began braking. Jago extended her hand for the cup.

Damiri?

Tabini's hitherto clandestine lover? Of the Atigeini opposition?

My God. Damiri had declared herself. Her relatives were going to riot in the streets.

And a *human* for Tabini's next-door neighbor, even temporarily, lodged in an area of the Bu-javid only the highest and most ancient lords of the Association attained?

A human didn't belong there. Not there—and certainly not in a noble and respectable lady's private quarters. There was bound to be gossip. Coarse jokes. Detriment to the lady and the lady's family, whose regional association had openly opposed Tabini's policies from the day of his accession as aiji-major.

Slipping indeed. He must have let his dismay reach his face: Banichi said, as the brakes squealed, "Tabini wants you alive at any cost, nand' paidhi. Things are very delicate. The lady has made her wager on Tabini, and on Tabini's resourcefulness, with the dice still falling."

Baji-naji. Fortune and chance, twin powers of atevi belief, intervenors in the rigid tyranny of numbers.

The car came to rest.

The doors opened. Banichi was easily on his feet, offering a hand. Bren moved more slowly, promising himself that in just a little while he could have a bed, a place to lie still and let his head quit buzzing.

Jago gathered up his computer. "I'll manage it, Bren-ji. Take care for yourself. Please don't fall."

"I assure you," he murmured, and followed Banichi's lead to the door, down again, off the steps, into what he assumed was tight security—at least as tight as afforded no chance of meetings.

"Bren Cameron," a voice echoed out, a female voice, sharp, human and angry.

"Deana?" Deana Hanks didn't belong in the equation. She'd been out of communication, the fogged brain added back in; he'd asked that her authorizations be pulled by the Foreign Office, and he'd assumed—*assumed* she'd gone home. His successor had *no* legitimate business on the mainland.

Had she?

Things had moved too fast today and she was late for the airport. Mad, he was sure. Technically she should have met him at the airport, giving the plane just enough time to fuel and take on cargo, and be airborne inside an hour.

All of which was at the rear of his mind as he extended a friendly left hand, glad she was all right. "This is a surprise. Thank you for the backup."

"Thank you, hell!"

One didn't take a hostile tone around atevi. Guards' hands twitched toward pockets, inside coats, both her security, and his.

"Hata-mai," he said quickly, *It's all right,* and lapsed back into the atevi language. "Deana, nadi, may we be a little softer, please? I'm sure the plane will wait for you."

"Softer, is it?" She was a dark-haired woman, pale-skinned, flushed about the face most times that he ever dealt with her. She wore an atevi-style coat and had her hair in the court braid, the same as he did. Her atevi escort made an anxious wall behind her. "Softer? Is the government caving in to blackmail now? Is this the best answer they could come up with? They deliver ultimatums and we jump?"

"Nadi, if you please—"

"I'll the hell speak Mosphei', thank you. I want a report. I want to know where you were, I want to know what you were doing, I want to know who you were talking to and what you reported to whom, and I'll talk in the office, this afternoon."

It must be the pain pill. He wasn't tracking that well. Maybe he'd personally affronted the woman—not hard, considering Deana's temper, but he was determined she be on that outbound plane. Two humans weren't ever supposed to be this side of the strait at the same time. "We can settle this by fax. I'll brief you. But you've got a flight to catch."

"Oh, of course, of *course* I have. —I haven't any recall order, Mr. Cameron. Of course, without communications, there's damned little I do hear but court gossip. —And threats against this office. I want written orders. I take it you brought them with you."

"I—don't think they've ever been required."

"Nadi Bren," Jago said. "Please. Let's be moving."

"You *take* orders, nadi," Hanks snapped. "This is a matter inside our office, no local concern."

"Ms. Hanks." She'd insulted Jago. That was the last straw. "You're not talking to building security, if you haven't noticed the braid. And if you want an order, you've got an order. You're relieved of duty, your codes are invalid, your presence is no longer required. Get on that plane."

"Get me an order from Mospheira. I don't take it from you. And I've received *nothing* from Foreign Affairs except the advisement you were going back to Mospheira on a medical."

"Well, clearly I'm back."

"Not officially, Mr. Cameron. Not to me."

"I suggest, nadiin," Banichi said, moving between, and addressing Hanks' guards, "that you take this woman out of Bren-paidhi's way or face administrative procedures. Or mine. You *are* in error, nadiin, don't make more of it—I advise you."

There was threat in the air. All of a sudden Bren sensed resistance from Hanks' escort, aggression from Banichi—who surely had authority. He felt his heart speed, which the pain pill didn't want to have happen.

But Hanks' escort moved to take her out of his path—

He didn't know how it happened—suddenly he had a maneuvering wall of atevi between him and the world, and no one even hit him, as far as he realized, but he felt a painful jolt as he stumbled against the concrete station wall. He cradled his casted arm out of the way as an ateva overshadowed him and seized his good arm.

He ducked to the side, to the limit he could, caught sight of Hanks and her guards. "You," he yelled out, "be on that plane, Ms. Hanks. You're entirely out of line!"

"Show me the order from the Department."

"I'll show you an arrest warrant, next thing *you* see."

"Bren-ji," Jago said, and with an inexorable grip on his arm, hurried him toward the lift, as he heard angry atevi voices behind them, Banichi ordering Hanks' guards to get her back to her residency and *not* to the airport.

Which countermanded *his* orders, ominous note; Banichi derived his authority and his instructions from Tabini; and Banichi was in no good mood as he overtook them at the lift door. They went inside; Banichi followed them in and pushed the lift button to take them up.

"Banichi-ji," Bren said. "I fear I aggravated the situation. Not to excuse it, but she believes she was slighted in the Department sending me here without notice to her. That was the gist of it."

"Nadi," Banichi said, still hot. "I will report that interpretation to those who can judge."

He'd never seen Banichi this angry, not even under fire, and he wasn't inspired to continue on the subject. It wanted extensive phone calls to straighten this one out—one hoped before the plane received orders to clear atevi airspace. Hanks had been, even on a second and third thought, entirely out of line back there. He couldn't read what was afoot—except that Hanks belonged on that outbound plane, and that, slow-witted as he might be thanks to the painkiller, he wasn't taking undue offense.

It wasn't a friendship. He and Hanks had never liked each other, not in university, not in the Foreign Office, not in the halls of the Department. Their candidacies for the office had had different political supporters. He'd won; he'd become Wilson-paidhi's designated successor. She'd ended up as alternate, being far less fluent—she'd had the political patronage in the executive of the Department, but he'd had her on technicalities and nuances of the language in ways the selection process couldn't ignore, no matter Hanks' friends in high places.

But that she met him, clearly in breach of the Treaty, and threw a public tantrum—God, he didn't know what insanity had gotten into the woman. It shook him.

Probably she'd been blindsided as he'd been—one branch of the State Department moving faster than Shawn Tyers in the Foreign Affairs branch could get hold of the paidhi-successor through the phone system, possibly this afternoon.

Or, equally a possibility during any crisis between atevi and humans or atevi and atevi, the phone system might be shut down between Mospheira and the mainland. An hours-long phone blackout was certainly no excuse for Hanks' outburst; it was precisely when the paidhi was most supposed to use his head. He hadn't *liked* Hanks, but he'd never considered her a total fool.

The arm ached from the jolt he'd taken against the wall. He wasn't up to physical or mental confrontations today. Banichi had apparently reacted in temper, a first; Hanks had blown up; and, what was more, Hanks' security had been set personally in the wrong, publicly embarrassed and outranked. You didn't do that to atevi loyal to you. You didn't put them in that position.

An atevi internal crisis, which he greatly feared could be the occasion of his precipitate recall—some shake-up ricocheting through atevi government—was no time to fine-tune his successor's grasp of protocols, especially when she went so far as to attack *him* in public and launch her security against his, who, on loan from Tabini himself, far outranked her middling-rank guards. This performance deserved a report and a strong warning.

More immediately, he needed to get on the phone to Tabini *and* Mospheira and get Hanks out of here. They could assuredly hold the plane for Hanks. There was no more important cargo Mospheiran Air carried than the paidhi and the paidhi-successor in transit, and it could sit there until they got Hanks aboard.

Two phone calls necessitated, Hanks and a security

glitch, inside a minute of debarking; God, he had much rather go to the apartment he knew, his comfortable little affair on the lower tier of the building. It had a bed he was used to and servants he could deal with—

And a garden door, which had, in the paidhi's suddenly critical and controversial rise to prominence in atevi society, become an egregious security hazard.

That fact came through to him with particular force as the lift cranked to a halt and he saw the floor indicator saying, not 1, the public level, but 3, the tightest security not only in the Bu-javid but anywhere on the mainland.

2

The Atigeini residence certainly lacked, in Bren's estimation, the charm of his single room on the lower garden court—but one couldn't apply a word like charm to a palace.

There was a staff of, Jago informed him, setting down his computer beside the reception room door, fifty. Fifty servants to keep the place in order.

Grand baroque, maybe. Extravagance, definitely.

Gilt and silver wash on the cabinets and tables.

Priceless murals. Gilded carvings. He only wanted a bed. A place, a closet, a couch to sit on, anywhere to let his arm stop aching.

"Nadiin," a woman said, bowing, as she met them in the foyer, "nand' paidhi. My name is Saidin, chief of staff. Welcome."

"Nand' Saidin," Bren murmured, and reflexively returned the bow, stiff arm and all. She was clearly a woman of dignity and proper decorum, even gifted on the sudden with a human guest. "I regret very much disarranging the staff. Thank you so much for your courtesy."

"Our lady is pleased to provide you comfort, nand' paidhi. Would you care to see the arrangement of the premises?"

Banichi frowned and looked to him for opinion—but one could hardly, under the circumstances of being offered a palace, decline the honor.

"I'd be delighted, nand' Saidin. Thank you."

"Please do us the honor," Saidin murmured, and walked ahead of him, Banichi and Jago close behind. Saidin was middle-aged, slender—her coat was beige brocade, her slippers matching, in the very latest fashion; her braid was a simple affair, incorporating pink and green ribbons in the heraldic style of centuries of service to aristocracy. She was of that class of servants, clearly, born, not hired, to the lifelong duty of a particular house to which she was possibly, though unofficially, related. He knew the type—the sort of woman, he thought, who deserved both respect for her position and understanding for her passionate devotion to the premises.

"This is the outer section, nand' paidhi, which serves all the formal functions, with the state dining room, the reception salon, the post-of-guard, which has been modernized. . . . The inner rooms are the master bedrooms, each with bath. The bedrooms all give out onto a circular salon surrounding the private dining hall. . . ."

Hand-loomed carpets and needlework drapes. The paidhi was never, in the interests of his job, a cultural illiterate, and the areas of his brain that didn't at the moment have all they could handle in etiquette, security and the animal instincts of balance, were respectfully absorbing all the nuances of regional and period design around him. Mospheira imported handmade as well as synthetic fabrics, some very expensive, but Mospheira had seen this kind of work only once, a single sample in a glass case in the War Museum.

And in this apartment, far more extravagant than Tabini's own, one walked on such carpets. In the reception salon next to the entry, one looked out clear glass windows past priceless draperies, intricately figured in muted gold, to the same view that Tabini's apartment enjoyed next door: the tiled roofs of the historic Old City spread out below the hill, the blue range of the Bergid— scantly visible on this stormy evening, beneath gray and burdened clouds. Wind, rain-laden, breathed through the apartment from open windows and hidden vents alike. He'd transited climates as well as provinces, begun to feel summer was decidedly over, and, now, felt as if he'd skipped across months and come in on another spring, another world, a situation months, not days, removed.

The paidhi was a little giddy. Doing surprisingly well,

considering. He wasn't sorry to have the tour. He'd grown not merely security conscious but security obsessive in recent days. He wanted to know the lay of the place, and whether there were outside doors, and whether a footfall echoing from one direction was surely a servant and from the other potentially an intruder.

"Are there other outside doors?" he asked. "Even scullery exits?"

"All external exits are to the foyer," Banichi said. "Very secure."

"There have been extensive revisions in the early part of this century," Saidin said. "You'll notice, however, that the stone and the wood matches exactly. Lord Sarosi did personal research to locate the old quarry, which presently supplies stone for other restorations within the Bu-javid, including the new west portico. . . ."

The rest passed in increasing haze—the salon, the solarium, the bedrooms, the dining area. The staff, all women, so far as he saw, appeared and vanished discreetly, opened doors and closed them as the head of staff silently directed, turned on lights and turned them off again, whisked imaginary dust off a sideboard and straightened a tasseled damask runner—forty-nine additional and mostly invisible servants, a propitious number, Bren was sure, to remain, safeguarding the historic family premises and maintaining decorum in the face of human presence.

And everything spoke of a mathematical calculation underlying the decor—the eye learned to pick it out, down to the color and number of the dried flowers in the frequent and towering bouquets.

Every measure of the place was surely propitious for the lady's family, down to the circular *baji-naji* figure centered in the beautifully appointed formal dining area: Fortune and Chance, chaos in the center of the rigid number-governed design of the rooms.

The room began to spin about that center, and the paidhi, in his private, pain-edged haze, suddenly hoped to not faint on the antique carpet. He was by now only and exclusively interested in the guest bedchamber, and the bed they said would be his, next on the tour—

He walked in, behind the gracious madam Saidin, into a room of immense proportions, with silver satin bedclothes, gold coverlet, gilt bedstead supported by gilt heraldic beasts—a bed wide enough for him and half the Mospheiran Foreign Office. The modern coverlet, Saidin said, exactly duplicated one of the fifty-eighth century, which had been on the bed when the last family occupant of the bedchamber, a fifty-ninth century lord, had met an untimely and probably messy end.

The family had declined to use it thereafter, but the numbers of the place had been altered to remove the infelicitous influences—two bluewood cabinets of precisely calculated dimensions were the addition that, the paidhi could be sure, guaranteed the harmony of the occupant. The chief of staff would be delighted to provide the figures, should the paidhi desire.

Six guest bedrooms, besides his own, each with its private bath; halls with doubtless felicitous arrangements of furnishings. He had no desire to question Atigeini judgment, and every desire to stay and prove the bed unhaunted, but the gentle majordomo was clearly proud of the next rooms, which she called, in her soft voice, "The most charming area of the house, lady Damiri's private residence," which she was sure the paidhi would find congenial to his work. Lady Damiri had, as an unprecedented favor, opened even her personal library and sitting rooms to her human guest—and he didn't find the will to deny Saidin, who might well have, in that stiff back and formal demeanor, concerns that a human guest would cast gnawed bones on the carpets and leave germs on the china.

Clearly he was going to be an inconvenience to the staff, genteel servants of a very highborn lady. And he wanted to begin with a good impression—knowing reports would be passed and that gossip would make the rounds if only inside the Atigeini family, in itself a security concern Banichi hadn't mentioned, but surely took into account. The last thing he wanted to do for his own safety was to alienate the staff.

So it was through silver-washed doors to the absent lady's private sitting rooms, a library with floor to ceiling shelves, a very fine book collection with an emphasis, he saw, on horticulture; and then, across the hall, a small, tile-floored solarium with a view of, again, the city and the mountains. Beautifully carved, windowed doors opened onto a balcony about which Banichi and Jago didn't look at all pleased—a balcony designed, Bren was sure, long before high-powered rifles had entered the repertoire of the Assassins' Guild.

Such thoughts swam leisurely through the paidhi's wavering brain, along with a sharp longing for his comfortable, quiet little garden apartment, and a fevered consideration of the lady of the apartment with her library of books on flowers—but, sadly, not a garden accessible to her—

He should recommend his lower-level garden to Damiri. She afforded him her hospitality. He could show her a charming place in the lower halls she'd likely never visited in her rich and security-insulated life.

In that thought the paidhi was growing entirely fuzzy-minded, and he really had rather sit down than go on to tour the breakfast room. He was certain, all credit to Banichi and Jago, that he had the very best and most secure guest room for himself. He was completely satisfied with the historic bed. He thought the library and the private solarium delightful. He couldn't bear a detailed tour of the other wonders he was sure abounded, which on another day he might have a keen interest as well as the fortitude to see.

There was a chair at the door of the solarium. He sat down in it with his heart pounding and mentally measured the distance back to the bedroom. He wasn't sure he could make it.

"Nadi Bren?" Jago asked as their guide hesitated.

"A fine chair," he breathed, and patted its brocade arm. "A very fine chair. Very comfortable. I'll be very pleased to work in this room. Please—convey my profound

thanks to lady Damiri for allowing me this very kind—
this very—extraordinary hospitality. I very much regret
her inconvenience. But I can't—" He wasn't doing well
with words at the moment. "I can't—manage any formality tonight. Please convey to Tabini-aiji my intention—to
be in my office tomorrow. It's just that, tonight—I'd like
my computer. And my bed. And a phone."

"We're both to stay here, nadi," Banichi said. "In these
apartments. Guarding you. We'll carry your messages."
They all towered above him, a black wall of efficiency
and implacable hospitality that seemed to cut off the daylight. "Tano will occupy the security station and the small
suite at the front door. He's already moving in—he has
arrived with your suitcase. Your belongings will be in the
drawers. Algini will join him in the security station, as
soon as he's back from the hospital—we estimate, within
a day or two."

"Not serious, I hope. . . ."

"Cuts and contusions. Perfectly fine."

"I'm very glad." His head was going around. He rested
his chin on his fist, elbow on the arm of the chair, to fix
a center of rotation in the environment, somewhere
around Jago's figure. "I was very glad—very glad you
came to the airport. Thank you. I wouldn't—"—wouldn't
have trusted, was the expression that leaped to mind. He
wasn't censoring quickly enough. He'd made himself a
maze of syntax. "—wouldn't have had such confidence in
strangers."

Damn, he wasn't sure how that parsed, either. He might
just have insulted Saidin and the whole staff. He couldn't
remember the front end of his own sentence.

"No difficulty at all," Banichi said. "Jago and I will establish ourselves in the red and the blue rooms, nearest
your own, if that's agreeable."

"Of course." He didn't know how Banichi stayed on
his feet: Banichi was walking wounded himself, limping
slightly all through their tour about the apartment, but
Banichi went on functioning, because that was the kind of
man Banichi was, while the paidhi—

"Nadi Bren?"

The room went quite around. And around. He shut his eyes a second, until it stopped, and he drew a shaky breath. "Nadiin," he said, determined to settle some details—what was going on, and why the extraordinary security, "is there anything else you can tell me about my situation? Is there a threat, a difficulty, a matter under debate?"

"All three," Jago said.

"Regarding the ship over our heads?"

"Among other small matters," Banichi said. "I regret, Tabini-aiji *must* see you as soon as possible, nand' paidhi. I know you'd rather be in bed, but these are our orders. I'll explain your exhaustion and your inconvenience, and perhaps he'll come here."

"What small matters? *What* matters? I haven't had any news since I left."

"The hasdrawad and the tashrid. The ship. Nand' Deana."

The hasdrawad and the tashrid he could guess. They were in emergency session. He'd understood he could postpone his speech to them by at least the term of his illness. The ship. That was a given. He knew that was why his presence and his ability to translate was so vital to the aiji. Touchy, the Foreign Office had said of the course of events with it. But—

"The aiji has not held audience with this Hanks person," Jago said. "He has not regarded this substitution as legitimate."

"But," Banichi said, "certain individuals have indeed approached Hanks-paidhi. Tabini wishes to talk to you about this situation as soon as possible. Within the *hour,* if you can possibly manage it."

He'd thought he hadn't the strength to get up. He'd thought he'd no reserves left.

But the thought of Hanks occupying his office, holding meetings, as Banichi hinted, with God-knew-whom on her own, making her own accommodations on questions he'd resisted, resisting what he'd already settled—in the middle of *this* crisis—

It *wasn't* a phone-call solution. He needed to know

what had happened between Hanks and Tabini before he dropped angry phone calls to Mospheira into the mix.

"I absolutely need to talk to Tabini," he said. "Now. I'll go there." The room might still be going around, but he had a sudden sense of what he had to focus on.

Like the apparition in the heavens—which put the entire Treaty in doubt.

Like a woman who'd consistently scored low on culture and psychology, who'd survived the academic committee winnowing process and gotten an appointment as paidhi-designate solely because she had high-ranking, narrow-interest support in the State Department—and a high-level finagle, he was sure of it, had landed her in a damned bad situation for novices.

"I'll advise the aiji," Banichi said.

3

Tabini's apartment, literally next door and centermost of the seven historic residences on this floor, was no strange territory: a young paidhi and an equally young aiji, both of them suddenly appointed to office with the demise of Tabini's father and the abrupt resignation of Wilson-paidhi—in private, where no politics intervened, he and Tabini laughed and held discussions far more easily than certain powers on either side of the strait might like to think. They were both sports enthusiasts—he skied and Tabini hunted; both single men in high-stress jobs—but he had Barb and Tabini had Damiri for refuge, and they compared notes.

They'd met in Tabini's apartment times uncounted. Scant days ago they'd been on vacation together, hunting in the hills at Tabini's country house at Taiben—where, in technical contravention of Treaty law, which forbade a human on the mainland carrying any sort of weapon under any excuse, Tabini had been teaching him target shooting. In the evenings they'd sat on the hearth ledge in that rural and peaceful house, looking forward to tomorrow and exchanging grandiose hopes for the future of human-atevi relations: a joint space program; trade city contact between their species, from the modest beginning of student computer exchanges—

Now, with their respective armed security drinking tea and socializing quietly in the foyer, the two of them took to the small salon aside from the entry of Tabini's residence—not a room he'd been in before, but Tabini had taken one look at him and ordered the little salon opened, so that, Tabini had said, the paidhi needn't walk another step.

It was a cozy chamber needing only a single servant, slight, bookish Eidi, who was probably a licensed assassin and undoubtedly senior security, himself—Bren had always suspected so—to pour tea and serve the traditional bittersweet wafers.

"Thank you for coming," Tabini said, protocols aside, and in the same moment Damiri herself turned up in the doorway.

"Nand' paidhi," Damiri said, offering a hand, and Bren began to struggle back to his feet, the very least of courtesy he owed his hostess and Tabini's official guest.

"No, no, please, stay seated, nand' paidhi. I'm so pleased you accepted my invitation. Has Saidin made you comfortable?"

"Quite, nai-ma. Thank you ever so much. I'm overwhelmed at such courtesy."

"An honor," she said, offering her hand, and taking it, he stayed entirely on his guard—at social disadvantage, of course, because he hadn't gotten up; which left her free to be gracious. The lady whom Tabini approved—the atevi expression—was neither ingenue nor scatterwit, and *she* defined the meeting, *she* spoke for herself, and not coincidentally for the Atigeini, whose consent or lack of it in the hospitality he had not a clue.

"I hope to be minimal bother to your gracious staff, daja-ma. It's an extraordinary courtesy you've extended to the paidhi's office." He was very careful about that word "office," *not* attributing the hospitality to anything personal, an instinctively diplomatic distinction which seemed to touch the lady's fancy.

"The aiji's guest is my guest," she said, and made a little bow to him, to Tabini, and left with some quiet word to Eidi.

"Assure her, please," Bren said. "I'm utterly in awe of the apartment. I swear to be careful."

"She's very curious about you," Tabini said, giving no cue whatsoever how much Damiri had just tried Tabini's patience, or added opposition support to his questions, or acted in any wise by his consent. "Quite in touch with her staff, I warn you. But only from curiosity."

Possibly a signal of the situation. Certainly a warning. "Then I hope they report well of me."

"I've no doubts. Is it chill for you? A front moved through this afternoon. One could easily light the heater."

"No. Not at all. It's quite pleasant. Thank you, aiji-ma."

"Is there pain?"

"Some. Fever. I think that's normal."

"I'm very glad to see you safe, nadi. How glad you cannot imagine."

"I should have stayed in Shejidan, aiji-ma. I'd no idea anything was in imminent motion. I earnestly wish you'd told me. I'd have stayed and talked to the hasdrawad immediately."

"I wanted you treated by your own doctors. That demanded I send you to the island. But I was extremely anxious, nadi. I swear I was anxious until I heard your plane was safely in our airspace."

"Aiji-ma." He was somewhat surprised, even touched by Tabini's expression of personal concern—and held himself mentally and emotionally still on his guard, not least because he was glad to *be* back and had to put the brakes on that warm little human reaction that answered *no* questions whatsoever that bore on atevi motivation.

Like—whether the Western Association was holding firm around Tabini.

Like whether all hell was continuing to break loose in the eastern regions of the Association, provinces where Tabini was most politically vulnerable. There'd been bombs dropping there as late as two days ago, to which he could personally attest—bombs that had killed men he knew. He didn't know to this hour how that set-to had come out, or whether the provincial lords, reacting to a strong move by Tabini and a shift of certain lords to Tabini's side, had taken a wait-see as he hoped had happened.

The side-switching could include the Atigeini, but he had no information whether or not lady Damiri had courted assassination by her own family for siding openly with Tabini, whom her association had at first opposed and then only coolly supported; and whether her family supported her in lodging a human guest in rooms hallowed in Atigeini history—when, for all he knew, his broken shoulder owed something to Atigeini suspicions of Tabini.

And he couldn't ask. He daren't ask until he knew more. There were conventions of politeness worth one's life.

"This ship above us," Tabini began.

"Yes, aiji-ma?"

"Mospheira is carrying on conversation with it. What's the general news? Were you able to hear anything?"

"Just that, as I understand, aiji-ma, there's no doubt in anyone's mind it's the same ship that brought us here. Where it's been for a hundred and seventy-eight years— that's a serious question. Someone on Mospheira may know the answer. I don't."

"Where do you guess it might have been?"

"Aiji-ma, all I know is what I've been told since I was a child, which is that it went out looking for the auspicious guide stars to find out where we are."

"Easy question. Here is *here*."

"Not from their view. As I understand. There's much more to it than that, but I confess, aiji-ma, as a student I didn't study the business about the ship with anything like the attention I should have. It just wasn't expected that the ship would ever come back."

"So. And what opinions are officials debating, now, in the high offices of Mospheira?"

The questions, besides being something he didn't know, tended a step over the edge of the aiji's need-to-know. The paidhi didn't, on principle, provide information on Mospheira's internal politics or Mospheira's moment-to-moment internal debates. The paidhi wasn't officially, at least, supposed to provide such information, as the aiji wasn't, by the Treaty, supposed to ask him.

"Tabini-ma, you know I can't answer that."

Tabini took up his teacup, balanced the fragile porcelain in his fingers. Atevi eyes were gold. Tabini's were a pale shade of that color. Some called them a sign of his father's infelicity. "Bren-ji, whatever we can and can't answer, whatever promises we make, many things will change now, between you on Mospheira and us on the mainland. Is this not a realistic assumption—that change is inevitable? And I ask the paidhi, who is supposed to interpret humans to atevi, in what direction those currents are flowing."

It was so, so quiet in the room, with only the voices from the other side of the foyer carrying through. He tried to gather a breath. Just a breath. He'd not thought of these things, not to the degree he needed to. He'd been preoccupied with a great deal of pain. And flying bullets.

"Tabini-ma, the Treaty created the paidhiin to be honest brokers for either side. Didn't they?"

Tabini took a sip of tea. "And for how many sides, nadi, can you be that honest broker? Are there three conversants, now—or still two?"

"I hope to give you an answer."

"Surely the paidhi can answer that one very simple question. Try this one: do you direct that ship? Or does that ship direct you?"

Adrenaline was definitely flowing. He'd literally bet his life on Tabini in coming back to the mainland. And he knew right now that in the condition he was in, he had no business coming in here to fence with Tabini. He should have taken another pain pill, no matter the urgency, and gone to bed where he belonged.

"Nand' paidhi? It seems to me a reasonable question. Am I unreasonable?"

"I just had my shoulder broken, Tabini-ma, I just had the hell beaten out of me by people who thought they could use the paidhi or get the paidhi to say things they could use. I held out against them. I—" He had to set his cup down. He couldn't keep his hand from shaking. "I would serve you and Mospheira both very ill if I injected my own half-minded interpretation of some official's hasty and possibly uninformed opinion into what I tell you or them. Especially if I myself were as underinformed as I am right now, aiji-ma. The aiji I've dealt with is too wise a man to destroy my value."

"Ah, flattery, now, Bren-ji. Not your usual standard."

"Honesty, Tabini-ma, is my only value. I stand *between*. I'll carry your messages to Mospheira. I'll tell you what responsible authorities answer after they've had time to think. But I won't inform on debates in progress, theirs or yours. Or the ship's. And, Tabini-ma, consider that I've been out of the information loop for days, I've been hours under anesthetic, I've had a pain pill and I'm not clear-headed at the moment. In such circumstances I can only—only stand by the strict interpretation of the Treaty. I would be ashamed to give you less than my best advice or, worse, to misinform you."

Atevi so rarely showed inner feelings. Tabini's face was an absolute mask, but it became a gentler one.

And, oh, Tabini could use the charm when he wanted to.

"I'm aware of your injuries. I asked for you back, Bren-ji, because I'm convinced of your good will, I rely on your candor, and I urgently need to know, before making any policy decisions, what this ship is saying and what Mospheira is saying to it. I need some warning what Mospheira will decide to do so that I'm not caught by surprise. I know that this may violate the language of the Treaty, but the collapse of the Association will abrogate the Treaty entirely and put everything in question. Believe me: we are in the midst of a crisis and, Bren-ji, let me urge upon you that I'm not the only one playing games with the Treaty when Mospheira sends me *two* paidhiin."

"It's ordinary when I'm not on duty. And I'd been out of touch for days. Surely you can't fault—"

"I'm aware of the scene downstairs. She claimed she was going to the airport, when in fact she had no travel pass and no clearance. Her intention was plainly to accost you publicly and create gossip."

"If it was to make dissent in the paidhi's office evident, I fear she succeeded."

"One fears so, yes. Bren-ji, I'd gladly have taken her to

the airport under guard; I'd gladly set her adrift in a row-boat, if I didn't feel such a dismissal would not better relations with Mospheira."

"I ask you to give her the travel pass, aiji-ma."

"Is this so? The Treaty says there shall be a paidhi. So since you won't answer my questions about their intent, at least tell me who are *you?* Do you still have the office, or does this woman hold it? Does her arrival have more to do with your absence from Shejidan—or with the appearance of that ship in our sky? Do you see the drift of my thoughts, Bren-ji? Who is in charge, now, in your government, and whom does this woman represent?"

He felt himself short of breath, putting together the threads—and not certain he had all of them. "There's no change in government or policy that I'm aware of. But I went straight from here to hospital. And my mind isn't clear, aiji-ma. Someone may have told me about Hanks' whereabouts. I—just—can't remember. I—can't—bring that back."

"The day you left for Malguri, your government requested you to answer a message sent to your office. You weren't here, obviously. More messages followed. One can guess their sudden urgency had somewhat to do with the apparition in our heavens."

"One would—indeed—think so, aiji-ma."

"On the third day an aircraft requested landing with this woman aboard. We saw the likelihood of close questions regarding your whereabouts, so we asked for the television interview with you, for—"

"For tape of *me?*" One didn't interrupt the aiji when he was talking. "Forgive me, aiji-ma."

"It was useful," Tabini said. "One learns about television, among other blasphemous possibilities, that it plays very interesting games with time, with scale, with numbers in general. An impious device. A box of illusions. But it did quiet some general questions about your good health. And it maintained the idea in the public mind that you'd never ceased in office. —But you keep evading my very serious question, Bren-ji. Have they sent you back merely to quiet my demands—or are you back with real authority?"

"The most of my authority, aiji-ma, is the plain fact that I speak the language of the chief atevi Association, and the equally plain fact that I'm here by your invitation and that you choose to deal with me. I assume that you deal with me."

"True."

"Have you dealt at all with Hanks? Is there an agreement? Are there negotiations in progress? Are there proposals on the table?"

"With the likes of Taigi and Naijo. With every damned potential conspirator in the Association—possibly. With me—no."

Appalling information. "Surely she's sought meetings with you."

"Shall I empower this interloper? I dealt with this woman once and only once, when I told her to tell Mospheira send you back immediately or I would have her shot. By the result, I believe she transmitted my message faithfully."

God—was the gut-level, Mospheiran reaction. But this wasn't Mospheira. Indeed Tabini could have had her shot. And if Tabini had threatened it—Tabini absolutely would have had to do it if Hanks hadn't complied.

"I have to ask for her safety," he said quietly. "Please, aiji-ma."

"Does the paidhi ask? Do you have the support of the Treaty?"

"I trust," he said, light-headed with the awareness he was hedging on a breach of Department rules *and* the Treaty, "that if persons in authority on Mospheira did send me, they sent me by the terms of your request, and by that, if they receive messages from me they'll know they're your messages faithfully and accurately rendered. I don't believe they consider me corrupt, or incompetent. Logically speaking, aiji-ma, if you choose to deal with me rather than with her, what can they do, if they wish to continue to receive your communications?"

"They can ignore my communications."

"No, aiji-ma. They can't. What atevi do and think is vastly important."

"Then why send this Deana Hanks in the first place? And why is she listening to unacceptable people?"

He temporized. "She is my legitimate successor. If I was gone—"

"She's a fool."

"Aiji-ma, the presumption on Mospheira clearly was that I wasn't on the job, for whatever reason, in what they knew was a very touchy situation. Possibly they sent her with absolute good will to you, as the best stopgap they could manage if some accident had befallen me— such as assassination at the hands of some opposition movement—"

"They needed to select a fool?"

"There are very, very few humans who speak the language, only three who can think in it."

"There are *two*. You and Wilson-paidhi. This woman does not *think*."

Tabini was damned mad. Clearly. And there was far more at issue than Hanks' life. Or his.

"Possibly—possibly, aiji-ma, once the State Department is sure I'm well enough to carry on my office, they may indeed recall her. And if they don't, I'll urge they do. I assure you."

"This woman is interfering in our politics. Where is their intelligence, nand' paidhi? Is this a deliberate act to violate the Treaty? Or is some other, perhaps ignorant, party now directing human affairs?"

It was a very frightening question, at depth—even confining the implications of that question to the State Department, which he knew wasn't Tabini's entire concern, considering that ship in the heavens.

More, the paidhi didn't have the definitive answer to give. The Foreign Office called talks with the ship *touchy*. "I'll make your displeasure very clear to the responsible parties, aiji-ma. In the meantime, please, no move to remove her by force. Let me arrange it, in my own way. I believe I can do it without disturbance."

"You're asking a great favor, Bren-ji."

"I know I am."

"And favors have returns."

"I know that too, aiji-ma."

"So what *is* the momentary thinking inside the President's office?"

God, his wits were hazed. He should have seen that coming.

And he did from time to time take chances on Tabini, monumental chances, once he'd felt out the ground underfoot—once they were both sure of the extent and purpose of the question.

And especially when the honest answer might give Tabini a reassuring insight into human mental processes.

"Aiji-ma, nothing I've learned on Mospheira inside or outside official channels has changed my initial impression: Mospheira is disturbed—not alarmed, but disturbed, for exactly the same reasons atevi are disturbed. No one planned for this. I agree: no government likes to be surprised. Mospheira was surprised. You were surprised. And I think that ship is surprised. It left a functioning station. It came back to a situation it can't have counted on finding, and a complexity of political arrangements it can't readily unravel."

"So what does this mean? Are there two human associations now, or one? And is the authority in our sky—or on Mospheira?"

Critical questions. Urgent questions. From a ruler who couldn't conceptualize geographic boundaries as valid. "Aiji-ma, my answer from my own understanding is—they're two authorities which once were one, not hostile to each other, each now with separate interests to protect. You've been monitoring transmissions. You surely have recordings."

"Such exist."

"Do you find them encoded?"

"Numbers and names are quite clear. I assume that you can translate the rest of the voice segments for us."

That it wasn't code was reassuring. He was entirely uneasy about an agreement to translate—but Mospheira *knew* he had that capacity, as they knew Hanks had when they'd sent her here: they weren't unwilling to have it done—or they hadn't indicated it to him that *he* could remember.

"I would think so, aiji-ma. I would naturally prefer to consult with the university on—"

"If the Mospheiran authorities put themselves in association with that ship, tell me, where would your responsibility lie?"

"I can construe no circumstance under which that would happen."

"I can. But perhaps my imagination is extravagant."

"Human associations are more and less hierarchical than atevi." An alarming thought occurred to him. "And they're not biological imperatives. I know it's difficult to construe this, aiji-ma, but on the basis of what I've lately learned, I have to tell you that we feel absolutely nothing about that ship that atevi would feel in our place."

"You haven't convinced me, nand' paidhi. I assure you, many atevi have already assumed a unitary human authority is unquestionably what we're dealing with. Where human biology enters into it—I confess myself at a loss. But that you say two authorities exist separated by time, and that you say there isn't hostility, does confuse me."

They were up against one of those walls—imperfect interface. Atevi gut feelings and human. Tabini didn't understand, absolutely didn't understand that there wasn't *man'chi,* loyalty in the atevi definition: a gut-level, emotional compulsion for Mospheira to join the authority represented by that ship, which looked strong, which had historically held authority—

Mospheira itself could have no comprehension how atevi would read the situation, either. Tabini was at least canny enough in the differences between atevi and human to know that, gut level, he might think he understood— but chances were very good that he wouldn't, couldn't, and never would, unaided by the paidhi, come up with the right forecast of human behavior, because he didn't come with the right hardwiring. Average people didn't analyze what they thought: they thought they thought, and half of it was gut reaction.

But because lately—very lately—the paidhi-aiji had tumbled across that line and lived far away from experts at making that interface, stayed among ordinary atevi in the hinterlands long enough for the paidhi to meet those gut-level reactions, he at least had awareness how and on what critical points Tabini was coping with him—and in the process changing the interface, unwittingly corrupting what the paidhiin thought they knew about atevi.

"Aiji-ma, wise and perceptive as you are, I'm reluctant to use the word *man'chi* as a human thought, even when it almost works, but it's very close to what Mospheirans feel toward this world. We think we have that feeling in common with atevi, not with the ship. A *man'chi* to this planet."

Tabini's pale eyes were unreadable and thoughtful. Interest in the concept was the best a human could guess.

And after a long moment digesting that idea or another, chin on fist, Tabini said, "Another why, nand' paidhi, when you say you feel no such emotions."

So, so much riding on the understanding. He felt the shakes coming on, a feverishness that made focus difficult. "Whys lead to whys. I should go to bed, aiji-ma, and let you ask me when I've thought it through. I've been through too much to give answers lightly."

"This answer, nand' paidhi. Don't toss me a lure of reassurance and then say don't follow."

"Aiji-ma, it's simply emotional, our attachment to the world. There's no logic. It just is. Like *man'chi*, it just is."

"You say there's been no preparation for this ship to occupy the station. No—hidden presence up there."

"*You* don't believe there's a human presence up there, aiji-ma."

"But there certainly is now, is there not, over our heads at this very moment?"

"True."

"So. Let me tell you: this is very serious business, Bren ji. Humans swooping down with death rays used to be bad television. Now it's speculation on the evening news."

It was slowly sinking in, how far his mission to the mainland had deteriorated in the passage of a few days: the structure of trust was—if not gone—at least badly bent. "Three days ago, aiji-ma, I'd have sworn I understood what sane atevi believed. Now—I *don't* know. I can at least swear to you there are no death rays."

"On Mospheira? Or on that ship? By the Treaty you agreed to turn over all your technology to us, in such steps as wouldn't wreck—what, our environment? Our cultural destiny? As I recall, our own Space Committee was talking about slosh baffles for a heavy-lift rocket and the launch facilities for communications satellites. I think these people are somewhat beyond that."

"Yes, aiji-ma," he said humbly. "They possibly are."

"And will you turn over *their* technology to us? I fear we're back to that question again: are these people part of your association, bound by the Treaty? Or are they not? Hanks has been talking recklessly about the expansion of the industrial base. About stars and the distances between stars—and faster-than-light travel, which, you are aware, defies the views of certain sects, even commits heresy."

He felt his head light, his thinking unstable. FTL. *Hanks* took it on herself—

"Pardon, Tabini-ma, was she perhaps speaking in confidence—or—?"

"In confidence, oh, yes. To lord Geigi. Coupled with suggestions that, with sweeping advances in technology, the oil price might rise."

"Oh, my God."

"Deity?"

He'd been so confounded he'd reacted in Mosphei'—of which Tabini knew at least a salient few words.

"Tabini-ma. The woman is a—"

"—fool?"

"Naive," he said faintly.

"Lord Geigi, as you know, is a Determinist. With immense oil reserves. Is she insulting his beliefs? Or promising him revenue—what do you say—under the table?"

"One could, if one were Geigi, be very confused."

"Especially since Geigi is heavily in debt. *Not* for public release. The man is desperate."

"God," he breathed, and a shaky, perilous vision opened in front of him—the Association tottering on uncertain communications, disaffection of the lords, numerology confounded. Faster-than-light was now a fact in certain atevi minds, God knew how far the rumor had spread. The Determinist numerologists would have heard about it: ultimately the astronomers and the space scientists were going to hear the transmissions from the ship. The seed, as the atevi proverb had it, would see the sun.

Then unless there was some clever face-saving device on which the Determinists might explain their embarrassing paradox, all hell was going to break loose. Important people would be called liars, respected authorities and culturally important systems would be overthrown by incontrovertible fact—possibly even taken down in bloodshed, since flesh and bone supported these glass structures of belief.

"I'll deal with Hanks."

"Faster-than-light." Tabini reached aside to let Eidi pour a cup of tea. "And do we, after all, deal with death rays next?"

"I trust not," he breathed, while his mind was searching wildly for justification, for rationalization with Departmental policy, for *something* that could let him tell Tabini the thoughts that hit a fevered human brain with sudden, rare, atevi-language clarity. He couldn't count on recovering the moment tomorrow, not the approach to both Tabini and the situation.

"Aiji-ma, here's the fact that occurs to me: atevi assume weapons. But weapons weren't the real threat in the War."

"Ask the dead."

"No, but they weren't decisive. We had the weapons—which did us no good. What hurt atevi—the very threat that hangs over Mospheira *and* atevi—is the mere shock of them being here. The numbers they deal with. Their bringing new things into the world faster than atevi can adjust. The same mistakes we made—and destabilized the society, the economy. Everything." The shoulder was giving him sudden, particular pain at the angle he'd chosen in the chair, and the threads of logic tried to escape him, but he hung on. "Worse, aiji-ma, we're not dealing with a slow information flow among atevi this time. Now it's instant information, instant crisis, instant reaction, as fast as television can throw it at the world. And if change comes at people so fast the electorate doesn't understand it, aiji-ma, if people can't plan for their own personal futures, if the businesses can't adjust to it—fast enough—"

"Baji-naji," Tabini said, and shrugged—which was to say, proverbially, that the random devil lurked in every design, and the numbers could inevitably forecast, but not infallibly predict. "We survived it once. We even, as you recall, won the resultant war."

"That, I swear to you, I *swear* to you without hearing them—isn't their intent. We don't want a war."

"War shouldn't have happened the last time. But how will we avoid it? Don't just tell me we're wiser. Or that you are. Tell me who Hanks is representing."

He drew a slow breath, only to win time to think. He'd led Tabini around to *his* argument; now, in a turnabout which confused a weary brain, he was back where Tabini had led him—feeling the dull ache spread from the newly fused bone, and sensing Tabini's belief in him, Tabini's expectations of him, riding on a knife's edge of attention.

"I don't know, but I'll find out, aiji-ma. Certainly she's not representing that ship. Or the Foreign Office, at this point. They sent *me* back. And I will *not* let everything we've worked for go down, aiji-ma."

"So. The paidhi will mediate. Is that what you say? The paidhi will convince the Mospheiran authorities, the Foreign Office and the internal authorities of this ship, and speak *my* arguments and *my* requirements?"

Tabini was pushing a sick man and Tabini damned well knew it. Tabini had his own job to do, for his people, and Tabini wanted information out of the best and readiest source he had.

Tabini also believed in truth under duress. Tabini would push in such sessions until he got something of substance from the paidhi and felt that sufficient truth was on the table. You couldn't put him off, not unless you were prepared to see Tabini pull far, far back.

The paidhi damned well knew that trait. And knew when to gamble.

"All right, aiji-ma, you want to know what course humans on Mospheira can possibly take. One—fall in line behind these people and end up negotiating with them for the ability of their young, their talented, and their ablest people to go up to the station and live, because—and I gather Hanks has raised the issue—neither you nor we have the industrial base to build a launch system. If we take their transport, we become passengers—on somebody else's space program. Or—"

Pain was coming in waves. He had to shift back in the chair and risk mistaken interpretation of body language. "I'm sorry, aiji-ma, a twinge."

"Or," Tabini said.

Primary rule: *never* leave an explanation for an ateva to fill in the blanks.

"Or, aiji-ma, the world can try, as I think Hanks is legitimately suggesting, aside from her oil industry estimates, to build the requisite industrial base under our own regulation, as fast as the world can deal with it, and refuse to go faster. Ordinary folk aren't going to give up their homes or their plans. The aiji in Shejidan can't trample on the opinions of a Wingin brickmason, no more than the President of Mospheira can tell some North Shore fisherman in my brother's town that he's going to go up into space and work on some orbiting fish farm. They'd have to come and get him. The same as your atevi mason."

"Ah, but what when these celestial visitors offer you cures for disease? Instant technology? Instant answers? It strikes me that Mospheira is in the same position we were in when you came floating down out of our sky. These people can offer you your dearest ambitions. These people can make you lords."

"Aiji-ma, these people should approach Mospheira and Shejidan both with *great* trepidation. You're absolutely right about the bait they'll use, consciously or unconsciously. But we can't take it. The Treaty is our collective safety, aiji-ma. You and I *have* internal differences, emotionally, logically, culturally, that these strangers don't know about. You have natural allies in humans who want to stay on this planet. We have to make Mospheira listen, and we have to make the ship crew listen to us."

"They might simply decide our objections were irrelevant."

"Unfortunately they don't need to do a damned thing— excuse me, aiji-ma—but rebuild the station and sit up there to preempt atevi *ever* achieving the future they might have had."

"So? Would this not benefit you—even your fisherman—in the long run?"

"Aiji-ma, we came down to build factories and make roads and transgress the lines of atevi associations with no sense of the damage we were doing. But that ship up there—that's not a chemical rocket. Believe me that it's just as disruptive of my world."

"Not your world."

"Then we've *nowhere* to belong, Tabini-ma." They'd gone past what he intended and he'd said far more than he meant to. He wasn't sure now what impression he'd created that he couldn't undo. His head was throbbing. He felt a wave of dizziness and nausea. He picked up the teacup, controlled action, trying to control the information he passed. "I *want* to go into space, understand, Tabini-ma. I want that—personally, for me, I want so much to go up there I can't explain it. But I won't sell atevi interests to get that ticket, and I won't sell Mospheira."

"*Sell* them?"

"Sell out. A Mosphei' proverb. One sells melons in a market. That's proper. But one doesn't sell one's duty to people who aren't qualified to have it."

"Sell one's duty. A curious notion."

"I said—for us it's not biological. Because it isn't, it can be sold, aiji-ma, for money, for other considerations. But good humans will *never* sell it."

"What then do they do with it?"

"They give it away, very much—but not quite—as atevi do."

"These not-quites are the very devil."

"They always are, aiji-ma."

"Indeed." Tabini set aside his empty cup and rested his chin on his fist. "Indeed. For this very reason I demanded you back, Bren-ji. You are a treasure. And yet you want me not to shoot Deana Hanks. Why?"

Pale, pale and oh-so-sober eyes. Tabini was calling him a fool, by atevi lights. And asking an honest question. There was everything at risk. And it was time to take the debate aside.

"Well, for one thing, Tabini-ma, —it would make one hell of a mess with the State Department."

Tabini gave one of his rare, silent laughs. "Don't divert me, clever man. You've given me nightmares of death rays. Let me spoil *your* sleep. Grandmother is in residence."

"God, I'd have thought she'd want to get straight home."

"Oh, this is *home*, Bren-ji. As much *home* as Malguri, at least in title."

"Is the situation in Malguri Province then quiet, aiji-ma?"

"If you mean have my forces stopped the gunfire, yes. If you mean have all the rebels come around to my way of thinking, and is there absolutely no likelihood that certain folk both noble and common would gladly assassinate you and me with one bullet, I fear the answer is no. Doubtless my grandmother will want to talk to you. Bear in mind her associations with the rebels. You have such a generous, unsuspicious nature."

"I'll remember that."

"Beware of her. I tell you, there are far too many people in the world who would wish to silence you."

"Has anyone filed Intent?"

"No. But I tell you this, nadi, I may be utterly mistaken, but I fear some of those individuals may reside on Mospheira. And do I understand, on Mospheira they don't have a law requiring a filing?"

He'd believe in betrayals of other kinds, perhaps, but not in physical danger from Mospheira.

Though silencing him need not be physical. He had sufficient reason for misgivings in his successor's presence on the mainland.

"Tabini-ma, I honestly—honestly don't think even my dedicated detractors would want to give up the only means they have of talking to you, now that they know you won't talk to Hanks. Not when—" He didn't know what happened to him. There was a black space. He wasn't holding the cup all of a sudden, and made a grab for it as it fell on the priceless carpet. It rolled—unbroken, but tea stood on the immaculate designs. He was appalled—he seized his napkin and flung it down on the spill, trying to bend to see to it himself.

But Eidi was there instantly, to recover the cup and to mop up the damage.

"Forgive me," Bren said, intensely embarrassed. "I've had terrible luck with teacups."

"Bren-ji, it's only carpet." Tabini made a furious wave of the hand, dismissing Eidi, dismissing the whole fuss. "Listen just this moment more. I need you as soon as you can possibly bring yourself up to date with this crisis, to go before the joint legislatures, explain these strangers in our sky and translate the dialogue between Mospheira and this ship. End the speculation. More—tell this ship the things atevi have to say to them. *That* is what I need of you, Bren-ji. Do you agree?"

"I—have no authorization to contact them, aiji-ma, not even to translate, and I would prefer—"

"You have *my* authorization, Bren-ji. The Treaty document said, did it not, there shall be one translator between humans and the atevi? Did it not say, the paidhi shall interpret humans to the atevi and atevi to the humans? I take this as the basis of the Treaty, Bren-ji. No matter the division in your Department that sends me *two* paidhiin, no matter they're in violation of the Treaty—*you* will make this contact and render our words honestly to these strangers."

"Tabini-ma, I need to think. I can't think tonight. I can't promise—"

"I requested Mospheira to send you back. Surely they aren't so simple-minded as to believe I wouldn't use your abilities, Bren-ji. Can you place any other interpretation on it?"

"But it may not be straightforward. That we do use audio records is going to slow linguistic drift, but the vastly different experience of our populations is going to accelerate it. I can't be sure I'll understand all the nuances. Meanings change far more than syntax, and I've no wish to—"

"Bren-ji, linguistics is *your* concern. The Association is in crisis. There must be some action, some assertion of the legitimate human authority. Every day you spend preparing—we may lose lives. Don't tell me about your problems. Mine generate casualty figures."

It was true. He knew what delay cost. He tried not to think too much on it—when worry only slowed the process. The human brain could only take so much. "Tabini-ma," he said. "Give me tomorrow to get my wits about me. Get me the transmissions."

"Bren-ji, understand, there's nothing in the world more dangerous than politics running without information. I have heads of security, heads of committees, clamoring at my doors. There's a meeting of committee heads going on right now—"

"Aiji-ma," he began.

"Bren-ji, tonight, before this can go further in rumor-making conjecture, at least go down and address that meeting, only briefly. This woman—this Deana Hanks—has created speculations, panic, angers, suspicion. Be patient, I say, wait for Bren-paidhi. And they're waiting, but the rumors are already running the corridors. I know you're in pain. But tonight, if at all possible, at least assure these people I haven't deceived them."

He'd thought he'd finished his duty. He thought he was going within the next few moments to his borrowed apartment and to his borrowed bed. The arm hurt. The tape around his ribs was its own special, knife-edged misery, growing more acute by the minute, and he couldn't do what Tabini wanted of him. He couldn't face it.

But Tabini was right about people dying while experts split semantic hairs; and God knew what rumors could be loose, or what Hanks could have said.

"Paidhi-ji, lives are at issue. The stability of the Association is at issue. The aiji of Shejidan can't *ask* help of his associates. It would insult them. But so the paidhi understands, across the difficulty of our association—" Tabini couldn't imply his associates didn't share his needs—without implying they were traitors; Tabini was doing the paidhi's job again.

"I understand that," he said. "But I don't think I can walk far, aiji-ma." His voice wobbled. He felt irrationally close to tears. The shock of bombs in Malguri was still jolting through his nerves, the spatter of a close hit: not just dirt and rock chips, but fragments of a decent man he'd grown to like—

"It's just downstairs," Tabini said. "Just down the lift."

"I'll try," he said. He didn't even know how he was going to get to his feet. But Tabini stood up, and ignoring the pinch of tape around his ribs, Bren made it.

To do a job. To make sense of the incomprehensible, when the paidhi hardly conceived of the situation himself.

4

A cable lift existed in the guarded back corridors of the aiji's apartment, a creaky thing, an antique of brass filigree and an alarming little bounce in the cables; but Bren rated it far, far better than a long walk. He went down with Tabini, with Banichi and with Tabini's senior personal guard, Naidiri, a two-floor descent into the constantly manned security post below, and out a series of doors which gave out onto a hall not available to the public.

By that back passage, one came to a small guard station with a choice of three other doors that were the secure access to separate meeting rooms which had, each, one outside general access. It was the closed route the Bu-javid residents used to reach the area where atevi commons and atevi lords met elbow to elbow, with all the vigorous give and take the legislatures employed.

On this route the lords of the Association, who held court at other appointed times, could reach their meetings safe from jostling by crowds and random, improper petitioners—and on this route one comparatively fragile and battered human could feel less threatened by collision in the halls.

More, the walk from the lift to the committee rooms was quite short, the room being, in this case, the small Blue Hall, which the Judiciary and Commerce Committees regularly used.

Jago and Tabini's second-rank security had preceded them down, were already at the doors, and briskly opened them on a noisy debate in progress among the twenty or so lords and people's representatives—the Minister of Finance shouting at the lord Minister of Transport with enough passion to jar the nerves of a weary, aching, and somewhat queasy human.

Perhaps they'd rather shout and finish the business they clearly had under consideration; and if he asked Tabini very nicely they might get him to his bed where he could fall unconscious.

But the debate died in mid-sentence, a quiet fell over the room, and lords and representatives of the Western Association bowed not just once to Tabini, but again to the paidhi, very clearly directing that courtesy at him.

Bren was taken quite aback—bowed before he thought clearly, and doubted then in muzzy embarrassment whether the second courtesy could be possibly aimed him at all.

"Nadiin," he murmured, confused and dizzy from the exertion, hoping only to make this short and not to have to answer more than a few questions.

Aides and pages hastened to draw out chairs and to settle him at the table, a flurry of courtesy, he thought, unaccustomed to the solicitousness and the attention, as if the paidhi looked to be apt to die on the spot.

Death wasn't an option, he thought, drawing a breath and feeling pain shoot through the shoulder, the wind from the air ducts cold on his perspiring face. But fainting dead away—that, he might do. Voices came to him distantly, surreal and alternate with the beating of his heart.

"Nadiin," Tabini said quietly, having sat down at the other end of the table, "Bren-paidhi is straight from surgery and a long plane flight. Don't be too urgent with him. He's taxed himself just to walk down here."

Came then a murmur of sympathy and appreciation, the tall, black-skinned lords and representatives who set a lone, pale human at a childlike scale. A small tray with water and a small pot of hot tea arrived at Bren's place, as at every seat, then a small be-ribboned folder that would be, like the other such folders, the agenda of the meeting. He opened it, perfunctory courtesy. He wanted the water, but having settled at a relatively pain-free angle, didn't want to lean forward to get it.

"We were hearing the tape," lord Sigiadi said, the Minister of Commerce. "Does the paidhi have some notion, some least inkling, what the dialogue is between the island and the ship?"

"I haven't heard the tapes, nand' Minister. I'm promised to have them tomorrow."

"Would the paidhi listen briefly and tell us?"

The whole assembly murmured a quick agreement to that suggestion. "Yes," they said. "Play the tape."

At which point the paidhi suddenly knew, by the suspicious lack of special ceremony to Tabini's arrival, and by the equally elaborate courtesy to the paidhi, that the committee had almost certainly seen Tabini earlier in the same session.

And that the paidhi had just been, by a master of the art, sandbagged.

But it was a relief to sit still, at least, after a long day's jostling about. Even in the brief spell of sitting he'd had in Tabini's apartment, he'd exhausted himself, and the Council of Committees demanded nothing of him more than to sit in this late-night session and listen to the week's worth of tapes he urgently wanted to hear and get the gist of.

Which made it necessary to keep every reaction off his face, while men and women of the Western Association, themselves minimally expressive and capable of reading the little expression which high-ranking atevi did show in public, were watching his every twitch, shift of posture, and blink.

So he sat propped at his least painful angle, chin on hand, facial nerves deliberately disengaged—the paidhi had learned that atevi art early in his tenure—listening to the numeric blip and beep that atevi surveillance had picked up from Mospheira communications to the abandoned space station, machine talking to machine, the same as every week before the ship had arrived out of nowhere.

"This is computers talking," he murmured to the committee heads. "Either stored data exchange or one computer trying to find the protocols of another. I leave the numbers therein to the experts, to tell if there's anything unusual. If the technician could go directly to the discernible voices—"

Then, with a hiccup of the running tape: *"Ground Station Alpha, this is* Phoenix. *Please respond."*

Even expecting it to happen, that thin voice hit human nerves—a voice from space, talking to a long-dead outpost, exactly as it would have done all those centuries ago.

But it was real, it was contemporary. It was the ship-dwelling presence orbiting the planet—a presence expecting all manner of things to be true that hadn't been true for longer than anyone alive could reckon.

"They're asking for an answer from the old landing site," he said, trying to look as blasé as possible, while his pulse was doing otherwise. "They've no idea it's been dead for nearly two hundred years."

On that ship might even be—his scant expertise in relativity hinted at such—crew that *remembered* that site. The thought gave him gooseflesh as he listened through the brief squeal and blip, computers talking again: as he judged now, searching frequencies and sites for response from what optics had to tell the ship was an extensive settlement. He was about to indicate to the aide in charge of the tape to increase the playback rate.

"What *of* the numbers?" Judiciary asked. Loaded question.

"I believe they have to do with date, time, authorizations. That's the usual content."

Then he heard an obscure communications officer in charge of the all but defunct ground-station link answer that inquiry. *"Say again?"*

Which he rendered, and rare laughter touched the solemn faces about the table—surprise-reaction as humor being one of those few congruent points of atevi-human psychology; he was very glad of that reaction. It was an overwhelmingly important point to make with them, that humans had been as surprised as atevi; he hoped he'd scored it hard enough to get that fact told around.

That recorded call skipped rapidly through an increasingly high-ranking series of phone patches until he was experiencing the events, *he* was waiting with those confused technicians—recovering the moments he'd missed while he was tucked away in remote places of the continent, and which, with Hanks sitting idle and unconsulted, atevi had had to experience without knowing what humans were saying.

After the first few exchanges, the realization that the contact was no hoax must have rocketed clear to the executive wing in less than an hour, because in a very scant chain of calls, the President of Mospheira was talking directly to the ship's captain.

"He's telling the ship's captain that he is in charge of the human community on Mospheira. The captain asks what that means, and the President answers that Mospheira is the island, that he is in charge ..."

He lost a little of it then, or didn't lose it, just whited out on a wave of acute discomfort. He caught himself with a tightness around the mouth, and knew he had to keep his face calm. "Back the tape, please, just a little. The shoulder's hurting."

"If the paidhi is too ill—" Finance said; but stern, suspicious Judiciary broke in: "This is what we most need to hear, nand' paidhi. If you possibly can, one would like to hear."

"Replay," he said. The paidhi survived at times on theater. If you had points with atevi you used them, and going on in evident pain did get points, while the pain might excuse any frown. He listened, as the President maintained indeed he was the head of state on an exclusively human-populated island—

God. It already hit sensitive topics. He was no longer sure of his own judgment in going on when he'd had a chance to stop and think; he thought wildly now of falling from his chair in a faint, and feared his face was dead white. But pain was still a better excuse than he'd have later.

"The captain asks about the President's authority. The President says, 'Mospheira is a sovereign nation, the station is still under Mospheiran governance. The ship's captain then asks, 'Mr. President, where *is* the station crew?'—he's found the station abandoned—and then the President asks, 'Why—' '" He tried not to let his face change as he played the question through and through his head in the space of a few seconds, trying not to lose the thread that was continuing on the tape.

"What, nand' paidhi?" the Minister of Transportation asked quietly, and Bren lifted his hand for silence, not quite venturing to silence an atevi lord, but Tabini himself moved a cautioning hand as the tape kept running.

"The President of Mospheira complains of the ship's abandonment of the colony. The ship's captain suggested that the humans on Mospheira had a duty to maintain the station."

And after several more uneasy exchanges, in which he *knew* he'd gotten well over his head in this translation, came the conclusion from the ship: *"Then you don't have a space capability."*

Bluntly put.

He rendered it: "The ship's captain asks whether Mospheira has manned launch capability." But he understood something far more ominous, and there seemed suddenly to be a draft in the room, as if someone elsewhere had opened a door. He sat and listened to the end of that conversation, feeling small chills jolt through him—maybe lack of sleep, maybe recent anesthetic, he wasn't sure.

No. Mospheira didn't have a space capability. Atevi didn't have, either. Not to equal that ship. And there was clear apprehension on atevi faces, expression allowed to surface; these heads of committee were steeped in atevi suspicion of each other—in a society where assassins were a legal recourse.

Damn, he thought, damn. He didn't know what he could do. The ship was *not* flinging out open arms to its lost brethren. The Foreign Office had called the exchanges *touchy,* and they were clearly that. His expression couldn't be auspicious or reassuring at the moment, and he hoped they attributed it to the pain.

"Cut the tape off," he said, "please, nadi. I think we

have the essential position they're taking. The two leaders are signing off. I'll give you a full transcript as soon as tomorrow, I'm just—" His voice wobbled. "Very shaky right now."

"So," Tabini said in the silence that followed. "What does the paidhi think?"

The paidhi's mind was whited out in thought after tumbling thought. He rested his elbow on the chair, chin on his hand, in the one comfortable position he'd discovered, and took a moment answering.

"Aiji-ma, nadiin-ji, give me one day and the rest of the tapes. I can tell you . . . there is no agreement between the ship and Mospheira on the abandonment of the station. It seems an angry issue." Set the hook. Convince the committee heads they were getting the real story. Make them *value* their information from the paidhi, not Hanks and not the rumor mill. "Please understand," he said in a very deep, very profound silence, "that I haven't heard the full text, and that the bridge between the atevi and human languages is very difficult on some topics such as confidence or nonconfidence, for biological reasons. Even after my years of study I've discovered immense difference in what I thought versus what I now realize of atevi understanding. Words I've always been told are direct equivalents have turned out not to be equivalent at all. But that I do understand gives me hope, even if—" he laid a hand on the sling "—it was a painful acquisition—that if my brain can make the adjustment to your way of thinking, then there must be words; and if I can find the words I can deal with this. Believe me, tonight, that what I hear on that tape disturbs me, but does not alarm me. I hear no threat of war, rather typical posturing and position-taking, preface to negotiation, not to conflict."

"Have they, nadi, not mentioned atevi?" The question, coldly posed, came from the conservative Minister of Defense. "Am I mistaken that that word occurs?"

"Only insofar as, nandi, in the discussion of territory, Mospheira asserted its sovereignty over humans."

"Sovereignty," Judiciary repeated.

Loaded word. Very.

"Sovereignty over humans was the phrase, nand' Minister. Remember, please, the President can't use the atevi word 'association' to them and make the ship's captain understand it. He has to use words—as do I in translation—which carry inconvenient historical baggage. We don't have a perfect translation for every thought. This is why the paidhi exists, and I will be very sure the President understands his Treaty obligations and that he's sensitive to implications in translation. The Treaty will stand."

Suspicions remained evident, but tempers were settling, judgment at least deferred. The shoulder ached, muscle tension, perhaps, and he tried to relax—impossible thought, when he was beginning to shiver in the draft from the doorway.

"There is a rumor," Finance said, "that humans have built more ships."

"I believe I can deny that, nand' Minister, unless someone besides the paidhi understands that from some tape I haven't heard." He said it, and *Hanks* landed on his mind like a hammer blow. "I ask you, nadiin, please, when you hear such things, make me aware of them, so that I can address them as they deserve in information I give to you. I'll certainly listen to the tapes with that in mind, nandi, and I thank you for the information."

Finance gave a mollified bow of assent, her face entirely expressionless as she leaned back and regarded him under lowered brows.

Meanwhile the room was swinging around and around, and there was no good trying to request to leave until it stopped—the waves of dizziness when they started having at least a few minutes to run. "Be assured," he said, "that I'm back in business—a little weak today, but don't hesitate to send me queries and information at any hour. That's my job."

"The paidhi," Tabini interjected, "is staying in the Atigeini residence for security reasons. You may direct your phone calls and your messages there. Hanks is not here officially. We have cleared up that matter and are proceeding to clear it up with Mospheira."

Some little consternation and curiosity attended on that remark.

"What of the Treaty?" Judiciary asked. "*One* human."

"They apparently thought I'd died," Bren said. "And since I'm alive, but injured, it's possible they left Hanks in place thinking I wasn't up to my duties. I left Mospheira very rapidly after surgery this morning, and it's possible they briefed me on a number of things immediately after I came to, but I fear I didn't retain them. I by no means dispute she's in violation, but it's likely only a confusion of signals in a very rapidly evolving situation. While I'm paidhi, I promise you, nadiin, ship or no ship, Mospheira will stay within the Treaty."

Triti, in the atevi language. Which they roughly defined as a human concept of association—as humans thought atevi association meant government or confederation, not *feeling* the instinctual level of it. Bandy "treaty" about in the atevi language in most quarters with any suggestion of it as a paper document and one risked real confusion of human motives.

"But this 'sovereignty,' " Transportation objected.

"Is a difficult word," he said. "A rebel word to you, but it doesn't have such connotations in Mosphei'. It applies to their relations with each other, not with atevi, nand' Minister. How does it stand now? Has there been much more conversation?"

"Not between these two individuals," Defense said, dour-faced, and finding preoccupation in his pen and a paper clip. "We do have numerous exchanges between what we suspect to be lower-level authorities."

"Probably correct, nadi." He felt a sense of panic, sorting wildly through two languages, two psychological, historical realities, trying to make them seamless. "The fact that they've turned talk over to subordinates doesn't mean a settlement or a feud, merely that there's no agreement substantial enough to enable two leaders to talk."

"Two leaders, nadi." Defense was unwontedly peremptory, even rude in that "nadi," evidencing disturbance in his voice. "Two, is it?"

"It's not certain." He fought for calm. It wasn't territory he wanted to explore. "Not at all certain, nand' Minister. I think they're trying to see if association exists. I think historically they'll conclude it does. But if they can't find it, I can't imagine that one ship could think it outranks the entire population of Mospheira. At worst, or best, the ship might withdraw to elsewhere in the solar system. I just can't—can't—be definitive right now—"

"The paidhi," Tabini said, "is very tired, and in pain, nadiin. Thank him for his extraordinary effort on this matter, and let him go to his bed and rest tonight. Will you not, nand' paidhi?"

"Aiji-ma, if I had the strength I'd stay, but, yes, I—think that's wise. The shoulder's hurting—quite sharply."

"Then I'll turn you back to your escort and wish you good night, paidhi-ji. I ask you to consider your safety extremely important, and extremely threatened, perhaps even from human agencies. Stay to your security, night and day, nand' paidhi."

Why? was the question that leaped up, disturbing his composure in front of a table full of lords and representatives, some of whom might have been in consultation with Hanks. He wished Tabini hadn't added that—and tumbling to why, he thought: to let the troublemakers in the Association think about the hazard of making associations no ateva understood—like Hanks.

Clever of the man, Bren thought. One could admire Tabini's artistry at a distance. One just didn't want to be the subject of it—and he couldn't protest to the contrary, or call the aiji a liar. He certainly couldn't say that Hanks was an innocent in Tabini's difficulties.

One just, with the help of the table, struggled to his feet, bowed to the assembled committee chairmen—and lost the coat off his shoulders—another twinge as he tried to save it.

Banichi quietly intervened to save his dignity, adjusted the coat, and the lords and representatives gave him the courtesy of bows from their seats, two even rising in respect of his performance, when he was less than certain it was credible or creditable.

"See he rests," Tabini said to Banichi and Jago. "Straight to bed. No formalities, no excuses."

The paidhi had no argument at all with that instruction. He'd believed only giddy minutes ago that he'd controlled that conversation at least enough to hold his own.

But once out of Tabini's immediate presence the spell was broken, the excitement ebbed, and adrenaline was shifting from second-to-second performance to the raw fear that he had a human situation on his hands and that he'd given atevi far too much information.

It hadn't been a total mistake to agree to Tabini's requests. Sometimes he'd gotten extraordinary results when Tabini pulled one of his must-talks. Sometimes he'd been able to skate along on dangerously thin ice, maybe giving just a shade more to Tabini's demands for information than the Department would ever feel comfortable with—

But, dammit, getting concessions back, too—more cooperation between this aiji and Mospheira in his few years in Shejidan than his predecessor had gotten from Tabini's father in his whole career. He'd won expansions of the Treaty, he'd increased trade—

He hadn't said anything that, by the Treaty, they weren't entitled to have, or done anything that he hadn't promised to do when he got back to Shejidan, but he walked the lower hall from the meeting room under the escort of Banichi and Jago, in increasing distress over the tone and tenor of the meeting—definite deterioration in atevi confidence. Definite unease. And maybe justified unease. He needed to talk to Hanks—find out what she'd done and said, and what she understood as the truth.

Meanwhile Banichi talked to someone on his pocket-com, the device against his ear, and directed him to an express lift he was well familiar with, the one he'd used on his other visits to the third floor. He rode it up with Banichi, seeing the conference room downstairs more vividly than the utilitarian metal around them—reviewing the nuance of remembered dialogue, and agonizing over how, without going back and forth with Mospheira, he was going to straighten out concepts.

More, there were names in the text, which made it a human Rosetta Stone for atevi grammarians. An extensive text limited to topics on which atevi already knew certain Mosphei' words—and knowing words didn't mean knowing the language. Words like loyalty that didn't quite mean *man'chi;* and propriety that didn't quite mean *kabiu;* and, on the atevi side, *triti* that, unknown to most humans, didn't mean treaty, but a homing instinct under fire—*damn* Hanks and her assumptions.

Her campaigning for atevi partisans of her own couldn't be Foreign Office policy. The faction behind Hanks had absolutely no interest in screwing up on that dangerous a level. *Hanks* wanted the job; Hanks wanted what she'd trained for all her life, *he* understood that— and she was flattered to be making real headway with the likes of lord Geigi and the hard-to-handle fringes of the Association, real proof of her competency, the hell with the university liberals who *couldn't* be right about the associational fringe elements . . .

Damn, damn, and damn.

They exited into the upper hall, near the door, walked the hand-loomed carpet runner past extravagant porcelain bouquets in glass cases.

He ought to call Mospheira and brief someone— tonight, if he could get a call through—if he could keep his wits about him to make a report, no surety at all.

Worse, he wasn't sure, in view of Hanks' being left here, that he dared pick up a phone to make a call or even receive one. He'd started down a course of action he couldn't backtrack on—and he couldn't afford to have the upper echelons of the Department pull the rug out from under the Foreign Office or the paidhi with any wait-for-official-decision or a mandated consultation with Hanks.

The paidhi had damned sure better have authority in the field. Atevi certainly thought he did. The aiji of Shejidan wouldn't talk to anyone who didn't have authority to make a decision stick.

It was a situation you had to stand on both sides of: for the currently serving paidhi, it meant living up to your ears in real-time guesswork.

And yes, sometimes even that paragon of Departmental rectitude, his predecessor, Wilson-paidhi, hadn't consulted.

The hall was a haze of gold carpet patterns and pastel porcelain bouquets and he felt increasingly sick at his stomach. He wanted to be in his bed without fuss, unconscious.

He wanted to wake up in the morning with an arm that didn't hurt and with a clear-headed, logical insight into how he was going to keep everything humans and atevi had built together from blowing up in their faces.

He also wanted, pettishly, to have had more personal time at home, dammit, before they dropped him back into the boiling oil. He'd won his time off: he'd planned to sit for at least a day on his brother's white-railed porch watching the waves roll in and letting his mind go to the zero-state it longed to achieve—

Paidhiin had taken fast action before to keep an aiji of Shejidan in power. But they'd never—never—handed over the human fall-back positions in negotiating before the State Department ever got to the negotiations.

God—he thought suddenly, as that hit, asking himself what he'd done. Or what he'd actually said, or they'd implied. He suddenly couldn't remember. It was all coming apart in his mind, bleeding into confusion as they reached his door, as Jago keyed through the lock into state-of-the-art security systems which could, if forced, deal death on an intruder in ways that made a human unused to such conveniences feel very, very queasy.

Tano met them in the foyer. That was a welcome surprise. Tano might have been chasing them since the airport, but he hadn't actually seen Tano since Malguri, and in the surreal flux of events around him he was ever so glad to see the man in good health. Tano was security the same as Banichi and Jago were: deadly and grim and all of that. But Tano was on *his* side, on Tabini's orders, more particularly on Banichi's, and Banichi ranked very, very high in the Guild of Assassins by all he could figure.

"Your luggage is safe, nand' paidhi," Tano said. "I've also set your computer in safekeeping."

"Thank you, nadi. I *very* much regret your difficulties. I hope to be a very quiet resident here and give you absolutely no adventures."

Tano took his coat. "One does hope so, nand' paidhi." Another, probably real, servant appeared a few steps ahead of the gracious nadi Saidin, captured the coat from Tano and whisked it away under Saidin's direction, one supposed for cleaning and pressing. "There are messages," Saidin said, indicating the reception table by the door, where filigree silver message cylinders in daunting abundance waited in a silver basket, along with one paper simply rolled and sealed.

"The paidhi is exhausted, nadi," Banichi objected, which was only sense. Bren knew he should let those messages alone, go to bed and sleep the uneasy sleep of the truly morally compromised, without knowing or imagining who would have sent him messages so urgently early in his return: every head of every committee he'd just talked to downstairs, he was certain; plus every atevi official who saw in his accession to this apartment, and his return to Shejidan, the new importance of the paidhiin.

And possibly ordinary citizens as far as Malguri had recently seen the paidhi on local television and seen the ship in their skies and just wanted to ask: Are we and our children safe in our towns?

Certain cylinders announced their nature at a cursory glance. And, dammit, he wasn't constitutionally capable of walking past that table without assuring himself there wasn't a life-and-death communication in the lot.

Or word from Mospheira.

"A moment, nadiin-ji. Just a moment," he said and, shaky with exhaustion, nipped out of the basket the ones in particular that had caught his eye—the plain, uncylindered one: that usually meant telegrams from Mospheira; then two more, one seal that he feared he recognized, and one he was damned well sure of. Other familiar seals he didn't need to question: the head of the Space Committee—who hadn't been at the meeting, and who would have urgent, businesslike and thoroughly reasonable questions to ask the paidhi, such as: Is there still a space program, nand' paidhi? What do we do?

And, dead sure, What can we tell the Appropriations Committee?

One certainly understood that good gentleman's concern. He saw the seals of Transportation and Trade, too—logical that they had questions for the paidhi: he hoped he'd answered them adequately downstairs.

But that cylinder of real silver was indeed the seal he'd thought it was, a diamond-centered crest he'd seen not so long ago and, in view of Tabini's warning, expected.

Grandmother.

The aiji-dowager.

Ilisidi had brought him to Shejidan. Saved his neck. And risked it. Awkward with the cast, he cracked the seal with his thumbnail, slid out the little scroll and pulled it open.

Nand' paidhi, it said, in a fine, spidery hand, *I swear to your safety. The return of this cylinder on whatever day you feel able will signal your availability for breakfast. You must keep me posted. An old woman can grow so quickly out of touch with the world.*

He really truly wanted to go to bed and not to think about Ilisidi.

But there remained the two letters, one with his own white ribbon and red wax seal.

I hope you are aware, it read, *that the aiji has resorted to threats of assassination against this office to secure your return to the mainland, while repercussions of your unannounced venture into the hinterlands are still disturbing the capital. In the present crisis, I have taken measures to smooth over the damage in public relations.*

Damn!

I am continuing to conduct business, to hold discussions with responsible parties, and to send regular reports to the Department as the sole functioning diplomatic officer. That the aiji has offered you his personal hospitality is beside the point. I have not received, nor under the present conditions expect to receive, nor can I accept from you, any instruction whatsoever. I shall con-

tinue as paidhi in Shejidan until I receive official recall from the head of the State Department.

He trusted he kept his face calm. He let the paper roll up and dropped it and his own, damn the woman, message cylinder with the paidhi's seal back into the basket, before he unrolled the paper he was glad to read, the one he was sure was a telegram from Mospheira—a communication from his family or from Barb, certainly not from the Department, which used other, more secure, means to reach him.

It said, in Mosphei'-to-atevi phonetic rendering, *Sorry I missed your phone call. Bren, I know it's probably not the time to tell you, but there's no good time and this mustn't go on longer. I've married Paul. Forgive me. I wish I could build a life on your visits, but I can't.—Barb.*

He couldn't believe it. He read it again. Then somewhere inside him a little autopilot tick of professionalism reminded him he was under the witness of atevi who had every reason to assume danger to themselves lay in telegrams from Mospheira.

So he rolled up the scroll. The steadiness of his own hands amazed him. He trusted his expression was calm.

"Is there a problem, nadi Bren?"

He hadn't managed, then. Jago saw through it.

"A personal one. My—f–f–fiancée—" Atevi language failed him. The word was just suddenly there in his mouth—no other atevi way he could think of to explain a long relationship and emotional investment. "—got tired of waiting. She married someone else."

There was silence around him. He supposed they didn't know what to say. He didn't either, except, "Hold the rest of the messages, Tano, please, I'll deal with them in the morning. The aiji-dowager's—is not that urgent."

"Was this expected?" Banichi asked him, not, he was sure, regarding the dowager.

He shook his head. Then remembered with a little trepidation where he was and to what a dangerous agency he was speaking. "No, nadi. But she's quite justified."

Another small, uncomfortable silence. He supposed

he'd passed their professional limits. He didn't know. Then Jago said harshly, "She was *not* justified."

"Jago-ji," Banichi said. "Go set up for the night with Security. The paidhi is retiring. The aiji was right. We shouldn't have delayed."

"Yes," Jago said, and quietly took herself off into the apartments, pocket-com in hand, back stiff, braid swinging, while Banichi waved a hand in the same direction, toward the inner apartments.

He'd never seen Jago blurt out anything so uncontrolled. But Jago was Banichi's business, and he was more than willing to take Banichi's direction and go to bed, where he hoped he was exhausted enough to fall immediately into a sound sleep. He couldn't take any more physical or emotional jostling.

He went with Banichi and Tano through the sitting room and on to the inner chambers. The rest of the rooms were a geographical jumble in his mind, but he knew where the bedroom was.

"Will the paidhi want a bath tonight?" Banichi asked. "Or had the paidhi rather go directly to bed?"

"Bed, nadi. I'm very tired." He was grateful that Banichi had reverted to formality, Banichi's cure for too much intimacy, perhaps: it cooled the air and quietly distanced him from the problems of the world, the most important of which certainly weren't the paidhi's botched-up personal life, the paidhi's nonexistent personal life.

The paidhi had had a lot else on his mind for no few days prior; Barb had probably been trying to reach his office in Shejidan time after time without getting him—chasing him down with a telegram at his Mospheira office had probably been her last resort. Barb wasn't an ungracious person—was a very kind, very gentle person, in fact, which was what he was most going to miss, and he hoped that Paul Saarinson appreciated what he'd won. He hoped there'd be a chance to take them both to dinner and wish Barb well.

The gracious thing. The civilized thing to do. God knew he was civilized. He took his losses with entirely professional perspective.

But, *dammit!*

"Nadi," Tano said, and wished to help him with his shirt cuffs. He'd never felt comfortable letting servants, or security only masquerading as a servant, dress and undress him. It was the one atevi convention he'd evaded.

But he was the prisoner of a cut-up, taped-together shirt, a human-style shirt the Department must have come up with, because the one he'd arrived in at the hospital had been a total loss, and the hospital had turned up the next afternoon with this, which they'd cut to accommodate the cast.

He didn't, come to think of it, know how he was going to get into a shirt in the morning, or how he was going to bathe except with a sponge. For God knew how long. He was numb.

It hadn't, he knew, quite sunk in yet about Barb.

It hadn't altogether sunk in yet about what Tabini had pulled, and what he'd done downstairs, either. It kept coming back to him in flashes, snatches of what he'd said and what Tabini had said, like a recurring nightmare.

He managed the trousers on his own, kicked the shoes off, and intended to sit down on the bed just as a female servant, arriving out of nowhere, flicked down the covers. He was so tired he flinched at the whisk of coverlet and sheets from under him and sat down suddenly, jolting the arm.

A servant tried to kneel—he bent to cope, one-handed, with the socks, before she took that over. He was appalled, locked, he began to realize, in an atevi lady's female household, with servants accustomed to do things he'd never wanted servants to do for him, and no provisions at all for a man's privacy.

"I'm terribly tired," he said in a wobbly voice, an appeal to Banichi for peace, for quiet, for some kind of guard against a troop of women relentless in their hospitality. "Please," he said. "I'd like a small light left burning, Banichi-ji. I've been in too many strange rooms lately, and I'm afraid if I have to get up, I'll walk into a wall."

"Perfectly understandable," Banichi said, though one

was certain Banichi would never do such a foolish thing; Banichi passed the requisite orders with more fluency than the paidhi could manage at the moment—and the women absconded with his clothes, shoes, socks and all.

"The shirt will be a problem in the morning." Small obstacles preoccupied him, looming up as insurmountable. He turned querulous, close to tears, for no sane reason. "I don't know what I'm going to do."

"The staff will have them adjusted, nadi," Tano said. "It's all taken care of. We'll manage."

"They gave me a folder for the doctors. —Pills. I'll want my traveling case by the bedside. Water."

Such things arrived, from one source and another, servants going hither and yon. He fumbled together a nest of pillows, there being no scarcity of them in the huge bed, and stuffed them about him to rest his arm and his shoulder, while Banichi and Tano and random female servants hovered over him.

"Do you want your medicine, nadi?"

"Not right now," he said. The arm ached—but he'd been moving about, and he hoped it would ease without it. He'd regretted taking the painkiller this afternoon. They hadn't warned him it would make him dim-witted. He'd made one mess of things this evening. He didn't want to wake up stupid in the morning.

As much as anything, he didn't want to move from where he'd settled, not until daylight, not maybe for the next five days.

Banichi laid a pocket-com on the table in front of his face.

"What's that for?"

"In case, nadi. Don't go wandering about if you need something. Please call. One of us will come, very quickly. Don't walk into a wall."

"Thanks," he said, and Banichi and Tano found their way to the door—put out the lights, but left the one he'd requested.

Barb was married. Well, he thought—hell. They'd talked about marriage, in a couple of foolish moments when, early in his career, he'd thought his life would be

so routine he could arrange regular trips to Mospheira.
But she'd said no, said she didn't want marriage—and
she'd probably known he was dreaming.

Paul Saarinson was stable. Solid. Paul would be there,
all the time.

The one thing he for damn sure couldn't give her. He
was the occasions, the events, the flying trips onto the island for a glittering weekend on a far from modest,
saved-up salary—then off again, with promises and dates
that somehow didn't turn out to be available.

She was right. You couldn't build a life off weekends.
He knew that. He guessed Barb just had never told him
what she really wanted.

He blinked. The dim light shattered, rebuilt itself. You
could get used to pain.

Part of the job, wasn't it? He seemed to have made
himself a hero to the atevi around him. *They* appreciated
him in their way, which hadn't anything to do with the
sense of human companionship he had from Barb; but it
wasn't a bad thing, if you couldn't have other things, to
be appreciated by the people you most associated with.

Appreciated, hell, tell that to Tabini. Tabini *appreciated*
him. Tabini appreciated him the way an atevi lord appreciated any useful, entertaining, personally pleasant re-
source you could put on the spot and get solid value out
of.

You couldn't say love, you couldn't say friendship, you
couldn't say all sorts of things that resonated off human
nerves and satisfied human feelings. That was a trap the
first settlers had walked right into, sure that atevi, who
laughed at the right times and seemed perfectly agreeable,
did, in their own way, understand such feelings; or thinking that atevi would somehow learn to understand, that
humans would teach these godlike, tall, reserved natives
of the world the way to access their own repressed emotions.

The simple fact was atevi weren't wired for what humans wanted, they weren't in the least repressed, and they
didn't feel all the same impulses humans felt. He couldn't
take Jago's little outburst of support for him in the foyer

and build off it the fantasy that behind that momentarily fractured reserve Jago felt anything like human sympathy. Jago felt. No question that Jago felt strongly about the situation, but you couldn't warp it into what a human wanted to understand, or you missed everything that was Jago.

And did her a great disservice in the process—one always had to remember that, on the other side of the equation. As the ateva she was, Jago was wonderful, reliable, and brave. Banichi—God love him, which Banichi wouldn't at all understand—Banichi had seen him in distress and saved him from total embarrassment out there in front of Tano and the staff, because Banichi had reacted to defuse a charged situation, for whatever reasons ran through atevi nerves, be it only Banichi's sense that protecting the paidhi meant protecting the paidhi's dignity.

A human wanted a familiar tag to call things, and Banichi was a lot of things that humans the other side of the strait would be scared to death to share a room with. So was Jago. And when they'd risked their lives to save yours, you could love them so much—if you didn't need to be loved back.

Like Ilisidi, the other ateva he'd grown close to—God, if he shut his eyes he could have nightmares of the bone snapping and ligaments tearing, which hadn't been the nicest experience of his life—but he figured if nothing else he'd won points with Ilisidi and her associates simply by surviving, and backing off that invitation of hers would lose everything he'd won.

If somebody did make a move to assassinate Tabini—and him—Ilisidi was one of the likeliest perpetrators. But she asked the paidhi to breakfast at his earliest convenience.

Made perfect sense.

Maybe, the thought came recurring to him during the course of a troubled, hallucinatory night, maybe he should nerve himself, swallow his pride, and call Barb. Maybe there was more to the Paul business than he understood. He didn't like it that he'd gotten the answering machine when he'd called—he didn't know where she'd have been but home on a work night. If she'd moved up-town to Paul's place, her number should still route her calls to her.

Maybe she'd left the answering machine on precisely because she knew he was flying home and just didn't want to deal with the news on the phone—she hadn't meant to blindside him back on the mainland with that letter. He refused to believe that.

That letter had, he was absolutely convinced now, chased him from his office to the hospital and back to his office, then transferred right across the strait on the auto-mated system. He'd messaged her that he was going into hospital for some minor repair work—he hadn't elabo-rated. Maybe she'd planned to see him before he left. She'd certainly had no way to know Tabini was going to request him to do a twenty-four-hour turnaround back to Shejidan.

And he couldn't blame her for the timing. There just was no good time to tell him a piece of news like that. There'd never been a good time to tell each other much of anything: that was the trouble, wasn't it? Never a way to discuss the future, no real complaint except that he'd worked too long and given too much to the job, and he'd always known the office he'd trained for was mistress, wife, mother and sister—he couldn't talk about what he did, he couldn't offload his troubles to anybody without an equivalent security clearance, and he damn sure wasn't romantically inclined toward the Foreign Secretary.

Time after time he'd come back wound tight as a spring and so atevi-wired he couldn't speak or think Mosphei' for the first few hours; and Barb would be the first refuge after the debriefing, someone who, unlike his relatives, never met him at the door with a list of must-dos and a catalogue of family feuds. He and Barb hadn't put a load on each other, that was the whole idea of R&R, wasn't it?

But maybe she'd been *too* good-hearted—she'd known from the start she was the refuge, the safety valve for an occasionally available and generally stressed public servant the whole human race relied on. She'd ask him no classified questions, which was almost everything he knew; she'd never met him at the door with her troubles, never complained about his job, having the sense to know that he and the job weren't ever separable.

She'd laughed and she made him laugh—and he'd lost that without ever imagining it was threatened. That was what felt unfair. To him. Not unfair, he told himself, to Barb.

Hell, maybe human caring was a survival disadvantage. Who knew? It sure screwed up lives.

And where in human hell did this Paul business come from? Paul—God, Paul was so damned *dull,* so damned *safe,* a real Department man, never any interest in anything but his computers. He couldn't imagine party-loving Barb sitting in front of the television knitting while Paul was off in computerland. The whole scenario was unbelievable.

If he'd only thought to call again, when he'd stopped by his office on the way to the airport. He'd been so anxious about the travel order, so worried about getting the computer commands in. . . .

He hoped those files he'd requested had all transferred. They'd rushed him, the car had been waiting on the street—he should have delayed to check the contents. He couldn't exactly call up Mospheira now and say, Hello, I'm planning to violate Departmental policy, and I need the files you didn't send me. . . .

The State Department was where actions the Foreign Office knew atevi wouldn't tolerate ran head-on into humans who wouldn't remotely understand the atevi view. The State Department refused to admit that the paidhi in the field had authority to negotiate, although it accepted his negotiations for debate; it believed since it selected the paidhiin, that the paidhi, meaning the Foreign Office, should take orders from the State Department, a small disparity in what the Treaty meant to atevi and what humans insisted was the legal reality on their side of the strait.

Translation was going to be worrisome, even paper

translation, let alone real-time dealing with the language with a raft of new concepts.

He could make semantic mistakes. He had no Mosphei' dictionary at all, a human-language dictionary being a forbidden item on this side of the strait; the Department and a university committee even censored the entirely atevi-to-atevi dictionary and semantic/contextual reference he could take with him across the strait, since there were, in the usage of certain atevi words (in the active imagination of the committee), ways the paidhi could deliver semantic clues Mospheira didn't want in atevi hands—or minds, as the case might be—until Mospheira was sure officially that they were there.

There was some sense behind that view—there were concepts, even nontechnological concepts, that the committee rated too risky, too culturally based, too biologically based to address in the current atevi-human context, even if the paidhiin had devised reliable ways to express them in answer to questions atevi themselves had asked him.

The whole university/Foreign Office review process meant that the words the paidhi used on the mainland often ended up not being, in the classified official dictionary, the same as what his predecessor had proposed. The damned thing was constantly out of date—or subject to revision once atevi, moving consistently faster than the committee, came up with their own expression in popular usage—

Which the committee still debated, as if they could veto what atevi themselves had decided to call a thing.

More, even the Mosphei' equivalents remained flagged for censorship in documents the computers let cross the strait, computers which made electronic lace out of documents—brilliant decisions like censoring the Mosphei' expression *air traffic control system,* because supposedly, in the astute minds of the committee, *air traffic control system* had Defense Department connotations—a censorship that had lasted until well into the implementation of an atevi ATC system on the mainland, part of which, on a technological level, he was still trying to get

installed past the objections of provincial atevi lords who
thought directing air traffic and assigning landing sequence smacked rather of associational preference, a bad
word on *this* side of the strait.

And *faster-than-light?*

God help him. They trusted him with a computer with
defense codes in its layered programs and restricted him
from comprehensive dictionaries.

Meanwhile atevi, miffed at *their* inability to gain a dictionary of human language (though atevi had compiled
one, he was dead certain) didn't allow comprehensive
atevi dictionaries into the paidhi's hands on this side of
the strait. And he'd bet his unused paychecks that there
were atevi who could marginally understand Mosphei'.
Banichi came equipped with a little understanding of
Mosphei', which surfaced just now and again; Jago had a
very little; Tabini very frequently surprised him with a
word he'd picked up.

More and more interest from atevi in learning Mosphei' in recent decades, when it became clear that computers, read *human number theory,* were all bound up in
that language, and, oh, damn, yes, even conservative atevi
were interested in knowing the human numbers that described the universe. They were avid and eager learners
of anything numerical—passionate in rejection of certain
human ideas, even ones that patently worked, where they
contravened some elegant and elaborate universal number
theory; and suddenly, in the last ten years, atevi were pre-
senting elegant solutions to classic problems that the
computer people and the mathematicians were still trying
to work into their own theory—and spy out further elab-
orations thereof.

The servants, the security that kept the paidhi safe,
doubtless spied on his library and kept it pure of atevi reference.

Damnable situation. A war of dictionaries. A duel of
conceptual linguistic ignorance—when the only thing that
had brought the real war to a halt was a farseeing aiji in
Shejidan and a scholar on the human side who had, in
fact, reached the concept of "treaty" as equivalent to atevi

"association" and thereby stopped the bloodshed and the destruction—the dictionary again, victorious.

Meanwhile Hanks stayed, in danger of an assassination that was apt to fracture the Treaty. And Tabini through, he was sure, no wish of his own, had the Association legislatures in session, not only the hasdrawad and tashrid, but the provincial legislatures, in districts whose lords were ready to make a grab for power at any moment Tabini remotely looked like stumbling.

Damned right Tabini needed him to do something fast; Tabini, damn his conniving heart, needed a miracle, ideally a piece of drama pulled off right in front of the joint legislatures—the whole atevi world was waiting for official answers from the Bu-javid, from the aiji and from the paidhi's office.

God only knew what Hanks had actually said. Inexperienced humans, even humans who'd sweated through advanced mathematics courses in the candidacy courses, never believed at gut level how quick atevi were to work math in their heads. The language with its multiple plurals set up a hell of a quick-reckoning system that was a major barrier to a human trying to learn it as a second language; Hanks wouldn't be the first translator who in the simple struggle to handle the verb forms in conversation had edged her way into deep linguistic trouble.

Thoughts like those chased each other in circles for what felt like hours, intermittent with the shoulder aching until he could only count the pulses of the pain and wish in vain for sleep.

Enough to make him think about the pill and the water on the bedside table. If he didn't need his brain tomorrow. But it was a toss-up how the lack of sleep was going to help find a solution, either. He needed a jolt of adrenaline. If he could just summon it up for about six hours tomorrow, he had a fighting chance of thinking his way through to what he ought to do.

Damn, he said to himself. Damn.

He wanted to go back and replay the meeting with Tabini and do it all differently.

He wanted to have made that second phone call from his office, before he'd gone to the airport.

Oh, Barb, you damn fool. *Paul,* for God's sake.

But when they'd broken his shoulder and he'd believed he'd die, he'd not been able to think about Barb, or Toby, or anybody—just the mountains. Just his mountain and the snow. . . . And he'd felt hollow, and didn't know why he couldn't think of Barb or find any feeling in himself. He'd found it disturbing that he couldn't scrape together any feeling about it—he'd tried, *tried* to reconstruct his feeling for Barb, but he couldn't get it back the way he remembered it being, not then—not when he'd gotten home.

He'd thought to call her.

He'd been worried when he couldn't reach her—last thought he'd had going under anesthetic, where was Barb? So he'd felt something.

He'd felt real pain when he'd read her message, felt it right in the gut; he was losing Barb—when he didn't know he'd ever *had* Barb, had no reason to think what they had amounted to a life, didn't know if he loved her—just—a feeling that blinked out on him under the gun in Malguri and blinked on again when he got back to familiar referents and places he was used to being.

So what was it? Love or a habit he'd gotten into? Or what in hell was the matter with a man who hadn't been able to remember Barb's face when he was in the worst trouble he'd ever been in? What was the matter with a man whose deepest feelings blinked on and off like that?

Too long on the mainland, maybe. Too long wrestling the demons of atevi emotions, until what he'd studied grew commonplace to him and what he'd been grew foreign. He was fluent, he was good, he could find his way among atevi by the map he'd made, *he'd* made, whole new understandings that humans hadn't had before—but he wasn't sure he'd charted the way back.

Snap. And he was playing by human rules and he loved Barb.

Snap. And he was deep in atevi thinking and he didn't know how to do that.

He was scared. He was really scared.

It was two hours before dawn, by the watch he'd pulled out of his office drawer. And he had to function tomorrow. He had to pull his wits together tomorrow.

He *had* to get some sleep. He daren't take the pill, now; he'd sleep half the day and drag through the rest and he couldn't afford that.

He tried counting. By hundreds. To the highest numbers he could think of.

He tried thinking about committee meetings, reconstructing lord Brominandi's speeches to the Transport Committee, sane lawmakers arguing for fifteen solid days whether requiring airports to maintain computer records on flights could accidentally assign infelicitous numbers and cause crashes.

He woke up dreaming about atevi shadows asking him questions, about an urgent meeting he had to get to—and woke up again with the impression of a beast leering at him from the bedroom wall. But the beast wasn't here, it was in Malguri.

He'd flown home. He'd flown back. He'd met with Tabini, that was where he was. The outlines of the room were strange. He was in an atevi lady's apartment, in a bed a man had died in. He was supposed to solve the ship problem tomorrow.

Stave off the invaders.

Hold the world economy together.

Try to shave and take a damn bath.

Thirty minutes before dawn. If the servant staff started moving about right now and woke him up, he'd have them all assassinated. He wanted at least two hours sleep. He wasn't budging until he'd gotten those two hours. Not if the ship orbiting over their heads started firing death rays down on the city.

Then he started worrying about the computer files and couldn't get back to sleep.

The servants began stirring about in the farther halls.

Don't touch me, he thought. Don't dare come in here. If I don't move, they won't make any noise. If I don't move, they won't bother me maybe till they think I'm dead.

But he had to find out whether the files had transferred.

And he *didn't* have that much time to prepare: Tabini had said it, people could die—and he had to be right about the translations, which couldn't—*couldn't* convey anything atevi could construe as irrevocable threat to them: the answer Tabini got back had to be something that would reassure atevi, not something that would hit the evening news with panic—he had to go over the entire vocabulary he'd allot himself in dealing with the matter; after that he could ad lib all he liked—but not until he was sure of extended and obscure meanings.

He stuck a foot out from under the covers; he got his working elbow under him, unstuffed pillows from under him and made a try to turn on the light.

Knocked the water glass over.

On the carpet.

The pocket-com followed. And the pill bottle. And the lamp.

The room lights went on.

"Nadi?" Jago asked, all concern, her hand on the light switch. "Are you all right?"

5

It was a strange perspective, either on the scale of human problems or human capacity for delusion, that one hour of daylight could dull acute, even rational, concerns and persuade an exhausted man he'd had a night's sleep.

At least he'd achieved a functional distance from the insanity he'd slept with, the carpet had survived the water, the lamp had survived the fall, a breakfast of tea and toast and jam to cushion the necessary antibiotics—not the pain pills—hadn't upset his stomach, and the breakfast room turned out to have a beautiful view.

More, life on earth had not after all ended with his relationship with Barb. He couldn't fix it from where he was, he probably hadn't the right to fix it—it was the old story: it was going to be too late for him to do a damned thing by the time he had a chance to do anything.

Meanwhile he had urgent work to do, and the context-sensitive language programs he needed to work out his translation appeared to have made it into his machine.

So after a tolerably leisurely breakfast in a privacy for which the paidhi's bathrobe was completely if informally sufficient, he sent Tano to attack the bowlful of mail, so that, excused by his injury, he could sit in said bathrobe in the solarium in view of the magnificent Bergid range, rummage through his Mospheira-origin computer message files and wait for the voice records Tabini had promised him would arrive as soon as possible.

The message download was immense. Whenever he logged on at his Mospheira office port he'd inevitably acquire, through the filter that censored and frequently made hash of what it let him have, a mishmash of messages, some official, some scholarly inquiries, some the advisories of the hard-worked staff that supported the paidhi's office, from the devoted crew that sifted the out-pourings of the phone-ins of every ilk, to the more reli-able information that came to him down official channels, and to the Mospheira news summaries, neatly computer-censored for buzzwords and restricted concepts the paidhi couldn't take with him across the strait. That he'd gotten anything on his flags reassured him that, Hanks or no Hanks, he was getting cooperation from official channels, and he did have his authorizations intact.

His message-load held personal letters from a list of correspondents he'd flagged as always full-text, at least as full-text as the censors let him have, ranging from uni-versity professors of linguistics and semantics, to old neighborhood friends giving him news of spouses, kids and summer vacations.

And came the State Department output, which was not, this time, highly informative: information on pensions. Helpful. God.

Some of it had to go—he ordered Explore, and saw the Interactives come back with characteristics and content of the files; he asked it next to Search ship/*Phoenix*/station/ history content, and it came back with lists.

And lists.

And lists.

With tags of correspondents both regular and names he didn't at all know: everyone with access to the For-eign Office had had an opinion and offered it when the news broke about the ship returning, that was what had happened—he'd done such a fast turnaround the staff hadn't had the time they usually had to weed and con-dense—meaning he had the whole damned load, God help him, every crackpot who could find the address in the phonefile.

Several of the files were absolutely huge. University papers. Theses. Dissertations.

He hadn't thought it possible to crowd the memory limits. It was a *big* storage. He checked through the over-lays, scared something might have started a memory resident to chewing up the available space, but nothing checked out as active but things that ought to be, and nothing was actively eating memory. It was just that much data he'd sucked up in his connection time.

It wasn't going to be an easy sift-out. The computer was going to have to search and search.

And there was one thing he had to do, before he sank all the way into study: he asked Saidin for a phone, sat down in his bathrobe and, calmly composed, called through the Bu-javid phone system with a request for Hanks-paidhi.

Not available, the operator said.

"Message to her residence," he said patiently, very patiently.

"Proceed, nand' paidhi. Record now."

"Hanks-paidhi," he said in the atevi language. "Kindly return my call. We have urgent business. End, thank you, nadi."

The bloody *hell* Hanks wasn't available. He took a deep breath, dismissed Hanks and her maneuvers from his list of critical matters, and went back to his chair and his computer.

He set his background search criteria, then, to his needs, defaulted to print-matches-to-screen at his own high-rate data-speed, which was damn fast when he was motivated and the criteria were subject-narrow: a lifetime of foreign language, semantics, dictionary work and theoretical linguistics gave him some advantages in mental processing and rapid reading, and what he did in his head with the files was a personal Search and Dump and Store that didn't even half rely on conscious brain. Just the relevant stuff reached the mental data banks, a process that rapidly occupied all the circuits, preempted the pain receptors, turned off everything but the eyes and the fingers on a very limited set of buttons.

What came through to him was an impression, variously derived from his university scholar correspondents and the mishmash from correspondents both authorized and not, of a degree of concern about the ship's long absence, and its careful questioning of Mospheiran officials.

He couldn't nail the specific questions: the letter that might have been most specific was full of censored holes.

But references abounded to that bitter dispute among the original settlers, whether to land on the one livable world in the system, or mine and stay in space. There were specific names of ship crew, which he tagged as useful—who had been in important positions versus where descendants ranked might tell him something about the difference between the power structures that existed two hundred years ago—the foundation of scholarly and governmental assumptions—and those that existed now: clues to the passing of power downward.

A university professor he'd thought long-retired offered him information about the final ship-station exchanges, a file which contained exact quotes. Those he dived after and read, and read, and read, at a speed at which his eyes dried out and his teacup stayed suspended until a deft touch removed it from his hand.

Banichi said, "Would the paidhi care for hot tea?"

"Thank you," he said, stopped the dataflow of that not-friendly exchange, and took a brief intermission to what atevi genteelly called the necessity.

A servant had meanwhile supplied a fresh teapot, a clean cup and a plate of wafers, and he restarted the dataflow three minutes before the interrupt point.

The sun inched up out of the window. Lunch appeared, sandwiches ceremoniously brought to his chair.

There arrived, with it, Banichi, and a message from Tabini that asked whether he had any questions Banichi and Jago couldn't answer. "No, nadi," he said to Banichi's inquiry. "Just the ground-station transmission records. Please. Do you have any idea the reason of the delay, nadi?"

"I believe they're changing format," Banichi said.

"Banichi, if I'm supposed to listen to the tapes, I don't need the intelligence people to clean them up. Peel the access codes out, I don't *care* about the numbers, I swear to you, I don't have to have their precious numbers—we're not 'counters here. Just get me the damn—excuse me—voice recordings. That's all I ask, nadi."

"I'll urge this point with Tabini. I need the paidhi's authority to approach him against other orders."

"Please do." He was frustrated. Time was running. Someone in Defense was apparently holding things up for real concerns or obstructionist motives. He couldn't guess. He couldn't let go of his thoughts. He'd built too fragile a web of translated conjecture. He'd never yet taken his eyes from his screen and the reminders of where he was in the structure; and when Banichi left, he reached for half a sandwich with the same attention he'd given his teacup, then dived back into his work, only moving a leg that had gone to sleep.

"Tabini-aiji asks," Banichi said at another necessity-break, "if the paidhi would care to issue a statement for the news. It's by no means a command. Only a suggestion, if the paidhi is able."

"Tell them," he said, floundering brain-overloaded in a sea of input, "tell them in my name that I would wish to speak to them, but I'm in the middle of a briefing. Whatever you can contrive, Banichi-ji. I can't possibly issue a definitive statement yet. I'm translating and memorizing as fast as I can. I'm drowning in details. —And they won't get me the records. What in hell are they doing, Banichi?"

"One is aware," Banichi said carefully. "Steps have been taken. Forgive my intrusion."

Banichi was a professional—at the various things Banichi did. The paidhi at the moment had one focus: data and cross-connection; reading for *hours* on end at unremitting scroll.

Figuring out how, with a limited dictionary, to explain interstellar flight in unambiguous words for the Determinists and the Rational Absolutists, whose universe didn't admit faster-than-light, was absolutely terrifying. *He* didn't understand FTL, himself, and finding two atevi-mentality numerical philosophies a linguistic straw of paradox to cling to, to keep two provinces of the Association from disintegrating into riot, made his brain ache. It was all a structure of contrived cross-connections and special pigeonholes for the linguistically, historically, mathematically and physically irresolvable—and he hoped to God nobody asked the question.

Especially when all the historical information contradicted itself—and indicated the Mospheiran records, God help him, were not infallible.

Paidhiin before him had elevated atevi science from the steam engine to television, fast food, scheduled airlines, and a space program—and he didn't know if the next step might be Armageddon.

So he bent himself again to his reading, seeing the Seeker had come up with a further digest of content— slow, memory-hungry operation, running slower than usual in the background—and had the summary of thirty-three trivial files, all inquiries, none informative.

That could go down to temp-store on a card. Free up memory. Make the computer run faster. The paidhi had other problems.

And, seeing that the Seeker had created another ship/ history thread through a chain of files, he said, "Thread, ship/history, collect," and saw the result rip past at his fast-study speed.

But the information wouldn't coalesce for him. He'd blown his concentration or there was something else knocking at the back door of his awareness, something large and far-reaching, all associative circuits occupied—

"Forgive me again," Banichi said, and Bren restrained a frantic impulse to wave it off, because he had almost realized there was something there.

But Banichi laid a recorder on the table—along with a message cylinder carrying the red-and-black seal that indicated it came from Tabini himself.

Thoughts went to the winds. He suffered a cold chill, murmured a, "Thank you, nadi, wait a moment," and opened the message cylinder, finding a note in Tabini's hand: *This is the complete record, paidhi-ji, with the numbers. I hope this proves helpful.*

He hoped to God. He found lunch not sitting well on his stomach. "Thank you, nadi-ji," he said, dismissing Banichi to his own business, and lost no time first in setting his computer to run full bore on the time-consuming

Seeker summary program, then in setting the recorder to play back.

The first of it—he'd heard last night. He sped past that and fast-played the computer chatter.

More voices, then.

It fit the suspicion he'd formed from the records he'd been handed—the parting nastiness of Pilots' Guild politics suddenly played out real-time in what had gone on while he was in the east: the Pilots' Guild, for reasons for which one had to trust the distinguished university professor's unpublished history, had cast some obstacles in the way of the Landing all those years ago, ostensibly to protect atevi civilization.

But, the professor's account suggested, the Guild had both promoted and double-crossed the operation, because the Guild's real objective had been to maintain the ship as paramount, over the station, over any planetary settlement. The Guild had intended to run human affairs—as it had done during the long struggle to get to the earth of the atevi.

Trusting any history for the truth in a situation rapidly becoming current was, by its very nature, trusting a sifted, condensed account of hour-by-hour centuries-old events that he couldn't recover—events sifted by somebody with a point of view rooted in his own time, his own points to prove. He doubted that the detail he needed still existed even in the computer records on Mospheira: the war had taken out one big mass of files.

The fact was—he knew far less about *Phoenix* than he knew about atevi; he knew *Phoenix'* present attitudes, inclinations and crew list less than he knew the geography of the moon. He didn't *know* what *Phoenix* meant, or intended, or threatened.

He didn't know the capabilities of the ship, whether it had traveled at FTL speeds or—considering the length of time it had been gone—sublight, which seemed a possibility.

But, ominously, the dialogue between ship and ground-station had gone from massively informative and high-level in the initial moments to, finally, the converse of under-secretaries and ship's officers niggling their way through questions neither side was willing to bring anybody to the microphone to answer.

What was the state of affairs, the ship asked, between Mospheira and the world's native population?

Mospheira wasn't answering that question. The State Department, the same close-mouthed upper echelon that backed Deana Hanks, was advising the President on an entity it didn't know a damned thing about; and the executive once it got involved was used to having weeks, months, even years and decades to study and debate a problem.

Mospheira didn't *have* or *want* rapid change. The social and technological dynamics meant what was, would be, foreseeably, for fifty, a hundred years, and its planning was always well in advance, a simple steerage of the world at large, atevi and human, toward matching technological bases, toward goals decades away. And if the executive got off its butt and moved—the sub-offices through which governmental communications ran weren't geared to decide faster than they did.

And if the ship knew what it wanted and pushed . . .

He listened, as back the two sides came to another foot-dragging exchange of minor ship officers demanding station records which they thought Mospheira should have; and after a day and a half, by the time markers, another exchange demanding in turn where the ship had been for two hundred years.

Damn again, Bren thought, hearing *Phoenix* ignore the question and then hail the world at large, wondering if anyone else down there was listening.

Phoenix was trying to make contact on its own. Thank God nobody in the atevi world understood enough to fire back an answer and begin a dialogue. Thank God the Treaty provided the paidhi at least as a unified contact point. *Phoenix* was unknowingly charting a very dangerous course.

After that the ship broke off transmissions for what seemed a long time, and atevi date notations on the tape confirmed it. The ship asked no questions and ominously

provided not one answer, not one clue to the President's
persistent questions: Where have you been? Why have
you come back? What do you want here now?

Mospheira had revealed a great deal to the incomers—
necessarily, with the whole planet spread out for the orbiting ship to see—a tapestry of railroads and lighted towns
and cities and airports, the same on one side of the strait
as on the other, which had not at all been the case when
the ship left. And he knew what the ship's optics were capable of seeing, at least the equal of what Mospheira had
been able to see through the failing eyes of the station—
hype that several times, for what a ship with undamaged
optics could pick up.

And there was no way to see inside the ship or the station.

While Mospheira had, he mused, knuckle pressed
against his lips, revealed more in its questions than it
might realize, too, certainly to him. He knew the Department, he knew the executive, he knew personalities—the
ship didn't, unless it discovered old patterns, but, damn,
he could almost detect the fingerprints on the questions,
the responses, the attitudes. It was Jules Erton, senior Policy; it was Claudia Swynton—it was the President's Chief
of Staff, George Barrulin: the President didn't *have* opinions until George told him what he thought.

The records became contemporaneous. Mospheira
talked. The ship continued its efforts at contacting population centers, Shejidan in particular. There hadn't been
contact between the ship and Mospheira for two days.
The ship was *not* currently answering questions from
Mospheira about its business or its activities.

The cold that had started with his arm had spread to a
general shivery unease and left him wishing—which he
never thought in his life he would wish—that he could
pick up the phone, call Deana Hanks, and say, amicably,
sanely, Look, Deana, differences aside—we have a problem.

Which was not, damn the woman, a comfortable proposition. The rift was not a resolvable rift between two
people, it was ideological, between two political philoso-

phies on Mospheira. The camp he feared now had thrown Deana Hanks onto the mainland was the same that had supported Hanks through the selection process no matter her test scores, and he suspected foreknowledge of key questions she *still* hadn't answered with as high a score as his, as well as outside help on the requisite paper. She was Raymond Gaylord Hanks' granddaughter, and S. Gaylord Hanks' daughter: that was old, old politics, a conservative element that had, ever since the war, argued that Shejidan was secretly hostile—the same damned suspicion among humans that, mirror-image among atevi, believed in death rays on the station, maintained that the atevi space program got atevi funding because, along with getting into space, atevi meant to take the station and use it as a base to deny access for Mospheira.

The fixation of the conservatives lately was the snowballing advances in technology during his and Wilson's tenure, both technological and social: the conservatives held that Tabini was hostile and using a naive paidhi for his own purposes.

That very conservative camp of human interests moldered away, not in obscure university posts, but in the halls of the presidency, the legislature: they were the old guard politicians, whose families had been in politics since the war, in an island community where politics had traditionally not mattered a damn in ordinary human affairs and nepotism got more immediate results.

In the State Department, most of the view-with-alarmers were at senior levels, entrenched in lifelong tenancies: they had never, ever accepted the official atevi assertion that Tabini was innocent of his father's assassination. It was a tenet of the conservative faith that Tabini had done it, and that Tabini had demanded Wilson-paidhi resign to get a new and naive paidhi to carry out his programs.

In brutal atevi fact, they were very probably right, granted Tabini's grandmother hadn't beaten him to it— but parricide didn't weigh the same on the mainland as it did on Mospheira. One just couldn't judge atevi by human ethics. Assassinate someone of the same *man'chi,* the same hierarchical loyalty? That was shocking.

Assassinate a relative? That was possibly a rational solution.

The damn trouble was—the paidhi had far better pipelines and mechanisms for dispensing new information into the atevi mainland than he had for moving public opinion on Mospheira. It had never been *necessary* before for the paidhi to convince Mospheirans. It had never been *necessary* before for the paidhi to campaign against the conservatives, because the conservatives had never had a crisis in which they could move members of academe, as he feared they had done, to interfere in the paidhi's office.

But the academic insulation that supported the paidhi and assisted in the decision-making—usually without the politicians involved in the process—was a politically naive group of people, who, confronted with panic, might have been rushed to put Hanks in a position where she could at least observe at a time when lack of information seemed very ominous.

He'd never taken Hanks seriously. He'd taken for granted that she'd drown quietly in academe and be so old if she ever got the appointment she'd likely decline it, immersed lifelong in Mospheiran ways and incapable of adjusting if she got here. He'd trusted the academics to just keep shunting his conservative albatross aside for decades, give her some tenured professorship in Philosophy of Contact or some other nap class. Ask him a year ago and he'd have said that was the future of Deana Hanks.

It wasn't.

The shiver that had started wouldn't go away. It wasn't fear, he said to himself. It was simply sitting in one spot in what he now realized, by the blowing of the curtains, was a draft from the windows, until his legs went to sleep. It was the aftereffects of anesthetic. It was the whole crisis he'd been through—

It was the whole, damnable, mishandled situation. He'd been in the eastern part of the continent, out of the information loop, when atevi needed him most. It might not be his fault; atevi might have put him there temporarily until they were assured they could rely on—not trust—him.

But for whatever necessary satisfaction of atevi suspicion, he had been kept in the dark, all the same, and now if he misstepped—if he was even apprehended to misstep, politically—or if he pulled a mistake like Hanks' mistake with lord Geigi, which he *still* had to clean up—

Hell. He'd made a few mistakes himself, early on in his tenure.

And hell twice—the woman had to have some sense, somewhere located. You couldn't get through Comparative Reasoning or the math and physics requirements if you hadn't at least the ability to draw abstract conclusions. He should give reason a try.

He extricated himself from the chair, bit by slow bit and, letting his foot tingle back to awareness, got up and pulled the bell-cord. Saidin answered it. He sent Saidin after Jago, and Jago to deliver two verbal messages. To Tabini: *I've learned all I'm likely to find out. I'm ready to talk to the public.*

And to Deana Hanks: *I will shortly issue an official position on the ship presence; you will receive a copy. We need to talk. Is tomorrow evening possibly agreeable to your schedule?*

Then he went back to his chair, tucked up, and shut his eyes. Amazing how fast, how heavily sleep could come down, once the decision was made and the load was off.

But he could afford to sleep now, he said to himself. Other people could deal with the scheduling and the meetings and the arranging of things. He half-waked when someone settled a coverlet over his legs, decided they didn't need him, that the ship hadn't swooped down with death rays yet, and he simply hugged the coverlet up over a breeze-chilled arm and enjoyed the comfortable angle he'd found.

He waked again when Jago came to him, called his name and gave him another message cylinder sealed with Tabini's seal.

It gave the time of the joint session as midevening, unusual for atevi legislative proceedings, and added, simply, *Your attendance and interpretations are gratefully requested, nand' paidhi.*

"Any other message?" he asked. "Anything from the island?"

"No, I regret not, Bren-ji."

"Did you talk to Deana Hanks? What did she say?"

"She was very courteous," Jago said. "She listened. She said tell you a word I hesitate to say it."

"In Mosphei', she gave you this word."

"I think that *go-to-'elle* is rude. Do I apprehend correctly?"

Temper—was not what would serve him this evening. He made his face quite impassive.

"I made no answer," Jago said. "I am embarrassed to bring you such a report. If you have an answer, I will certainly carry it. Or we can bring this person to your office, Bren-paidhi."

Tempting. "Jago-ji, I've sent you to a fool. You will get an apology, or satisfaction."

"There are less comfortable accommodations than your old apartment, Bren-ji."

"She's in *my* apartment?"

Jago shrugged. "I fear so, Bren-ji. If I were handling her security, I'd advise otherwise."

"I want her moved *out*. Speak to Housing. This is not a woman without enemies."

Jago made a little moue, seemed to be thinking, and finally said, "Her security is very tight—for such a sieve. In terms of live bodies, quite a high level. I speak in confidence."

"I've no doubt. *Tabini's* security?"

"Yes. Which the aiji can relax at will."

Meaning leave her completely unprotected. Jago didn't breach Tabini's security on a whim. That Jago told him anything at all on a matter she didn't need to mention was troubling.

"Did Tabini tell you to tell me this?"

Jago's face was at its most unreadable.

"No," she said.

Which meant narrowly what you could get it to mean—but when Jago took that tone, there was no more information forthcoming.

6

Plastic bags, scavenged from the post office down-stairs, the female servants declared in triumph; and tape from the same source. It was Tano's idea, so that a disreputable-feeling human, pushed beyond an already-fading interspecies modesty, could enjoy a real, honest-to-God hot shower, with all the bandages and the cast protected: "Nand' paidhi, you don't want to get water under the cast," was Tano's judgment. "Trust me in this."

He did. Waterproofed, he leaned against the wall in a real, beautifully tiled, modern bathroom, shut his eyes, breathed the steam, and felt the world swinging around an axis somewhere in the center of his skull.

He was possibly about to commit treason. Was that what you called it, when it was your species as well as your nation in question?

He was at least about to do something astonishingly foolhardy, going into this speech without one written note card for vocabulary, trusting adrenaline to hit and inspiration to arrive in his brain, when it wasn't entirely certain that he owned the strength necessary to make it down-stairs or a vocabulary more extensive than occurred on that card. It was the evening, the fairly late evening, of a very, very long day, and the shower and the steam were reducing him to a very, very low ebb of willpower.

"Nand' paidhi," Tano called to him from outside the shower. "Nand' paidhi, I regret, you should come out now."

It was an atevi-engineered luxury, that literally inex-haustible hot water supply. And he had to leave it. Unfair. Unfair. Unfair.

He delayed the length of two long sighs, went out into the cruel brisk air and suffered the tape peeled; allowed himself to be unwrapped, toweled and, by now robbed of all modesty—and with the servants quite properly and respectfully professional—helped into his clothes: a silk shirt, re-tailored with a seam and fastenings up the arm, his coat, likewise sacrificed; soft, easy trousers of a modest and apolitical pale blue, a very good fit.

Once he'd sat down, too, a further toweling of his past-the-shoulders hair and a competently done braid, the only thing for which he'd habitually relied on his servants.

That was when the nerves began to wind tight. That was when he began to feel the old rush of adrenaline, a lawyer going into court, a diplomat going into critical negotiations. He was sitting, feeling the tugs at his hair as Tano plaited it, when Jago, wearing a black leather jacket despite the summer weather, arrived with a written message from Tabini, which said simply, *There will be news cameras. Speak the truth. I have all confidence in you.*

News cameras. One *didn't* damn the aiji to hell with the servants listening, no matter how one wanted to.

"Where's Banichi?" he asked. He was slipping toward combat-mode. He wanted everything that was his nailed down, accounted for, tallied and named. He *knew* Tabini in his slipperiest mode. He wanted Banichi on his side of the fence, not Tabini's. He wanted to know what orders Banichi had, and from whom.

"I don't know, nadi," Jago said. "I only know I'm to escort you, nadi, when you're ready."

There was body armor and a weapon under that black leather coat, he was well sure. With feelings and suspicions understandably running high, it was entirely reasonable. And if Banichi wasn't with him, Banichi was up to something that left his junior partner in charge—possibly serving as Tabini's security, which Banichi also was. He had no way to know.

And no choice but the duty in front of him.

He gathered himself out of the chair and let Tano and the servants help him into the many-buttoned formal coat—which occasioned a little fuss with the discreetly placed fastenings that made the sleeve look relatively intact, and in order for the all-important ribbon-distinguished braid to lie outside the high collar. There were tweaks, there were adjustments, there were sly, curious and solemn looks.

He stood, to the ebon, godlike ladies around him, about the size of a nine-year-old. He felt entirely overwhelmed and fragile, and hoped, God, hoped he retained the things he needed in his head, and wouldn't—God help him—say or imply something disastrous tonight.

"Jago-ji, if you'd bring the computer—I don't think I'll need it, but something might come up."

"Yes," Jago said. "Are we ready, nand' paidhi?"

"I hope so," he said, and was surprised and even moved when Saidin bowed deeply, with: "All the staff wishes you success, nand' paidhi. Please do well for us."

"Nadi. Nadiin." He bowed to the servants, who bowed with more than perfunctory courtesy. "You've made my work possible. Thank you ever so much for your courtesy and care."

"Nand' paidhi," the general murmur was. And a second all-round bow, on the tail of which Jago took him in charge, picked up the computer and headed him toward the outer chambers and the door. Tano, wearing a uniform identical to Jago's, overtook them just before the foyer.

Then it was out into the hall of porcelain flowers and down to the general security lift, which all the residents of the top two levels used, down the three floors to the broadest, most televised corridor in the Bu-javid, the entrance to the tashrid.

He was accustomed to the territory. His own office wasn't that far removed. But the halls were lighted from scaffolds supporting television cameras and crews, echoing with the goings and comings of staff and aides. If he'd felt overwhelmed by the servants, he was far more so here, in the entry to the hall itself, where the tall, elegant lords of the Association gathered and talked—more so, as silence fell where he and his escort walked, and became a quiet murmur at his back.

There was a lesser corridor, for the privileged not wishing to be accosted in the aisles, a way into the tashrid, the house of lords, down the division between that and the much larger chamber of the hasdrawad, the commons. The screen which divided the two chambers was folded back, affording direct access to the joined chambers, where he could walk past the stares and the murmurous gossip of the members, down the slant of the figured carpet to that small set of ornately carved benches set aside for dignitaries and invited witnesses and petitioners.

There on the front row of the dignitaries' gallery he could sit alone with his single note card, with the reassurance of Jago and Tano hovering in the standing area near him.

The lords of the Association and the elected representatives of the provinces were drifting in rapidly now. He directed his attention to the card he had yet to memorize, a handful of words that could convey what he wanted to convey without unwanted connotations, a handful of atevi-language definitions he'd devised. FTL was an absolute ticking bomb. He *didn't* want to handle it tonight. He hoped to steer away from technicalities.

From a third of the seats filled there was a sudden abundance of legislators in the aisles, moving with some purpose, and he was not at all surprised, once that influx had found seats, that Tabini-aiji arrived by the same entry he'd used—but Tabini walked to the fore of the chamber. The gallery was jammed with observers, and while Jago and Tano stood steadfastly on guard near Bren, Tabini walked to the podium.

"Nand' paidhi," Tabini said, the speakers echoing out over both halls.

He got up, picked up the computer Jago had set near him, and began his trek down the aisle while Tabini received the standing, silent courtesy of the joint houses, and then declared that the paidhi would, for the first time in this administration, address the houses of government and the provinces conjointly, "to provide expert information on the event in the heavens."

He came up to the secondary microphone with no other

fanfare, bowed to Tabini, bowed to the tashrid, to the hasdrawad, and set the computer down.

"Ladies and gentlemen of the Association," was the correct address, and, "Nand' paidhi," he heard back, as the members bowed to him in turn, then sat down.

He drew an insufficient breath, and found a convenient place to lean a supporting arm on the lower rails of a speaker's platform far too tall for him.

A sea of dark, listening, variously expectant faces confronted him.

"A long time ago," he began, "nadiin, a ship set out from a distant world, intending to build a space station at a place they thought they were going to live. But some accident sent the ship out of sight of all the stars the navigators knew, into a place so heavy with radiation it was deadly to anyone working outside the hull. Very many of the crew died gathering the resources they had to have to take the ship to safety. The workers who were only passengers on this mission had no skills to save the ship: they voted the ship's crew extraordinary privilege and power so long as it was ship's crew who went outside the hull."

Atevi audiences didn't emote in a formal presentation. They sat. They kept impassive faces and absolute, respectful silence. They didn't cue a speaker what way they were thinking, or whether they were understanding, or whether they wanted to shoot the speaker. Atevi audiences just *listened*, disconcertingly so.

But the reason for the granting of rank and privilege was absolutely important to atevi thinking. And while privilege could arise from ancestral merit, it had to have constant merit, or it was suspect: *that* was the groundwork he was laying. Deliberately.

"Nadiin," he said, and fought for breath over the constriction of the tape around his ribs, damnably unforgiving of the fact the wearer was scared, needed to project his voice, and needed more air. "Brave people mined the fuel they needed to fly the ship to a more favorable and healthful place, which they had to choose on very little data. This world—" One avoided more precise cosmology. It had to come soon. Just, please God, not tonight. "This world was promising. But once they entered orbit here, they were vastly upset to learn it was an inhabited planet. They'd spent all their fuel. They'd lost so many lives they were growing fragile as a community. The ship crew wanted to withdraw to the fourth planet from the sun and build a station in orbit, thinking it then might be a long time before atevi discovered human presence—but after such a dangerous journey—"

Another pause for air, and he still had no reaction at all, good or bad, to what was mostly old information, with insights that weren't in the previous canon. "After such a terrible journey, nadiin, and so many lives lost, people were afraid of travel and harsh, unknown environments. They reasoned if they built their home in orbit around a life-bearing world, and if something went wrong in space, there was the planet below as a last resort. They saw that atevi were civilized and advanced—their telescopes told them so. They felt much safer where they were, and they voted against the ship's crew.

"But some Mospheirans say the crew of the ship was anxious to maintain the reason for their rank and privilege, and that was their real reason for wanting to take the ship back into deep space.

"Some argue, no, it was a true concern for disturbing atevi lives.

"Still others say that they simply were a space-faring people and saw themselves constricted by this long time at dock.

"But for whatever reason, the crew of the ship wanted to leave and wanted fuel. The workers' representatives opposed more expenditure of effort for the ship in a venture in which they saw no advantage for themselves. That was the point at which the association on the station truly began to fragment.

"Some said they should go down to the planet and establish a base there.

"Some said all resources should go to the station as a permanent human home in orbit, and that they wouldn't divert resources to a landing or to the ship for any new venture.

"Now there were three factions, and the situation demanded compromise.

"The ship sided with the workers who wanted to maintain the station, because they needed the station for a dock and a source of repair and supply; but taking the ship out into deep space, which was their highest priority, demanded an immense amount of the resources the station wanted for itself. The workers who wanted to land on the planet switched sides and voted with the ship's crew, at least one human scholar suspects, in return for secret assurances the spacefarers wouldn't let the station dwellers block their activities.

"The human community became a nest of intrigue as the new sub-associations pulled each in their own directions. The ship sided with the would-be colonists to get the resources it needed—

"But, because in this three-way standoff, the pro-Landing people couldn't get funding or resources for advanced landing craft, no one believed they could land, especially since the Pilots' Guild refused to fly the designs they had for a landing craft—or—the Landing faction began to suspect, any design they would ever come up with.

"So—that group built landers with old technology that didn't need Guild pilots. In effect, they fell toward the planet and parachuted in, the petal sails of the old account. Mospheira looked to them to have a lot of vacant land, and they thought if there were trouble, it would be easy to live in the north of the island and make agreements with atevi to the south in what they thought was an island government."

Atevi calm cracked in scattered laughter. Certain members clearly thought it was a joke. It *was* funny, if lives on both sides hadn't paid for it; he was relieved: they were following his logic. They were understanding this very critical point of human behavior.

"It actually got worse, nadiin. The Guild thought the Landing would lose credibility, either operationally, due to crashes, or practically, in atevi unwillingness to allow them on the planet.

"But the first down landed safely. The world seemed perfectly hospitable. Even the station workers and the Guild now believed, since atevi hadn't objected, that all the empty land on the planet was unowned land, where they'd bother no one.

"That, nadiin, was the situation when the ship left. That's the last it knows. It knows nothing about the war, it knows nothing about the Treaty, it knows nothing about the abandonment of the station and it knows nothing about the reasons that bar humans and atevi from dealing directly. You are faced, nadiin, in my estimation, with both marginal good will from the ship and an ignorance equaling the ignorance of my direct ancestors in that year, in that day, in that *hour* of their departure.

"Nadiin, humans in the early days had no idea how they'd disturbed atevi life—they didn't understand they'd transgressed associations when they'd followed a geographical feature they believed was a boundary. They blundered through association lines, they built roads with no remote thought that they were creating a problem, they brought technology to one association with no remote idea they were altering balances, and, *baji-naji,* there are humans on Mospheira who *still* can't make that leap out of their own mentality and into atevi understanding, just as there are doubtless atevi who dismiss human behavior as complete insanity.

"But we have that ship up there that left a planet with atevi just developing steam engines. Now it looks down on railroads, cities, airports, power plants alike on Mospheira and the mainland, and sees nothing there to tell it what the agreements are that let this happen peacefully.

"I report to my great regret a hitherto harmless minority of officials in my government, a faction who take the demands of cultural separation in the Treaty agreement as a major item of their belief: we call them separatists, but some of them go much further than mere cultural preservation, and believe that humans should exclude atevi from space, which, along with advanced technology, they view as their exclusive heritage. They may see the ship as a chance for them to recapture the past. They may try to urge the ship's crew that I'm a gullible fool and that they're being threatened by atevi, whom they have always apprehended as seeking to destroy human culture.

"The most serious danger is not the ship. It's in offering a reckless minority of my own people on this world the belief that they have alternatives to negotiation with atevi *if* they can mislead the crew of the ship to their own opinions, and particularly if they can get a presence of their own persuasion brought up to the station.

"I've not completely traced the origins of the human separatist movement, or analyzed its membership: in fact, most won't admit to it. But recall that the station had to be abandoned because of failing systems and lack of resources, that the faction which wanted the station maintained is on this planet with us, and I think likely the pro-space movement among humans logically contains those who wish we'd stayed in space. They in particular may be lured into an association with the separatists because the separatists could offer them a return to the station. It involves conjecture on my part, but I fear an association may suddenly be possible involving these two groups with a human return to space as its unifying purpose. I am utterly, morally, opposed to seeing a handful of Mospheirans go back into space with borrowed technology and entering into agreements that convey political power again on the ship crew. The space program this world develops must be jointly human and atevi, and control of the station must be jointly human and atevi.

"I know that some atevi also ask, Why human presence at all? And, yes, ideally no human would ever have come down to this planet; but since humans *have* no other planet in all of space around which to center their activity, and since humans are in orbit around this planet, it's reasonable that the ship, representing many factors of higher technology than any this world can manage right now, is up to activities that will inevitably involve this world on which atevi live. For that reason it becomes imperative that atevi secure a vote in human space activities.

"Nadiin, I do *not* intend to let a minority of humans put themselves forward as the only voice speaking for this planet. I wish to put forward the Treaty as the operative association of humans and atevi.

"I am willing to translate atevi voices to the ship, in order to see to it that whatever the ship wants or whatever the Mospheiran President or Mospheiran factions of whatever nature may do, the ship will not be conducting business in the same ignorance that led to the War of the Landing.

"I do know humans, nadiin, from the inside. I can assure you as I know the sun will rise tomorrow, that the ship crew won't be nearly as naive about Mospheira's humans as they may be about atevi. It's going to be very hard for any Mospheiran faction to persuade the ship that they're without ulterior motives, and very hard for any faction on Mospheira to persuade the ship to any course, not alone because the ship will suspect factionalism, but because the ship itself may have internal factions whose siding with one faction or the other on Mospheira may absolutely paralyze decision and produce new subassociations with the potential for truly dangerous compromises.

"For that reason I foresee that the human government on Mospheira will respond to evidence of division among atevi with paralytic inaction on the part of the government, frenetic activity on the part of those out of power, and no rational decision will result.

"I therefore recommend, nadiin, that atevi speak with one voice when they speak to humans on the ship and on Mospheira, that your inner divisions and debates remain strictly secret, and that you treat Mospheira and the ship as two separate entities until they themselves can speak with one voice. I recommend you claim, not demand, *claim as a fact* an equal share in the space station . . . for a mere beginning.

"I recommend that you speak to the ship directly and soon. I am the paidhi the Treaty appointed to deal between Mospheira and the atevi of the Western Association. I ask the Association to appoint me paidhi also to deal with the ship. This triangular arrangement—" one was never without awareness of the all-important numbers "—places the Western Association on equal footing with Mospheira, who has already delegated spokesmen to deal with the ship.

"The ship knows it must understand Mospheira as well as atevi before it can be confident of its actions. The permutations of advantage and disadvantage in this arrangement are complex, and I am convinced that atevi can secure equal advantage for themselves, particularly by securing agreements with both the elected government of Mospheira *and* with the ship's authority. Again, a trilateral stability.

"I hope for your favorable consideration of the matters I've brought before you, my lords of the Association, most honorable representatives of the provinces, aiji-ma. Thank you. I stand for questions."

There it goes, he thought, made the requisite formal bow, and suffered a shortness of breath, a sweating of the palms, and a fleeting recollection, of all things, of Barb on the ski run: Barb laughing, all that white, and the whole world stretching on forever—that time, that chance, that life—

Gone—maybe gone for good, with the moves he was making.

And he had, with that disoriented sense of what now? and where now? a consuming fear that he hadn't been entirely dispassionate in his judgment, when he most, God help him, needed to be.

Slowly, in the way of atevi listeners, a murmur of comment had begun, then:

"Nand' paidhi." It was a distinguished member of the tashrid, rising to question, in the custom of the chambers. "Has your President assigned you this action against human interests in some sense of numeric balances?"

An intercultural minefield. Had the human government found inharmonious numbers for the whole situation or did it wish to create them for atevi? And the gentleman of the tashrid damn well knew humans didn't count numbers: he was playing to rural atevi paranoia and he was playing straight to the television.

So could he.

"Lord Aidin, I by no means see Mospheiran and atevi best interests as conflicting. Consider, too, my government returned me, in a crisis and under medical circumstances which clearly justified my staying on Mospheira for weeks—cooperating because Tabini-aiji requested my return. They know that if there weren't a paidhi, or if the aiji should break off relations with the paidhi-successor, as the aiji has done, no communication at all would be possible between atevi and humans. Had Mospheira wished to hold me hostage and cut off communication they might have done so. My return, literally rushing me from surgery to the airport, signals a very strong human desire to maintain communication with the mainland and their firm acknowledgment that the aiji is the ruler of the Western Association."

Lord Aidin sat down, having planted what he'd chosen to plant, all the same, for minds set on number conspiracies, damn him; but he'd gotten his own little drama in front of the cameras, too.

Then, in the evenhanded alternation of questions, a member of the hasdrawad rose, a woman he didn't know, with an abrupt: "Then who, nadi, sent Hanks-paidhi?"

Nadi, to an official speaker on the platform, was not fully respectful, and it roused a rare stir in the chambers—a sharp look from Tabini.

He answered, nonetheless, to an ateva who might have either been offended by Hanks, or leaned to Hanks as a source and now found herself embarrassed in Hanks' lack of authority:

"By the Treaty, nadi, there is only one paidhi. And, nadi, nadiin, Hanks is my successor-designate, doubtless confused by the rapidity of events. She should have received a recall order, but events have moved perhaps faster than ordinary lines of communication. She has as yet received no such orders, and feels it incumbent on her to stay until she does. I've requested of the aiji to allow her presence temporarily. If you have doubt of the delivery of your messages to the paidhi during this transition, please don't hesitate to resend. No slight is intended, nadi."

So, so quietly posed. It was really the most byzantine atevi warning he'd ever managed to deliver, and he was quite satisfied with his performance—injecting into the atevi consciousness at basement level an insight into human decision-making, and not just the hasdrawad and the tashrid, thanks to the television cameras. He had had the option, being only human, of ducking the after-address questions ordinary for an atevi speaker; but he saw those cameras, and daunting as they'd been at the outset, he'd managed, sure in his own mind it was useful for atevi out in the provinces to see the paidhi and get a sense of his face, his reactions, his nature.

"Nand' paidhi." It was a conservative member of the tashrid, rising to speak in turn. "What do *you* believe the ship is doing up there?"

Old, old, lord Madinais, blunt, and very common-man in his approaches. A respected grandfather, he always thought of the man; but that misapprehended the real power Madinais had, through seniority in a network of sub-associations many of which *were* common-man, broad-based and powerful.

"Lord Madinais, I can only conjecture: *I* think the ship broke down again. *I* think they've managed to fix it, get it running, and get back to what they hoped would be a thriving human community. It is thriving—but it's certainly complicated their position."

Dissident interests, not far from lord Madinais, had tried to kill Bren last week. But there was nothing personal in it.

"What about the trade rules?" a member of the hasdrawad shouted out. "What about the negotiations?"

"I don't think there'll be any progress in the trade talks until this ship question is settled, quite frankly, nadi. Although—"

Behind the glare of television lights someone else was on his feet, in the hasdrawad, and that wasn't by the rules.

Nerves twitched, hesitated at alarm— Fall down, his

information told him; but, Possibly mistaken, his fore-brain was saying.

At that moment a body hit him like a thunderbolt from the casted side and a shot boomed out and echoed and re-echoed in the chambers.

He was on his side, with a sore hip, a bump on the side of his head where he'd hit the podium, and a crushing atevi weight half on him—Tano, he was suddenly aware. He was grateful, was stunned and apprehensive: he didn't see Jago. But he didn't see damn much of anything but the base of the podium and Tano's anxious face looking out toward the chambers. He didn't even protest to Tano that he was in pain, Tano's attention being clearly directed outward for hostile movements—but by the buzz of talk and the tenor of voices in the chamber, he could guess there'd been at least one fatality, and that the crisis was done, meaning the fatality was the person who'd threatened the paidhi.

Confirmed, as Tano began to get to one knee.

The recipient of such devoted guardianship knew he should still keep his head down and better his position only with extreme care. But he hurt. Members and security alike were converging on the podium—Tabini himself among them, which surely meant it was safe to get up, and he began to, first with Tano's help, then with Tabini's, and last with Tabini's security holding his arm and being very careful of his bandages and the cast.

"I'm very sorry," he said, embarrassed, not realizing the microphone was on. It boomed out over the hall and provoked laughter. Provoked, more, the solemn, unison clapping of hands that was the atevi notion of formal applause—

They hadn't been sure he was alive. They were pleased that he was. At least—the majority seemed to be.

Clearly there'd been one vote to the contrary.

The network television clip showed Tano's tackle and take-down, the sight of which sent repeated shocks through his nerves, and a house camera showed the gun-man, who'd put a bullet into a thirteenth-century chande-

lier when Jago had put a bullet through his head. They
ran it, ran it back and ran it again and again in slow motion.

Bren, elbow on the counter, put his knuckle in front of
his mouth and tried to be objective. He'd *seen* shots fired
before, he'd seen people hit, he'd felt the ground he was
standing on jump to far heavier ordnance, and he told
himself he ought to take it in an atevi sort of calm, safe
as he was in the security station.

He didn't feel that at all.

The chief of Bu-javid security laid a black-and-white
photo on the desk, showing him an older man, a man who
ought to have had sense.

"The representative from Eighin," the chief said,
"Beiguri, house of the Guisi. Any personal cause with
this man or the Guisi?"

"No, nadi." His voice came out faint. He sat up, tried
to ignore the pain of bruised ribs. "I know him—as politically opposed to the trade cities. He's never shown any—
any such behavior. He's never been impolite. . . ."

Tabini was out in the chambers, vehemently pressing
his point. There was talk of a vote on the paidhi's repre-
sentation to the ship, a debate on an initiative to Mospheira. The police and Bu-javid security were rounding
up Beiguri's aides and office staff.

The tape around the ribs was hell. He hoped Tano
hadn't popped stitches, bone, or seams. He hurt. Tano
kept hovering, worse than Jago, who hadn't used him for
a landing zone; and Jago—

Jago was suffering the aftermath, he thought: the
awareness how easily she might have missed that snap
shot. She quivered with unspent energy and anger, she
hugged it in with arms clenched across her chest, and she
wanted, Bren was sure, to be out there scouring the representative's office for what the junior security agents
were most likely going to lay all too-casual hands on, in
Jago's probably accurate estimation.

Jago wasn't senior in her own team. She was probably
also worrying about Banichi's opinion. Or Banichi's
whereabouts.

Or *knew* where Banichi was. And still worried.

More investigators came into the security station, reporting that the death office had taken the body away. A respectable and sensible man, a father of children, an elected representative of his province, had died trying to take the paidhi's life.

Bren shivered. Tano set hands on his shoulder and argued with the police that the paidhi would be perfectly safe upstairs in his own bed, and should be there.

"The aiji—" the chief of police began.

"We have the aiji's orders," Jago said shortly, taking her eyes from the constant replay. "And we have the responsibility, nand' Marin. It's been a very long day for him, and yesterday was longer. If the paidhi wishes to go upstairs—"

"The paidhi wishes," Bren said. He put himself on his feet as a way to accelerate matters. He wanted his room, he wanted his bed, he wanted quiet.

And he'd seen enough of the television replays.

He'd not have given anything for his chance of enduring police questions and playback after playback of the event, which assumed a surreal slow motion in his mind.

But after deciding one impossible thing after the other was the order of the hour, he had to do it, that was all. The next walk, Jago assured him, was only down to the lift—the press was excluded from this area, under special order—Tabini-aiji would handle the reporters in a news conference to follow his speech, and upstairs to his room and his bed was the direct order of business.

He made the lift, found himself with Jago and Tano alone in the car, and gratefully collapsed back against the wall. Tano was quiet; Jago was still in a glum, angry mood.

"Thank you," he said to her and Tano. He wasn't certain he *had* managed somehow to express that.

"My job, nadi," Jago muttered, somewhat curtly, if a human could judge. If a human could judge, Jago was distracted in her own glum thoughts, maybe about Banichi's whereabouts, and the fact she'd had to peg a risky shot clear across, God help them, the halls of government. Maybe she'd gotten a reprimand from senior security, he wasn't sure.

It more than shook him. It whited out his logic about the situation. He realized Jago still had his computer, was still carrying it. Jago didn't make mistakes. Jago had had custody of his computer in the instant she was killing a man—and hadn't lost track of it.

More than the paidhi could say, who'd lingered on his feet analyzing why a man had risen out of turn—stood there, like a fool, and put Jago to making that desperate shot.

The lift let them out on the third level, and they walked the hall of porcelain flowers: ordinary homecoming, quite as if he were coming back from a day at the office, he thought in dazed detachment, standing at the door which Jago had to open with her device-disabling key.

The other side, in the pale, gilt foyer, the soul of atevi propriety, Saidin was there to take his coat.

"Just bed, nand' Saidin," he said. "I'm very tired." He deliberately didn't look at the message bowl. He didn't want to look.

"I think," he said, ticking down that mental list of things he'd reserved as priority, absolute must-dos, "I think I have to return the dowager's message tonight. Maybe we'd better talk very soon."

"You need your rest," Jago said severely.

"The dowager's goodwill is critical," he said. "Tomorrow morning would be a very good time. If there are repercussions—I can't let the dowager interpret my silence and my absence, Jago-ji. Am I mistaken? I believe I understand the woman."

Jago thought about it. Still wasn't pleased. Or was worried. "There is a danger, nadi. You know I can't go there."

"I don't think they're ready for open warfare. Therefore I'm safe."

Jago was not happy. Not at all. "I'll convey your message," she said. So Jago found his logic acceptable, atevi-fashion. And he thought he was right.

But the visible universe had shrunk to the immediate

area of the foyer, and his sense of balance was uncertain—maybe relief, maybe just exhaustion. He felt quite shaky, quite short of breath in the constricting bandages.

"I'll go to bed, then," he said. "I think I've had a long day."

"Nand' paidhi," Tano said, and accompanied him.

He'd been amazed at his ability just to cross the speakers' platform without falling on his face.

But the bedroom was close, and he had not only Tano but a handful of female staff helping him, snatching up the laundry and murmuring that they were very glad the paidhi was unharmed. They'd seen the television. They were appalled at the goings-on.

He'd not had a review of his performance. "Nadiin," he said to them, "did you hear the things I said? Did they seem reasonable?"

"Nand' paidhi," one said, clearly taken aback, "it's not for us to offer opinion."

"If the paidhi asked."

"It was a very fine speech," one said. "*Baji-naji,* nand' paidhi. I don't understand such foreign things."

Another: "It was very risky for your ancestors to come down here."

And a third: "But where is this dangerous place, nand' paidhi? And where is the human earth? And where has the ship been?"

"All of these things, I wish I knew, nadi. The paidhi doesn't know. The wisest people on Mospheira don't know."

A servant lifted her hand, encompassing all things overhead. "Can't you find it with telescopes?"

"No. We're far, far, out of sight of where we came from. And there aren't any landmarks up there."

"Would you go there if you could, nand' paidhi?"

He faced a half dozen solemn female faces, dark, tall atevi, some standing, some kneeling, shadows in the light. He was the foreigner. He felt very much the foreigner in these premises.

"I was born on this planet," he said wearily. "I don't think I should be at home there, nadiin."

The faces gave him nothing.

"I regret," he said wearily, "I regret the matter to-night. He was a respectable man, nadiin. I regret—very much—he died. Please," he said, "nadiin, I'm very tired. I have to go to bed."

There were multiple bows. The servants went away. But one turned back at the door and bowed. "Nand' paidhi," she said, "we hold to your side."

Another lingered and bowed, and in a moment more they were all back in the doorway, all talking at once, how they all wished him well, and how they hoped he would have a good night's sleep.

"Thank you, nadiin," he said, and began to arrange his nest of pillows to prop his arm as they went away into the central hall.

From which, in a moment, he heard a furious whispering about his white skin and his bruises, which he supposed he had more of, and remarking how he'd joked when Tabini had helped him up, and how he had very good composure.

Joked?

He didn't remember he'd done so well as that. He'd been scared as hell. He'd had to have Tano's help to get down the steps. He hadn't been able to walk up the aisle without his knees knocking—knowing—knowing the attempt was not only against him, who could be replaced, but against the entire established order. Atevi knew that. Atevi understood how much that bullet was supposed to destroy—

Hell, he said to himself, exhausted, so exhausted he could melt into the mattress. But, dammit, the mind was threatening to wake up.

He started replaying the speech, the assassination attempt, the police questions, asking himself what they'd suspected and what they'd meant.

He readjusted the lumpy pillows, stuffed more under his arm and fell back in them, asking himself if maybe aspirin would help.

But that gradually became a dimmer thought, and a dimmer one, as the ribs stopped hurting, having found some bracing against the pillows that kept the tape from cutting in. He wasn't sure it was sleep, but the thoughts began to be fewer, and fewer, and he wouldn't move, not while he'd found a place where he actually had no pain.

7

You couldn't see the orbiting ship in Shejidan. City lights obscured all the dimmer stars—granted a clear sky, which it looked to be, a return of late summer warmth above the city, mountain winds sending a few wisps of dark cloud across a pink-tinged and bruised-looking dawn.

Ilisidi liked fresh air, and ate breakfast on her balcony, here, as at Malguri, and Bren couldn't help but think of Banichi's disapproval of the balcony in lady Damiri's apartment—which, if he looked directly up from the table, he thought must be the balcony above this one.

The venture into hostile territory, as it were, would give a sane man pause, and he'd had more than a twinge of doubt in coming here, but it gave him, too, a strange, fatalistic sense of continuity, things getting back on track, reminding him vividly of Malguri, and now that he was here, the butterflies had gone away and he was glad he'd accepted the invitation. The old ateva sitting across from him was so frail-looking the wind could carry her away—her servants and her security around her; Cenedi, chief of the latter, standing to Ilisidi in the same position Banichi, when he wasn't standing watch over the paidhi, held with Tabini.

Banichi wasn't here. Banichi still hadn't come back; it was Jago who'd delivered him into Cenedi's hands at the door—and Cenedi who'd delivered him to Ilisidi's company. Cenedi, who directed every sniper who had a motive to consider the Bu-javid's balconies, and who, if someone transgressed Cenedi's direction, would take it very personally: a Guild assassin, Cenedi was, like Jago, like Banichi. For that reason he felt safe in Cenedi's hands, not at all because Cenedi happened to owe him, personally—which Cenedi did—but precisely because personal debt wouldn't weigh a hair with Cenedi if he were called on—professionally.

So the paidhi sat down with the aiji-dowager, the most immediate arbiter of life and death, possibly in collusion with the man who'd tried to kill him last night, at a table outside on a balcony he was sure was as safe and no safer than his own upstairs. White curtains billowed out of the room beyond them in a dawn wind that lacked the cold edge of Malguri's rain-soaked mornings. The wind carried instead the heavy musk of tropic diossi flowers from somewhere nearby, possibly another balcony.

Potential enemies, they shared tea first.

And small talk.

"Does it hurt much?" the dowager asked.

"Not much, nand' dowager. Not often."

"You seem distracted."

"By thoughts, nand' dowager."

"This fiancée?"

Damn the woman. There was decidedly a leak somewhere, and there was absolutely nothing chance about Ilisidi's revealing it as an opening gambit: that she did so might be a gesture of goodwill toward the paidhi.

It was definitely a demonstration of her power to reach inside Tabini's intimates' living space.

"Her action is nothing I can complain of, nand' dowager." He took satisfaction in giving not a flicker of emotion to a wicked old campaigner. "She was certainly within her rights."

"No quarrel, then."

"None, nand' dowager. I regard her highly, still. Certainly she would have told me—but business, as you know," (pause for no small irony) "kept me on this side of the strait. That's certainly the heart of her complaints against me."

"The woman's a fool," Ilisidi said. "Such a personable young man."

One couldn't argue opinions with the dowager. And a

sparkle of warmth and enjoyment was in Ilisidi's eyes, twice damn her, the smile on thin, creased lips just faintly discernible.

He said graciously, "My mother thinks so, I'm sure, nai-ji. So does Jago. But I fear both are biased."

A servant laid down two plates of food—eggs, and game, in season, to be sure—muffins—the muffins were always safe.

"Human ways and human choices," Ilisidi said. "You have no relationship with this woman they've sent?"

"Deana Hanks."

"This woman, I say."

"I have none such," he said. "Not the remotest interest, I assure the dowager."

"Pity."

"Oh, I don't think so, nand' dowager." He applied cream to a muffin, or tried to. A servant slipped in a little deft help and he abandoned the effort to the servant.

"Such an inconvenience," Ilisidi said.

"Lack of appeal in my professional associate—or the broken arm?"

Ilisidi was amused. A salt-and-pepper brow quirked on an impeccably grave black face. Gold eyes. "The arm, actually. When are you rid of that uncomfortable thing, nadi?"

"I don't know, aiji-ma. They sent me instructions. I confess I haven't read them."

"No interest?"

"No time. I'd quite forgotten to read them." The ice had broken and other topics were permissible. He steered in his own direction. "Your grandson was anxious to have me back."

"My grandson would have traded three lords and an estate to get you back, nand' paidhi. Drive a hard bargain with him."

"The dowager is very kind."

"Oh, let's be practical. We've a damned foreigner ship in our sky, the rural lords are in revolt, someone tried to kill you, the religious see omens in the numbers, and the television tells us absolutely nothing. Fools sit out at night on their rooftops with binoculars, armed with shotguns."

"If you had eyes to see to Mospheira, you'd see the same, aiji-ma. As I said in the joint meeting, opinion as to potential benefits is vastly divided."

Ilisidi's head cocked slightly—she had one better ear, Bren had come to think; and certainly Cenedi lurking at the double doors was taking mental notes on every inflection, every nuance, everything said and not said.

"Nand' paidhi," Ilisidi said, "what you want to say this morning, say to me, straight out. I'm curious."

"It's a request."

"Make it."

"That the dowager use her influence to assure the Association's stability. I know how much that entails. I also know you've weighed the cost more than anyone alive, nand' dowager."

He touched the old woman to the quick. He saw Ilisidi's eyes shadow, saw the darkness of a passing thought, the map of years and choices on her face, the scars of a long, long warfare of atevi conscience.

With two words and the skill of the assassin behind her, this woman could take the Association apart, wreck the peace, topple lords and assure the breakup of everything humans vitally concerned with the peace had to work with.

And she refrained. Atevi lords weren't much on self-denial. They were a great deal on reputation, on being respected. Or feared.

Twice the hasdrawad had passed over Ilisidi's claim to be aiji of the Association that effectively dominated atevi affairs. They'd passed over her as too likely to curtail other lords' ambitions. Too likely to launch unprecedented worries.

Little they'd understood the men they'd installed as (they hoped) more peaceful administrators: first her son and then Tabini aiji in her stead, and oh, how that rankled—her grandson Tabini reputed as the virtuous, the generous, the wise ruler.

Ask 'Sidi-ji to remain a shadow-player to posterity, as well as the past generation?

"I haven't knifed the mayor or salted the wine," Ilisidi muttered. "Tell my grandson I'm watching him, nand' paidhi, for like good behavior." Nothing fazed Ilisidi's appetite. Four eggs had disappeared from her plate. Her knife blade tapped the china, and two more appeared from the quick hand of a servant. "Eggs, nand' paidhi?"

"Thank you, nand' dowager, but I'm still being careful with my stomach."

"Wise." Another tap of the knife blade, this time on the teapot. The empty one was whisked away, another appeared, the cosy removed, the dowager's cup refilled. "Not disturbed about last night."

"I regret the loss of life."

"Fools."

"Most probably."

"Uncertainty breeds such acts. Debate, hell. What *else* is there to do but deal with these people? What are they *voting* on?"

"I'm sure I agree, nand' dowager."

"It's amazing to me, nand' paidhi, at every turn of our affairs, just at our achieving the unity we sought and just at our developing the power for the technology we could have developed for ourselves—lo, here you fall down from the skies and give us, what, television and computer games? And at our *second* opportunity to adjust the terms of the association, coincidentally with our efforts toward space—behold, this ship in the heavens, and another moment of crisis. There are damned important atevi issues, nand' paidhi, which have repeatedly been set aside for the sake of unity in the face of human intrusion, issues which have *no* import to humans but vast import to atevi. And it's not just because the hasdrawad thinks I'm a bloody-handed tyrant, nand' paidhi, no matter what you may have heard from my, of course, clean-fingered grandson—there are reasons I was passed over for the succession that speak a great deal more to the political climate at the time my son demised and left Tabini and his junior cronies in position to vote us down. So here we are again, nand' paidhi." The knife whacked the plate, commanding attention. "Listen to me. *Listen* to me, paidhi-ji, damn you. You ask forbearance. I ask your full attention."

He'd been paying it. Completely. But he understood her. "All my attention, nand' dowager."

"Remember Malguri. Remember the world as it was. Remember the things that should survive."

"With all my mind, nand' dowager." It was the truth. Malguri wasn't that far away in his mind. He didn't think now it would ever be: the uncompromising cliffs, the fortress, half primitive, half modern, electric wires strung along ancient stones. The wi'itkitiin crying against the wind, gliding down the cliffs.

The towering threat of riders on mecheiti, shadows against the sun.

"Yet one more time," Ilisidi said, "the hasdrawad bids me step aside for progress. I am *old,* nand' paidhi. My associates are old. How many more years will there be to hear us? How many more years will there be, before everything is television and telephones and satellites, and there's no more room for us?"

"There will be wi'itkitiin, nand' dowager. I swear to you. There will *be* Malguri. And Taiben. And the other places. I've seen. If a stone-stubborn human like me can be snared by it—how can atevi not?"

For a moment Ilisidi said nothing, her yellow eyes lifeless in thought. Then she nodded slowly as if she'd reached some private decision, and made short work of another egg. "Well," she said then, "well, we do what we can. As we can. And these atevi, these humans sitting on their roofs this dawn, nand' paidhi, what would you say to them?"

It was a question, one without a clear answer. "I'd say they shouldn't panic yet. I'd say no one on this world has an answer, except that wholeheartedly I'll speak as the aiji's translator, nand' dowager, to the humans above and the humans below. And I'll make you personally aware as I can what I'm hearing."

"Oh? Is that Tabini's word on it?"

"I don't know why he didn't stand in the way of my being here."

"Clever man."

Argue with Ilisidi, and you needed only supply the cues. She was amused in spite of herself.

"I *will* get word to you somehow, nand' dowager. It's a frightening job to be an honest man."

"A dangerous job, among fools."

"But neither you nor Tabini is a fool, nand' dowager. So my life is in your hands."

"You claim no debts, nand' paidhi?"

"I'd be a fool. You're also honest."

"Oh, paidhi-ji. Don't ruin my reputation."

She touched such dangerous and human chords in him.

"The dowager knows exactly what she's doing," he said, "and the world *won't* forget her, not if she did nothing more than she's already done. She needs nothing else."

Ilisidi's brows came down in a thunderous scowl. But didn't quite stay that way. "You are reprehensible, nadi. It was a marvelous performance last night, by the way. I don't say brilliant, but the faint was a nice touch."

"I honestly don't remember what I answered the gentleman."

"Damned reckless."

"Not if I went out there to tell the truth—as I did. Too many sides in this, nand' dowager. It's hard enough to track the truth. And if the paidhi once begins to shade the truth at all, the difficulties I can make for myself are absolute hell. Please, nand' dowager, never read anything atevi into my actions. It's very dangerous."

"Wicked, wicked man. You're so very skillful."

"Nand' dowager, in all seriousness, Malguri touches human instincts, so, so deeply."

"What, greed?"

"Respect, nand' dowager. A sense of age, of profound truths. Respect for something hands made, that's stood through storms and wars and time. It persuades us that things we do may last and matter."

"That's the best thing I've ever heard said about humans."

"I assure you it's so, nand' dowager."

"More tea?"

"I've a meeting I shouldn't be late to."

"With my grandson and the Policy Committee?"

"The dowager's intelligence is, as usual, accurate. May I ask a favor?"

"I don't say I'll grant it."

"It's to all our good. Nand' dowager, be frank with me constantly. I value your interests. Give me the benefit of your advice when you see me stray, and I swear I'll always trust the tea at your table."

Ilisidi laughed, a flash of white teeth. "Away with you. Flatterer."

"Aiji-ma." He did have the appointment. Jago had told him. It took effort to get up. He made his awkward bow, and Cenedi showed him toward the door—"Nand' paidhi," Cenedi said, when they reached the front hall, "take care. There are more fools loose."

"Is it a specific threat?"

"I can't name names."

"Forgive me." He didn't know the inner workings of the Guild.

Cenedi shrugged, avoiding his eyes. "My profession allows no debts, nand' paidhi. Understand. Ask Banichi."

"I haven't seen him."

"Not unrelated."

"Guild business?"

"That might be."

"Is he in danger?"

They'd reached the door, and two more of Ilisidi's security were on duty there; men he knew, men he'd hunted with, ridden with.

"Never worry about us," Cenedi said. "I can only say that fools have moved—several are dead fools—and there are voices in our Guild who speak for the paidhi. Contracts have been proposed, and voted down. I've spoken more already than I should. Ask Banichi. Or Jago. *They're* within your *man'chi.*"

"I'm very grateful for your concern, nand' Cenedi."

"In all matters," Cenedi said, "I take instruction from the aiji-dowager. Understand this. A favor given weighs nothing in my Guild. But if the paidhi were to come to grief in Shejidan *not* by the dowager's express order, certain of the Guild would sue to take personal contract."

"Nadi, I am vastly moved to think so."

"Do you understand, nand' paidhi, the burden you've placed on 'Sidi-ji?"

"I can't," he said. "I can't possibly, nadi, but I can't refrain from it—because she's essential to the peace. Capable of ruling the Association, I've no doubt. But her place in these events is greater than that. Which you and I both know—and I can't tell her that, nadi. I want to, in so many words. But she'd toss me right out her door. Deservedly—for my impudence."

" 'Sidi-ji knows her own measure," Cenedi said. "And her value. She defends herself very well. Come. I'll walk you down to neutral ground, nadi."

"Where," he asked Jago sharply, when Jago picked him up after the committee hearings downstairs, "where, nadi, is Banichi?"

"At the moment?"

"Jago-ji, don't put me off. Cenedi says there's trouble. A matter before the Guild. That I should ask you and Banichi. —Is that where Banichi is?"

"Banichi is involved in Guild business," Jago said, the first that she'd actually admitted.

"About me?"

"It might be."

"Is that reason to worry?"

"It's reason to worry," Jago said.

"So why can't you tell me?"

"Not to worry you, nadi."

"You'll have noticed," he said, "that I *am* worried. I think I have reason to worry. Is he in danger?"

Jago didn't answer. They'd reached the door, and Jago spoke on the pocket-com to Tano, inside, asking him to open.

Bren said quietly, standing by Jago's side, "The dowager knew Barb had broken with me."

And, casting that stone into the pool, he gave Jago something of her own to worry about. She did. She cast him a frowning glance.

"How, do you suppose?" he asked as Tano opened the door.

Jago didn't answer. They walked in, and servants wanted to take his coat. "Nadiin," he said to the servants, "I'll just pick up my work. I'm on my way down to my office."

"Nadi," Jago reproved him.

"To my office," he said. He'd never gone against Jago. But he'd never had Jago give him an order not regarding his performance of his job.

"No," Jago said, "nadi. I can't have you do this."

"Where am I supposed to get work done?"

"One has this rather extensive apartment, nand' paidhi, which I might remind the paidhi includes ample rooms and resources."

He was halfway stunned—was dismayed at his situation, Jago making him out an ingrate, or in the wrong, or somehow at odds with reasonable behavior. There was so damned much—so damned much to do: there were papers to write, there were positional statements to prepare. . . .

There were, Cenedi had warned him, serious matters before the Assassins' Guild, in which Jago had warned him Banichi was occupied.

There was a man dead, last night, an otherwise decent man, by all the information he had on the subject; he'd had a long morning, a trying, tedious meeting rehearsing details and eventualities that only meant more letters to write; a towering lot of letters to write and no staff he could rely on for clerical work, the paidhi never having had the need for a staff because very few people had to consult the paidhi—who had been very safe in a minor office in a minor job in the Bu-javid doing very routine things and scanning trade manifests and long-range social concerns, before a human ship decided to pull up at the human station and multiply his mail by a thousandfold

and his avenues of contact by the same, with no—*no*—
proportionate increase in his resources. He saw no way
over the stack of paper, he'd gotten three new jobs during
the meeting with Associational lords who were asking
questions all of which he could answer, but not without
being sure of the numerical felicities of the situations they
described. He was feeling desperate as it was, and all of
a sudden he saw his whole job circumscribed by Jago,
and Cenedi, and Banichi, and Tano, and assassins and
their precautions, and no means to *do* the things he
needed to do—the mail and the messages alone were
stacked up to—

"I am very sorry," Jago said quietly, "and I offer the
paidhi all respect, but I cannot permit him in an unsecured area."

He'd done rather well in an unsecured area this morning, he thought. He'd gotten through the breakfast with
Ilisidi with a sense of actual accomplishment, in that he
thought he might have made some progress toward reason
with the other side of the shadow-government that doubtless inspired his would-be assassins, a power that kept a
cohesion of political forces that opposed the aiji scarcely
in check—lately in open rebellion, but currently in check.
Waiting. Dangerous. But, dammit, he'd drunk the dowager's tea. They got—

—along.

Human interface again. The emotional trap. Cenedi'd
sucked him right into it. He didn't *think* atevi knew what
they were doing.

But if any did understand, Ilisidi and Tabini were the
likeliest.

"Forgive me," he said to Jago, and patched *that* interface. But he'd crashed on that reflection, plunged right
into that hollow spot that existed in the atevi-human relationship, the one that couldn't ever work, and it took a
second, it just took a second not to be angry, or hurt, or
desperate, or to feel like a prisoner hemmed in at every
turn.

"Bren-ji?"

Tano was standing there, too, not knowing how to read

what was going on; Jago was embarrassed, he was sure, and Jago would walk over glass to protect him. Jago would even make him angry to protect him. It was daunting to have that kind of duty attached to you. It was hard, when one was frustrated and desperately afraid one couldn't handle the job, to be worth someone like Jago.

"One's been a fool," he said, calm again. "I know I've resources. I apologize profoundly."

"I was perhaps rude," Jago said.

"No. Jago, just—no."

"All the same . . ."

"Jago—it comes of *liking* people, that's all."

He surely puzzled Tano. He puzzled Jago, too, in a different way, because Jago had met the human notion of *liking* as an emotion. Banichi had, too, and still protested he wasn't, as the atevi verb had it, a dinner course.

"Still, one feels betrayed," Jago said. "Is that so, Bren-ji?"

"One *feels* betrayed," he said, "and knows it's damned nonsense. Tano, nadi-ji, you've been through the mail. What's the nature of it? Are there things anyone else can possibly handle?"

"I have a summary," Tano said. "Most are officials, most are anxious, a few angry, a few quite confused. One could, if the paidhi wished, find staff to prepare replies, nand' paidhi. Perhaps even in the household there are such resources. I can, too, go to your office and bring back necessary materials."

He'd embarrassed himself thoroughly. His staff was well ahead of the game, trying their best, and he was, he realized, in pain from the tape about his ribs, from long sitting, from long speeches, impossible demands on his mental capacity, and utter exhaustion. "Tano-ji, please do. My seal, a number of message cylinders. I'm very grateful. I need a phone, a television—Jago, is it possible to have a television without offending the harmony of this historic house?"

"One can arrange such things," Jago said, "I've been advised that the paidhi may bring in whatever he needs, only so long as we protect the walls and woodwork."

A courteous, well-lined gilt-and-tapestry prison. One with his favorite people and every convenience. But at Malguri, equally concerned for the historic walls, they'd let him ride, and hunt, and he'd had fear of the staff, but no anxiety about where their reports of him were going, as he did here—every smiling one of the women either analyzing him, watching him, or holding secret communication, he was sure, with Damiri. And one of whom, Ilisidi had let him know this morning, was feeding information to someone who talked to Tabini's rivals and enemies, among whom one had to count Ilisidi and her staff.

He felt, in the aftermath of that realization this morning, somewhat shaky in returning to the apartment. And lost. Jago and Tano, at least, wouldn't betray him. Last of all, they'd betray his ...

Trust. Which didn't, damnit, exist for an outsider among atevi. He wasn't in their *man'chi*, their *group*, beyond loyalty, all the way over to identity, except as he was Tabini's ...

Property.

He felt a crashing, plummeting depression, then: one of those glum moods that came of too much vaulting back and forth between the cultures.

Or too much medication. He couldn't afford any medications with depressive side effects, not doing what he did, and whenever he was on medication he distrusted such mood swings. God, he didn't need this on top of the workload he'd been handed.

"Nadi, go do those things," Jago said to Tano, and Tano agreed and quietly left, while he unfastened the cuff tab that secured his coat sleeve and began to try to get out of his coat, since he wasn't, after all, going anywhere.

He wanted to go sit down and not think and not deal with his well-meaning guards for a moment. But he ought to be making a couple of critical phone calls.

He *ought* to go look at his medical records and find out what he was taking, and make absolutely sure it was only antibiotics. He let Jago help him off with his coat, which she did very carefully.

"I'm terribly embarrassed," he said. Sometimes it

seemed to be the only way to make cross-species amends. "Forgive me, Jago-ji. I'm tired. My ribs hurt."

She eased his coat sleeve free. Easy to evade her eyes, easy to glance down when she stood so much taller.

But not when she touched his good shoulder and wanted his attention.

"The distress is ours," Jago said. That plural again. The group. The collective to which he was always biologically external.

He'd been inside at Malguri, briefly. Inside, in all senses, the one glimpse he'd ever had of what he couldn't have, couldn't *be*. That was what Ilisidi and Cenedi had touched.

Barb had fairly well finished the human attachment he had, but he couldn't replace it with Jago or Banichi.

Certainly not much of an emotional life, he had to admit. Clearly Barb had found it pretty thin fare, enough that Paul Saarinson had looked to her like a far better bet. Barb had gotten the signals: youth ending, the rest of her life starting—at twenty-whatever, five?—and no prospect of his coming home, not only soon, but ever—because he valued the job, he valued things he couldn't talk about to her.

He valued relationships he couldn't have, with atevi he couldn't talk to, either, but at least—at least he was where he could do some good, with knowledge that could do some good, and people who at least wanted to listen to him.

He gave a sigh, that was what his emotional storm was worth, now it had found its real and honest grounds: he hadn't any right to Barb's life, he'd gone into the job with his eyes open, and he was tolerably well armored, once he got his sense of perspective adjusted.

So he could ask Jago for his computer and for access to the Bu-javid phone system, and sit down at the security station desk, which had the same relation to this foyer as Tabini's small sitting-room, next door. It was a comfortable little nook, with the phone, and, God, stacks and stacks of little unrolled message scrolls, all flattened with the ornate lead weights atevi kept for such troublesome but traditional duty.

Six stacks of message scrolls, sorted, he imagined glumly, into categories of criticality—assassination threats, suicide threats, committee complaints, school project requests; God, he didn't know, but he felt acutely sorry for his outburst in Tano's vicinity. The man was doing his absolute damnedest on a job he wasn't even trained to do, and without staff. He could explain to Jago, who'd at least gotten used to the paidhi's occasional frayed nerves, and to Banichi, who'd likely ask him what he wanted done about the sky falling; but poor Tano just sat and handled things, and the paidhi thanked his efforts by throwing a fit.

He set up his computer on the desk, with Jago's patient help, made the phone connection and let computers talk to each other for a moment until his call and its authorizations had rung through the Bu-javid board, the provincial board, the Mospheiran entry board, the Capitol board, and all the way to the Foreign Office.

Then:

"This is Bren Cameron," he said, and a voice on the other end said:

"Mr. Cameron, the Foreign Secretary is very anxious to talk to you. Please hold."

Another sigh. Damned right the Foreign Secretary was anxious to talk to him.

"Quite," he said, and hardly a breath later, had the Secretary himself.

"Bren. Bren, this is Shawn. Are you all right?"

"Doing well, thank you." He chose to misunderstand Shawn Tyers' concern as health related. "You may know the situation here's been rather dicey, but we're just fine, with one complication. What's going on with Hanks' visa? She's expired, she's still sitting here, violating Treaty law. Our hosts are extremely miffed, and she's used my seal without my permission. Could we have a clarification of her position?"

"Bren, you may know there's some disturbance in the

upstairs Department, both about your address to the legislatures last night and the shooting."

"Not surprised. Very high feelings on the mainland, I assure you. Hanks isn't helping."

"How's business otherwise?"

Right past his question. Meaning was Tabini solidly in power. But definitely ignoring his question. "Thriving. In spite of the weather. Listen, Shawn, other matters aside, can you find me an answer about my redundancy here?"

"That's a wait. You're sawing off limbs, Bren."

As clear a warning as the Secretary could give. So Hanks' presence and continued presence in a critical situation went above the paidhi's office, and went above the Foreign Secretary's office. He knew where, right down to the fancy wood door. Durant was the name, Secretary of State Hampton Durant, possibly Erton's office, possibly higher than that.

"Advisedly," he said to Shawn's warning. "But the tree's overcrowded. Somebody has to. Send me what you can."

"What I can," the Secretary said; and Bren said, the all's-well sign-off, "See you."

But he didn't at the moment think so. Ever. He had a slightly sick-at-the-stomach feeling about that conversation, in which the Foreign Office, *his* office, couldn't give the paidhi in the field any remote assurance it could get Hanks unassigned, even with all the signals he'd flashed about atevi displeasure.

Freely translated, the State Department, in charge of the Foreign Office, doesn't give a damn what atevi think.

He called through to the Bu-javid telegraph, said, "This is Bren Cameron, nadi, from the third floor. Ring Hanks-paidhi, please, wherever she's lodged."

The phone call went out. And rang. Someone picked up.

"Deana?" he asked.

The receiver slammed down. *Bang!*

He took several deep breaths. Professional behavior. The dignity of the paidhiin. The appearance of human unity.

He signaled the operator. "This is Bren-paidhi again. Ring again."

"Was this incorrect, nand' paidhi?"

"Just ring."

More rings. And rings.

And rings.

"Nand' paidhi, I have no answer."

"Operator, kindly ring until she answers. One long four shorts two longs. Until she picks up *and* talks."

"Yes, nadi."

He sat. And sat. And put the constant ringing on speaker, and sat, and called up the text program and wrote the necessary letter to Foreign Secretary Shawn Tyers, that said, in code, *"Hanks has met with dissidents against the government and offered them such unauthorized concepts as FTL, the repercussions of which I will have to handle among the devout of lord Geigi's province. She has made unauthorized and unsubstantiated offers of trade, which may have been apprehended as a bribe. Hanks refuses my phone calls. She refuses my order to withdraw. She has revealed classified information, ignored atevi law, and alienated atevi across completely opposite political lines, endangering her life and mine. I do not know how to characterize her actions except in the strongest terms: not only dangerous to the peace, but incompetent even among atevi whom she would probably wish to have on her side. She is in personal danger. She has offended atevi of very high rank and unlimited resources, and shows no disposition to make amends to them or to listen to advice from me. I urge you to seek clearance for her immediate withdrawal from the field."*

He didn't send, however. He stored the damning message to file, and sat, and sat, and waited. And waited.

He heard the line pop again, then bang, with a receiver slammed down.

He shook his head, restraining his own temper, unable to understand—remotely to conceive of—the stupidity of the island-bound, island-educated, culturally insular mentality that ran the Department, that ran so well at its lower levels—unable to conceive of the mentality that abandoned concern so far that political ideologues could toss the job he'd traded his whole human life for into the hands of an arrant, politically motivated, opinionated, and prejudiced *fool*.

He *didn't* believe it. He refused to believe the powers actually in charge, sitting above a university that, most of the time, knew what it was doing and what it was advising, were that damnably ignorant of the critically dangerous differences of atevi culture, atevi life, atevi politics.

But the ones with the power over Mospheira itself didn't give a damn. The people they put in charge of the upper echelons of the State Department didn't give an effectual damn. *They* had their position, *they* had their power, *they* had their access to the President, *they* called it State Department business when they opened an appliance factory on the North Shore, and *they* were wined and dined by the company execs, also in their social set, for the petty approvals and the official stamps and the environmental clearances and the power-brokering that shepherded projects through what in atevi terms ought to be the Ministry of Works and the Ministry of Commerce.

But, no, among humans it was the business of the State Department, because some human official just after the war had seen the development of Mospheira as an internationally sensitive matter that had to go through *somebody* who presumably understood the impact it was going to have on atevi relations and the window it was going to provide for atevi to figure out (atevi being clever) *what* humans had and could deliver to reproduce on the mainland. And somebody else had said they should be appointed by the President.

The result was a Department whose highest officers knew a lot more about political patronage than they knew about factory effluents—whose highest officers rarely exercised their power at operational or foreign office levels, but they sat as a political, contribution-courting roadblock to every railroad, every highway, every item of new commerce and every extrapolation of Mospheiran domestic technology. They knew a damn sight less about atevi policy: they shunted incomprehensible intellectual problems like atevi affairs and atevi grants of technology and atevi cultural and environmental impact studies off to the university Foreign Service Study Program and that far-down-the-hall office of the lowly Foreign Secretary, who didn't contribute to their party's campaign and therefore didn't have to be bothered except occasionally.

Which meant neither the paidhi in the field nor the Foreign Secretary had the easy, routine access to the President that the Secretary of State had.

A Secretary of State with his technocrat cronies who hadn't waked up from fairyland since Tabini came to power, except for his cocktail parties, his influence-trading, his shepherding of special bills through the legislature and his social schedule and his attendance at the soccer nationals and—oh, yes, oh, God, yes—the opening of the Space Research Center, where the Heritage Redevelopment Society, also with an officership populated mostly by wealthy conservatives, consumed enough alcohol to power an airliner into orbit and lamented humanity's losses in the historic war. The HRS annually commemorated the departure of the ship, listened to engineers talk about revitalizing the space station and consistently refused to put speakers from International Studies on the program, even when they wrote papers that directly impacted proposals that the HRS was going to come out with in the next session of the legislature. He'd personally *tried,* this last spring, being invited by a handful of the Foreign Office and some junior members of the HRS who wanted to get someone of stature to make their point in favor of the trade cities project: the higher echelons of the HRS had politely lost his application and failed to review his paper, which meant he could come and attend, if he could get the time, if he wanted to pay the conference fee, but he wasn't on the agenda.

Deana Hanks had gone to the conference as a guest speaker. Deana Hanks had sat in the meetings and, on personal request of the conference chair who said the conference wanted to acknowledge the paidhi's office, made a polite little speech about human advancement to space and human retention of human cultural heritage.

God, he wanted to kill somebody. Filing Intent on Deana Hanks definitely came to mind. On this side of the strait, total fools didn't last long.

He sat a little longer, then rang the Bu-javid operator again. "This is Bren Cameron. Are we still ringing Hanks-paidhi?"

"One will, Bren-paidhi. Yes."

"Thank you."

He punched in the speaker and heard the repeated ring.

A second time the phone was picked up and slammed down.

"Operator?"

"Nand' paidhi?"

"Do this constantly until I advise you I've had a satisfactory answer. Pass the instruction to the next shift when it comes on. I will have an answer eventually."

"I am so very regretful of the difficulty, nand' paidhi."

"Please account it to human sense of humor, nadi, and thank you so much."

8

He composed his further messages and answers in the sitting room, while Tano, armed with the paidhi's own message cylinders and seal, answered the simple and the routine.

He expressed the wish for a simple, in-house lunch, and settled down to Tano's summation of the clerical situation: three of Damiri's staff were perfectly competent— more competent, serving in a noble house—at etiquette to answer routine inquiries, with Tano to handle the substance and himself to catch the odd or difficult ones.

A telegram, from a primer-school class in Jackson City, requesting the paidhi to assure them that there wouldn't be a war. No, he said. Atevi are quite as anxious as humans to keep the peace.

Too damn much television.

He asked the staff to scour up a tape of the news coverage. He made a note to send Ilisidi the translation transcripts.

He wrote a note to Tabini that said, *Aiji-ma, I am doing well today. Thank you for your kind intervention last night. I hope for your success in all undertakings.*

Meaning grandmother hadn't served up the wrong tea, Tano hadn't broken his ribs last night, and he was waiting, hoping for information.

Hanks, meanwhile, hadn't cracked. Wasn't home, contrary to security's expectations. Or had flung herself on security wires rather than listen to the ringing.

He sent his brief message to Tabini; and the one damning Hanks to diplomatic hell to the Foreign Office.

He had his sandwich: the Bu-javid was always *kabiu,*

strictly proper, and the game allowable in the season was
by no means his favorite: that left fish and eggs, the allowable alternatives, as his diet until the midpoint of this
month, which was, thankfully, almost on them.

The Bu-javid, relatively modern among atevi antiquities, but shared by various atevi philosophical schools,
was more meticulously *kabiu* than Malguri, in fact, where
wise chefs put by a cooked roast or two of this and that.
Atevi never shot game out of season, one never trafficked
in—unthinkable—domestic meat and never sold meat out
of season, but Malguri cannily managed to have leftovers
enough to stretch through the less palatable months. A
civilized solution, in his reckoning and, one suspected,
the original custom of which the strict *kabiu* of the Bu-
javid was the rigid, entrenched rule, probably more to do
with early lack of refrigeration than any ceremonial
reason—but the paidhi wasn't about to suggest such a solution to the very *kabiu* Atigeini chef. The paidhi had
enough controversy on his hands, thank you, and such a
suggestion might set him on the side of some provincial
philosophical sect bloodily opposed to some other one
critical to the union the Bu-javid represented.

He took to the afternoon reports, wondering now where
Jago had gone. She'd just not turned up in the to-do with
the office. Add that to Banichi, who wasn't here.

Tano, meanwhile, God help him—coped.

Someone arrived at the door; he hoped it was Jago or
Banichi, if only to have the important parts of his household in one place and within his understanding.

But a trip to the door proved it to be another batch of
messages—one from the installation at Mogari-nai, which
received the transmissions from the ship, which he was
anxious to get. That transmissions existed showed, for
one thing, that the ship was talking again, and offered a
possibility that something might have budged. So he took
the tape from Tano, walked back to the study where he
had the recorders set up, put it in and set it to play.

The usual chatter of machines talking to machines.

And past that exchange of machine protocols, more
chatter, involving, this time, the transmission of docu-

ments or images—he wasn't sure, but it was digital, and he was sure the atevi machinery could spit it out, the same as atevi documents ended up intercepted by Mospheira, where there was a listening station: spying on each other was a full-time, well-funded operation, an absolute guarantee of employment for the practitioners.

Tano came in bearing a stack of paper: more correspondence, he thought. But Tano said, quietly:

"I think this must go with the tape, nadi Bren."

It certainly did. He saw that when he opened it, and no wonder the machine-to-machine talk went on and on: Mospheira had elected to go to written transmission, and the transcript . . .

It was a nonphonetic Mosphei' transcript. On this side of the strait.

It was—he had no trouble recognizing the text—the first chapters of *The History of Contact,* by Meighan Durna, a work that laid out every action, every mistake of the Landing and the war.

It released a devil of a lot of intimate knowledge about Mospheira and atevi in the process, which he had rather not have had happen on Durna's occasionally incomplete understanding of atevi motivation—but he didn't totally disagree with the decision to transmit the book. It was certainly a way to bring the *Phoenix* crew up to speed, or at least as far as most of Mospheira itself knew the truth: every school on Mospheira studied it as foundational to understanding where Mospheirans were and who they were, all three hundred and more pages. He jotted down a background note to the ship, for transmission at the first opportunity: *The* History, *while expressing the origin of the Mospheiran mindset, could not accurately account for atevi behavior and should never be used to predict or explain atevi motivation* . . .

He wanted to get on with the tape. At home, he could have used voice-search. The atevi machine didn't have that luxury. He fast-forwarded and listened to the pitch.

There *was* indeed a voice section.

He sat and listened, then turned on his second recorder, the one with a blank tape, and used the directional mike to make a running commentary and quasi-translation for Tabini.

"Mostly operational protocols, discussion of the gap in relays. Schedules of contact."

Then it was something else. Then it was a ship captain asking to speak to the President of Mospheira.

Almost immediately the sign of a break, and probably an interval in which they patched the communications link together.

The President came on.

The captain said, after preliminary well-wishes, *"We're very impressed, Mr. President, with the extensive development, on both sides of the water. Peace and prosperity. You're to be congratulated."*

"Thank you, Captain," came the answer. The President quite comfortably taking credit for all of it. Leave it to him.

"The condition of the station is such," the captain continued, *"that we can with effort bring it up to operational. We'd like to offer you a cooperative agreement. As I understand—you trade with the atevi, technology, raw materials, anything you want."*

"There are limits, Captain. Nothing that destabilizes the society or the environment."

Good, Bren thought. The man at least said that.

Then:

"You're preparing," the ship captain said, *"a return to space. You are making efforts in that direction."*

"Yes. Considerable effort. The circumstances that forced our landing—"

"Yes. I'm aware. On the other hand—we can provide a far shorter route to orbit. We'll provide the design. You provide the manufacturing, build the ground-to-orbit craft and we can put this station back into full-scale operation. . . ."

Bren took deep breaths to calm his heart. With what resources? He shaped the words with his lips, willing the answer, hoping it wasn't a package dropped in from space, free of effort.

"We can make secure habitat for five hundred workers

to start with; ten thousand in three years, then—then there's no practical limit, Mr. President."

That's labor crews, Mr. President, do you hear it?

"You should know, you're not unique in space. We've got another station, near to this star, small operation, but we're growing. This is prosperity, Mr. President. This is the human future we came for."

There was a lump of ice in Bren's chest.

"You're saying," the President answered slowly, *"that you've already built another station. Out there. Somewhere."*

"A mining and repair operation, self-sustaining food supply. Humanity is in business in this district of space, Mr. President. We're asking you to rejoin the universe. We don't dispute whatever arrangements you've made down there. It clearly works. All we're interested in is the station."

How nice. How magnanimous. How *concerned* for everyone's rights.

"We can restore what we had. We can build, Mr. President. All you've got to do is get up here: a share of the station, exactly what the original mission charter calls for, to all the builders and their descendants."

"I have to consult," the President said. *"I have to consult with the council and the Departments."*

Depend on it. God, the man couldn't executive-order a fire drill.

"That's fine, Mr. President. I'll be here."

So what are you going to do *now*, Mr. President? Consult about what?

Strangers to our whole way of life are on the station. They're sitting up there in possession of it, and now they want manpower, Mr. President. They want what they wanted from us two hundred years ago, and you don't even know for a fact there's another station, the way they claim. We've got their word for it, don't we, the way we've got their word for everything else in space.

The way we had their word for it they'd let the station-builders and the miners run the station once they finished it, and you know how much say we had over what they did with the ship, and how much say we had over policy on the station. They double-crossed the station-keepers to get fuel for their ship, and now they're mad that the station-keepers couldn't keep the station going?

The good ones in the crew, the heroes—they'd volunteered to go out into the radiation hell of the star we came to after the accident, to get us to a kinder sun. The brightest and the best, they died *way* young, back when Taylor was captain.

The heroes weren't in charge when the scum that let them do the dying made all the later decisions.

The real heroes in the crew died and left the self-saving sons-of-bitches to run the thing they died for, Mr. President: don't believe these people. What they're dealing for is not just a ticket to fly. The idealists, the dreamers, the engineers and the nose-in-a-data-table scientists, are all in the same basket with *this* generation of sons-of-bitches who want off the planet, the ones who want their political party up where they control real power—power not to deal with atevi except down the barrel of a gun, a laser, whatever state of the art they've got up there. After that, nobody but them gets up there—

They're still fighting the damn war, Mr. President, but they don't let me on conference programs to call it what it is—they're still nursing a hatred of atevi that has nothing to do with the facts either present or past. They're the ones who write the letters about plots in atevi advances. They don't see anything but war. They think God made them perfect, in His image, and atevi . . .

Atevi can't love, they have no feelings, the separatists told those willing to listen—they couldn't expound it on television: the censors bleeped them off as inciting to break the peace; but they said it in places where people gathered who wanted to listen—not many people, because Mospheirans weren't political, weren't discontent, didn't give a damn so long as water came from the tap and they could observe their annual cycles of vacation at the shoresides, winter break for the mountains, total employment, pensioned retirement—the bowling societies, the touring societies, the dance societies, the low and the fashionable nightclubs, and the concern, if they worried about anything, over the weather, their health, their social standing, their vacation schedules, their kids' schools, and their various annual community festivals. *That* was the public the activists of whatever stripe had to deal with, a public that didn't grow exercised over any situation until it inconvenienced their plans: that was the Mospheiran political reality, in a system without real poverty, real threat, real anxiety, a system where stress was a rainy spell during your harvest celebration. Nobody got involved in politics except the few with an agenda, and lacking sources for funds and door-to-door campaigners, politics became a land of long-term benevolent chair-warmers and occasional agenda-pushers.

You only hoped to get the chair-warmers in office. And the pro-spacers, who were generally idealistic sorts— except this small, this hitherto mostly laughable nest of people who believed atevi were secretly building rockets to hurl at Mospheira—had been a private lunacy, not practiced in public, so the Secretary of State was secretly scared of atevi. It wasn't critical to the operation of the Foreign Office, which was Treaty-mandated, therefore set in concrete, and university-advised, therefore too esoteric to matter to the purveyors of corporate largesse that fed the successive Secretaries of State.

Until now.

There was public ignorance out there—fertile ground for fears.

There were people who'd never bothered to educate themselves about atevi because it wasn't their job to deal with atevi. The public just knew there was a different and far more violent world beyond their shores; the conservative party, which made a career out of viewing-with-alarm and deprecating esoteric scientific advances as costing too much money—those whose whole political bent was to conserve what was or yearn for what they thought had been, feared progress toward any future that didn't fit their imaginary past.

And they played to an undereducated populace with their demands for stronger defense, more secrecy, more money for a launch vehicle to get humans off the planet—which, of course, they could get by spending less for atevi language studies, and nothing at all for trade cities, as giving too much to atevi.

Lately the conservatives had tried to get three perhaps ill-advised university graduate students' grant revoked for teaching atevi philosophy as a cultural immersion experience for human eight-year-olds.

And in the ensuing flap, the more radical conservatives had tried to get all atevi studies professors thrown off the State Department's university advisory committee. Everyone had thought that an extreme reaction. Then. Before the ship.

The list of attempts to nibble away at the edges of intercultural accommodation went on and on, and it all added up in the paidhi's not apolitical mind to a movement that wasn't in any sense a party, wasn't in any sense grassroots, an agenda that only a minute fraction of the population agreed with in total.

But the closer atevi and human cultures drew to each other, the more the radicals, turning up in high places, generated issue after issue after issue—because the majority of humans, while not hating atevi, still had just a little nervousness about their neighbors across the strait, who did shoot each other, who looked strikingly different, who were ruled by a different government, who couldn't speak Mosphei; and people, be they human, be they atevi, always wanted to feel safer than they did, and more in charge of their future than they were.

The fact was, living on an island and hearing for nearly two hundred years of their government turning more and more sophisticated technology over to atevi—and lately knowing that the highest tech humans owned was on the negotiating table, and that within their children's lifetimes, the remaining technogap was going to close—could one wonder that humans who hadn't made atevi studies part of their education were becoming more than a little anxious?

On the atevi side of the strait, an atevi who sincerely believed there were secret human spaceships lurking on the great moon was very likely to be outspoken, to be known throughout the structure of his *man'chi* as holding those opinions, and *not* be appointed to office.

But on Mosphiera nobody had ever asked, when a candidate stood for public office, or stood for appointment, whether that candidate was a separatist. A State Department appointee could believe that atevi were stealing human children to make sausages, for God's sake, and none of that belief could turn up in the legislative review of fitness for office, because it wasn't a belief polite people expressed in public.

From totally insignificant, in the one *hour* of that ship's arrival, the separatists had come within reach of the kind of power that could keep them, they were sure, safe.

Because up there any human could deal with the Pilots' Guild for political power, for management authority over the station, while hiring the pro-spacers and their own malcontents to go risk their rears doing the real work.

The Pilots' Guild didn't know the situation on the planet, even if it had the best intentions in the world: it had to trust what it was told, and by all the history he knew the Pilots' Guild didn't care that damn much what they dealt with so long as it agreed with their agenda. The number of times the Guild had switched sides back in the debate over the Landing—even double-crossing the station management, then to patch things with the station, double-crossing the Landing faction—damned well *ensured* that the station population would be so bitterly divided and angry at each other that negotiation became impossible: *that* was the state of affairs he'd learned from his professors' unpublished notes. The station's demise had been virtually certain once the ship left, because station management was, in the view of the workers, compromised, untrustable, and lying through their teeth.

Screwed over, screwed up, and now the great holy Ship was back, offering paradise in space and the sun, the moon and the stars to anybody who'd come up there, risk their necks in the service of the all-important ship.

The same damned business all over again.

The same damned lot that had—perhaps not shoved Gaylord Hanks' daughter over here—

But certainly bestirred itself to keep her here. Maybe—they were not even aware as yet the degree of trouble she was stirring up, but just pushing their candidate in place, and pushing. A blow-up in atevi relations might be *exactly* what would put a finish to Bren Cameron's liberal dealings, could render the atevi interface unworkable and, in the minds of the opposition, put everything in *their* hands at a time when there was power to be had.

It was too stupid to be a reason. It was too far removed from sanity.

But his political sense kept up a persistent itch that said: A, Given ignorance in the mix, stupidity was at least as common in politics as astute maneuvering; B, Crisis always drew insects; and, C, Inevitably the party trying to resolve a matter had to contend with the party most willing to exploit it.

He found himself, with this voice-tape, sitting in possession of information that led him places he didn't at all want to go—conclusions that on one level were suspect, though informed: a set of conclusions that—even if they didn't fit present reality—still described its behavior—and the Hanks situation—with disturbingly predictive accuracy.

If he went down, humanity was in for a long, long siege of trouble—and might not win the ensuing civil wars, the breakdown of atevi peaceful tech and the acceleration of weapons development: witness planes in Malguri dropping homemade bombs, when Mospheira had made every design attempt to keep atevi aircraft stall rates where it would discourage that development. Humans *never* reckoned on atevi ingenuity, and even the best of the academics kept relying on human history to predict what atevi would logically come up with next.

But atevi ability to solve math problems, applied to design, meant everything you gave atevi mutated before sundown.

And some humans thought you could double-cross

atevi, outnumbered in *their* solar system, and keep them planetbound and out of the political question?

That, or there were people with notions of dealing with atevi that the paidhi didn't even want to contemplate.

Departmental policy said: Don't discuss human politics. Don't discuss internal and unresolved debates.

It wasn't the paidhi's business to steer atevi policy to oppose a Mospheiran choice. He didn't have that level of information. He wasn't appointed by any election or process to do that.

But he was elected—and appointed—and trained—and briefed on an executive level on this side of the strait. He *did* know atevi on levels that nobody else, even on the university advisory committee, could inform the State Department.

He sat for a while, while the tape ran down to its end, and there was no more information, there were no more bombs, but the one was enough.

It wasn't that the President had *chosen* to accept the offer—it was that the political process of decision had been set into motion, and the process was going to be dirty, full of fast-moving politics a slow-moving government wasn't going to stay on top of. Thanks to that apparently generous offer, very dirty, very destructive elements were going to push an agenda that could, if somebody didn't take fast action, crack Mospheira's insular, safe little world apart.

Meaning issues that didn't have a damned thing to do with reality. Mospheira didn't understand atevi. Mospheira had never needed or wanted to understand atevi. Just the paidhi did. That was why they appointed him. That was what they paid him to do. So they didn't have to.

And he had to talk to Tabini. Before the legislatures formulated policy. Before they took a public position.

He cut off the first recorder and went in search of Saidin, his coat, and Tano.

It was already a trying day: an unscheduled but urgent luncheon briefing in Tabini's own residence that post-

poned a scheduled agricultural council meeting downstairs in the Blue Hall and probably started a flood of rumors.

And trying through that stressful affair to convey—to a
man who could with a word start an interspecies war—
some sense of the dynamics at work in the Mospheiran
population: the small percentage of the opposition involved, the substantial danger to atevi interests and
claims on the space station of letting relations deteriorate,
and the need to hold firm and resolved in the face of hys-
terical or bribe-bearing voices on either side of the strait
who could only want to aggravate the tensions.

That meant coming up with an atevi negotiating position that took into account the things humans were going
to need: the paidhi could count off on both hands, at least
if not more knowledgeably than the President of Mospheira, critical raw materials and some finished goods
needful to the space effort that humans didn't have available on the island—and the paidhi knew what humans either on Mospheira or on the ship would be able and
willing to trade—namely money, designs, and full atevi
participation in space, once human prejudice and patronage had had its say and sober realization set in—in order
for the ship to get what they had to have: workers in numbers going up to that station.

Meaning atevi had to be willing to shut down trade and
go to unified bargaining with Mospheira or with the ship,
depending on which party proved reasonable.

"That doesn't allow Hanks-paidhi to deal with lord
Geigi for oil," Tabini instantly pointed out. "Does it?"

"The antithesis, I assure you, of what we want, aiji-ma.
No province should make independent deals for anything.
Everything in this emergency should go through Shejidan, just as Shejidan approves roads, rail, bridges and
dams—trade should go through Shejidan, for the good of
all the individual provinces so there isn't, for one thing,
undercutting of prices and selling of goods for less than
their fair value. Pool all trade, all shipping: establish market value, pay the suppliers, the workers, the shippers on
that standard, no exceptions, no profit for the central gov-

ernment, but no getting past it, either. The provincials have to understand they can lose money; and they have to understand the hazard of speaking with more than one voice when they deal with humans, exactly as I said in my speech, aiji-ma. Humans may quarrel among themselves: atevi can't afford to. This is where atevi make up the technological disadvantage: atevi know what they want, they've already voted their consensus, and they can vote, hold fast as a bloc, and be ready to deal while the President of Mospheira is still consulting with committees. Be fast enough and the ship folk may well choose to deal with you rather than Mospheira. At least you can scare Mospheira enough to get a better deal than they'd have given otherwise—and they're still your more natural ally, having dealt with you for two hundred years."

"Interesting," Tabini said. Tabini clearly *liked* that notion. The provincial lords wouldn't like it half as well, count on it. The lords of the provinces—and call a province a convenience of the map that only marginally described the real complexity of the arrangement—were always pulling in various directions for their own profit and for their own power if they could manage it.

"The provincial lords," Bren said, "have to find specific advantage for themselves."

"Believe me that I can find such advantages, in ways they will understand."

Meaning—the paidhi hoped—that the aiji would use bribes, fair, historically negotiated division of revenue, and not bullets.

The paidhi was about to pursue that point—when lady Damiri happened in, sat down at the table, set her chin in her hand, and declared that she couldn't help but overhear.

"Daja-ma," Bren said in confusion.

"Perhaps you'll persuade just *this* provincial, nand' paidhi, of the means with which the Atigeini should deal with Mospheira."

"I—can only urge my host that the Atigeini are in the same position as every powerful house in the Association—that if atevi don't deal as a unit, atevi will be at the mercy of the weakest and most desperate lords who *will* deal with humans when the aiji would urge—"

"When the aiji would urge," Tabini said, "that the provincial lords not sell to the humans, except at a price we agree, and under conditions we agree—with conditions which above all guarantee us access to the space station."

"What will we do with it?" Damiri asked—*not* the feckless question it might seem. "How do we come and go to this possession without this marketplace haggling over transport?"

"Atevi are ready," Bren said, and broke a chain of departmental rules, "for a major leap forward. Atevi are capable of safeguarding their own environment, their own government, and their own future. Atevi will secure access to materials and processes that go far beyond the designs we've already released. Atevi *will* have state-of-the-art earth-to-orbit craft, right along with Mospheira, and the paidhi hopes that atevi do better with advanced power systems than drop bombs on each others' heads, nadiin-nai."

"Does your President say so?"

"Aiji-ma, I say so. You have the Mospheiran President hanging on a frayed rope: there's no way for Mospheira to get critical materials without dealing with atevi. The ship could mine the moon, if it had workers to get the materials to build the robots to get the materials, but that's not practical. It needs supply and it needs workers. There's no way that Mospheirans can come and go at will on their own craft and the paidhi allow atevi to remain only passengers. But—a big *but*, nadiin—we *must* rely on computers. We *must* file flight plans. There *must* be air traffic control up there. Or whatever one calls it. There will be changes, in short, in atevi thinking, in atevi concepts. The paidhi can't prevent that."

Tabini was amused. The experienced eye saw it in the minute lift of a brow. An actual smile chased it.

"Weinathi Bridge in the heavens?"

A notorious air crash—which had persuaded even most provincial lords that precedence in the air couldn't rely on rank and that filing flight plans and standing by them no matter what was a very good idea. Especially in urban areas around major airports.

"We have only one station," Bren said. "Humans and atevi must live there. Beyond trade cities—the station is very close living, very close cooperation."

"This place that killed so many humans. That humans couldn't continue to occupy. Should atevi die for it?"

"The station itself is suitable for living. And can be made far safer than it is. This is a possible place, daja-ma. This is a place where atevi and humans can find things in common, and work in peace."

"A place with no air. No earth under one's feet."

"Just like in an airplane, daja-ma, one seals the doors and pumps air in."

"From where?"

"In this case—I suppose we bring it in tanks from the planet. Or plants can create it. Engineers know these things. The paidhi is an interpreter. If you wish to see plans, daja-ma, I can say they'll no longer be restricted."

"And the working of this ship?"

Not a simple curiosity, he thought, and was on guard. "Not the actual numbers and dimensions and techniques, daja-ma. I know liquid and solid-fuel rockets very well. But what powers this ship, what kind of technology we may have to create down here to bring us up to date with that ship—I don't know."

"Can you find out such things?" Tabini asked. "Can you get them from the ship?"

"I can tell you that I'll try. That eventually—yes, we'll find a way."

"Find a way," Damiri said.

"Daja-ma, in all my lifetime I've always been able to look around me on Mospheira and see the next technological step. For the first time—Mospheirans and atevi will be making whatever next step there is together, into a future we both don't know. I can't promise. I don't know. But atevi will have their chance. That's what I can work toward."

"There is no word," Tabini said, a question, "what this ship wants—beyond maintenance for the station."

"On a mere guess," Bren said, "the ship's crew is far more interested in the ship and in space than it is in any planet. What they do out there, where they go, what their lives are like—I suppose is very reasonable to them. I suppose it's enough—to them—to have the ship working."

Damiri asked, "Can the ship up there *take* what it wants?"

"I think," Bren said, "daja-ma, that it might possibly, as far as having the power; but what it wants just isn't so simple as to rob all banks on the planet and go its way. I can't foresee all that it might want, but I can't imagine it taking raw materials and manufacturing things itself. It never did, that I know."

"So what will it want, nadi?"

His hostess *never* accorded him the courtesy of his title. There was always the imperious edge to the voice; and he glanced at Tabini, ever so briefly, receiving nothing but a straightforward, interested attention.

"Bren-ji," Tabini said, with a casual wave of his fingers. Tabini wasn't unaware. Be patient, that seemed to mean, and he answered the question.

"I think it wants the station to fuel it and repair it if it needs repair."

"Why?"

"So, perhaps, it can leave us for another two hundred years. In the meanwhile—we have the access to the station."

"This is quite mad," Damiri said.

"Bren-ji," Tabini reproved his unadorned answer.

"Daja-ma, the ship puzzles all humans. I can say it would be very much simpler for it to have Mospheirans work for it and not have to deal with atevi. But that would allow Mospheira power that would unbalance everything the Treaty balanced. I completely oppose any such solution. Even if atevi had rather not deal with them—I don't think it wise to take that decision."

"The paidhi *is* human."

"Yes, daja-ma. But most Mospheirans don't want to have their affairs run from space. I can't speak for every official in office, but among ordinary people, and many in office as well, atevi have natural allies. Mospheirans stand to lose their authority over their own lives if certain other Mospheirans, very much like rebel provinces, have their way. To answer your very excellent question, nai-ma—I don't think the ship intends violence. By every evidence, they need the station. They want it the cheapest way possible. We have to prevent some humans from providing it too cheaply, without atevi participation. That's the situation as plainly as I can put it. And we have the leverage to prevent it."

"Bren-ji characterizes the Mospheiran government as indecisive. Incapable of strong decision."

"Is this so?" Damiri turned her golden eyes to Tabini, and back to him. "Then why are they fit allies?"

"Daja-ma," Bren said, "Mospheirans have a long history of opposition to the ship. Second, there's no strong dissent on Mospheira. There never has been, in any numbers that could cause trouble. The government isn't used to dealing with the tactics of opposition—which I feel this time there will be. Shejidan, on the other hand, is used to dissent and rapidly moving situations. The President of Mospheira can't conceive of what to do next, many but not all of his advisors are selfishly motivated, and he urgently needs a proposal on the table to give him a tenable position he can consider—results that he can hold up in public view. Publicity. Television, aiji-ma, that demon box, can draw his opposition into defending against the proposal you make rather than pushing their own program."

Tabini rested his chin on his hand. The two of them were mirror-images, Tabini and the prospective partner in his necessary and several years postponed heir-getting. One had to think of Tabini's lamented father, and the dowager, and breakfast.

And all that atevi talent for intrigue.

"Such a reprehensible, furtive tactic," Tabini said. "Can we not just assassinate the rascals?"

One suspected the aiji was joking. One never dared assume too far. "I think the President believes his alternatives are all human. I think he would welcome a well-worded and enlightening message from Shejidan, particularly one suggesting workable solutions."

"Interesting," Tabini said. And didn't say he had to consult. One had the feeling Tabini's brain was already working on the exact text.

In the next moment, indeed, the forefinger went up, commanding attention: "Say this, Bren-ji. Say to your President, Tabini-aiji has raw materials indispensable to your effort. Say, Tabini-aiji will sell you these materials only if humans and atevi are to *share* the station. Say that to him ... in whatever form one speaks to presidenti. Make up words he will understand and will not refuse." The fingers waved. "I leave such details of translation to you."

Tabini said, further, "We'll call the ship this evening, Bren-ji. Be ready."

He almost missed that. And didn't know what to say, but, "Yes, aiji-ma."

9

Tabini had made up his mind. Tabini was going to move, which notoriously meant a string of moves so rapid he kept his opponents' situation in moment-to-moment flux. It kept his aides in the same condition, unfortunately for the aides, and dealing with Tabini in that steel-trap, no-pretenses mode, trying to think what that chain of actions was logically going to be, always upset his stomach. He wrote out the best wording he could think of for Tabini's message to the island, atevi-style, reasonably simple. Lawyers had a practice, but never dominated the making of agreements—it might be the fact of assassination.

Being ready for whatever came, however, meant not only delivering the message but querying the Foreign Office one more time to catch up to whatever events were proceeding on Mospheira—assuming that the Foreign Office might know by now that the ship had made an offer to Mospheira.

One assumed something consequently might be going on in the halls of government and that Shawn might find a clever way to say so.

But whatever the Foreign Office might know, the Foreign Office wasn't admitting to anything. Shawn . . . didn't want to come on mike, but Bren kept after it, and asked bluntly,

"Shawn, do you know anything about an offer from the ship?"

"No. Sorry."

"Are you sure? I'm dealing with some specific information."

"We don't have any advisements," was the limp and helpless sum of what Shawn could say, and no, to his subsequent query, the Secretary of State wasn't available and, no, the undersecretary and his secretary's secretary weren't available.

That didn't inspire him to trust what the Foreign Office or the paidhi's office under him was currently being told by the executive; and along with that, anything he was being told by the Foreign Secretary—who wouldn't necessarily lie to him, but he had the feeling Shawn was signaling hard that he wasn't getting information.

He didn't have backup. Now he didn't have advice.

He said, "Shawn, you'd better record this. The ship's been talking, Tabini knows what's going on, and Tabini has a message to deliver to the President to the effect that if trade's going to continue, he has conditions which must include assurances. I'm telling you now in paraphrase in case communications mysteriously go down. Tabini-aiji has a message for the President personally, and if anything happens to the phones can you kindly get somebody on the next flight over here to pick up the aiji's message in writing? I'm going to transmit at the end of this message, and I want you to get somebody to courier it over to the President, in person. This *is* official. There are people on Mospheira who may not want this message to reach the President. Do you read me?"

"I'll carry it myself."

He sent. It said, *Mr. President, a message from Tabini-aiji. The offer from the ship makes no mention of atevi Treaty rights on the station. Tabini-aiji suggests that to accept this offer would negate the Treaty and stop trade of materials needful to carry out any accelerated building program.*

On the other hand, Tabini-aiji suggests that the inhabitants of this world, both atevi and Mospheiran human, enter into agreement to withhold our consent and cooperation until our needs are met. Clearly the ship wants workers, and has made an offer which may not be to either your advantage or the advantage of the Association.

Recognizing this political reality, Mr. President, Tabini-

aiji is willing to accelerate the pace of atevi technological development in order to promote atevi presence on the station and atevi natural interests in these affairs in the space around our planet and our sun. In short, Mr. President, we suggest a partnership between Mospheira and atevi which may secure the economy, the civil rights, and the political stability of both Mospheira and the Association as a whole. You will have your heavy-launch manned vehicle, and we will bear a half share of the station operation and maintenance.

We have many cultural and biological differences, but we share a concern for a stable economy and the rights of our citizens to live in peace on this planet. If that now means cooperation in orbit above this planet, we trust that atevi and humans can reach a just and rapid accommodation.

The aiji, speaking with the consensus of the hasdrawad and the tashrid, awaits your reply.

He received an acknowledgment from Shawn. But he'd bet—he'd just about bet—the phones between Mospheira and the mainland would go down within half an hour.

He'd stretched the point. A lot. He'd used words nobody could say in an atevi language. He'd played on the concerns he was sure the President felt over shifts in internal politics which could throw him and the majority of politicians on Mospheira out of office.

He had a headache. His stomach was upset from lunch. Or from the thought of what he'd implied in that message.

Or from the knowledge he had to go real-time tonight and talk to the ship himself.

Meanwhile he had a handful of troublesome official letters Tano had pulled from the pile of atevi correspondence, one of which was from the restricted-universe Absolutists, a sect of the Determinists, mostly from Geigi's province, though there were—he consulted his computer file—others from small, traditional schools. They attached moral significance and their interpretation of human and atevi origins to a hierarchy of numbers that didn't admit FTL physics—God save him: if he couldn't find a numerical explanation of FTL, thanks to Hanks, the Determinists were going to rise up and call him a liar and insulting to their intelligence for claiming the ship *wasn't* a case of humans lurking on the station for two hundred years in secret and preparing to swoop down with death rays.

Banichi was missing. Jago had gone somewhere. That scared him to death. He had no idea, but he assumed the two absences were connected: Cenedi had hinted at serious trouble in the Assassins' Guild, which could, as far as he knew, threaten Banichi's and Jago's lives as well as his. He hadn't been able to ask Tabini, especially since Damiri had shown up and sat down—assuming admission to any meeting, any affair going on in the apartment.

He'd had a question in the back of his mind when Damiri had intruded, and in his general haste to get the matter restated for this most influential—and clearly pricklish—of Tabini's private advisors, he'd not found the opportunity to ask Damiri her meanings, her secrets, or her implications; and, damn, he didn't know what it meant, or what rights Tabini had granted her—who wasn't Tabini's social equal, and who had constantly pushed not only at the paidhi's dignity but at Tabini's authority in that interview. Was there some cue he should have taken? Was there something he'd done in the apartment that had set Damiri off?

Cenedi had said there were people trying to file Intent on the paidhi. Which gave no idea on exactly what issue was involved or whether the paidhi was surrogate for Tabini in the atevi politics of assassins and intrigue.

He resolved at least that he was going to take the advice of the security Tabini had provided him, and meant to take no chances with his personal safety.

The bright spot in the entire day thus far was an unexpected ring of the phone from Bu-javid Security, reporting that Tano's wayward partner was actually downstairs in the Bu-javid subway station, and that, lacking specific instruction, Security was double-checking

Algini's assignment to the sensitive Bu-javid third floor and questioning a "considerable amount of baggage." That assignment and the baggage apparently needed someone's authorization, and in the absence of Banichi and Jago, Tano evidently not being qualified to recognize his own partner, it had to go all the way up to Tabini himself.

Which Tabini, called out of yet one more committee meeting, was patiently willing to do for the paidhi—resulting, within the hour, in Algini's entry into the foyer with an amazing accompaniment of baggage, a towering pile of responsibility which had Saidin and the household servants whispering together in urgent dismay, as strong Bu-javid security personnel delivered stack after stack of baggage belonging to a broad-shouldered ateva with bandages and plaster patches glaring white on his skin, not in uniform, but in clothes more appropriate for a hike through the hills—small wonder Security downstairs had blinked.

Tano himself was so glad to see his partner that he actually patted Algini on the shoulder—not, Bren sternly reminded himself, that Tano felt the way he would under similar circumstances.

But—but—and but. It was another tantalizing pass of that camaraderie that atevi did have, that Jago and Banichi he would swear had given him: more warmth in all than Tabini was wont to show, although—one had to remind oneself—in assessing atevi emotion, one might be dealing with individual differences.

But he found himself watching Tano and Algini with a certain tightness about the throat and thinking he almost *had* something like that with Banichi and Jago, whatever it was and whatever it felt like; a level of feeling that at least let a man believe his back was defended under all circumstances and that he wasn't come hell and high water alone in the universe—more emotional attachment of whatever kind and more loyalty than he'd had from humans he could name. More dangerous thoughts, around other humanly, emotionally charged words. He was *not* doing well today.

That, after his session with Tabini, calmly laying out for Tabini what he'd heard, what he suspected, what he thought were the only available human choices—in short, treason, of a virtually unprecedented kind so far as the history of the paidhiin. The act had hit a particularly sensitive spot in his nerves, with, in all that trying session, Tabini never showing any emotion but somber thought or amusement, never thanking him or reassuring him of the peaceful, constructive, wise uses to which the information he'd given would be put.

He found himself with very raw, very abraded sensitivities this afternoon, wanting not to feel as alone as he felt, and here Tano and Algini held that lure out in front of him, a demonstration that, yes, there was feeling, yes, it was almost—almost—what a human could access. He'd touched it. He'd tasted it. He'd relied on it for life and sanity in Malguri, and it might be all he could damn well look to for the rest of his life, thanks to choices he was making in these few desperate days.

And it wasn't, wasn't, *wasn't* reliable emotion. He could play voyeur to the experience of it; he was glad it existed for them. He was very glad for Algini's safety.

And perhaps that was the cold, sensible, atevi thing to feel right now. Perhaps it was all Tabini, for instance, would feel, or that Jago and Banichi would feel, if they were here.

Algini came to him and bowed with a pleasant, even cheerful face, unusual on glum Algini, and declared proudly, "I brought your baggage, nand' paidhi."

My God, was *that* the contents of the pasteboard boxes and cases piled on the antique carpets? All the things he'd left behind in Malguri, literally all he owned in the world, except a few keepsakes he'd left with his mother. He'd thought there was a remote chance of getting some things back, in the regret of a favorite sweater, his best coat, his brush, his traveling kit, the photos of his family—that was his whole damned life sitting in those boxes, and Algini had just brought it back, from his shirts and socks to the rings and the watch that Barb had given him.

"Nadi-ji," he said to Algini. The vocabulary of atevi

gratitude was linguistic quicksand. "—I'm very surprised." He still wasn't hitting it. "Much as I value these things, I'd give them all to have you safe. It's very good, very dutiful, very—considerate of you to have brought them."

Which must have hit something. Algini looked astonished, grim and silent as he tended to be, and said, "Nand' paidhi, it's my job," the way Jago would sometimes remind him.

Even Banichi and Jago respected Algini—Tano, who'd taken until after Malguri to show his expressions, had him for a partner—and in this moment Bren saw qualities in Algini that he'd either been blind to, or that Algini hadn't let *him* see before; qualities which said this was, in human terms, a man who did his duty because that was what he expected of himself.

And all those boxes. Saidin was observing from the doorway, and he gave the matter into her hands. "Please," he said, "have the staff do the arranging. I have all confidence in your judgment, nand' Saidin. Algini, please rest. Banichi and Jago aren't here. I don't know where they are. But I'm sure they'd say so."

"Nand' paidhi," Algini said quietly, "one would be glad to do that, thank you, yes."

A hell of a household, he said to himself, the lot of them in bandages and patches. Algini was ready to collapse on his face, by all he could figure, but before they could clear the boxes out of the vestibule, the light at the door flashed, the security wire went down, the door opened and Jago came in.

" 'Gini-ji," Jago said, in some evident pleasure, and there were more bows, and even more shoulder-slapping than between Algini and Tano. "One is glad. One is very glad."

But straightway Jago looked to have remembered something forgotten, said, "Bren-ji, pardon," and gave him a message cylinder, one with Tabini's seal.

Bren halfway expected it. He stood in the sea of boxes, with his security looking on, with the staff beginning to carry away this item and that, and saw the date and time as this evening and the place as the blue room.

He wasn't ready, not emotionally—maybe not mentally. He hadn't been ready for anything they'd thrown at him yet, except in the conviction, already taken, that he had to try and he couldn't, on the moment's bereaved, deranged thought, do worse than Mospheira's President and experts had done, so far as falling into what the paidhi, the unique individual actually experienced in foreign negotiation, saw as a trap.

The paidhi could be wrong, of course.

The paidhi could be wrong up and down the board.

But he went out at the appointed time with his notes and his computer, and went to the lift in Jago's company. Now, if never before in his career, he had to focus down and have his wits about him.

And he was scared stiff.

He had to think in Mosphei' in a handful of minutes, which required a complete mental turnover—granted they could raise the ship at all, had to go back and forth between the two languages, which required a compartmentalization he didn't like to do real-time.

The official document delivered to him had chased Tabini's note: the formal announcement of decision on his request, a parchment heavy with ribbons and legislative seals, which he was requested to return, and which he carried in his hand. The legislatures had argued their way past midnight last night and concluded a general resolution to see where contact might lead: Would the paidhi, that immense document said in brief, kindly intercede and convey the salutations of the Association to the ship, the aiji willing?

Tabini's note had put it more succinctly, had given him the hour of the meeting and said: *The legislature will re-enter session today on a special motion from the eastern provinces.* That meant the rebel provinces were raising some issue.

And Tabini's note had continued: *By suppertime the*

whole matter must be fait accompli by way of Bu-javid systems or we will be awash in additional motions.

Chimati sida'ta. The beast under dispute would already be stewed, as the atevi proverb had it: the aiji and the paidhi-aiji had authority granted by the vote last night until some vote today negated it or delayed it for study or did something else creatively pernicious to Tabini's interests. Therefore the haste.

The vote, however, did not convey authority from Mospheira—who had sent no response to his messages, no response to Tabini's message to the President of Mospheira. He *had* hoped, he had remotely hoped—and knew he was creating serious trouble not only for himself, but for everyone in the Department who backed him, in proceeding without authority. He regretted that as a personal, calculated and depressingly necessary betrayal.

But the committee that would have to answer him had the nature of committees even on this side of the strait, and possibly throughout the universe: ask it a question and it felt compelled to make a formal ruling, which in the time frame of a Mospheiran committee, far worse than the ones he dealt with here, might arrive next year, once the message had hit—the President's council hardly moved faster.

If They, meaning the senior officials in the State Department, hanged the paidhi for it—at this point, *chimati sida'ta,* they had to catch him first.

If They wanted to talk to atevi, and he knew that, regardless of public posture, all but a handful of mostly-talk ideologues had no notion in the world of breaking off talk with atevi—again, *chimati sida'ta.* If Tabini moved fast, They had no choice but to deal with what was, and They still had to talk to Tabini through him, since Tabini wouldn't talk to Hanks, wouldn't talk to Wilson, or anybody else in the Department they could hasten through to promotion. By now, Hanks would have been dead, he greatly feared, if he hadn't specifically asked Tabini not to deal with the affront to his nation atevi-fashion; at any second violation of the Treaty he might not be able to ar-

gue Tabini out of a demonstration of atevi impatience
with opposition to the paidhi they chose to deal with.

So if even temporarily the more pragmatic and politically savvy separatists in State should fall from grace and
the true concrete-for-brains ideologues gain temporary as-
cendency, he'd vastly regret the damage he'd have done
the foresighted, loyal people at lower levels who backed
him. But he had ultimate confidence the rabid ideologues
would have short satisfaction, and shorter tenure, when
they couldn't get information or cooperation—or raw
materials—out of the mainland.

So even if they made their deals with the ship aloft,
they were screwed—

And so was the ship, ultimately, until it dealt with
atevi. He didn't like the position he was forced to. He
didn't like the responsibility, but circumstances had assured he knew, and Mospheira didn't, and it was a position no conscientious diplomat ever wanted to be put
into—

Because he *was,* dammit, trained to consult, *was* loyal
to his nation if not the Department; *he* was following the
course decades of paidhiin and advisory committees had
mapped out, step by step, down to what technology could
go in at what stages, and why.

Which made him, walking the lower corridor at Jago's
side, realize three things: first, that he wasn't altogether
alone in his resolve. No matter who was presently in
charge of events back home or aloft, he had behind him
all the structure and decision of all the past paidhiin-
aijiin that had ever served, along with all their advisory
committees—predecessors who were being betrayed by
present expediency and the present administration.

Second, that to protect the situation they currently had,
he had to get Hanks home quietly.

And, third, that he was really going to do it, really going to make a break with the Department as it was presently constituted. He would have to accelerate what his
and Tabini's very wise predecessors had determined as
the necessary rate of turnover of human technology to
atevi far faster in its last stages than the planners had ever

remotely envisioned as wise. He would have to push the world toward a more direct and more risky exposure of culture to culture than the exploratory Trade Cities proposal had ever remotely contemplated. The Trade Cities bill had been designed to educate the two populaces on an interpersonal, intercultural level; and to find out what the problems would be in an exposure which the best Foreign Office wisdom held as a very, very difficult interface.

That interface would be far more difficult in orbit—with two very set-in-their-ways cultures trying to adapt to a new environment as well as to each other, difficult even *if*—and a big if—the crew of the ship up there didn't intend to double-cross the station-builders and station-workers one more time to fuel that ship and leave everyone betrayed and angry. The ship crew might think they could play the same game with new players.

They would think wrong.

If last night his speech before the legislature had provoked an assassination attempt, what he had formed as his intention now might bring out assassins in droves. If last night's speech had turned on every light in the presidential residence, tonight's work was going to keep them burning for weeks.

10

It wasn't a matter of going out to the installation where the dish was: they would, Tabini's message had said, relay to Bu-javid systems, which meant anywhere convenient, and the meeting room was the same that Tabini had called him to the night he arrived.

Jago preceded him as he maneuvered his casted shoulder past the converse of aides at the door, into a meeting room crowded with technicians, communications equipment, and lords and representatives, two of the senior members of the print media, and a camera crew of uncertain but undoubtedly well-funded affiliation.

"Nand' paidhi," Tabini said, inviting him to the place of prominence, and Tabini's aides hastened to draw back his chair and settle him at Tabini's right, while Jago quietly set his notebook in front of him and his computer beside his chair. Technicians were making last-moment adjustments and set a microphone in front of him. He saw that it was switched off and cast a nervous look at the cameras. "Are they network, Tabini-ma?"

"Legislative," Tabini said. "We want meticulous records, not alone for posterity."

Preservative, he thought, of all their reputations, considering all the rumors that were bound to arise.

And useful in mistakes the paidhi might have to set straight. He felt more at ease with the cameras and the press under that understanding. He decided he wanted them there, rumor tending, as it did, to exaggerate every unaccustomed event. "Have we made technical contact yet?"

"The technicians are working on it. Everyone should

understand—" A hush was rapidly settling in the room as lords and representatives strained to overhear them. "This entire evening's effort may be without result. But the contact between us and the ground station is clear. —Are we settled, then?"

There was a murmur from around the table as the last two members quickly assumed their chairs.

"Speak, nand' paidhi. We hope the ship will listen: your microphone will reach the operator at Mogari-nai."

"I'll do what I can, aiji-ma." He drew the mike closer, flipped the switch to On and felt his stomach uneasy. "Mogari-nai, this is Bren-paidhi. Do you hear?"

"Nand' paidhi, we can put you straight onto the dish."

Dreadful syntax. An assault on the language. The traditionalists objected to these enthusiastic technocrats. It likewise jarred the paidhi's nerves.

"Yes. Thank you, Mogari-nai. Am I going through now?"

"You're going through."

"Phoenix-com, this is Bren Cameron, translator for the atevi head of state based in Shejidan. The aiji of the Aishi'ditat has a message for the captains. Please acknowledge. —Nadiin-sai, machi arai'si na djima sa dimajin tasu."*

Keep playing that until further notice, that was.

He looked at Tabini. "I've asked the ship to answer, aiji-ma. No knowing whether there's a captain immediately available—there's probably more than one—or whether anyone's monitoring the radio. Sleep and waking hours up there aren't necessarily on—"

"This is Phoenix-*com,"* came through the audio, in Mosphei'—or at least a dialect with origins common to his own. *"Do you read?"*

He'd felt reasonably steady a heartbeat ago. Now his very surroundings looked unreal to him. He moved the microphone closer, and his pulse seemed to shake his bones and preempt his breathing.

"I hear you quite clearly, sir. To whom am I speaking?"
"This is Robert Orr, watch officer. Please give your name and identification."

"Mr. Orr, this is Bren Cameron, translator between humans and the Western Association—which *is* the largest nation and the only nation with which humanity has regular, treaty-bound contact. As a matter of protocol, as the translator, I can negotiate with you as a ship's officer. The person for whom I translate, on the other hand, the elected head of state of the Western Association, wishes to speak with the seniormost officer on the ship. This is a matter of protocol. The atevi head of state is present, well-disposed, and waiting to speak. Can you advise your senior captain and see if we can put him and the atevi head of state in direct contact during this conversation?"

"Yes, sir. I'll inform him." There was a little quaver of disturbance in the voice, a hasty, apparently afterthought: *"Stand by. Someone will be back to you in just a minute. Don't lose contact."*

"Thank you." He looked at Tabini. "Aiji-ma. I was speaking with a person of middle rank. I asked him to alert his highest authority. He wishes us to be patient; I believe he's gone in search of someone qualified."

There was absolute silence down the table, not the rustle of a paper.

"How do you judge the reply?"

"This is a respectful, proper answer to the proposition of someone of rank. They've every reason to deal sensibly, and to find someone—"

"Mr. Cameron."

A different voice.

"This is Stani Ramirez, senior captain. I understand you're speaking for a native government. Is this correct?"

"For the elected head of the Western Association—which covers more than three-quarters of the world's largest continent, and all industrialized culture whatsoever. I'm speaking from the capital of Shejidan. Please hold." Language switch. For a moment he suffered mental whiteout. "Tabini-ma. This is Stani, house name Ramirez. He is the highest authority over the ship. He's waiting to speak to you."

"Explain the Treaty. Inform him we consider this the appropriate association with humans."

"Yes, aiji-ma." Switch back. "Captain Ramirez. The aiji wishes me to explain that the Western Association considers that relations between all humans and atevi are governed by a Treaty which the aiji accepts as the appropriately safeguarded conditions of human-atevi interaction. I'm prepared to transmit a copy to you at the end of this conversation. The Western Association asks you to follow its terms as the only mutually agreed means of protecting both human and atevi cultures from misunderstandings."

"We'll have to consider this document."

"Yes, sir, but I believe you know that the first atevi-human contact led to war. The issues are biological, not cultural, and all persons experienced in atevi-human contact will advise you these issues are not resolvable. Atevi are not hostile. They wish to communicate directly with the ship, for protection of their own interests, but communication channels have to be confined to persons educated to interpret what's being said: that's the whole gist of the Treaty."

"Tell him," Tabini interrupted him, lifting a hand, "to appoint a mediator like yourself, Bren-paidhi, whom you will instruct. This translator will deal with you and come down to Shejidan in person as soon as possible."

He froze for what felt like a long, stunned moment. There were sinking instants in which he was *sure* Tabini knew more Mosphei' than Tabini ever admitted to, and then he said to himself that Tabini had done nothing more than take a rational decision in advance. An appropriate decision. A Treaty-suggested decision. The committee heads shifted anxiously in their seats at his delay— perhaps at the dismay that might have gotten to his face. It wasn't for the paidhi to rule on the aiji's decisions, no more than he made policy for Mospheira. He translated. He interpreted. That was all he was supposed to do. It was just—

Tabini had injected a completely unplanned, unknowable variable into his calculations, and with the aiji's powers to dictate first and have the legislature review it later, Tabini had done exactly what he'd suggested Tabini do: act.

"Sir," he said to the captain.

"I read you clear."

"In regard to what I was saying, in your reading of the Treaty, you'll find all translation and mediation between atevi and human authority rests in a single appointed translator. Let me explain: it's a difficult, biologically impacted language interface." One couldn't even assume, he thought on the fly, that ship personnel knew *anything* about languages other than their own. One couldn't assume, over elapsed centuries of restricted, probably small population on that ship, that they even retained the concept, let alone the experience, of different language—let alone had persons able to grapple with the facts of a language with almost no word-by-word congruency with Mosphei'. "The language expresses vast differences in psychological concepts, in basic biology, which we've worked out peacefully and reasonably. The leader of the atevi invites you to appoint a candidate to take instruction from me in necessary protocols as well as language. The aiji requires this representative be sent to the capital at Shejidan as soon as possible."

"You're saying, appoint a protocol officer to be in regular contact with you. To land on the planet."

"Sir, yes: send down a person with authority to make agreements which you may ratify. A diplomat."

"What does Mospheira say to this?"

"Mospheira is a member state of the Western Association. The island is a province among other provinces. It does not speak for atevi or for this planet. It's required to abide by the decisions of the Western Association regarding foreign policy and trade. Such things are easy to set up—there are channels, appropriate routes, that kind of thing. There are abundant agreements attached to the Treaty which handle protocols, shipping points—I understand you're looking for some manufacture and supply that lies on the mainland. A protocol officer could facilitate that—but a real aptitude for language is a must. I can provide short cuts, but there has to be a natural ability."

There was a silence. Damned right there should be a moment of silence. Then: *"I have my own council to consult. How will we contact you?"*

God, it sounded like Mospheira. One thought the captain of a working ship could make a decision. "The ground-station operators will be aware of my whereabouts. We have one gap in the relays which I imagine you will have noticed: the satellite went down a considerable time ago. The operators are aware of that and can work around it."

"Are these native operators?"

"They are atevi, yes, sir. They won't understand your operators, but the Western Association is linguistically homogeneous and I'm well-known. Use my name and they'll have no doubt that you're looking for contact. I suggest another call tomorrow at local midday. Can we expect that?"

"It may take longer to go through this document. What's your sending mode?"

"Standard to the station. Atevi communications are identical systems to the ones you've been reaching on the island." Yes, Captain, we are receiving what you say to Mospheira, but you don't know at what levels and how legitimate or thorough our penetration of ship communications is, do you? "You'll find the document very brief, in the style of atevi legal documents. The details rest in specific subsequent agreements. If you need me at any hour of the day or night, you can reach me simply by calling the earth station. They can patch me right into the local phone system, wherever I am."

"Mr. Cameron, this may be late to bring up—but what assurance do we have that you're authorized, or even a real official?"

It was at least one thing he'd thought of in advance. "Sir, if you've located the source of transmission—" and I'll bet you're doing that, sir, and trying to figure what it is "—you'll find it a very large, very official installation which regularly monitors the station's telemetry. In point of fact, there are only three or so humans in the world fluent in the atevi language, there're no atevi fluent in the human language, and there's no other channel appointed by the Treaty for contact except me. Call anywhere on the planet you like: you'll get no answers but from me and Mospheira. The big dish at a site called Mogari-nai is the only place besides Mospheira that can put you in touch with anyone who understands your language." He cast a glance at Tabini, who'd been quite patient. "Aiji-ma, jis asdi parei'manima pag' nand' Stani-captain?"

"Masji sig' triti didamei'shi."

"First atevi word to learn, sir, is aiji. That's the title of the atevi president—more powers than 'president,' but it's the closest translation. His personal name is Tabini: call him Tabini-aiji, and call that name whenever and every time in a conversation you say a sentence to him: it's basic courtesy. He'll await and expect your acceptance of the entire Treaty. Atevi don't understand making exceptions during initial agreement: please consider the Treaty document as a sweeping statement of principle, closer negotiations to follow. Atevi law is based on equity stemming from such broad agreements. —Have you any special word, sir, to the aiji of the Western Association?"

"Tell him we hope for friendly contact and we'll stand by for your document transmission."

"Thank you, sir. I'm concluding now. —Daiti, nadiin tekikin, madighi tritin distitas pas ajiimaisit, das, das, das, magji das."

"Pai sat, paidhi-ma."

He set the computer on the table, with the last-moment help of an aide, flipped up the screen, pulled out the line to the phone connector on the table.

Then he called a file; actuated; and the Treaty document flew, presumably, to the atevi earth station and bounced to the ship.

That simply, that easily, from a phone connection on a desk in the Bu-javid.

Mind-boggling even to the arbiter of technology.

And evidently mind-boggling to the heads of committee at the table. Usually at a meeting there were half-attentive looks and the momentary fidgets or a consultation of notes or aides. Not this time. There was solemn anxiousness, absolute quiet. They might not yet realize what had happened. They certainly didn't know what all that chatter back and forth had been.

"So what did he say?" Tabini asked.

"I asked, aiji-ma, what he would say to the aiji. He said, quote, 'We desire peaceful contact and we'll stand by for the Treaty agreement transmission.' End quote. I sent it. I did substitute one word in that: his 'peaceful' contact carries an expectation of nonwarlike interaction that has no atevi equivalent."

"Does it change the meaning of contact?" the head of Judiciary asked.

"It expresses routine politeness. Sometimes it has a casual and not highly specific application, meaning not-war, or, equally, can mean a real yearning for association. It's that word *friend,* nadi, the one that always confuses translations."

"A pest of a word," Tabini said.

"Always, aiji-ma. Even another human has to figure out how the other human means it at the moment."

"Intended confusion?"

"It can be." The atevi leap to suspicion was possibly hardwired. It was at least fast. "I could have predicted he'd use it—in a way I find it reassuring that he did use it. But he doesn't realize you won't know its nuances. I suspect there's no one on the ship that's ever met another language. They want to know about the Treaty document—and I can equally well predict they'll ask if they got it all. They won't expect it to be that short. Their own legal documents try to nail down every minute exception and possible eventuality in advance."

"This seems excessive trouble," Tabini muttered.

"Tradition. Law—I'm not sure I know the history behind it. But they try to think of all the problems that could come up."

"Negative thinking. Is this not your expression?"

"But they will almost certainly do it. I confess I'm daunted, nadiin, aiji-ma. I just hadn't realized operationally until I talked with this man how far back I have to start explaining our mutual history of relations. Clearly

I'm *not* dealing with the university on Mospheira: I'm going to have to interpret very heavily. No one on the ship is going to know how to avoid troublesome concepts. I'll have to explain them as I go."

"How accurate can this interpretation be?" Judiciary asked.

"As accurate as the paidhi's recognition there's a difficulty, nandi, which is why I must ask, if you hear something disturbing, please interrupt and object. Context makes a vast difference. So does historical background. I'll advise you of the words I find suspect; and I find the idea of creating a specialist from among them—startling as it was to me—is an excellent notion, aiji-ma. Granting they can find someone with the ability and if I can teach the right ideas to this person—it may be a vast help." He found himself more nervous than if he'd been facing guns and grenades. One *didn't* second-guess the aiji. Or any other atevi lord. But he had to supply the objection he saw. "But if I detect the person isn't capable or that the interface is getting worse—I request the authority, aiji-ma, nadiin-ma, to shut this person off immediately from information and to reject this contact. If that should be, we may be thrown back on the resources of the university. And we may have to go to them, if I find I can't deal with the translations alone."

"This would have severe implications," Tabini said. "And I would rather you succeeded, paidhi-ji."

"I would most earnestly rather I succeeded, aiji-ma." He'd been more anxious than he knew. A number of conclusions were coming home to roost, one of them a surmise that, since he'd put himself on very shaky ground with the university and the Department, he might still have to deal with Hanks as the representative of Mospheira and himself ... God only knew. As Tabini's, he supposed.

It wasn't a situation he wanted. But that little jarring note in the negotiation had rung alarm bells all up and down his nerves: not that he hadn't expected it, but that word *friendly,* that no regular contact he used would have dared use, advised him of dangerous problems.

Friendly contact.

The War memorials and the fact that humans lived on an island weren't part of the ship captain's growing up, the captain's constant awareness, the captain's conceptual reality. He didn't know that lives were in danger. Or didn't know that they were in danger for the reasons that they were. Mospheira had transmitted a history of the war. But knowing the details of history wasn't the same as stopping for that minute of silence at 9:16 A.M. every Treaty Day; or seeing that time frozen on the clock in the photos of Alpha Base. He'd been there once. Every paidhi went there once.

"Aiji-ma," he said, "I'll prepare another document for transmission. A handbook of protocols, by your leave. I can assemble it by tomorrow, out of the dictionary."

"As the paidhi will," Tabini said. "Whatever the paidhi deems necessary."

It was an appalling grant of power. It meant—in atevi terms—he bore direct responsibility, along with that grant of power.

He folded up his computer quietly, thinking, God, he'd put his neck in the noose now. After that it came down to operational details, a handful of answers he needed to give, a confirmation of meeting dates, all of which he had to sit through, but his mind wasn't on committee housekeeping, or even the few questions committee members asked.

It was the moment, in a curious retreat of his mind, in which he really, definitively said good-bye forever to Barb. In which he thought of the letter he'd write to his mother, and Toby.

In which he held himself and his motives and his mental condition entirely suspect. The aftershocks of an irrevocable, previously confident decision were rumbling through the mental landscape, disturbing precarious balance. He felt slightly sick at his stomach. He questioned his motives and his sanity this time from hindsight, not theoretical actions. Reality always put a texture on things, a chaotic topography of imperfections, that imagination had foreseen as smooth and featureless. Now it was all in past-tense conversation between two minds, not one mind reasoning with itself. Now it was interaction with a very potent and distance-wise inscrutable third party, as well as a Department that was going to ask the paidhi what in *hell* he thought he was doing.

"Nadiin," Tabini said, "we are adjourned. Nand' paidhi, thank you."

"Aiji-ma," he murmured, and with one aide to help with the chair and another to help with the computer, he gathered himself up, still with that hollow feeling inside, and collected his belongings.

Lord Eigji of the Commerce Committee cleared his path to the door—perhaps in consideration of his small stature and his necessary awkwardness with the outward-braced cast—but such a reversal of ordinary protocols of rank required first the acknowledgment of a bow of the head, then puzzled afterthought, so deep a thought he knocked the doorframe with the cast in leaving and, expecting Jago, didn't look up quite enough: his view was suddenly and entirely black leather and silver metal.

"I have it," Banichi said, and collected the computer from his hand.

"Where have you *been*, nadi?" was his first unthought question, while they were still blocking atevi lords from the doorway.

Banichi led him aside before saying, "Sleeping, nand' paidhi. One has to, eventually."

It wasn't at all the truth. He gave not-the-truth back to it. "I never was sure you did that."

He amused Banichi. That Banichi could be amused was a reassuring stroke in itself: if Banichi was in good humor then something that was security's concern must have gone right.

One had to wonder, on the other hand, where Jago had gone now, and he wasn't at all sure it was back to the residence, but the recipient of their duty couldn't pursue the question, even in the most security-conscious area of the Bu-javid—

Or especially because they were here, in an area where anxious, life-and-death interests hung close about them.

They walked toward the lift not quite elbow to elbow with the lords of the Association, but possibly within earshot.

"I have to go to my office, if not today, tomorrow," he said, off his balance in this switch of personnel; he'd mapped out how to deal with Jago. And atevi had changed the situation on him again without warning. "I have to find out what's been done there—I need to consult with Hanks."

"I thought you'd declared war on her."

"Not—quite that far. Understand, please, Banichi-ji. I don't want her to come to harm."

"You must be the only one on the mainland," Banichi said, "to say so."

"We can't allow it, Banichi. Can't. Daren't. —Where *is* Jago?" They'd reached a relatively isolated area by the lift that served the more securitied floors, and he pounced on the first chance for the question. "Algini's back, did you know? You go, Jago goes, you come back, Algini's got the foyer stacked with my luggage—"

"Shush." It was the word one used with a child. "You're due upstairs. Rest, Bren-ji. It is a physical necessity."

"Cenedi said there was trouble going on."

Banichi had pushed the call button. The car had arrived, but Banichi lingered to cast him a curious look. "Cenedi said," Banichi reiterated.

"Cenedi said—he'd stand with you in the Guild, if he had a choice."

"*Did* he?"

They had to take the car or lose it. Banichi swept him inside and followed.

With no intent, it seemed, of answering his question, even in general. But he thought Banichi had been at least taken off his guard by that information.

And gave nothing back.

"Banichi, dammit."

Banichi found it convenient to watch the floor indicator. Banichi was dressed fit for a council meeting: official, impervious, unruffled by whatever was going on.

"A man died last night," Bren said sharply.

"One heard." Banichi still didn't look at him.

"Banichi—one could arrange one's affairs ever so much more wisely if one's security told him something! I am *not* a fool, Banichi, don't treat me as one."

Banichi offered a small, frayed smile. "Bren-ji, it's your task to deal with ships and such. It's ours to see you aren't diverted by extraneous matters."

"The man had a family, Banichi. I can't forget that."

The car stopped. The door opened.

"We can't discuss it here. Not a secure area, Bren-ji."

"What is? Besides the apartment I'm borrowing from—" But the microphones which evidently worried Banichi, which Banichi had equipment to detect, surely all that were in this hall served Tabini, and therefore were accessible to Damiri.

It was that small uncertainty that stopped him.

And why? he said to himself. *Why* could there be any question about third-floor security that Banichi couldn't make sure of?

Who was up here, with access to this floor, but staffs that held *man'chi* to Tabini, to—

To the Atigeini woman who'd offered him her hospitality—and whose family opposed Tabini.

Banichi stopped at the door to take out his key, and said, under his breath, "More than one man is dead, Bren-ji. Amateurs. I swear to you, it's amateurs will bring us down. I'm sure it's television. It plants foolish ideas in foolish heads that otherwise couldn't remotely conceive such plans."

"You mean the representative from—"

"One means that the Guild has refused arguments, bribes and coercion to undertake contracts against the paidhi." Banichi opened the door into a foyer miraculously void of boxes. "Jago's aim was accurate. His damaged a historical artifact. *That*—is the difference, among others. Kindly stay out of crowds, nadi."

The Assassins' Guild operated by strict rules. They accosted you in hallways, they turned up in your bedroom, they met you on the steps outside, but they didn't endanger bystanders, they didn't take out accidental targets, and most of all they required the person who hired them to meet certain criteria of responsibility and to file Intent with the authorities. Who notified you. Formally. In some ways—in their Guild deliberations on what contracts to accept and what to reject—they *were* atevi lawyers.

But the paidhi hadn't acquired an assassin of Banichi's and Jago's class; he'd touched off some middle-aged man with a family.

And probably nobody in the world remembered what he'd said last night. They'd just seen a man die, and nobody might even remember the difficult points he'd had to convince them of—the points he'd spent all his credit with his own government to make—and that thought brought a crashing depression—an aftershock, maybe—but with it a sense of being in well over his head.

He walked into the apartment with Banichi and found the message bowl overflowing onto the table. Tano met their arrival; so did madam Saidin: Saidin with grave courtesy, Tano with relief evident.

Which said to him Jago was *not* simply napping. And neither had Banichi been. Algini came from inside the security quarters, and Banichi and Algini were quite professional, quite matter-of-fact in their meeting.

The tenor of which said to him that Algini's presence in no way surprised Banichi and that Banichi just might have been at the airport when Algini came in.

"Nand' paidhi," Tano said, meanwhile, "Hanks-paidhi has called. Three times."

Oh, God, he hadn't countermanded the call and recall order. The operator had been ringing Hanks since the afternoon.

"Did she leave any message?"

"She was extremely angry. She said she wanted to speak with you personally."

"I do apologize, Tano."

"My job, nand' paidhi. I'm glad to intercept it. There are telegrams from Mospheira. Three, nand' paidhi. I wouldn't mention any business I could manage without consulting, but—"

He was tired. He was suddenly drained, and shaken, and he couldn't take his own damn coat off himself. The servant had to help him with it—her name was—he'd heard her name—

"I can't," he was forced to admit, and found his voice wobbling. "I can't—Tano, I'm sorry, I can't deal with these things tonight."

"Bren-ji is exhausted," Banichi said as the last of the tape came free of the sleeve and Bren escaped the coat. He just wanted his bed. Just that. Soft pillows. No questions.

But he was scared what might have come in those messages. He hoped one of them was from the President, accepting his position. He hoped it wasn't damning him for a fool and ordering his recall for arrest.

He had at least just to glance through those three and know what they were. He broke the seal on the first one, in his awkward, arm-braced procedure. It was from Barb.

Bren, it said. *I didn't know. I feel so bad. Please call me.*

He was numb, at first reading. Then he tossed it casually back into the message basket. He was angry—maybe as angry as he'd ever been at anyone in his life.

Or hurt. He couldn't decide. He couldn't ask himself for coherent judgment right now, least of all to judge Barb. He opened the second telegram, which proved to be from his mother. It said, *Sorry I missed you at the hospital,* but after that, the censors had made lace out of it. Not a damned sentence in the thing was intact but that, and whatever his mother had meant to say—God knew. He couldn't decipher anything from the I's and a's and the's.

Which meant his mother had said things critical to security—and his mother never knew anything critical to security. There was nothing she ever had to say to him that the censors would reasonably block, it just wasn't in her knowledge of the universe.

Something could have happened at home, maybe something they didn't want him to hear right now—but then why did the censors let that one line get through, when they could have stalled the whole letter? They could have sent the telegram down a black hole and he wouldn't have known it and his mother wouldn't have, until they could compare notes— so why worry him, if they were just trying to save him from worry in the first place? He didn't understand what was going on. They hadn't censored Barb, who'd certainly disturbed him, and those personal matters weren't likely secret from Departmental censors. It didn't make sense.

The third was from the State Department. It began, *Field Officer Cameron:* the title the State Department accorded him, though there was only one field and only one officer; it launched straight into *The Department advises you on behalf of the President that it is taking your report under advisement. In the meantime, it orders in the strongest possible terms that you make no further translation of intercepted transmissions as . . .*

Oh, well, he thought, that's all. He was too numb to give a damn and too far along the course to damnation to think it mattered. He tossed that telegram straight into the wastebasket, to the shock of Tano and bystanders, then gathered up Barb's and his mother's and chucked them after it.

Ilisidi's message cylinder had come back again. He opened that last. It said, *An old woman desires your company on any morning you feel inclined. You improve our circulation. And you have such pretty hair.*

He read it three times, with a lump in his throat and the illegitimate and fatal satisfaction of believing one living being in the universe enjoyed his company; one lord of the Association didn't want to buy him, kill him, or use him—or wasn't assigned by Tabini to protect him. Very opposite things were the possibility. But, dammit, at least he knew what and why.

He gave that cylinder to Tano. "Nadi, a courteous appreciation to the dowager, with my desire to join her at breakfast sometime very soon. Tell the lady dowager— tell her I treasure her flattery. Please see it delivered tonight. Order a felicitous arrangement of flowers with the message."

He surely shocked Tano, on more than one account.

Then he wandered off, out of the foyer toward his own bed, forgetful until he was in his own doorway that he'd left Banichi without a second look or a word of courtesy—but Banichi probably had his own instructions to give to Tano and Algini, or maybe Banichi just lingered to share a cup of tea with people who didn't ask him unanswerable questions.

At least Banichi was back—and Jago had vanished, if she wasn't in her room asleep, as Banichi had claimed to have been.

Maybe, he thought muzzily, they took waking turns at whatever they were doing, which he knew in his heart of hearts was Tabini's business, and Tabini's security. They'd never left him alone, nor would. He could rely on that. Popular as he was making himself—he had to rely on it.

He'd made Hanks mad. He was too tired to deal with it. Hell, he probably could start by apologizing, but he wasn't interested.

He undressed with the help of a half dozen demure servants, made his requisite nest in his bed, propped his cast with pillows, and only as he lay down realized they'd installed the television he requested, against the far wall, and a turn of his head found not only the requested water glass but a television remote within his reach at the bedside table. His nerves were one long buzz of exhaustion, his senses threatening to blank out on him, which he wished would just happen: he wanted to shut his eyes and let his mind spiral down to the sleep he'd won. But, *Please call,* Barb said.

Bloody damn hell. Call. Calling might have been in order, all right—for her to call him when he was in town—at least to have called the hospital. She'd probably been off on her honeymoon.

He'd forgiven her—everything but that "Please call," the way she'd always say when they'd disagreed. She knew the hours he kept in a work crisis, she knew she should call in the morning if she wanted to catch him with a personal problem. But, no, he should call her. Tonight. *He* should call *her.* He should do the negotiating, meaning cajole her into doling out this little reaction and that little reaction until he guessed his way through her crisis and placated *her*.

For *what*? For getting married? He wasn't in the mood.

He reached irritably for the television remote, flipped it on to find out what was on the news, and saw himself, sitting at the council table, heard himself, and knew that Mospheira could pick up that broadcast quite nicely—as the mainland regularly picked up whatever Mospheira let hit the airwaves.

There was footage of damage to something somewhere, but that wasn't bomb damage from Malguri; it seemed to be nothing more than a windstorm taking the roof off a local barn. A machimi play was on the next channel, a machimi he knew, a drama of inheritance and skullduggery, the resolution to which lay in two clans deciding they hated a third clan worse than they hated each other—very atevi, very logical. Lots of costumes, lots of battles.

Glassy-eyed and fading, he flipped back to the news, hoping to hear the weather, wishing for a cold front to alleviate what promised to be a still, muggy night.

The news anchor was saying something, this time without footage, about a parliamentary procedure recalling members of the Assassins' Guild to the city, a procedure which a spokesman for the Guild called an administrative election.

The hell, he thought, disquieted. They censored his mother's letter and Banichi was gone for a day and a night on administrative elections, while Cenedi said it was a crisis in the Guild? Jago also had a vote. And might be casting it.

And Banichi had said something about the Guild rejecting contracts on the paidhi. Disturbing thought. By how much, he wondered, had they voted down the contracts? And what would acceptance of those contracts have meant to Tabini's stability in office?

He found no comfort in the news. He could watch the play, which at least had color and movement. But the eyes were going and the mind had already gone or he wouldn't contemplate staying awake at all.

He was aware of dark, then, a suddenly dark room, and he must have slept—the television was showing a faint just-turned-off glow and a large man was standing in front of it.

"Banichi?" he asked faintly.

"One should never acknowledge being awake," Banichi said. "Delay gives one just that much more advantage."

"I have a house full of security," he objected. "And I haven't a gun any longer."

"Look in your dresser," Banichi said.

"You're joking." He wanted to go look, but he hadn't the strength to get up.

"No," Banichi said. "Good night, Bren-ji. Jago's back now, by the way. All's well."

"Can we talk, Banichi?"

"Talk of what, nadi?" Banichi had become a shadow in the doorway, in the dim light from some open door down the hall. But Banichi waited.

"About the election going on in your Guild, about what Cenedi found it his duty to warn me about—about what I suppose I'd better know since I've accepted another of Ilisidi's invitations."

"With suggestive grace, nadi. One *is* surprised."

"I like the old woman," he said shortly to a silhouette against the doorway, and well knew the word didn't mean *like* in the humanly emotional sense. "And there, of course, I have information I don't get here."

"Because you think the aiji-dowager is a salad and you value information from those most interested in disinforming you?"

He knew he should laugh. He didn't have it in him. It came out a weak moan, and his voice cracked. "Nadi, I think she's a breath of fresh air, you're a salad, yourself, and I'm collecting everything I can find that tells me how to make humans in the sky not fly down tomorrow morning in satellites and loot the Bu-javid treasures—I'm so damned tired, Banichi. Everybody wants my opinion and nobody wants to tell me a damned thing, how do I know she's disinforming me? Nothing else makes sense."

Banichi came and stood over him, throwing shadow like a blanket over him. "One has tried to protect you from too much distraction, nadi."

"Protect me less. Inform me more. I'm desperate, Banichi. I can't operate in an informational vacuum."

"Jago will take you to the country house at Taiben, at your request. It might be a safer place."

"Is there anything urgently the matter with where I am?"

That provoked a moment of troubling silence.

"Is there, Banichi?"

"Nand' paidhi, Deana Hanks has been sending other messages under your seal."

"Damn. Damn. —Damn." He shut his eyes. He was perilously close to unconsciousness. So tired. So very tired. "I don't mean to accuse, but I thought you had that stopped. What's she up to?"

"Nand' paidhi, she's in regular communication with certain of the tashrid. And we don't know how she got the seal, but she is using it."

He had to redirect his thinking. Three-quarters of the way to sleep, he had to come back, ask himself why Taiben, and where Hanks got a seal.

"Came with it," he said, "a damn forgery. Mospheira could have managed it."

"One hesitated to malign your office. That thought did occur to us. Equally possible, of course, that the forgery was created by our esteemed lords of the tashrid. And I don't say we haven't intercepted these messages before sending them on. They're some of them—quite egregiously misphrased."

"Dangerously?"

"She asked the lord of Korami province for a pregnant calendar."

Pregnant calendar and urgent meeting. He began to laugh, and sanity gave way; he laughed until the tape hurt.

"I take it that's not code?"

"Oh, God, oh, God."

"Are you all right, Bren-ji?"

He gradually caught his breath. "I'm very fine, thank you, Banichi. God, that's wonderful."

"Other mistakes are simply grammatical. And she speaks very bluntly."

"Never would believe you needed the polish." Humor fell away to memories of Deana after the exams, Deana in a sullen temper.

"We are keeping a log. We can do this—since it's our language under assault."

He laughed quietly, reassured in Banichi's good-humored confidences that things couldn't be so bad, that they could still joke across species lines, and he was fading fast, too fast to remember to question Banichi about the weather report, before, between flutters of tired eyelids, he found Banichi had ebbed out of the room, quiet as the rest of the shadows.

He hoped it would rain again and relieve the heat, which seemed excessive this evening, or it was the padding he was obliged to put around him.

Still, he was sleepy, and he didn't want to move—Banichi was all right, Banichi was watching, and if he waited patiently there was, he discovered, a very slight and promising breeze circulating through the apartment, from open windows, he supposed, perfumed with flowers he remembered—

But that was Malguri, was it not? Or his garden.

He shut his eyes again, having found a position that didn't hurt, and when he felt the breeze he saw the hillsides of Malguri, he saw the riders on tall mecheiti.

He felt Nokhada striding under him, saw the rocks passing under them—

The ominous shadow of a plane crossing the mountainside . . .

"Look out," he thought he said, jerking about to see, and feared falling bombs.

But after that he was riding again, feeling the rhythm of a living, thinking creature under him, feeling the damp cold wind.

He wanted to be there.

In a dream one could go back to that hillside.

In a dream one could find his room again, with the glass-eyed beast staring at him from the wall.

And his lake, of the ghost-passengers and the bells that tolled with no hand touching them.

That was what he wanted to save. That and the cliffs, and the wi'itkitiin—and Nokhada, that wicked creature. He wanted to go out riding again, wanted to be in the hills, just himself and that damn mecheita, who'd knocked him flat, jarred his teeth loose, and several times nearly killed him—wanted to see the obnoxious beast, for reasons of God-knew-what. He even wondered, in this dream, if he'd saved up enough in his bank account, and if he could get the funds converted into atevi draft, and if it was honorable of the aiji-dowager to sell Nokhada away from Malguri.

But then, still in this dream, which turned melancholy and productive of estrangements, he realized the mecheiti had their own order of things, and that he couldn't take Nokhada from the herd, the flock, the—whatever mecheiti had, that atevi also had, among themselves. Nokhada belonged there. A human didn't. Nokhada didn't understand love. Nokhada understood a tidal pull a human didn't, couldn't, wouldn't ever have.

In his dream he almost understood it, as a force pulling him toward association, weak word for the strongest thing atevi felt. In his dream he almost discovered what that was. He was walking in the hills, and he watched the mecheiti travel across the land, watched ancient banners flutter and flap with the color of the old machimi plays, and saw the association of lords as driven by what he could almost feel.

In this dream he saw the land and he felt human emotions toward it. He supposed he couldn't help it. His need to feel what atevi felt was a part of that human emotion, and more than suspect.

In this dream he sat down on a hillside, and his Beast walked up to him, still angry about its murder, but curious about the intrusion on the hill. It wanted part of his lunch, which he'd brought in a paper bag, and he shared it. The Beast, black and surly, heaved itself down with a sigh and ate half a sandwich, which it pinned down with a heavy forepaw and devoured with gusto. He supposed he was in danger from it. But it seemed content to sit by him and snarl at the land in general, as if it had some long-standing grudge, or some long-standing watch to keep over the fortress that sat on its hill below them. The sky was blue, but pale, making you think of heat, or new-blown glass. Anything might come from it. Maybe that was what the Beast watched for.

Wi'itkitiin launched themselves from the rocks. And far, far below, an atevi in black came walking, climbing up among the rocks, alone. He thought it was Jago, but he couldn't prove it from this distance.

The Beast watched, head on paws, snarling now and again, because it would, that was all. And no matter how long the figure below climbed, it came no nearer, and no matter how anxious he became, he was afraid to get up and go down to it, because he knew his Beast would follow and hunt both of them. It was safe while he kept it fed. As long as sandwiches came from that mysterious place in dreams from which all necessities emerged. The figure below was safe as long as it followed the unspoken Rules of this dream, which demanded it make no progress.

So was he. That was what he was doing here. He did a lot of dangerous things. But he wasn't going anywhere. He was stuck on this hillside, overlooking things he couldn't have. And the sky was free to rain havoc. The sun was shining now, but it wouldn't in a few hours. The sun was the only thing that did progress, the only thing that was free to move—except his Beast, and it was waiting.

11

The last thing he wanted in the morning on waking was a phone call, especially one from Hanks, before he'd so much as sat down to breakfast. Saidin notified him that Tano had notified her, and he asked for tea, went to the phone in the lady's small office, and took the call.

"This is Bren Cameron. Go ahead."

"I take it you're the one playing pranks with the phone, you son of a bitch."

For some things the nerves in the morning wanted preparation. And his weren't steady yet, nor was his diplomatic filter in full function.

"Deana, let me tell you, you've got a choice. You can be civil and get a briefing on what's going on, or you can sit it out until everything's beyond your useful input. Make a career choice."

"I'm not solving your problem for you! I'm here by Departmental mandate, I take everything that's happened including the damn phone as something you know about and something you arranged, and you listen to me, Mr. Cameron. You can hang yourself, you can work yourself in deeper and deeper, or you can listen to somebody."

"I'm listening, Deana." Past a certain point temper gave way to a slow simmer in which he could accept information, and he didn't give a particular damn about his source. "Give me your read on the situation. I'm listening with bated breath."

"Son of a bitch!" They were speaking Mosphei', Deana's choice from the moment he'd picked up the phone. *"You're going to hear from more than me, mister. I heard your speech. I heard the whole damned sales job.*

You go off to the interior and hold secret meetings, you sell out to the atevi overlord that wanted you back, and threatened my life to get it—"

"Sorry about that. But you weren't invited. You're playing with fire, Deana. This isn't our justice system. The aiji is well within his rights to remove a disturbance of the peace—"

"You—"

"You shut *up*, Deana, and get it figured this *isn't* Mospheira, it's not going to be Mospheira, and I don't care what you think your civil rights are on Mospheira, these people know their law, it works for them for reasons we don't have the biological systems to understand, far less come here and criticize. If *you* don't know what you're asking for when you go against atevi authority, I assure you, you don't belong here."

"Oh, and you do. You're working real hard at belonging, and damned right they moved heaven and earth to get you back, you'll give them anything they want. I heard your speech, I heard every damned word of it. I get the news. You want a list of the regulations you've broken?"

"I'm fairly well aware of them."

"Our internal politics, our policy disputes, all out waving in the wind—that's not just against policy, Mr. Cameron, that's against the law! You've incited atevi to act against our government—"

"Never against our government. Against your political backers, maybe."

"Don't you talk about my political backers. Let's talk about yours, let's talk about selling out, Mr. Cameron."

It wasn't getting anywhere. "What about lunch?"

"Lunch?"

"Let's have lunch."

"I'm locked in this damn apartment, you rang my phone for twelve hours straight—"

"Sorry about that."

"You've got the nerve to ask me to have lunch?"

"I think it might be productive. We've done rather too much shouting. And I'd like to know where you got the seal you're using."

Silence on the other end.

"You're not in office," he said, if she missed the point. "You're alive because Tabini-aiji is a patient and fortunately powerful man who can afford a nuisance. A less powerful aiji would kill you, Deana, because he'd have no choice. I suggest you have lunch with me, act less like a prisoner and more like an official guest—"

"And *be in public with you. And compromise my interests.*"

"Thank God you do understand. I'd begun to fear you'd *no* notion of subtlety. In private, then."

"*I'm not coming to your apartment*—which *I understand has scandalized the Atigeini as is, speaking of subtlety, Mr. Cameron. I'm not being gossiped about.*"

"Watch your mouth! There's no swearing there are no atevi that understand you. Edit yourself, for *God's* sake, or I can't protect you."

"*Protect me, hell!*"

"You *are* a fool."

"*No.*" Evidently not quite such a fool. The tone was quieter. "*No, I'll meet you for lunch. When?*"

"Noon. In this apartment. And you will be courteous to the lady's and my staff or I'll pitch you out on your head, Ms. Hanks. We're not playing games. I'm trying to salvage your reputation and prevent you doing another foolhardy thing that may get you killed. I can't say at the moment I feel overmuch sympathy for the mess you're in, but if you want to continue to watch the news for reports on the situation, you're quite free to rely on that."

At times he shocked himself. Maybe it was atevi court manners that took over his mouth when he suffered whiteouts of temper—court manners with all the vitriol that attended.

"*Barb Letterman's married,*" Hanks said. "*Did you know?*"

"How kind of you to let me know. Please bring me your seal. Or I'll have your apartment *and* your person searched."

The receiver went down. Hard.

Tag.

Which didn't make him calmer. But he had the phone, he had the moment. He took a sip of tea and called the Bu-javid operator.

"Nadi, this is Bren-paidhi. Please ring the Mospheiran operator."

"Yes," the answer came back; he heard the relays click. And abort.

"Nand' paidhi," the operator began, *"the connection—"*

"Is having a difficulty at this hour. Yes. Thank you. Would you give me the telegraph service?"

"Yes, nand' paidhi," the operator said, and a moment later, a new operator came on, with:

"This is the telegraph, nand' paidhi."

"Please send to the following numbers: 1-9878-1-1, and to 20-6755-1-1, and to 1-0079-14-42. Please voice-record for transcription."

"Ready, nand' paidhi, go ahead."

"Beginning message. Am doing fine. Are you all right? Last transmission was garbled. End message."

There was no fighting the phone system. It was part and parcel with the security problem—it went when you most needed it. And it could be retaliatory against him; it could be precautionary; it could be atevi doing. He couldn't know, as long as it was down.

That had gone to his mother in the capital, to Toby on the North Shore, and to his office in the capital. And presumably they'd know to resend. And possibly his mother's message would get past the censors this time, or possibly Toby would phrase things more obliquely. Their mother was not a diplomat.

Barb—

Barb could get on with her life. He didn't want to rake over that set of feelings before breakfast. He didn't know how much of what he was feeling was Hanks' meddling and how much was being, still, mad at the way Barb had gone about it, and mad at that edge-of-his-bedtime "Call me."

He sipped the remainder of the tea, decided he wouldn't dress yet, and went off to the breakfast room, advising the staff on his way that the paidhi was ready for his breakfast, thank you, and meant to take his time and, which he didn't mention, to let his headache and his temper settle. It did him no good to wake up his nastier side before breakfast—he started the day in attack condition and he found it hard to escape it. Particularly with the notion of sitting down at a table with Deana Hanks before afternoon.

He hadn't seen Banichi this morning. He hadn't seen Jago. He hoped he had security still in the apartment, and that the mysteries that were going on around him had no truly sinister import.

He had, for one very major point, to requisition materials on Determinism, and try to coax a human brain to handle concepts of physics Deana Hanks herself hadn't remotely understood when she'd lightly tossed off the concept of faster-than-light without Departmental approval.

He didn't know folded-space physics. He was doing damned well to get chemical rocket design down. He didn't understand Determinists.

But he had to before the week was out.

Tea and seasonal fruit, eggs and buttered meal, chased by toast and another pot of tea—with the distant blue vista of the Bergid range floating unattached above the tiled roofs of Shejidan, the curtains blowing in the long-awaited breeze, and the crises seemed suspended, the world peaceful and ordinary.

If one didn't know what was in the heavens demanding attention, and beyond the sunrise demanding attention, and across the water demanding attention. He'd like to go to the library after the cup of tea, spend his entire day looking through the antique books on horticulture, taking advantage of the rare opportunity the apartment and all its history presented.

But on that very thought Tano arrived bearing a tray of letters for, one hoped, mere signature and seal.

"Routine matters," Tano said.

"You've been a vast help," Bren said. "I truly am grateful."

"Thank the lady's staff. These are simple courtesies. There are others the aiji may perhaps lend staff to answer. Tabini-aiji gave us a verbal message that the paidhi should not by any means be obliged to distract himself with schoolchildren."

"The paidhi finds in the schoolchildren the best reason for keeping this job," he muttered without censoring, in the growing confidence that Tano bore no tales and Tabini would understand anyway. "Ask Banichi about salads. Jago *is* back this morning?"

"Asleep."

"Where's Algini?"

"He had to go—"

"—out? What in *hell* is going on, Tano?"

"There's a vote in the Guild we must attend."

"Ah." One clear question to the right source. "About assassinating the paidhi?"

"No, nand' paidhi. That's already been defeated."

It didn't even rate a blink. "Then may I ask?"

Tano looked distinctly uncomfortable. "Please ask Banichi, nand' paidhi."

"Forgive the question, Tano-ji. Thank you for what you've told me. Will you wait for these, and share a cup of tea with me, or have you urgent business?"

"Nand' paidhi, I am of junior rank."

"High in my personal regard. Please. Sit with me. —Saidin?"

Saidin always seemed in earshot. "Another cup," he decreed as the head of staff appeared in the doorway, and Saidin departed without a word as Tano settled uneasily into a separate, fragile chair, perched as if for ready escape.

"I intend no improper or unwelcome questions," Bren said, and affixed his seal to one after the other of the documents on his small table. "You looked as if you could stand a round or two of tea. And more mindful courtesy. I'm very abrupt, Tano-ji. When I'm bothered and in a hurry I can become quite preoccupied. I hope you never take it for intended rudeness."

"Nand' paidhi, you are extremely courteous."

"I'm quite glad."

"I assure the paidhi the votes against his detractors were overwhelming."

"Tano, you are not here for me to ask you more improper questions."

"I've no difficulty speaking about a past vote, Bren-paidhi. You have very many supporters. It hurts nothing at all that both Banichi and nand' Cenedi alike spoke for you."

"Cenedi." He *was* surprised.

"Nand' paidhi," Tano began, seeming uncertain of himself or his permission. But in that moment the tea and the cup arrived on two trays with two servants to carry them. The tea tray in the corridor, on the cart with all the electrical connections, seemed to maintain hot water at all moments.

And Tano had lost his momentum in the gentle courtesies of tea service. He balanced the fragile porcelain in his hand and looked down as he drank.

"Tano," Bren said, when the servants—one with lingering attention to Tano—had departed, "please don't feel obliged. I only want company this morning, just a voice. Tell me when your leave is coming, tell me what you'll do, tell me where you're from and where you go—talk about your job. I'm interested."

"It's very uninteresting, nand' paidhi."

"It's *very* interesting to me, Tano-ji. I wonder if people have happy lives. I hope they do. I hope they're doing exactly what they want to do, and that I haven't snatched them up out of something they'd rather be doing, or diverted them out of a course they'd rather be following."

"I assure the paidhi not. I'm very content." Something seemed to linger on Tano's tongue, and drown in a sip of tea.

"You would have said?" Bren asked.

"That I only worry about failing. About making some mistake that would cost immensely."

He'd not thought. He'd not measured Tano's steadily increased responsibility. Or the worry the paidhi put on his assigned guards, when he insisted on breakfasts with the aiji-dowager and lunch with Deana Hanks.

"I promise," he said, "I promise, Tano, not to do anything to make your job harder. I've put upon you shamefully. You weren't set here to manage stacks of paper. I've leaned on your support because I felt you had the judgment to discriminate the emergencies—I never meant to let it grow to this size."

"If the paidhi can concern himself with these papers, the paidhi's security can certainly value them."

"But answer them in stacks? Tano-ji, I've misused your courtesy."

"It's all quite instructive, paidhi-ji. I've learned who you contact, I've learned who are your associates and who are petulant and ill-disposed. I've learned that the paidhi considers the letters of ordinary citizens to be answered seriously. —So when I voted in the Guild, I also spoke about that, nand' paidhi. I'm not supposed to tell you that, but I did. Also Algini flew back from Malguri early, so *he* could vote in your behalf."

"I'm in his debt. Does the Guild call in absent members—for all proposed contracts?"

"When a contract involves matters so high as this, yes, it does, nand' paidhi: it goes to the total assembly of the Guild, as this had to, once members filed in opposition. I'm not forbidden to say that."

"Then thank you, Tano-ji. And thank Algini."

"You've become very well reputed among the Guild, nand' paidhi."

Some statements deserved wondering about.

But if "well-reputed" involved his staff and the dowager's staff speaking for him, he took it for a compliment. He finished his stack of seal-signatures, and gave it to Tano with the plea to see if, with the transferred funds which the paidhi had in the Bu-javid accounts, he might hire a temporary staff adequate to handle at least the citizen inquiries—

"At least for a few days, Tano. I'm not willing to impose on you further."

"One will inquire," Tano promised him. "But, nand' paidhi, I wonder if the letters will really abate in any number of days. They're holding two sacks of mail down in the post office, and most are from atevi children."

"Two sacks. Children."

"Many say, I saw you on television. The children, nand' paidhi, mostly ask whether you've seen spacemen and whether they'll send down machines to destroy the world."

"God, I've got to answer that. A computer printer. If I give you my answer—God, staff." His mind flew to the island-wide Mospheiran computer boards, the jobs-wanteds and jobs-offereds; but the Bu-javid *wasn't* an ordinary office and it wasn't Mospheira, and you couldn't just bring outsiders in. There had to be clearances. "I've never had to have staff before."

"I would suggest, nand' paidhi, if the paidhi hopes to answer sacks of mail, he certainly needs much more than the security post and a handful of household servants, however willing. He needs, I would guess—a staff of well above fifty, all skilled clericals, and a sealing machine. Most of the letters from citizens have subjects in common, fears of the ship, curiosity."

"Threats, probably."

"Some threats, but not many. —You've received two proposals of marriage."

"You're joking."

"One sent a picture. She's not bad looking, nand' paidhi."

"I'll—see if I can transfer sufficient funds. I may have to appeal to the Department." Not a good time to do that, he was thinking, and asked himself if he could secure atevi funding and decided again that such a source of funds wasn't politically neutral and wouldn't be seen as such.

He had, what?—his personal bank account. Which, lavish as it was for a man who couldn't be home to spend his salary and whose meals and lodging were handled by the

Bu-javid, couldn't begin to rent and salary an office of fifty people for a month. "Thank you, Tano-ji. I value your advice. I'll find out what I can do. I'll draft a reply for the children."

"Shall I make inquiries about staff?"

"I don't know how I'm to fund it—but we have no choice, the best I can see."

"I'll consult the appropriate agencies. Thank you for the tea, nand' paidhi."

Tano excused himself off to that task. Bren settled to stare out at the mountains, trying to imagine how much it cost to rent an office, hire fifty people, and pay for phones and faxes.

Which he couldn't do. He simply couldn't do it on his own, not if the letters came in sacks.

He had to come up with the statement for the children. That wasn't entirely easy.

He had to come up with a report for the various committee inquiries he was facing, one of which involved lord Geigi, and finding some way to explain FTL for the Determinists, who had to have a universe in unshakeable balance.

He had to have lunch with Hanks at noon—and, God, he'd asked for a call from the ship at the time he'd invited Hanks to lunch. He didn't know how that was going to work. But it might be an escape. Feed Hanks and dive off for a private call.

When he'd, given his leisure, like to go down to the library himself and spend the entire morning looking for astronomy references, until he felt he had some grasp of things he'd never had to wonder about. He was reaching into information he hadn't accessed since primer school—and it might be accurate: he didn't think astronomy had changed that much, but he didn't think a primer-school student's grasp of information was adequate to advise a head of state or argue with atevi number-counters, either.

He was drowning in details, none of which he seemed able to get to because of all the others, all of which argued he should have staff—but even having staff wasn't going to put enough knowledge into the paidhi's head to know where the ship might have been and how far it might have come or how he was going to explain it all to a province ready to erupt in disorder. The failing was in himself. He could *use* help from somebody like Deana Hanks, if Deana weren't an ass—which was an irrefutable condition.

He felt a mild headache becoming worse and called for another pot of tea.

And sent one of the servants, Dathio, on down to the library looking for references. The air didn't stir. Sometimes, in his experience of Shejidan summers, that heralded a hell of a storm.

But the one he expected at noon was sufficient.

Another bout of tape, a shower, a meticulous braiding of the hair—two servants to do that, who spent more time fussing than Tano would do, but Tano was clearly busy—Banichi and Jago the staff alleged to be awake, but both of them were immediately off somewhere about business. Algini was back, sore, stiff, preparing to take over the security station from Tano, who was off, Algini said, seeing about office space—so Algini had the post, and security had to be on duty if strangers were due in: Algini had certain inquiries to make just getting Hanks onto the third floor.

All of which left the paidhi alone and at the mercy of the staff.

If the paidhi had modesty left, at this point, he'd forgotten where he'd put it. He suffered the tape-up at the hands of pleasant and not entirely objective women, he had his shower, and thereafter abandoned himself to a pair of servants who thought his hair a complete novelty and argued over the job of braiding it; then a trio of dressers who, learning he was going to meet Hanks-paidhi, insisted on his best shirt, insisted on a little pin for the collar.

Last of all madam Saidin came to survey the result, disapproved of the pin and installed a larger, more expensive one the provenance of which he had no idea.

"That's not mine, nand' Saidin," he protested, viewing

the result in the mirror, asking himself whether that jewelry was Damiri's, or some antique Atigeini motif he was going to catch hell for if someone saw it. He'd no reason to distrust Saidin. He'd reason not to trust all the staff, counting rumors that had drifted out to the dowager's household, but he'd hoped Saidin herself was Damiri's and not serving any other interest.

"It's perfect," Saidin declared with senior authority, and he was left with a feeling of being trapped into Saidin's judgment, once she'd taken a position contravening three others of the staff.

Perhaps he shouldn't be so naive or so accommodating. But it was only Hanks, who wasn't likely to discriminate a pin he owned versus one he'd borrowed illicitly.

So he let it stay and paced the sitting room, waiting for calls from space or an explosion from Hanks, he wasn't sure which. He'd drafted a letter to Mospheira, a letter to the President, which said, in sum, that atevi unease over the appearance in their skies had generated a flood of mail which was being directed to the paidhi, and which consequently required the paidhi to answer, and which the Mospheiran budget should pay for, as otherwise it compromised the Mospheiran nature of the paidhi's office.

The President was going to read that one several times before he figured out it wasn't a joke, and the man who'd just broken Departmental regulations, defied an order from the Department's highest officers, and revealed privileged and sensitive information to the atevi leadership in a nationally televised speech, was asking the Mospheiran government to fund an expansion of his office.

He heard the front door open. He forbore to go out to the foyer. He strayed deeper into the apartments, hearing the to-do he could detect as Deana Hanks, Deana's Tabini-imposed security, Algini laying down the rules of the house. Servants passed him at a fair clip, delaying for the bows that were the rule of this house, on their way to the kitchen.

He'd decreed the lesser dining room, an intimate lunch, a small staff, though he'd been tempted to install Hanks at the opposite end of the state dining table. And, coward that he was, he hoped Saidin's unflappable courtesy could at least take the edge off the woman—his nerves were not at their steadiest, he had too much on his mind to spare attention to a fool's bad behavior, and he thought Hanks might behave herself civilly, at least, without the provocation of his oversight.

So, having walked the length of the hall down to the library and the pleasant view from the windows, he walked the slow course back again, judging by the flow of servants, this time to the lesser dining area, that Hanks had made it that far without destruction of the porcelains and the bouquets.

He walked into the dining room—which forced Hanks, already seated, to rise, in strict atevi etiquette. She sat, which the servants couldn't but remark, her human face and pallid complexion in stark contrast to the whole world he expected to deal with. The dark coat did nothing to diminish the effect; dark coat, dark hair—in the requisite and modest braid.

He bowed. She didn't so much as nod, just sat there, sullen and sober.

"FTL," he said, still standing. "Shall we dispose of that, in Mosphei', and say we've said you made a mistake? Or have you an excuse for that, too?"

"What about it?"

"You mentioned it? Or did Geigi just add figures you gave him?"

Hanks' face remained impassive. "So?"

"So. Is that your excuse? So?"

"I don't have to stay here."

"You can go home in a box if you act the fool much longer. I'm still trying to save your neck."

"From a situation you created."

"I created." A line of servants was piling up at the door, bearing plates. One had to toss the fool into the outer hall or sit down and let the servants do their best to put a social patch on the event. He smiled. He sat. He gathered up all the calm and social grace he had. "Deana, you *are* amazing. I don't suppose you've devised a universe construct to go with it."

"With what?"

"You can only go so far on bluff, Deana. You're scared. Or you should be. I'd be, if I knew as little as you do. You've not made yourself popular and the servants in this house haven't received a good first impression, so smile." He changed to the atevi language. "Nice weather. Isn't it?"

There was no smile. "I don't have to stay for this."

"No, you can whimper your way home to your apartment." The servants were setting out the plates. "Ah, we've changed seasons today. And the kitchen is doing its best. I *am* sorry about the phone, Deana. I didn't intend that, but it was my fault."

That only seemed to make her madder. At least the frown deepened. But she stayed put, smiled grimly at the servants who offered her condiments and, the initial flurry of serving out of the room, filled her mouth with the kitchen's not at all bad cooking.

Certainly fancier than the Bu-javid kitchen's fare.

"I wanted actually," he said, "to get a list of persons you've dealt with and what promises you think I should honor. By the way, where's the seal?"

She laid down her utensil, reached into her inside pocket, and pulled out the small metal object. Tossed it at him, on the casted side.

He didn't even try to catch it. He heard it hit the wall. A servant left the doorway to retrieve it, and having looked at it in some dismay, offered it to him.

"Thank you, Madig. It's quite all right. Hanks-paidhi is a little on edge today. Would you deliver that to Algini and tell him what it is?"

"Yes, nand' paidhi," the servant said in a very quiet voice.

"You seem to have quite the life here," Hanks said sweetly.

"Yes," he said, in the atevi mode, unadorned, the sort of thing Jago was wont to do to him. "Quite frankly speaking, Deana, I'm sorry about the phone. I hadn't meant that, but it is my fault. If it were possible for us to ignore the politics that divide us—"

"Mosphei'," she said sharply.

"No, Deana-ji, I don't think our hosts can make sense of us without that critical point of information. I've made it clear we have political differences, I've some hope that after all our interests are the welfare of Mospheira *and* the Western Association, and I hope that we can manage to do some work together. As long as you're here, I'd like to offer you the chance to patch up our differences."

"Of course."

"I'm quite serious."

"So am I."

He looked down the table at a very nice human face with a very reserved and inoffensive expression, the sort you practiced along with the language.

"Fine. *Do* you know anything about the ship that I don't know?"

"I'm sure I don't."

"Deana."

"Bren, I don't know. I know you're in contact with them."

"Your sources keep you well posted?"

"I've no sources. Just occasional contacts."

"Like hell, Deana. But let's be pleasant. And let me tell you, if you embarrass the people who are dealing with you, you can make very, very serious consequences for them, not to mention yourself."

"Don't talk to me about dealing against regulations."

"I hadn't mentioned regulations. Regulations aren't what's at issue here."

"Damned right *you* don't want to talk about regulations. Let me make a proposition to you, Mr. Cameron. You get me contact with Mospheira and we'll see what we can work out. You get the guard taken off my hall. You get me a meeting with Tabini."

"I'd be lying if I said I could get that. You've offended the man, and there's no patching that without action on your part, not mine. I might relay a message of apology."

There was no greater friendliness. There was, however, sober thought.

"Tell him I regret anything that may have offended him. I was afraid he might have done away with you."

"I'm touched."

"Which is the truth, damn you. I didn't know when I came over here whether you were dead, delirious with fever, or held hostage. I did the best I could under the circumstances. I talked to people who might give me other than official information. I *tried* to get you out of whatever you'd gotten into, in addition to doing your job."

That was at least plausible. Even a reasonable answer. He stared at her, unable to figure if it was something she'd only just thought of or actually the course she'd followed.

"Meaning," he concluded, "you wanted to be a damn hero. The service requires the *job,* Hanks-paidhi. Just the job, adequately done, nothing flashy."

"So where in hell were you? Malguri? Hunting in the hills with the dowager? Playing the damn hero?"

Nailed him. He didn't flinch from her level stare, but he didn't find anything to say, either, but, "Yes."

"So?"

"Point taken."

A tone of contrition. "I'm terribly sorry I tried to save you."

"I have it coming. Thank you for trying. Now can I persuade you to fly home? I might be able to get you a travel visa."

"I don't think you can, point one. I think the aiji is keeping me in reserve in case things blow up with your negotiations, or in case the next assassin is on target. And, point two, I'm no use there to anyone."

"It's a fairly accurate assessment. I still think I could get you out as a personal favor."

"Don't use up your credit on my account. There's still point two. I'm not going."

In Mosphei': "It's your funeral."

In Ragi: "Funny. Very funny, Cameron."

"If you'd make yourself just halfway useful—"

"Oh, tell me how."

Assign Hanks the mail. Let her affix *her* name to it, as if she had the office he was bound and determined to see her out of? Not likely. There wasn't damned much else she could touch without being a security risk to Tabini.

"You could write the everlasting reports."

"I could make the television speeches."

"I'm sure you could. But you do have areas of expertise—"

"I write them, you put your own gloss on them and look good."

"You write them, I delete the nonsense and the speculation and if they're useful I may moderate the report I've already sent in on your actions."

"Son of a bitch."

"That's ruder in Ragi than in Mosphei'. You really should watch the cultural contexts."

"You just can't say a pleasant word."

She was quite serious. He had to laugh. The servants took that for a moderately safe cue to refill the tea-cups.

"I tell you," Hanks said, in Mosphei', after a mouthful of paté and wafer, "high scores and all, I think there's a reason you're such a miracle of linguistic competency. I think you dream in Ragi."

It happened to be true, increasingly so. He found no reason to say so. Hanks was heading for some point of her own choosing.

"Did you know Barbara was going to marry?" Hanks asked in Ragi.

"No. It wasn't one of those things we discussed."

"What did you think? She was going to be there whenever you chanced in, for the rest of her life?"

"Actually, we'd raised the question. But that's Barb's business, not yours."

"I'm just curious."

"I know you are." He had a sip of tea. "You'll have to stay in that condition."

"You know your face doesn't react? Even when you're on Mospheira, you're absolutely deadpan."

"You lose the habit."

A tone of amazement. "You've really adapted, haven't you?"

Nothing Hanks meant was complimentary, he had no doubt. He didn't like this sudden pursuit instead of Parthian retreat, but he had a notion he was about to get an opinion out of Hanks, and maybe an honest one.

"What are you going to do, Bren-nadi? When are you going to come home? Or *are* you going to come home?"

"I'll come home once I'm sure some fool isn't going to screw things up, Ms. Hanks."

"How do you define fool?"

"I don't attempt it. I wait for demonstrations. They inevitably surpass my imagination."

"Oh, you've done more than wait." Hanks propped her chin on the heel of her hand and looked at him. "You're just so good. Just so fluent. Just so damned perfect. Look at you. You don't even question your ethics, do you?"

"Continually. As I trust you question yours."

"You're slipping, you know it? Going right over the edge. What happened to you in Malguri? What happened to the arm?"

"It broke."

"Who broke it?"

"A gentleman who didn't like my origins. That's always a danger."

"You'd rather be atevi, hadn't you?"

They were down to what she'd been stalking, he decided that: it was a tactic, it was no more sincere than the rest, but it still worked a little irritation—there were the servants in earshot, the woman's associations were closet bigots from the outset, and he didn't want Saidin or the staff exposed to that human problem.

"Ms. Hanks, you're a guest. Try courtesy. You'll like the result."

"I'm perfectly serious. I'm asking what happened at Malguri. What they did to you."

"Ms. Hanks—" He was exasperated. And halfway began to suspect the woman was serious. "They were courteous, sensible, and generally but not universally careful of our small size. I'm sorry to disappoint your well-intentioned though prurient curiosity, but I enjoyed the hospitality of an atevi estate, I made the acquaintance of a very gracious lady, we had to run like hell when rebels hit the place, and doubtless my fluency and my riding and my grasp of atevi numerical philosophy improved under fire, but I don't view myself as other than conscientiously human, irrevocably dedicated to the same objectives of technological parity that Wilson and paidhiin before me pursued, and thoroughly convinced that parity will through no fault of our planning occur in our lifetimes. Speak to the ship up there about the schedule if you don't like it. It's given us no damned choice but accelerate and given us a damnably difficult balancing act not to disrupt our economy or the atevi economy. I recall you did your thesis on economic dualism, Ms. Hanks. Let's see you do some creative work on real numbers, real provinces, real production figures. I'll give them to you. Plug those into your computer, produce some changes, and let's see if you're as brilliant without Papa's research staff as you are with it."

"I resent that!"

"My God, the woman has a sensitivity."

"Linguistics isn't the whole picture, Mr. Cameron. Give me the contact to *get* the figures. Don't hand me your lame assemblage of data and then blame my results."

A phone line in Deana Hanks' reach wouldn't please his security. Or Tabini's. It didn't please him.

But Deana's one solid expertise—which wasn't his—was alleged to be finance.

Inherited it from Papa, some said. Or cribbed it from Papa's staff. He'd always believed she had. But the indignation was moderately persuasive.

Maybe there was actual, uncredited ability. Maybe there was substance.

"All right," he said. "I'll see what I can turn up for you."

"To put your name on!"

"Deana—" They were down to the bitter wafers and tea, and he swallowed one mostly whole and washed it down. "If you can work us out a course that won't shipwreck us, if you can even get a hint of acceptable schedule, nobody in the Department's going to think *I* did it. It's your chance, Deana. It's what you do that I can't. Points to your side."

"Damn you." Her clenched fist came down on the table, but it came down in prudent quiet, and the language was Mosphei'. "Damn you, you're promising them everything, you're giving away for *free* everything we have to bargain with."

"Naighai maighi-*shi*, Deana-ji. *Urgent meeting.* Prepare your damn vocabulary in advance." He kept his voice ever so calm, didn't look at her, and poured his own tea, no servant venturing near. "You give me the economic report out of the numbers I'll give you in such abundance your head will swim—you pull that off and I'll recommend you for an audience with Tabini, a council citation and a civic medal. Use university resources, use *any* source you like, atevi or human, that's not hot for profit on the situation, and put your theory on paper. I'll listen."

"I need the phone," she said in a civil tone.

"I'll talk to security." He took a large swallow, and switched back to atevi. "But if you launch out on this notion, Deana-ji, and if you hold yourself up to the aiji as competent to do this and he extends you the credit and the contacts to try—you risk, should I fall down the stairs and break my neck, becoming the paidhi who couldn't deliver. Shortly thereafter—the ex-paidhi. Possibly the late, dead, deceased paidhi. Does that worry you?"

"No," Hanks said sharply, though there seemed by now a little prudent fear in that tone. "Not your breaking your neck and not my ability, *Mr.* Cameron. I want the phones to work. This afternoon."

"I'll do what I can. Note, I don't *say* I can. On this side of the strait, it's best to hedge one's promises. You should learn that. But you're in it. Good luck." He stood up, having decided that lunch—and his patience—was over. Hanks stood up, and he walked her to the door.

Jago was there. Jago, who delivered him an absolutely impassive stare and stood aside for him to show Hanks-paidhi to the foyer, into Algini's keeping.

He felt Jago's eyes on his back the entire time. She'd been here again, gone again, and came back, specifically, he suspected, to stand in the hall and listen to the negotiations with Hanks-paidhi, who had not made a good initial impression on Jago, not down in the subway and not by any behavior Jago had just heard.

"Algini-ji," he said to Algini, when he reached the foyer, and the station where Hanks' security, likewise Tabini's, waited. "Hanks-paidhi will go back now. —Good afternoon, Deana."

He offered his hand. He didn't think she'd take it. She surprised him by a light, strong grip and, in Mosphei', "It's *Ms*. Hanks, Mr. Cameron, thank you very much, I'm not your sister. Try smiling. You look so much nicer that way."

He didn't smile. He didn't appreciate the insulting coquetry, in front of staff, but she escaped with that. He wasn't interested in warfare, now, just the cursed numbers however she came up with them.

And interested in keeping her busy. Giving her a way out with her credibility intact. She had to know that it was an honest offer. It was a critical time, and paidhiin weren't that easy come by: the Foreign Office had years invested in Hanks, and she *might* learn—if she learned fast enough.

Noon had come and gone and he hadn't gotten his call from the ship—which, when he realized it, didn't improve his mood. There were a thousand possible reasons, including procedures aboard the ship, including long debates, including a ship that ran exactly like Mospheira, with no one willing to make a decision.

All the same, he'd hoped for sane and rapid agreement. Tabini had hoped. Doubtless the Space Committee would have hoped, and he had that committee scheduled for this afternoon.

He'd almost rather have Hanks' company instead. And that was going some.

12

The paidhi didn't regularly speak at committee meetings. He usually sat in the corner in silence—he had a veto, which he didn't intend to use. He had no right to speak, except by invitation of the chairman ...

"One understands, Bren-paidhi, that there will be changes, and rapid change. And clearly everything we've done and all materials in production—are subject to cancellation. We've promise of a building program that has no specifications, no design, that we've seen. Does the paidhi have any more information?"

"Nothing yet," he said. "I hope, nadiin, as you all do, that when information comes it will be thorough. Like you, I'm waiting for responses to questions. I'd say— there will be certain materials we'll use; we may go ahead with the launch program as a way to lift materials into orbit. There's still the construction for the launch site, maybe with modifications for the landing craft, unless whatever they propose can land at Shejidan Airport. Which isn't totally outside possibility. But we've yet to see."

"And Mospheira? The phones are down again." That was the representative from Wiigin, coastal and in a position to know when trade wasn't moving. "We take this for ominous."

Clearly Wiigin wasn't the only one to take that for ominous. Lord Geigi was on this committee. He wasn't one that Tabini had wanted on the committee, but lord Geigi did have the mathematical, and more, a scientific background rare for the tashrid.

Geigi didn't look happy. Geigi hadn't looked happy during the entire meeting.

"Nand' paidhi," another member asked, "what of Hanks' advice to expect far-reaching change?"

"Hanks-paidhi has decided to work with my office in certain areas in which she has considerable expertise. Economics, chiefly. She's not expert in space science. Nor, you may have gathered, fluent enough to pick up certain shades of meaning. It was brave of her to come across the strait to take up duties while she believed I might be dead—" He saw no reason to demolish Hanks' reputation with atevi, and gave her her due. "But she's straight out of an office on Mospheira and acquiring experience on the job. Thank you for offering her the help you have." That was for the opposition party, whom he didn't want to embarrass. "I think it exemplary of the peaceful system we've worked out that the office was able to function during the crisis, and I thank you in particular for your patience."

"Her advice has run counter to yours," Geigi said bluntly—and rudely—without the proprieties of address. "What are we to think? That juniors are free to advise us?"

"Our advice should not be that different." He felt giddy, blood as well as breath insufficient, or the heart not beating fast enough. Which seemed impossible. Like falling off a mountain. Like a fast downhill, on an icy slope. You could stop. But you didn't come up there to stop. He'd determined on his attack. He launched it. Cold and clear. "Let me be more clear, lord Geigi: in the State Department, there are divergent opinions: those who view that atevi and humans should always stay separate, a view which Hanks-paidhi has held; and those who believe as I do, that there's no unraveling a society that has become a whole fabric. I'm aware that certain atevi are equally apprehensive of true technological parity as if it were a subterfuge for cultural assimilation. That is the point on which Hanks' party and mine do find agreement: that cultural assimilation is not the ideal and not the target. The traditions and values of atevi are for atevi to keep. We know that attractions and change come with advances—"

"Television," a conservative representative muttered.

"Television," he agreed. "Yes, nadi, television. And we should *not* have provided the formats for broadcast and news. Maybe the television stations shouldn't broadcast full time. Maybe we've made mistakes. I'd be the first to agree that following our pattern is attractive, both culturally and economically—my predecessor vetoed the highway bill *because* he viewed it as casting atevi into a human development pattern destructive of atevi associational authority, and, pardon me, he found extremely strong opposition to and resentment of that veto. I've moderated my own view on the matter, I understand that there were and are local situations that should receive exceptions, but that's beside the point: one can't carry local situations into a major, continent-spanning development of a technology that's going to disrupt atevi life. The paidhiin have always opposed that kind of development."

"But the damage is done, nadi. And *where* are our traditions?"

"Nadi, I've recently been to the heart of the mainland, to a fortress built before humans ever left their earth— I've lived, as far a modern man can, the life atevi had before the world changed. I didn't come back unscathed, as you see. —Nor did I come back unaffected in my opinions. The course humans and atevi have followed has preserved such places and the land around them, and when we were struggling together for our lives, nadiin, with the shells flying around us, we found our instincts could work together and that we could fear for each others' lives as well as our own."

"All of this aside," the lord of Rigin said, "some would say this was no place for a human."

"Some would say the same of atevi on the station. I disagree, nadi. I agree it's a shaky cooperation. It will *be* a shaky cooperation, with exceptions to rational behavior, and it will be a carefully circumscribed cooperation, for our lifetimes at least, but consider, nadiin: there is one orbital space, one natural environment in which ships from this planet hope to operate, and we must each adapt to this new environment."

"With your designs. Your history. Your technology. Your path."

"Nadiin, there is one air, and one gravity, and one atmosphere through which airplanes move—atmosphere designs the planes, people don't. Some designs move through the air and stay in the sky more efficiently than others; and if humans had never come here at all, the airplanes you designed would work—in principle—exactly like our airplanes, because they operate under similar conditions. As they grew more efficient, they'd look more and more like our best designs, their controls would look very much like our controls—and the need to communicate about those machines at their speed would change your language, as it has, and change your attitude toward computers, which it has. Computers would have to exist. Television, whether or not you used it for general broadcast, would have to exist to give you efficient sight of things far off. And the ships you built for space would look very like the ship up there, once you've pared away all the nonessentials and adjusted the design to do what you need."

"These needs are still cultural decisions," the head of committee said. "That's why this committee exists. That's why we don't take your lordly designs, nadi, and go and build them exactly as you built them."

"Wisely so, my lord." God, he saw the cliff coming. Geigi was listening, chin on fist, glowering, and he took the jump, knowing the danger. "But cultural needs are one thing. There cannot be mathematical differences in our universes, my lord of Rigin. Physics is physics, whether accommodated by humans or by atevi."

"There is one universe," Geigi muttered.

"As efficient machines are what they need to be, no more, no less. To be efficient in a given environment, they turn out to look very much alike, nadiin, and manuals for running them turn out very similar, and people who run them eventually think very similarly, apart from their philosophical beliefs. Given that humans and atevi need similar machines to explore the same environment, we will grow more and more alike in our thinking. Physics guided even the wi'itkitiin, in their evolution, to have wings and not fins, to adjust their wing-surfaces in flight, as airplanes do, as atevi and human pilots do; in short, nadiin, neither humans nor atevi are immune to the numbers of the natural world. And atevi who live in space will use true numbers to understand its demands, and therefore enter harmony with the behaviors of humans who likewise live in harmony with those numbers. Numbers rule us all, nadiin. We admire atevi minds and your language that so readily expresses the harmonies of numbers: atevi have that advantage over us. We can admire. We respect atevi ability. We want association with atevi not least of all because of your remarkable language and your faculty with numbers, which may well develop new understandings in this new environment."

"Not when ships violate natural law," Geigi muttered. "I want to hear an explanation for your ships moving faster than light, nand' paidhi. I want to see the numbers."

Tension hung heavy in the conference room. Civil peace and civil war hinged on that question. Lord Geigi posed a demand the answer to which could shatter his belief, his political stability, the existence of his house and the institutions it supported, and he did it in public, with his personal fortunes at absolute low ebb—a man with nothing to lose but the philosophy on which he pinned his beliefs.

"Nadi-ma," Bren said, "I will find you an answer. I promise that. Mosphei' doesn't express such concepts easily, which hampers my understanding of the physics as well as my attempt to translate."

"Does that ship exceed the velocity of light?"

"Mosphei' expresses it in that way." The paidhi was desperate, and the tape around his ribs made him short-winded and probably pale as a sheet. "But the human language often approximates more complex situations, lord Geigi, since we have no convenient way to express what the atevi languages do—especially in high numbers and spatial concepts. We're entering on a field of math that

I've never tried to express." And never damn well understood. "Let me work on the problem a few days. I'm sure there's a better way of putting it than either I or Hanks has done."

Lord Geigi was not a happy man. Perhaps he'd hoped for the paidhi to deny it outright. There were uneasy looks elsewhere at the table.

But the Minister of Transportation moved for the paidhi to undertake such a study, the committee expressed confidence in the paidhi's research on the matter, and they went on to specific topics like the cost estimates on the launch facility and what they ought to recommend to the legislature on continuation of the rocket engine project, in serious doubt pending the receipt of far more modern design, with the contractors justifiably besieging the legislators' doors and demanding some payment on work already completed.

He thought—he *thought* that FTL encompassed areas of math he'd never completely understood, and he thought at least he knew where his deficiencies began. The paidhi had to have mathematical ability: it went with the job, and one learned it right along with a language that continually made changes in words according to number and relationship— sometimes you needed algebra just to figure the grammatically correct form of a set-adjective, when the wrong form could be infelicitous and offend the person you were trying to win. You formed sets on the fly in your conversation just to avoid divisible plural forms, like the dual or quad not offset by the triad or monad, and in learning rapid conversation, even with the shortcut concepts the language held, your head hurt—until you got to a degree of familiarity where you could chain-calculate while holding a conversation, and no restaurant ever got away with padding your bill. He'd slid out of higher math in desperation for more study time, found later that he could sight-solve the problems in the math he'd skipped if he thought in Ragi, and the university had given him six credits he'd never sat in class for.

But by everything he could access at this point, looking through the window of truly esoteric math from the out-

side, and studying atevi philosophy from the outside, and
without the neural hardwiring atevi had, he didn't know
how in hell to translate what didn't, emphatically didn't,
fit into the ordinary framework of the language. There
had to be forms as yet not in the dictionary, or acceptable
forms had to be created that wouldn't violate felicity—

Which wasn't exactly a job for a human proceeding
past the limits of his own education.

And if pedestrian and literal-minded atevi (and there
were such) believed that computers through demonic
processes assigned infelicitous numbers to airplanes, he
didn't know what he was going to do when the numbers
began to describe processes of an imperfectly perceived
universe.

Atevi demanded perfection in their numbers. It was the
demon in the works, that both kept atevi from sliding
back into dark ages once they'd made an advance: and
kept atevi from advancing as fast on a single front—
because they had to adjust *all* their philosophy to accommodate new concepts. The numbers of a situation entered
philosophy, integrated with it—and numbers could take
forever to find proof enough for someone to try a new
thing.

Or they could, absent the gadfly effect of human presence and human tech that patently and demonstrably
worked, stop all progress while atevi worked out perfection, while amateur 'counters and philosophers rose up
to claim the space program would puncture the atmosphere—

I detest amateurs, Banichi had said, in so many words.
The paidhi thought the same. God save them all from
paidhiin who revealed translight physics with no understanding that to atevi the math involved was far more
earth-shattering than the ship was; no understanding that
atevi would take the mathematics of folded space and
integrate it at every level of their languages, their philosophies, their thinking, until, if humans had trouble understanding atevi logic now, humans were in for a century
of real, devastatingly confusing adjustment, right when
the whole world had a lot else to adjust to.

It was a wrench in the works for sure. If he'd spent months thinking of exactly what mathematical concept he wouldn't want to toss into the atevi-human interface at this precise moment in history, he thought that folded space would probably sit at the top of the don't-mention list. But it was all on the negotiating table now.

Not everyone they had to deal with had Geigi's brand of courage. He *liked* the man. The same recklessness that had gotten Geigi into financial difficulty had evidently moved Geigi to that blunt, public question, and if there was an influence among the opposition to Tabini that deserved preservation right along with Ilisidi, Geigi's blunt willingness to confront the paidhi and demand a truth that might wreck him had the paidhi's respect.

With a word in the right ear—he might be able to help Geigi. He was moved to help Geigi—and damned right the paidhiin occasionally took wide decisions, and played, he hoped, lifesaving politics without consultation. He checked it through the professional filter: he believed he acted independently of human emotion, though human emotion appreciated what Geigi had done; intellect evaluated Geigi's character. And the value of a man who asked reasonable questions, he was convinced, did cross species lines. Any way he could take to help the man—he resolved to use the channels he did have.

Adjournment proceeded, on a vote of the committee, to reconvene in five days for a presentation by the paidhi on FTL.

The paidhi smiled and looked, he hoped, serene in the prospect.

It wasn't what the paidhi felt. And if Hanks had financial expertise, and if, *if* he could rely on her, Hanks still couldn't rescue him from this one. Financial modeling just didn't exactly suit the problem.

Jago had walked him down to the meeting, since Algini, who might have drawn the duty, was still feeling the effects of his injuries. Reasonably, he expected Jago to be waiting outside to walk him back to the apartment, but it was Banichi instead, standing with his shoulders against the wall, easing, one suspected, the stress on his lately injured leg.

"Banichi," he said, and Banichi stood upright quickly enough, though caught by some surprise, which one could rarely do with Banichi, as the committee adjourned without the usual fuss and members walked out the door.

Banichi was tired and in pain, Bren suspected. That rarely showed, either. One could almost guess Jago was taking the walking jobs and Banichi was handling those that didn't require that much; he'd sent Tano, the other of his security with two good legs, off looking for offices, another job his security shouldn't have to do.

"That was well done," Banichi said as they walked toward the lift.

"I hope so," Bren said.

"Tabini was pleased."

"How did he know?" He was startled into asking the unaskable; and Banichi returned:

"In the Bu-javid? Of course he knew."

Possibly through Banichi, who knew? Banichi carried a pocket-com that might have a sensitive enough mike. Banichi didn't say. But Banichi next spoke to someone on the pocket-com, probably clearing their passage to the lift: security's code was verbal and seemed to change day by day.

"Do *not* take gifts with you into secure areas," Banichi said.

"What gift?" he asked, like a fool.

And remembered.

"The pin." He was utterly chagrined.

"Fortunately it's Tabini's."

"Why?"

"He was anxious about Hanks."

"As if she'd leap on me? Hardly."

"One wasn't certain."

"She might have use. She might use better sense. I don't know."

They were still using the back ways, avoiding the main hall and any ordinary traffic that threatened the casted arm; but the paidhi was considering other things than his

224 / C. J. CHERRYH

surroundings—until he waited at the lift, watching the faces of other committee members, covert glances that came his way, all speculative: a small group hung about Geigi and his aides, and looks came his way.

He found his breath freer, despite the damned tape that went on binding and chafing. Matters came into clearer focus on all fronts. Hanks would do what she had to do or Hanks would go straight to the worst of the conservative elements on Mospheira, but Hanks, as a problem, was not *the* problem, not the one that could harm atevi. The problem that could blow the Western Alliance apart was standing right over there—that was why he hadn't been able to see a path through the rest of it.

It was magical, how freely the mind jumped once a burden of necessity was off the little problems. He couldn't do what Hanks did. He wasn't capable of replacing the entire university advisory committee. Neither was Hanks, and before all was said and done, no matter if Hanks turned up the most brilliant paper of her dubious career, he knew where the real bombshells lurked and he knew the paidhi had to be forearmed.

But as the lift took them in, and Banichi pushed the button to take them to the third floor:

"Banichi-ji, I have an odd request. I need to talk to mathematicians. People whose math describes space. The shape of the universe."

"The shape of the universe, nadi?"

"Universe" was difficult in the atevi language. It as well described the Western Association as stars and space. "Stars. Physics of stars, velocity—space. That universe."

"I know of some very respected mathematicians, some resident in the Bu-javid. But none that deal in such things as that. The shape of the universe. Bren-ji, I know no such things."

"Galaxies and distances." Atevi made no constellations. Stars were stars. "The physics of light."

The lift let them out into the hall. Banichi said:

"Maybe humans have such things. I'd expect them to."

"This human doesn't have these things with him; the

phones are down on Mospheira's side of the strait, and anyway, I don't think the human answer would help me that much. The math of fields and physics, Banichi. How atevi view the universe beyond the solar system. What it's shaped like. What's out there, beyond the last planet. What light does in long distances. The shape of space."

"The shape of space." Clearly that thought didn't make sense to Banichi. "Pregnant calendars?"

He laughed. "No. I've got the right word. I'm sure I've got the right word."

They'd come to the apartment door; Banichi had his key and let them in past the security precautions, to the ministrations of the servants and Saidin's oversight— "Nadiin," Bren said, and to Saidin, who evidently considered it her duty to meet her lodger at all his comings and goings, "nadi-ji."

"Will the paidhi care for supper in, tonight?"

"The paidhi would be very grateful, nadi, thank you." God, was it that late? He caught a look at the foyer table, where messages had overflowed the bowl and stacked on the table surface in Tano's absence. "God—save us."

"Nand' paidhi?" Saidin asked.

"An expression of dismay," Banichi said.

"Tano's looking for office space," Bren said. "And professional staff. I don't know how I'm to deal with it otherwise."

"The staff can sort these," Saidin said, "if the paidhi wishes."

"The paidhi would very much like that, daja-ji, thank you. We hope to have staff soon. If the phone lines clear. If—God, I don't know."

"The paidhi would like tea?"

"The paidhi is awash in tea. He just got out of a committee meeting. The paidhi would like something much stronger. Without alkaloids. Thank you, daja-ji. —Banichi, I have to have the mathematicians. I'm desperate. I need to talk to people who understand the shape of space itself. Astronomers."

"Astronomers?" Banichi gave him a frowning, considering look, and he suddenly remembered Banichi, all-competent Banichi, was from the provinces; there was that back-country mistrust of the astronomers—the old failure. If there were humans in the heavens, how could the astronomers have failed to find them? If numbers ruled the universe, as devout atevi believed, then how could atevi astronomers, measuring the universe, have numbers with discrepancies in them, as they argued about distances?

In some religious minds, that was heresy. The numbers of the universe *had* no discrepancies. That was the very point the Determinists and the Rational Absolutists fixed as unshakable.

"I fear that's who I need to talk to, yes, astronomers."

One rarely saw Banichi at a loss. "There's an observatory in Berigai, in the Bergid. That's an hour by air."

"None closer? The university? I mean legitimate astronomers, Banichi. Not fortune-tellers. This is a legitimate observatory in the Bergid, there's a school—"

"There is. We can call them. We can ask."

"Would you—" The paidhi was tired, and the security station was at hand. "Would you mind terribly giving them a call, asking if they have anyone who can answer my questions? I'll write my essential question out, given faster-than-light flight and the Determinist objection, and if you could ask them if there's anyone who can answer it—"

"No," Banichi said, which meant he didn't mind—one answered the question asked, not the question implied, as the paidhi's tired brain should have recalled.

The paidhi went to sit in the sitting room, write down his question for Banichi, and have the servants bring him a drink. He wished the ship had called. Or his mother had called, or someone. He took the little glass the servants offered, sat and stared at the Bergid, floating in its misty serenity above the city, wondering whether Banichi was having luck getting anyone, or whether he was totally on his own.

Atevi philosophy had used to hold, with misleading but reasonable argument, that the farthest events in the heav-

ens were the least changeable, because you could see
more of them.

And he supposed if there weren't atevi constellations,
as the paidhiin had from the beginning known there
weren't—no constellations such as humans from age im-
memorial had made out of the brighter stars, and still
tried to make out of the atevi sky—then it followed that
ordinary atevi *didn't* grow up with much curiosity about
the night sky—hard, without those pictures, and without
popular names for them, to tell where one was in a sea-
sonally changing sky. Ask a farmer, maybe. Maybe a
sailor, among nonscholarly types.

But, point of constant difference with human history, a
significant part of the atevi food supply didn't depend on
the stars and never had: they domesticated no food animals. They counted the winds from the sea, the turning of
the wind from the south, as a reliable marker for seasons.
Animals bred as animals pleased and the stars had nothing to do with it.

And in fact there was a dearth—he had heard it in
school—of reliable bright stars, compared to the sky of
the long-lost human earth.

Certainly the elite of the Assassins' Guild wouldn't
take overmuch time memorizing random lists of stars and
locations, except perhaps as it did affect navigation. But
the far-faring ships of atevi history had, another long-
understood point of atevi science, always hugged the
coasts and felt out the abiding currents for direction.

A significant point for the paidhi's journal to pass on to
the university: nobody had made a real study of atevi
star-lore, because there *wasn't* any atevi star-lore to speak
of. Though they'd marked the appearance of the Foreign
Star, as, a most strange event in atevi skies, the ship had
built the station—astronomers, in those days a cross between fortune-tellers and honest sky-charters, had correctly said it foretold something strange, and maybe
fearsome.

But atevi astronomers hadn't known what it was, and
they never had recovered their popular respectability,
which the paidhiin knew. But the paidhiin had, so far as

he knew, never risked the topic of atevi astronomy—
never dared seek out astronomers—because they didn't
want the specific questions astronomers could ask. He understood a risk in the undertaking that was precisely of
more and closer questions than Geigi knew how to ask.

Or in wasting time with a discipline allowed through
benign neglect to wander off into star observations and
fortune-telling, a discipline which was, as far as he knew,
half philosophy.

But that might be exactly the sort of people to talk to
the Determinists. *Someone* at that level had to have made
the kind of rationalizations that answered the Geigis of the
world. He only hoped not to bog down in sectarian disputes and abstruse systems. He hoped not to waste a great
deal of time on a matter which he wanted quietened, not
expanded to side questions and, one always risked it, controversy between philosophies.

Banichi finally came to him, looking perplexed as a
man might who'd just had to discuss warped space with
academics.

"There is a man," Banichi began.

"Have a drink," Bren said, and gestured toward a
chair—the servants must perch on the edge of visibility at
all times: it was almost predictable that there was a young
lady at Banichi's elbow before his weight had quite settled into the cushions. Banichi ordered one that was alka-
loid, straight, and propped his injured leg on a footstool.

"This man?" Bren said.

"Very old. They say he's brilliant, but the students
don't understand him. They wonder if he'd be of any help
to the paidhi."

"Banichi, among other things that have changed overnight, it's suddenly become relevant what stars lie near
us, what concepts atevi hold of the wider universe, and
the paidhi isn't studied up on these things. Ask me about
rocket fuel baffles. Ask me about low earth orbit and pay-
loads. We're dealing with near stars and solar systems."

"This faster-than-light controversy?" Banichi said.

"Very much so. Asking humans does me no good. I've
consulted the words I do have, in what study I can make

of it, and I don't know I can find what I want—I'm not sure the average atevi knows, if any atevi at all know what to call it."

"Faster-than-light. Doesn't that say it?"

"I mean concepts. I need mathematical pictures. Ideas, Banichi. I'm not sure that faster-than-light is the best word. Mosphei' has no precision about it."

"Translate. Is that not what the paidhi does?"

"Not when there may be precise atevi words."

"For faster-than-light?" Banichi was clearly doubtful.

"For foundational concepts. For the numbers. For ways of looking at what nature does."

"I fear the astronomers aren't the best method. They invite the paidhi to come in person and talk to this venerable. But—"

"But?"

"Such a meeting could generate controversy in itself."

"You said they were respectable people."

"I said they were scholarly. I didn't say they were respectable, nadi-ji."

"And are atevi astronomers still fortune-tellers? We've released a certain amount of astronomical data to your universities—measurements, data about stars, techniques of measurement—I doubt that the numbers your astronomers have are vastly different from our numbers. I don't see how they could be. I want to find out how they express the math. I want to find out if someone can take Hanks' statement and resolve the paradox the Determinists make of it. Clearly they see things differently than humans. Possibly it's simply terminology."

"There will still be controversy."

"Do they still tell the future? I'd be vastly surprised if they did."

"Certain ones do."

Bren took a sip of the liquor, found his hand trembling considerably: fatigue, he supposed. He was tired. He thought he'd found an answer and it was turning itself into a further problem. "I assure you our data does no such thing," he said, but he saw how astrology might still have greater attraction than astronomy for some atevi, and how the paidhi's simple inquiry after better terminology might offend other, more learned atevi. "We have far more uses for star data than telling the future, I assure you, and I would assume at least some atevi share that interest. Perhaps this old man."

"Their mathematics is reputedly highly suspect, Bren-ji, at the university. That's all I know."

That wasn't good news. For more than scientific reasons. "The university itself doesn't believe them?"

Banichi drew a long breath. Had a sip. "They hold that the stars should agree with the numbers humans provide. There are, I'm told, discrepancies. Changes."

"Banichi—" He was exasperated, and asked himself whether he might do far better looking into the truly eosteric corners of atevi physics, not observational astronomy—but that, considering the topic Hanks had broached, was a source of questions he wanted less than the ones observational astronomers might ask. "Banichi, stars move. Everything's moving. So is our observation point. We've put this forth time and time again. It doesn't mean the astronomers are wrong."

"I don't say it makes clear sense," Banichi said, "not to me."

"The earth goes around the sun. In winter it's at one point of its orbit and in the summer it's the opposite. If you're looking at a star and want to know its real numbers, you can measure by taking the numbers from the earth at opposite extremes of the earth's orbit. But the margin of error rapidly gets larger than the measurement itself. We're dealing in very great distances, Banichi, very big numbers, and they have nothing to do with forecast or philosophy: stars have to do with burning hydrogen, that's all."

"Then what use are they?"

"The sun's rather useful."

"What's the sun to do with anything?"

He was perplexed, now, and flung out the obvious. "The sun's a star, Banichi-ji. Close up, the stars look like the sun."

"I believe you," Banichi said after a moment. "I can

see your point, I think. But do you wish to add philosophical extremes to the debate? I counsel you, nadi, surely you can come up with something else."

"The ship up there has been to other stars, Banichi, almost certainly. We came from another star very much like the sun."

"This may be true, nadi, and I surely wouldn't dispute the paidhi's word."

He'd gone beyond impatience. He was arriving at curiosity himself, on topics the paidhiin *didn't* often ask atevi. "Well, where did you *think* we came from?"

"From another star, nadi."

"Like one of those little points of light up there."

"Actually—" Banichi said, "one had rarely wondered."

"Did you think we lived *on* a star?"

"Well . . ." Banichi said with a shrug. "People just don't ask such questions on the streets, nadi-ma. I think if you want such explanations for lord Geigi, you're only going to confuse him."

"I've got to do better than that, Banichi. Geigi at least has a scientific background. He understands the solar system."

"Better than I do," Banichi said. "But still, in public, I wouldn't make a great issue about the sun, nadi. I don't think many people will understand you."

He took a slow sip. He'd never in his administration had access to the astronomical faculties, never had recourse to them—he supposed Wilson-paidhi hadn't, nor—if one went on—earlier paidhiin—and that got into increasingly more primitive science. No one in the prior century would have wanted to raise questions of cosmology—or provide, God help them, heavily mathematical data to atevi—except the information that more or less accompanied certain stages of technology, much as knowledge of the ionosphere went along with radio, and the solar wind and the source of auroras would be, he was well sure, a part of current science curriculum—since it mattered. But, but, and but—no study he'd seen had ever speculated on the reach of systematic knowledge of cosmology into the popular understanding—

Of—damn—course. Atevi mentality integrated smaller systems quite well. But atevi truly didn't readily think of the whole earth, didn't have a word for universe that didn't equally mean one's immediate personal world. Atevi didn't have a real interest in understanding the theory of Everything, just in getting the right numbers on their individual circumstances. Philosophers were there to care about larger systems while ordinary atevi adhered to the dominant philosophy of their personal set of associations and trusted the philosophers to get the big picture right—that was exactly what was at stake with lord Geigi, who understood his philosophy better than the average atevi. Geigi had been led deep into that understanding because he'd pursued a scientific education, and he'd been forced to integrate astronomy into his personal system. What fell outside that meticulously ordered system—challenged that system. What couldn't be integrated—challenged that system.

And no wonder people with busy lives, people like Banichi, were content to let the philosophers hammer out the major, theoretical problems, and—in Banichi's and Tabini's case—take all philosophy with a large grain of salt, possibly because they dealt with multiple philosophies, and thought of them in terms of atevi political motives, not underlying fact. Tell Banichi the sun was a star? All right. It didn't shatter Banichi's world. He wouldn't lie awake thinking about it tonight. He might think about it when he had leisure. But he wouldn't worry about his personal universe falling apart because he couldn't integrate that information.

But those atevi who'd invested the time and hammered out the highest, most tenuous and difficult interrelationships of knowledge would lose sleep. And if *those* people were shaken in their confidence and debate filtered down past the pragmatic sorts like Banichi and became public doubts—a lot of people had invested heavily both financially and politically in what they considered fortuitous systems. A lot of people had paid money to numerologists who'd advised them to certain personal, political and financial courses in which, depend on it, they had a lot of emotional as well as monetary investment. Tell a man that his world wasn't as secure as he'd paid money to have it be, and damned right he was upset.

The paidhiin were well in touch with that fact of atevi life. The paidhiin walked around that kind of minefield all the time. Just—so far as he knew—no paidhi had ever checked up to see if astronomical and cosmological information had been filtering its way into atevi public consciousness to the same degree it had done among human beings who did have constellations, and whose history was tied up with the stars in one form or another. Just one of those myriad little differences that paidhiin stumbled over in operation and wrote some obscure paper about so that ten or fifteen years down the road some committee on Mospheira would take it into account in planning the introduction of some new technological system.

Usually the differences weren't critical. Usually there weren't so many changes at once. Usually there was a ten- to fifteen-year study behind a technological move.

And right now it seemed every unattended detail left for tomorrow by paidhiin of generations past was going to come due on his watch.

"I'll certainly take your advice, Banichi, at least as regards what people know: it's invaluable to me. I think—I'd better accept the venerable's invitation."

"His staff's invitation. I fear the venerable's attention is only for the stars. These foreign suns. Whatever they are. I'll look at the sky tonight and think of strangers. It's quite appalling."

"Inhabited planets must be very rare. I've heard so."

"One hopes. One does hope so, Bren-ji. I don't think we could bear another such onslaught of benefits."

"I've found an office, nadi Bren," Tano reported by phone. *"And by the earnest endeavor of the personnel office—twenty-seven discreet and experienced staff, of clear* man'chi *to Tabini-aiji, and one managerial, a retired gentleman, one Dasibi, out of Magisiri, who would be greatly honored to be called back to Bu-javid service. I explained that all positions might be temporary, pending*

changes in the volume of the paidhi's mail, but none objected to that. The standard salary seems to be Cari Street market privilege at six thousand a year, medical at two, housing and transport at four, pension at two, and incidentals at two-five. Nadi Dasibi agrees to the same plus six additional stipend. This seems fair and in line with standard. But they all do understand that the offer is conditional on funding."

Fifteen thousand five a year for twenty-seven people. Twenty-one five for another. Office payments. Faxes, phones, computers—

"I've not that much in personal savings," Bren said with a sinking heart. "I'd thought of one or two assistants. If we can apply to the general office—I don't know, Tano. I don't know that I *can* get funds out of my government. They may well want to shoot me instead."

"I've concluded nothing as yet, nand' paidhi. But I have all the figures. I can file a requisition through personnel. I'm sure it'll go straight up to the aiji."

"I'm sure it will." He didn't want to have the office funded through the Bu-javid. If he had a shred of propriety left in the office accounts, he shouldn't be accepting any more funding from atevi, who had far different standards for what the aiji's court demanded in dress and style than what the Mospheiran government wanted to fund for what they viewed as a civil servant. But— "Do it, Tano. I've no other recourse but leave the correspondence piling up. There's another stack. The household staff is sorting through it."

"One isn't surprised at more mail, nand' paidhi. But I'll be a while at the requisitions. I've forms to fill out. A lot of them."

"I'm grateful for your doing it, Tano. Everything's fine upstairs. Algini's resting, there aren't any emergencies. Take time for supper. Please. As a favor to me. If it doesn't all get done today, it'll still get done. We're searching out the volatile ones. We'll take care of it."

"Thank you, nadi-ji." Tano said.

He hung up the phone, working the numbers in his head without half thinking and coming up with a budget that wasn't by any stretch of the imagination going to get clearance without a fight. Mospheira wasn't going to understand why the paidhi, when all previous paidhiin had made do with no staff on the mainland and a staff of ten or less on Mospheira, suddenly needed this kind of operation. Long before Wilson, Mospheira in the executive branch hadn't wanted to admit that the paidhiin were anything but a convenient appendage to the State Department's other, internal business—saw them as bearers of messages, generators of dictionaries, or perhaps as mostly engaged in generating tenure in university posts.

And without executive branch support, figure that the legislators were never going to leap to drain money from their constituencies for an office that had never needed it before, for a paidhi that didn't have friends in high places.

God . . . help him. He didn't have the funds. In the absence of Mospheira suddenly seeing reason, he knew where the funds were going to have to come from: Tabini. Which, on principle, he didn't want, but if the ship answered—if the ship would just, please God, answer Tabini, and call him, and tell him that they were going to agree to Tabini's proposals. . . .

He was in the lady's small office, where he had a phone and some privacy. Supper was in preparation. He hadn't enough time to start any letter or anything else useful. He resolved to try the Mospheiran phone system again, and called through to the operator with his mother's number.

The call went through. Or sounded as if it were going through.

It didn't.

He listened through the phone system Number Temporarily Out of Service message, and couldn't even get the damn central message system to leave her a "Hello, this is Bren."

He called through again, this time to Toby's home, on the North Shore.

"Toby? This is Bren. Toby. Pick up the phone. Pick up the damn phone, Toby."

The daughter came on. A high clear voice called, *"Papa? It's Uncle Bren,"* and in a series of thumps somebody came down the steps to the front hall.

"Bren."

"Toby, good to hear a voice. What's the matter with Mom's number?"

"What's the matter?"

"I'm getting a Temporarily Out of Service."

There was a moment of silence. *"Maybe they're doing repair."*

"I tried to call this morning. I got a telegram from her. It was censored to hell. Is everything all right?"

Silence. And more silence.

"Toby?"

"Yeah, everything's fine. How are you doing? The shoulder all right?"

"Best I can tell. —Toby, how's Jill?"

"Oh, Jill's fine. We're all fine. Weather's a little soggy. You'll probably catch it tomorrow."

"We could do with some rain. Cool it off a little. Have you talked to Mother in the last few days?"

Silence. Then: *"You know Mom. She doesn't like change."*

"Toby?"

"I've got to hang up now. We're going out to supper."

"Toby, what in bloody hell's going on?"

"Mom's been getting some calls, all right? It's not a problem."

"Not a problem. What kind of calls?"

"I'll drop her a message on the system, tell her you called. It's all right, Bren, it's all right, don't worry about it. —I've got to go. Jill's waiting. We were just going out the door."

"Yeah," he said. "Yeah. Thanks, Toby."

Something's wrong, those silences meant. Something was wrong regarding their mother.

He hit his hand on the paneled wall. Which did nothing but summon a concerned servant.

"Nand' paidhi?" She was one of the youngest, very earnest, very anxious.

He carefully removed expression from his face. And tried not to feel the acid upset in his stomach. "It's all right, nadi. It's nothing."

"Yes," the servant said, and bowed and went her way.

The paidhi gathered up the nerves he had left and tried to divert his mind back to office budgets and folded space.

The change of season meaning a more palatable meat course, the cook was inspired, to judge by the meticulous arrangement and green-sauce spirals on the appetizers. And the paidhi, the object of so much attention, should have had a ravenous appetite, counting the chasing about he'd done, and the lunch he hadn't but picked over.

But he couldn't take his mind off Toby's informative silences, picked over the appetizers, too, and decided finally he'd rather try to eat than answer cook's hurt feelings.

He wished he hadn't called at all. He couldn't do anything. He couldn't get there. Toby could, but Toby hadn't, which might mean Toby wasn't that worried.

But "Getting some calls." What in hell did that mean? Some random crazy?

A movement touched the edge of his vision. And stopped, which the serving staff hadn't done. He looked toward the door.

"Nandi," he said, seeing Saidin standing, hands folded, expectant of something. With more staff behind her.

With a serving tray.

Probably the season's inaugural dish. It was a very formal house. And he *couldn't* offend the cook. He gave the event his full attention.

The servants brought the tray in and set out a very large flat bread, with an amazing array of foods atop, all appropriate, all seasonal. But on a green vegetable sauce.

"This is a new dish," he remarked.

And evidently set the staff somewhat aback—when cook herself had come into the hall, and waited—clearly—for his reaction.

"It's quite nice," he said, trying to salve feelings.

"What do you call it?" He tried to learn new words and new things as they presented themselves. It was what the paidhi did in the ordinary course of his job.

"Pizza," the youngest servant blurted out. "Is this not in correct season, nand' paidhi?"

"Of course it is," he said, at once. "Of *course*, pizza, nadi. I'm just—quite surprised." He could have broken into laughter—if he hadn't control of his face, and his voice. "It's wonderful."

"We hadn't the red sauce," cook said. "We're told it will come, but the plane was delayed by weather."

"One did think," madam Saidin said, clearly part of the conspiracy, "that after dealing with that unpleasant woman this noon it was a good day for a traditional food."

"It smells very good," he said. "Would the staff share? It's traditional to pass it around."

The servants looked excited. Saidin looked dubious, but cook said, "There're eight more in the kitchen. One had provided for the staff, nand' paidhi, by your leave."

"Call Algini. And Jago." The notion of an Occasion made him positively cheerful. "Might we have drinks, nand' Saidin?"

Even Saidin was falling into it. Cook declared that she could whip up more in short order, there was serious question about what the felicitous number of pieces should be for the cutting, and servants were scurrying after various members of the household, awake and asleep—nothing would do but that everybody come in, and flowers be found, and the state table be laid out with the second-best silver.

Jago was nowhere about, but Algini came from the security station—and sampled the dish, and went back again, with plain tea to drink—but several of the staff became quite happy, someone put on music, and in the hallway a couple of the servants began a solemn, hands-behind-the-back line step, which in no wise endangered the fragile tables or the porcelain. He left the dining room to watch, and the servants would happily have taught him, but madam Saidin was scandalized, and advised them the paidhi was much too dignified for that.

The paidhi wasn't, as happened, but one didn't defy madam Saidin's judgments in front of her staff, and the paidhi stood in the doorway sipping a drink he knew was safe. They *had* tomatos and potatoes, peppers, onions and herbs on Mospheira they didn't allow to cross the strait uncooked, for fear of seeds and starts and the mainland ecology, although atevi who'd tried tomatos found something in tomatos and potatoes and peppers they relished, and there was a seasonal trade; but the ubiquitous green sauce, peppery and sour, went well with the bread and atevi foods piled atop so thickly a single slice was gluttony—and there was plenty of that among the staff.

"What does the dish celebrate?" a servant wanted to know, and the paidhi rapidly searched his mental files and said, shamelessly, "Success in hard work."

That pleased everyone, who congratulated each other, and even Saidin was pleased with herself.

Then Algini came in, in greater haste than Algini's injuries or Algini's habit usually afforded, with:

"Nadi Bren!"

There was a sudden hush, except of the music from the tape system. Security was all but impossible, as Algini said, "A phone call, Bren-paidhi. From Mogari-nai. They say the ship is calling you. They say they'll patch through."

"This is Bren Cameron," he said, still out of breath from reaching the office phone, "Go ahead, Mogari-nai."

"It's going through, nand' paidhi. Stand by."

He was still a couple of drinks to the worse and cursing his bad judgment, because, dammit, he'd known a call from the ship was at least still pending, and he'd assumed—assumed—it wouldn't happen. He took deep slow breaths, trying to pull his scattered wits together.

The next voice was thinner. *"Hello?"* it said. *"This is* Phoenix-*com. Bren Cameron, please."*

"This is Bren Cameron. Go ahead, *Phoenix*-com." He could hear the rippling murmur of gossip underway among the servants down the short hall, but the party had quietened, Saidin, at least, being as aware as Algini what was at stake in this phone call.

"Mr. Cameron, this is Ramirez."

"Good evening, sir."

"Good evening. Sorry to miss your 1200 request. We've been sifting through a swarm of material, yours, theirs—I just got off the com with the island, and the President is claiming you haven't any authority to negotiate, I should tell you that first."

Damn, was the thought. He said, he trusted calmly, while juggling the phone receiver on his good shoulder and trying at the same time to reach the record button with the good hand—he punched the button—"The President has no authority to negotiate for atevi, sir, by the meaning and intent of the Treaty, the text of which you have. By grant of Tabini-aiji, sir, I *do* have the authority, and while I don't imagine—" God, the alcohol was making the room too warm, or the tape was cutting off his wind "—while I don't imagine the President is too pleased with that situation, I'm going to continue to provide translation between you and the atevi authority."

"I think we've come around to that point. What's the aiji's position on dealing with us?"

"Entirely open-minded." This wasn't a diplomat he was talking to. He picked up the bluntness and matched it. "The deal's been integrated economies, equal technological levels. Atevi and humans were building launch facilities before you arrived, to share renovation and operation of the station. That's the deal in progress. The aiji sees no cause to change that."

"Is he receiving this?"

"I can arrange it in a matter of minutes."

"No need, if you'll inform him we certainly want a good relationship with his government and we've selected the representative to go down there, at his request, on two conditions: one, our representative gets official status and official protection; and, two, there'll be an immediate application of resources to getting up here. I

want an official confirmation from him that this will be the case."

"You'll get an official confirmation of both points, sir, but I can say there'll be no problem with that."

"We're dropping two representatives, one to you, one to Mospheira."

"No problem with that, either, sir."

"Good. We've got the volunteers. —Jason? Jason Graham. Bren Cameron."

"Mr. Cameron." A new, younger-sounding voice. *"This is Jason Graham. Glad to make your acquaintance. I gather I'm likely to be seeing you soon."*

"Looking forward to that. You've got a landing craft, then?"

"Well—we've got one. I'd like to call tomorrow, your choice of times, and get some feeling about what I'm dropping into."

"Delighted." He was. "Local daybreak's easy to figure. We left your clock when we landed. Tomorrow morning?"

"Daybreak. Dawn. Sunrise. All those words. Tomorrow dawn, it is. Good night. Do you say that?"

"Good night," he said, with the least small unease of realization that those were all dictionary words to the man. Conceptually dead. Three hundred and more years away—and daybreak was conceptually a dead word to him.

He signed off with the technicians at Mogari-nai, snatched the tape out of the machine before anything could happen to it, and phoned Tabini's private phone with, "I just had a brief ship contact, aiji-ma. They've apparently agreed to everything we want. I'll get you the full text."

"This is very good, Bren-ji. This is very good."

"They say they've got a landing capability of some kind and two people are scheduled to come down, one for the mainland, one for Mospheira. I'm going to talk to their representative at the crack of dawn tomorrow and I'll have more detail: the conversation was very brief. They want, they said, good relations with the atevi government. That's about the limit of the conversation, but it was cordial and positive."

"Very good news, Bren-ji. Good to hear. —Bren-ji?"

"Aiji-ma?"

"One hears of celebration over there."

"I'm terribly sorry if I've disturbed you, aiji-ma."

"No, our walls are quite thick. Enjoy the evening, Bren-ji."

"Thank you," he said, bewildered, as Tabini hung up.

Then it slowly came to him that there was something changed, and they might have reason to celebrate—the threat to the world might have taken a turn toward real, productive solution.

He walked out to the dining hall where a hushed assembly of servants stood waiting—hushed until he arrived: then the staff began to ask all at the same time, "Did you speak to the ship, nand' paidhi?" and "Did it go well, nand' paidhi?"

"Hush," Saidin said, scandalized. "Hush! This is by no means our business."

"But it did go well, nand' Saidin," Bren said. "If we can believe what I hear from the ship." He dared not claim to have reached any agreement, although he was sliding giddily toward believing it himself, for reasons that had more to do with where the resources were than any confidence in innate generosity in orbit over their heads. For that, he counted more on Mospheira, and that, very little and in offices not in ultimate authority over anything.

But around him there was growing excitement on faces. Algini was still in the group, and the crowd in the dining room and the hall numbered, he was sure, every servant on staff. Even Saidin and Algini seemed to catch the enthusiasm when he'd said as much as he had said, and someone put a glass in his hand, which accounted for all his ability to hold anything. It smelled at least like the safe variety, a wary touch of the tongue didn't have the queasy rough taste the truly dangerous drink had, and while he was engaged in deciding that, Saidin snatched it from him with an exclamation of dismay and replaced it with another, Saidin berating the glass-giver in the same instant for unwarranted carelessness with the paidhi, who everyone knew had a delicate stomach and a delicate constitution and was, moreover, Saidin's harangue continued, a virtual invalid lately wounded in the service of the Association, beside the hazard to lady Damiri's reputation in their carelessness.

The music had come up again, and cook's cart had arrived, this time with trays of chilled sweetmeats, probably a month's provisions, on which the servants descended and stripped tray after tray. Saidin was nibbling a sweet herself, and Algini had a number of very nice-looking young ladies backing him against the wall and firing questions at him, doubtless on his recent adventures and the reason for the bandages.

Then, ominous, dark and formal in her uniform, Jago arrived in the midst of things, and surveyed the situation without expression.

"Bren-ji," she said, moving up beside him, "one heard, down in Security."

"About the ship? It sounds good so far."

A servant would have given Jago a glass, but she ordered tea; there was still food to be had, and while Jago wouldn't drink, she took down a piece of pizza in short order, and listened to the music, standing by him with a solemn and on-duty stare at the proceedings as dancers, twenty or so of them, this time, wound down the hall.

"It—rather well grew, nadi," Bren said, feeling foolish and completely responsible. "I hate to tell them no, but I fear we're disturbing the peace."

"No," Jago said in her somber way. "Though Cenedi, downstairs, made inquiry for the dowager's sake."

"Oh, damn."

"And Banichi and Tano demand a share saved for them." Jago's tea arrived, with suitable deference, and Jago stood and sipped tea. "They'll be in later. Cook is going to be beset for the recipe. Pieces made their way down to Security, over to Tabini, and down to the dowager. One hopes this contravenes no ceremonial propriety."

"No," he said solemnly. "By no means. God, is nothing safe?"

"The recipe?" Jago said.

"The information. Everything I do—"

"We do watch, Bren-ji. But don't rely on it too far. Banichi says get to bed in good season, don't proposition the servants, and don't break the ancestral porcelains."

"Where *is* he?"

Jago cast a glance aside, then said, "He's got your plane arranged."

"Plane."

"To the observatory," Jago said, as if, of course, he should have known.

Which he should. The paidhi wasn't tracking as well as he ought. Probably it was the third glass. He was relatively sure it was the third.

"Day after tomorrow," Jago said, and sipped her tea. And hadn't, he realized a moment later, answered his question about Banichi's whereabouts at all.

Dammit, he thought. He got more information out of Cenedi and Tano than he did out of either of the two security personnel he counted closer to him.

But it wasn't the time or the place to insist. Banichi would turn up, probably as Jago disappeared somewhere, as they'd been doing. Jago'd mentioned a security station, and somehow Jago and Tabini *and* Banichi knew every move he made and every breath he took, which might indicate the nature of the security station they were occupying and the fact that the porcelains might be listening.

Which might indicate that, with a country at risk, or what passed for one in atevi reckoning, Tabini might not find it within his conscience to take him totally on his word.

Or dared not, with the amount of controversy he'd generated, and apparently a major crisis in the Assassins' Guild, leave him unwatched for a second.

Celebration might be in order. But solutions didn't fall into your hands, strangers didn't agree with you for no reason of advantage to themselves, and aijiin, presidents, and likely ship captains as well, when they had constituents at issue, didn't just do the logical, straightforward, economical—or trusting—thing.

Not that he'd ever observed.

13

"I've got a very little of a few languages," Graham said, on the phone patch-through. "I'm as close as we could come. I'm a history hobbyist. That's how I'm elected to the atevi side of this—I've got a background in history. The other of us, going to the human population— she's got all the technical background you want, but no study in languages at all. Nobody has, much. We don't have different languages. I just got into it because I was interested in history, and I got curious. And I teach, too. It was something I thought I ought to know."

"You're a teacher?" Bren asked, and poured a cup of tea from the pot on the office desk, with growing visions of a gentle, professorial young man, politically naive, dropping into political hell.

"Well, computers most of the time, but somebody's got to write the lessons for the kids. I gave them language study. I thought it was good for them. But not too many were interested."

"Know a noun from a verb?"

"Yes, sir. Conjugations, declensions, participles—"

"That's going to be useful. I've prepped another data-load for you this morning, atevi-Mosphei' grammar notes with at least the basics—you're not going to understand half of it. A handful of phrases in the remote case you have to communicate with somebody other than me. We're not dealing with a human grammatical structure, as you'll find out. Good in math?"

"Up to a point, sir. Why?"

"Because you have to do some calculation constantly. The number of persons in a polite sentence isn't by head count, it's by calculations of rank plus real number, and there are forms you use to avoid jinxing somebody when you *have* to use an infelicitous number of persons. You'll love it. I'm *so* glad to have somebody from the ship who's going to understand that this isn't a straightforward matter of word-for-word translation. I've been trying for years to make my department heads understand that answers one time aren't the answers the next time. If I haven't scared you by now, you may do."

"I'm at least daunted."

"Good judgment. Atevi and humans have deep but solvable conceptual differences, moderately significant psychological differences, and I'll tell you, we were just on the verge of important breakthroughs including space missions when you turned up in the sky scaring hell out of the children. Any background in negotiation? Politics?"

"History. Just—history."

He had an academic on his hands. God help them. Or a dilettante.

"Good vocabulary?"

"A pretty good one. Better than some."

"I've asked your captain to give you real authority to negotiate. And stand behind you. Will he?"

"I've heard what you said. He told me just—call if I had a question and I'm supposed to get a thorough briefing before I go down, on what we're going to need, on the lift vehicle and after. I'll need regular communications with the ship. I can get the technical details in download."

Either the captain was naive—a possibility—or the captain was sending them somebody who didn't know enough to spill anything under interrogation.

But Jason Graham wasn't stupid. A man who made a hobby out of history and languages wasn't stupid.

A fool, maybe. That was a different matter.

"You have any concept of politics, Graham? How do you make critical decisions up there? What's your procedure?"

"Guild vote, sir. The captains lay out what's to be done,

or sometimes the technicians do, and then we all lay out what our choices are—it's not like a whole country, sir, it's a lot more like we've got information, and we've got what we don't know, and we've got to figure."

"How did you decide to come back, for example?"

A silence for a moment. *"Well, we were always going to. And we decided it was a good time."*

"Why was it a good time?"

"Well, because we've got another station, and linking up the two of them could give us a lot more options where we could go."

"Fueling, you mean."

"And supplies."

"What are you going to trade for?"

Another small silence. *"I don't know, sir. I think that's something that's still pretty far off, the way the station looks right now."*

Meaning the station needed population, the station needed workers, and the ship—

The ship, as it always had, wanted refueling. The ship wanted provisions. And the world was supposed to provide that, free of charge, one could guess, after one hell of a lot of man-hours of dangerous effort producing what the starship could drink down at one gulp and leave.

But as Jason Graham said, there were things to do first. They were stuck with the ship as a factor. They had a station decaying more rapidly by the year, the ship was a shortcut to saving it—which was worth something, damn sure.

And the ship—couldn't get anything off the planet. By everything he knew—it couldn't get anything that wasn't brought to it in space. That meant the world had leverage.

"Meaning they'll send down their figures as they develop them."

"Essentially, sir, but—can we talk very frankly?"

"Anything you want to talk about. Go ahead."

"I'm volunteering because I want to do something more with my life than push keys, which is the job I've got, but I don't want to get my throat cut, and I don't want to end up somebody's hostage. Neither does Yolanda. It won't

work, for one thing. The captain says he won't deal there to get us back. If anything goes wrong we're on our own. So—how safe are we?"

"You'll have the protection of Tabini-aiji. That's very safe. I can't say about your companion, but Mospheira's quiet to the point of tedium under most circumstances. I'll make every effort to meet you when you arrive. Are you coming down at the same time?"

"That's what we plan. If we can get one of us a way to get to the other place."

"Easily. By the next plane."

"Mospheira says—speaking frankly, sir—that atevi can shoot you for no reason. Legally. That somebody just tried to kill you. Twice. That we're much safer landing on the island. You're telling me otherwise."

"I—equally frankly—advise you that landing on Mospheira would create special problems for you. Yes, there are some very different customs here, and assassination is legal, but it's also strictly regulated. The attempts against me were illicit, they were met by the aiji's security and stopped. In fact, if you land on the island, it would make you much less safe: Tabini-aiji has a great stake in your protection if you land where he asks you to, on his invitation—he's given you his personal assurance of safety, that's one thing. For another, he considerably outranks the Mospheiran President, and accepting the Mospheiran invitation over his would be very bad protocol. Atevi would take it for a calculated insult, or collusion and secret arrangements, which would start you off very badly. Please pass that word into your decision-making process."

"I will, sir. —Second question. Mospheira says the situation where you are is chaotic. They say you might not be acting of your own accord. That a woman who was supposed to be replacing you has disappeared."

Maybe not so politically naive. Or at least not incapable of asking questions.

"Can I believe you, sir, that's the question. The island says you've violated orders and you're giving unauthorized information to the atevi."

"Yes. I have done that. So has the woman they say has disappeared. You'll discover once you get down here that Mospheira moves incredibly slowly on decisions and translators in the field sometimes have to move very fast. Your ship showed in the sky, atevi feared Mospheira was going to abrogate the Treaty and that it was some kind of plot—damn right I had to take steps to calm things down, among people who didn't feel they had gotten honest information. That necessarily included my explaining what couldn't wait for some committee on Mospheira to approve. Mospheira is sending very contradictory signals. They want me here. They know I'll act. Now State is mad. Fine. If you want the blunt truth, I'd rather offend the President of Mospheira and not have the whole atevi and human relationship blow up over what I could solve, in a situation the facts of which they'd have to rely on my judgment to find out in the first place."

"What about this missing woman?"

"Deana Hanks? She's not missing. I ordered her to go home and she told me she was waiting for formal recall from Mospheira, which Mospheira hasn't sent."

"Why?"

"Because—you want the truth?—she belongs to an opposition party on Mospheira that's trying to get Tabini to accept her credentials; and he won't. She's fine, I had lunch with her yesterday, we argued as usual, but we've agreed to keep it in bounds."

"That's certainly not what we're getting from Mospheira."

"What are you getting from Mospheira?"

"That the situation there is very dangerous, and you might be lying, bluntly put, sir."

"You know where this transmission is coming from?"

"Yes, sir, a station on the coast."

"You think stations of that size are private? Or that it belongs to the atevi government?"

"To the government, I'd say, sir."

"I assure you that's who I'm speaking for, Mr. Graham. I'm the translator, the paidhi, the only human appointed by the Treaty to mediate between atevi and humans. The atevi legislature asked me to perform the same office between you and them, in which capacity I'm now officially functioning. Yes, I work for the Mospheiran government; by the nature of what I do, I also work for the atevi government. That means that it's my job occasionally to say things Mospheira doesn't want to hear. But if I don't say it, it doesn't get said, the situation festers in silence, and we can all end up with real trouble. Plainly, there are Mospheirans that don't like atevi, and they don't like me, either. But that opinion is never going to get atevi to cooperate. Not till hell freezes over, as the saying goes. So tell your captain he can listen to people on Mospheira who either get their information from me or from their own guesswork, or he can ask me firsthand and get the information directly. There's no other choice, because there's no other human authorized to contact the atevi. You're about to become the second. Welcome to the world of politics."

"*Are they—easy to get along with? Can you talk to regular atevi? Or are you pretty well guarded?*"

"I deal mostly with government people, but not exclusively. Atevi are honest, loyal to their associates, occasionally obscure, and occasionally blunt to the point of embarrassment. I'll be delighted to have another human face besides the one in the mirror, but I don't live a deprived life here. Let me ask a more technical question. What are your landing requirements? What do you need? A runway?"

"*Actually—not, sir. I wish we did. We're using one of your pods.*"

"You're kidding."

"*Afraid not. They found a couple in the station, packed up and everything.*"

"Good God. —Excuse me."

"*So we've got no way back up again if somebody doesn't build a return vehicle. Between you and me, sir, in language you wouldn't tell my mother, who's not real happy with this—what risk am I running?*"

"I'd sure want to know why those pods didn't get used."

"Mospheira says they were redundancies. There were three last ones. Because the last aboard the station were only six people. And if anything had gone wrong with one, they couldn't have built another. They had a rule about triple redundancy."

"That sounds reasonable. But I can't swear to it."

"So—if we have to build a ship that can get off the planet, how long is it going to take to get us back up again?"

"If we started today, if things went incredibly right, and that was our total objective in the program, we could maybe launch a manned capsule to low orbit inside a year, year and a half, on a rocket that's meant to launch communications satellites. No luxury accommodation, but we could get you up to low orbit and probably down again in one piece."

"But to reach high orbit?"

"Realistically, and I know this part of it, because I'm the technical translator, among my other jobs, if we want a meaningful high-orbit vehicle, we'd be wasting time building a small-scale chemical rocket. I'd much rather negotiate an orbit-and-return technology."

"And how long for that?"

"Depends on a lot of factors. Whether the materials meet design specs. How much cooperation you can get from the atevi. I'd say if you don't want to grow old down here, you'd better land on this side of the water and be damn nice to Tabini-aiji, who can single-handedly determine how fast the materials are going to meet design standard."

"That's—very persuasive, sir."

The whole business of haste—the rush to risk lives—bothered him. "A parachute two hundred years old? The glue on the heat shield—"

"We know. We propose to refit it. They say they can improve on it. Put us down pretty well on the mark. I don't personally like this parachute idea, but I guess it beats infalling without one."

"You've got more nerve than I'd have, Mr. Graham.

I'll give you that. But our ancestors made it, or we wouldn't be here."

"I hate to ask, but what was the failure rate? Do you have any stats on that?"

"Percentage? Low. I know that one sank in the sea. One hard-landed. Fatally. One lost the heat shield and burned up. They mostly made it, that's all I know. But with all your technology—isn't there some way to take a little time, at least modify that thing into a guided system? Nothing you've got can possibly serve as a landing craft?"

A pause. Then: *"Not for atmosphere. The moon—no problem. But that's a deep, deep well, sir."*

"Gravity well."

"Yes, sir."

It wasn't just Mospheira versus atevi that had a language gap. He guessed the shortened expression. And out of the expertise the technological translator necessarily gained in his career, other, more critical problems immediately dawned on him.

"Mr. Graham, I hope to hell if they unpack that parachute to check it, they know how to put it back in its housing. There's an exact and certain way those things have to unfold. Otherwise they don't open."

"You're really making me very nervous, sir. But they've got specifications on the lander. That's in the station library, they tell me."

"When are they sending you down here?"

"About five, six days."

"God."

"I wish you'd be more confident."

"Five days is pushing real hard, Mr. Graham. Is there a particular reason to be in a hurry?"

"No reason not to—I mean, we've no problem with ablation surfaces. We can do better in no time. I'm less sure about the parachute, but I have to trust they can tell from records. That's all. I have to trust it. And they'll be done, they tell me, in four days. And they can shoot us out there on a real precise infall, right down the path. I don't know what more they can do. They say it's no risk. That they've

got all the results. When did they lose the three they lost? Early on?"

"I think—early on. They didn't lose any of the last ones." A slight gloss of the truth. But the truth didn't help a man about to fall that far.

"I'll tell you, I'm not looking forward to the experience. I keep telling myself I'm stark raving crazy. I don't know what Yolanda's thinking. But if we just get down—"

"The atevi would say, Trust the numbers. Get fortunate numbers out of the technicians."

"I certainly intend to. —What's that sound?"

"Sound—?" He was suddenly aware of the outside, of the smell and feel of rain in the air. And anxiety in Graham's voice. "That was thunder. We're having a storm."

"Atmospheric disturbance."

"Rain."

"It must be loud."

"Thunder is. Can be. That was. It's right over us."

"It's not dangerous."

"Lightning is. Not a good idea to be on the phone much longer. But one thing I should mention before I sign off. We've never had much of a disease problem, there's not much we catch from atevi, and we were a pretty clean population when we landed. But on general principles the aiji will insist you undergo the process our ancestors did before they came down."

"We began it last watch. My stomach isn't happy, but that's the least of our worries."

"Sorry about that. I'll relay your assurance to the aiji and I assure you the aiji will be happy you've taken that precaution on your own initiative. You'll impress him as considerate, well-disposed people. I'll also inform him about your companion needing to get to a plane without delay, assuming that will be her wish. I'll fax up a map with the optimum sites marked, with text involving advantages and disadvantages. You can talk to your experts and make a choice, but it's just more convenient to the airports if you can come in on the public lands south of the capital."

"I'll pass that word along. I'd like to talk to you fairly

frequently, if you can arrange it. I want to look over this material you're sending up. I'll probably have questions."

"I'll fax up my meeting schedule. Tomorrow I'm going to be traveling out to an observatory in the mountains. I'll be back by evening. But if something comes up that needs information from me, wherever there are telephones, they can track me down. Even on the plane."

"To an observatory. Why?"

"To talk to a gentleman who may be able to answer some philosophical questions. Your arrival has—well, been pretty visible to anyone in the rural areas. And call it religious implications, as well as political ones. Say that concerned people have asked me questions."

"Is that part of the job?"

"I hope we'll be working together."

"I assure you I hope we'll be working together, sir. I'd just as soon they dropped us someplace soft."

He couldn't help but grin, to a featureless phone. "I'll pick you out a soft one, Mr. Graham. My name is Bren. Call me that, please. I've never been 'sir.' "

"I'm Jase. Always been. I really look forward to this. After I'm down there."

"Jase. I'm going to be very depressed if you don't make it. Please have those techs double-check everything. Tell them the world will wait if they're not sure. The aiji will. Under no circumstance would he want you to compromise your safety."

"I'm glad to know that. But I guess we're on that schedule unless they find something. To tell the truth, I'd just as soon be done with that part of it."

"We're on the end of our time." Thunder crashed, shocked the nerves. "That was a loud one. I should sign off now."

"Understood. Talk to you later. Soon as I can, anyway. Thanks."

The tea had cooled. The wind from the open doors was fresh and damp. Toby'd been right, the storm had swept right on past Mospheira and on to them in all its strength. The plane with the requested tomato sauce probably still hadn't made it in, and the paidhi had let his tea cool in that wind, talking on the phone with a man born in space at a star other than the sun.

A star the man still hadn't named for reasons that might not be chance.

Jason Graham claimed twenty-eight as old Earth measured years. The faxed-down information that preceded the call gave his personal record—his and his companion's, Yolanda Mercheson, thirty-one and an engineer trainee. Nice, ordinary-looking woman with what might be freckles: the fax wasn't perfect. Jase had a thin, earnest face, close-clipped dark hair—which was going to have to grow: atevi would be appalled, and understand, because, different from centuries ago, they understood that foreigners didn't always do things for atevi reasons.

But two people of a disposition to fall miles down onto a planet and be separated from each other by politics, species, and boundaries for reasons common sense said surely weren't all altruism, or naive curiosity—he didn't understand such a mentality; or he thanked God it wasn't part of *his* job. He supposed if they talked very long, very hard—

He still didn't know, and he believed Jason Graham saying he was scared. The ship had come up with its volunteers very quickly. Which might be the habit of looking down on places, and the nerve it took to travel on such a ship—he had no remote knowledge what their lives were like on the ship. It was all theoretical, all primer-school study, all imagination. Atevi occasionally had a very reckless curiosity. But he didn't think that curiosity was all that motivated Jase Graham and his associate: humanly speaking, he couldn't see it, and he couldn't find it in himself to believe someone sounding so disarmingly— friendly. For no reason. No—

—reason such as he had to trust the tea he was drinking. Because the woman who served it had *man'chi* to Damiri ... he was relatively sure; and Damiri had, toward Tabini, whatever atevi felt for a lover ... he was relatively sure. Above all else ...

He supposed the ship folk had their own set of

relatively-sures, and were prepared to risk his on his say-so. That that was the case . . . he was less sure; but it was the best bet, the only bet that led to a tolerable future.

It was just daybreak, and he was sitting in the absent lady's office. He shot his dataload up to the ship. Another war of dictionaries.

Of grammar texts and protocols.

He started, then, to phone down to Hanks, and stopped himself in time, remembering the hour was still god-awful, and Hanks would justifiably kill him.

Doubtless Ilisidi was at breakfast, on her balcony be-low his. She might accept a visitor at this hour. He almost wished he were there. But Ilisidi's was a company too chancy for a man grown suddenly human and vulnerable this morning. He wished for bright sunlight, for the atevi world to take shape around him and make his existence rational again. He couldn't afford the impulses that were running through him now, things like instinctual trust, ir-rational belief in someone on a set of signals that touched something at a level he no longer trusted existed. Not re-ally. It was safe to believe in some other business.

But not in international politics. Not when there were people, human and atevi, who were very, very good at be-ing credible, whose whole stock-in-trade was sounding so straightforward you couldn't doubt. He wished to hell Jase Graham had affected him otherwise. But the man scared hell out of him—scared him *for* Jase Graham, if he could believe the man, and scared him how ready he was to jump to those instincts, inside. If it was real, he hadn't time to give to another set of human relationships than the ones he had, flawed as they were, and it wasn't fair of fate to hand him a human being he could learn to like, that could waken instincts he couldn't otherwise trust, that could divert his attention from a very vital job—

Ironically—it was something like atevi described, that damned flocking instinct, that biological something that intervened in the machimi plays, and diverted some poor damned fool from the *man'chi* he'd thought he had to the *man'chi* he really had, and the poor damned fool in ques-tion stood center stage and agonized over the shattering of his mistaken life and mistaken relationships—before he went on to wreak havoc on everything and everyone that remotely seemed to matter to him.

A human watched the plays, trying to puzzle out that moment of impact. A human studied all the clues and knew there was something there.

A human might have finally found it on his own doorstep, in this unformed dawn, this gray, slow-arriving day, shot through with lightning flashes.

One could see the Bergid, now. One could see the earliest lights in the misting rain.

He hadn't premeditated the invitation to informality, but he'd felt comfortable with Jase Graham, even—

Even knowing now that dawn and sanity were arriving, that he had a daunting task in the man—someone who might—what? Trail years behind him in fluency, have a different cultural bias, a constant matter of explaining, defining, reexplaining, a lifetime of study crammed into— what, a handful of years, after which the ship left and another human link went away, left, went dead.

They might not even get here if the pod failed. The thought upset his stomach, unsettled him at some basic level he wasn't accessing with understanding. It was beyond self-pity this morning, it was all the way to stark terror: he was feeling lonely and cut off from humanity, and that—say it—*friendly*—voice had shaken his preconceptions, gotten through his defenses. He ought to know better. You wanted something and it never, ever quite—

Matched up to expectations? Hell, he wasn't the first human in the world to marry a job, break off a human relationship. He talked to a human being he marginally responded to and all of a sudden his brain was scrambled and he was facing that parachute drop along with Jase Graham as if he had his own life riding on that chute opening.

All those forbidden things he'd disciplined himself to write off, except Barb, who'd turned out as temporary as he'd planned at the start of their association, and he couldn't fault that in Barb. He was the one who'd gotten too close, broken the rules, come to the end of what he shouldn't have relied on lasting in the first place.

And he was damned close to another dangerous precipice, an expectation of some outcome for what he did. Write that off double-fast: it didn't happen, any more than for the paidhiin before him, that he'd ever look back at the accomplishments of a lifetime and say, We won; let alone, It's all solved. It wasn't that kind of a job: it didn't just happen in one paidhi's lifetime. Atevi in space, humans returned to the station, the whole bispecies world enabled to break down the cultural and psychological barriers and live and work together in some utopian paradise of understanding—

That was the God complex they warned you about when you embarked on the program and reminded you of it anytime you grew extravagant in your proposals to the committee. They showed you the pictures of the dead and the wounded in the war and they told you that was where too much progress too fast led you, right down the fabled primrose path to the kind of damage atevi and humans could do each other now that atevi and humans had much more advanced weapons—not only because certain ideas could be dangerous, but because change had to reverberate slowly through atevi society, and that it wasn't wise to add another set of vibrations before the first set had dissipated down to harmlessness, or one risked an untoward combination of effects that humans just weren't able to foresee.

Damned sure it wasn't the moment to lose his head and start expecting things were going to work. It was his job constantly to anticipate the worst, and to expect the parachute wasn't going to open. Most of all, *baji-naji,* the demon in the design: never expect common sense on both sides of the strait at the same time.

He walked out of the office and toward the breakfast room, as servants, some doubtless nursing hangovers, paid rapid bows and hurried off to that communications network they had that assured him if he sat down at the table his breakfast would turn up very soon.

He opened the glass doors onto the balcony and enjoyed the cool, damp wind. He had to brief Tabini, he ought to brief Hanks, he ought to brief Mospheira if he could get a call through to the Foreign Office.

God knew—he really ought to call the presidential staff and explain to George. Take a couple of antacids and see if he could work up the stomach to talk directly to the head of staff on the phone—assuming that Mospheira let the phones work this morning, and that the FO could get him patched through.

But he had a Policy Committee meeting before noon. He had a meeting with Tabini to set up. He had an interview upcoming with network news—a request had been waiting for him with the morning tea, and he'd confirmed it: the news service had found out, one assumed, that the paidhiin were holding conferences, that there were answers, that there was, in fact, another Landing imminent. He had a flight out to the Bergid and back staring him in the face.

He ate breakfast while he ran a voice-to-written copy of the tape, one of the mind-saving as well as finger-saving pieces of software he'd cajoled the censors into allowing across the strait. The program wasn't worth using for dictation; he was far more fluent without thinking about it and the damn thing mistook phonemes with no consistency or logic whatsoever, that he could discover: it took more headwork to figure out what word in Mosphei' the thing had distorted than it did to do it in the first place, but on a transcript of a considerable amount of recorded speech it was a help.

Especially if it let the paidhi have breakfast while it ran. And a little fuss with spell-check and a visual once-over let him fix the truly inane conversions that had gotten past the software and send it through the second phase translation, that at least gave him a framework to render into atevi script.

Half an hour's work and he had two sets of copies: of the tape itself, for the Foreign Office, for his records, and for Hanks—*With my compliments,* he sent to Deana, expecting a retaliatory note. And, while he had a line to

Mospheira, with his mother's number: *Drop me a line on the system. I'm worried about you.*

Of the translation—a copy first to Tabini, with: *Aiji-ma, I find the tone and purpose encouraging. I have undertaken to meet their descent and to find a suitable landing site such as serves for the petal sails. I wonder is the plain below Taiben suitable and reasonable, being public land?* To the hasdrawad: *Nadiin, I present you the transcript of my first conversation with the chosen paidhi from the ship. I find him a personable and reasonable man.* And to Ilisidi, with: *One has reason to hope, nand' dowager.*

To his own security, then, via the house security office: *I am encouraged by the tone and content of my initial conversation I have had with this individual. I hope that he and his companion make a safe descent. I look forward to dealing with this gentleman.*

"This seems a judgment of feeling," Tabini observed, when they had a chance, over lunch, to talk in Tabini's apartment. "Not of fact. There is no actual undertaking on their part to perform in any significant regard—and they're dealing with Mospheira. One would think they mean to bargain down to the last moment."

Right to the soft spot. Count on Tabini.

"I've tried very analytically to abstract emotion from my judgment," Bren said. "I agree that there's a hazard in my interpretation: I'm apprehensive of my own instinctive reactions to the man I talked to, aiji-ma, and I'm trying to be extraordinarily cautious at each step. I do judge that these are brave people, which makes them valuable to their captain, there's that about them: among humans, their willingness to take risk means either the risk is small, they're sensation-seeking fools—neither of which I think is the case—or they're people with an extraordinary sense of duty above self-interest."

"This *man'chi*-like 'duty.' To whom?"

"That's always the question, aiji-ma. They're very plain-spoken, very forthcoming with their worries about the descent, their worries about being stranded down here. They asked straightforward questions . . . well, you'll see when you read the transcript. We discussed landing sites. I did warn them very plainly they should land here rather than Mospheira, and that it was a matter of protocol. I hope I was convincing."

"This choice of Taiben," Tabini said. It was a private lunch, only Eidi to serve them, while Tano waited outside with Tabini's other security. The violence of the morning storms had passed and the daylight was, however gray, far stronger beyond the white gauze of the curtains. "Taiben—is an interesting idea. Among other sites with other advantages. Let's see what the ship people think important. Speed of transport—Taiben certainly has. And with public lands, there's no clearance to obtain."

"The south range is flat," Bren said. "And unwooded. It's a very dangerous thing they're attempting. I've serious doubts they understand this technology very well. There's a knack to stone axes, so I'm told, that makes it no sure thing for moderns to do."

"Why, do you think, they've no better choice?" Tabini asked. "Are these not the lords of technology? The explorers of the bounds of the universe?"

"I find it—though it's only a guess, aiji-ma—very logical that they have no means to go down into an atmosphere. Our ancestors left their home planet to build a station in space, not to land on a world. They certainly had no craft adequate when our ancestors wanted to come down here. The station folk refused to build one then: if they had, all of history would be different. And if the Pilots' Guild had been willing to fly the craft, those who did land might have built better. The landing capsules, the petal sails, were the only alternative my ancestors had, then—and it's ironic that they're all that exist now."

"All this vast knowledge," Tabini said, "and they fling themselves into the world like wi'itkitiin off the cliffs."

"Without even the ability to glide." A thought came to him. "I halfway suspect they don't know how to fly in air. It surely takes different skills. They wouldn't be trained for it. Flaps and rudder. They don't work in space."

"Meaning these lords of the universe can't land? They

only exist in space, where you say is no air, no breath at all? They've forgotten how to fly?"

"In storms like this? There aren't any in space, aiji-ma. Other things, other dangers, I'm sure—but weather and air currents have to be very different for them."

"Which means all the pilots that *can* navigate the air— are Mospheiran humans and atevi."

"Meaning that, yes, I would suspect so."

One saw the estimation of advantage dawning in Tabini's eyes. Thought, and plan.

"There is, then," Tabini said, "—if one builds this go-and-return craft you talk about—a point at which it is actually an airplane, dependent on air and winds."

"Yes, aiji-ma."

"I *like* this notion, nand' paidhi."

Nobody put anything over on Tabini. And one had to count on Tabini understanding exactly where his advantage was.

They talked also about the office expenses. Tano had sent a proposed budget, and Tabini passed it off with, "Household expense. Doesn't the Treaty say we would bear such expenses?"

Household expenses. A member of the tashrid had that kind of staff. A lord of a province. The paidhi was embarrassed—literally—and said, "Thank you, aiji-ma," very quietly, mentioning no more of it.

Tano, meeting him at the door, simply said, "One thought so. The elderly retired gentleman will be very pleased. He's of my clan."

"Ah," Bren said. On Mospheira one called it nepotism. On the mainland, one was simply relieved one understood where *man'chi* lay, definitively and absolutely. *No* elderly retired gentleman would disgrace even a junior member of the Guild. "What is he retired *from*, actually, Tano-ji?"

"He was Senior Director of External Communications for the Commission on Public Lands, and very skilled at politics," Tano said. "The commission has very many serious disputes and inquiries."

"That seems appropriate," he said. "I'm very grateful,

Tano. I'll meet with the people as soon as they've set up the office. Please tell them so. Does one send flowers?"

"It's not strictly required, but a felicitous arrangement and good wishes from the paidhi, also ribbons, if there were time—"

"Can we do it now? Before the press conference?"

"One could. I could find the ribbons. I could work the seal, nadi Bren."

One-handed sealing was a problem. But atevi set great store by cards, ribboned with the colors of office or rank, and stamped with official seals, as keepsakes, mementos of service or meeting.

"We should have them for all the staff, too," he decided. "Those that have served as well as those that will."

"That's a good thought," Tano said.

"I wouldn't offend the security staff if I gave them ribbons?"

Tano looked actually shy, at the moment. "One would treasure such a gift, nand' paidhi."

"You saved my life, Tano-ji. If ribbons would please you—by all means. Or anything else I can do."

"Nand' paidhi," Tano said, and caught-step and bowed as they walked the hall. "If *you* give a ribbon, my father will believe I've achieved distinction. Give me one for me to give to him, paidhi-ji, and I'll hear no more of being an engineer."

Such gestures counted. He'd never thought of doing it for the staff, and wished he had. He had a list, by now, of people he should send cards to. Everyone on staff at Malguri. Certainly every man and woman who'd risked his life for the paidhi's.

That had grown, he realized with some dismay, to a very long list.

14

The reporters had notepads full of questions: having found a chance to have the paidhi-aiji alone to themselves in a room, they'd naturally come armed with very specific and sometimes unanswerable questions, such as, Where does the ship come from, nand' paidhi? And: What does the ship want, nand' paidhi?

The first of which he couldn't answer, and didn't dare try to surmise: he didn't want to touch the topic of stars and suns; he segued desperately to the second question, which he could answer honestly enough on a level anyone not on the ship could possibly know: "Nadiin, by all it's said so far, the ship folk want the station restored to operation. They expected to find things the way they left them. And of course nothing's the same, not even the station they expected to be waiting for them. They're puzzled, and they're trying to find out what's happened to the world since they left."

He didn't mention the ship's desire to get a fair number of workers from the planet up to orbit, and left that to the reporters to ask if they thought of it. But one reporter asked how he viewed the Association's economic outlook, and what the impact was on relations with Mospheira.

To which he answered, "Nadiin, the Treaty was never more important to us or to Mospheira than it is now. Experience shows us how we can moderate the effects of change: history tells us that atevi will, in the long run, profit from this event, and the ones willing to research their investments thoroughly—I stress 'thoroughly'—should fare very well in industry. Space science is not a new proposition in Shejidan. Many companies already have important positions in space-age manufacturing, communications, and commerce.

"I also have a message for all the thousands of children who've written to the paidhi, asking if the machines will come down again or if the station will come down and shoot at people. And the answer is, No, the machines won't come down. No one will shoot at anyone. Tabini-aiji and the ship captain and the President of Mospheira are all talking by radio about how to fix the space station so that people can live there again—as I hope some of you may live there when you're grown. I've talked to a man on the ship who'll come down very soon to live in the Bu-javid, and be paidhi for the ship and the atevi. He's a young man, he's quite pleasant and polite, and he wishes to help atevi and humans to build a ship that will fly back and forth between the station, something like an ordinary airplane. You may see this ship-paidhi soon on television. He's been a teacher, just like your teachers in school, and he's coming to learn about atevi so he can tell his people about you.

"Ask your parents and your teachers about living in space, and what you'd do if you lived there and looked at the world every day from much higher up than an airplane flies. I may not be able to answer each and every letter you send to me, but I do thank you for writing and asking, nadiin-sai, thank you very much for your good questions."

He drew a deep breath. And thought—God help us. Where do you start with the kids? What are they seeing but invasions and battles on television?

He said to the reporters, "Nadiin, please urge your station managers to think carefully what the children see on television, at least until the news is better. The paidhi asks this, on his own advice, no other."

"Bren-paidhi, what *is* this news about another paidhi?"

"Two, actually, a man who'll come to Shejidan and a woman who'll go to Mospheira, each invited, each anxious and willing to assure a good relationship with the planet. Our talk was, as I've said to the children, pleasant, informative, and dwelt on the good of both humans and atevi. They've no other way at the moment to descend to the planet but to use the petal-sails our ancestors used. Only two such craft remain, and they'll use one for the two of them to come down—as early as five days from now. It's very dangerous, to my thinking, but perhaps ship folk believe they can moderate the dangers."

"Paidhi-ji, where will they come down?"

"That's under discussion. But they will land by official invitation, and I stress that only two people are landing, in a very fragile and navigationally helpless craft, and they'll be here at the aiji's request, observing all appropriate courtesy and respect of property and authority. That's all I can tell you at the moment. Thank you for your questions, and please request another conference if you see that anything varies from what I've told you. I will hold a formal news conference as soon as I've met with these people, which I hope to do soon. Thank you."

"Paidhi-ma," one said, and several bowed as he concluded the conference, as they would for a person of rank and substance, which the paidhi didn't quite expect—so he thought he'd at least made the necessary point, and maybe satisfied the questions, and maybe calmed some fears. He didn't know. But he returned the courtesies, and felt he'd escaped at least for a little while.

He'd dodged around the one first question, the one that was a disaster waiting to happen—thank God no one had asked, specifically, How far did they come?

But someone eventually would ask, besides lord Geigi. And since even atevi children worked sums in their heads very, very rapidly, once they had asked, as the average person didn't ask, yet—not having much grasp of a larger universe—there was no stopping them.

Not once the average atevi knew that the numbers of that wider universe were impacting their lives. Wait till the number-counters got their hands on those figures.

He was still signing cards, late, still stamping and sealing, after a supper attended only by the servants, until he'd reached those for staff, the staff solemnly coming by fives to receive his formal thanks.

Which seemed appropriate for the evening of a day— after which, he said to himself, he'd be so engaged in meetings and preparations he wouldn't have time to draw breath. He wanted to acknowledge the staff.

He'd gotten a note from Hanks, which said, *Message received. I've sent data to Mospheira and trust the phones will remain available at least from this side.*

He received one from the elderly gentleman of Tano's clan, which said, *You have prolonged my life as well as my livelihood, nand' paidhi. I hope at all times to render satisfactory service.*

One from Ilisidi, saying: *The flowers are delightful, but nothing replaces the sight of a young man in my apartment in the morning.*

One—he hoped might be a telegram from his mother. But it was another one from Barb, saying, *Bren, please call. I have a new number. It's 1-6980-29-82.*

He sat through another cup of tea, signing the very last cards, affixing ribbons and seal with the help of a pleasant older servant, a woman to whom he had already given a card, for her help with the messages.

He sat, he signed, he stamped, while Lamiji, which was the woman's name, held the card steady for his one-handed effort; and he delivered the last few thank-you's to junior staff, who expressed themselves as very, very pleased.

It was good, it was more than pleasant, to deliver gratitude to honest people who well deserved it.

He had replied to the dowager with, *Please accept my intentions to attend breakfast on the 15th, to which I look forward as the reward of a long work schedule. I would be there every day, but my days break with phone calls and emergencies. I reserve the 15th with determination not to be cheated again of the pleasure I find in your company.*

"Is it too forward?" he asked Tano, his arbiter of protocols. "Tell Cenedi to read it and send it back if it won't be well-received. One doesn't know how far I dare go with the dowager. But I esteem her greatly."

And back came the message from Ilisidi herself, saying, *If we were more reckless we would cause rumors, nand' paidhi. Come early on the fifteenth. Watch the dawn with me. Let us worry the nosy old woman of the balcony next. I know she suspects the worst.*

One could truly adore the old reprobate.

But in the world not of an atevi lord's whimsy, one had to deal with a mother who didn't answer the phone, didn't answer telegrams, didn't answer messages on the island-wide system, and hadn't been in communication with Toby since his message.

Or if she had, Toby hadn't seen fit to call through. And he generally expected better of Toby.

He went back to the lady Damiri's office and put through a call to his mother's number, which, as he expected, got the same recording.

Then he called the personal-emergency after-hours number at the State Department, which raised a junior assistant, whose answer to his query about threats against his family, specifically against his mother, was, "I really don't know, sir. I don't think I've heard of any trouble." And: "I don't have an authorization to call the city police, sir. I'll give you their number." With the sound of rustling paper.

"I have their number. Put me through to the National Security Agency." He swore a change in procedures in State if he survived long enough in his job. He listened through the clicks and thumps as the call transferred to the agency and got another nighttime junior assistant officer.

"This is an emergency number," that one started off.

"I'm aware it's an emergency number. This is Shejidan calling. This is a senior State Department officer who's advising you of a security problem."

"What's your name again, sir?"

"Bren Cameron. In Shejidan." His tone was more patient, the madder he got. "This is the paidhi. I want you to call a senior officer. I want you to check—"

"Just a second, sir. I need a report form. Is this a complaint or a—"

He was a diplomat. He understood forms and reports. He wasn't in the habit of slamming the phone down on confused juniors.

"Mister—what is your name?"

"Jim."

"Well, Jim, I want you to get me Sonja Podesty. Now."

"Ms. Podesty's at home, sir."

"I know Ms. Podesty's at home. I want to ring Ms. Podesty right now, and put me through. If I lose you off the phone, I want you to file a report of threatening anonymous calls against my family, namely my mother, possibly my brother, possibly Ms. Barbara Letterman and Mr. Paul Saarinson."

"Would you spell Saarinson, sir?"

"Approximate it. Just ring Podesty."

"Yes, sir." There was a period of ringing. And ringing. And Podesty's answering system. He repeated the names, the message, and lost the NSA off the line.

He thought in fact of calling the civil police, which would get another agency involved in what didn't need publicity. He'd already stretched the point. He wasn't sure threats existed. He wasn't sure about anything he surmised, but it didn't cure the worry.

He called Toby, up on the North Shore, and Toby's message service said he was unavailable. The phone was making that sputtering sound that said there were real, not political, interruptions possible, and that the phones, installed early and not the most modern of Shejidan's modern conveniences, might go down at least temporarily due to weather.

The paidhi on his schedule of meetings, interviews and briefings wasn't having damned much luck making calls to relatives and official agencies at hours when people were in or officials who could do anything were doing business at all. Mospheira's usual emergencies were drunken college students. Its criminals were mostly pilferers, card fraud and divorce cases; its lunatic bigots were legislators and department chairmen who generally kept their rank and file in line.

Except the occasional quiet sort who did try to bomb some legislator's garage with garden chemicals. With moderate, even dangerous success.

He had official numbers left to call. There was one private number for someone who really ought to know what was going on, who at least could take the bus across town and find out for him—if he really, really wanted someone to do something reliably, and wanted to pay the price of such information.

He gave the operator the number. And waited through the relays. And the rings. Six of them.

"Hello?" Barb said, then; and his heart, unreliably informed that things were different, did a rise and crash.

"Hello, Barb. How are you doing? Congratulations."

"Bren, I'm so glad you called. I hope you're not mad at me."

"No. . . ." Maybe it wasn't the most flattering, most truthful thing he could say. "Paul's a nice fellow. I'm glad you're happy. Sorry I missed the wedding. Congratulations."

"Bren, I—really want to talk. I mean, I just couldn't, we never could talk."

"Yes, well, I know that. Nature of the job, Barb, I never made it out to be anything different than it is."

"Bren—Bren, it's not, I mean, Bren, I don't know, I'm not sure, I'm just not sure anymore."

"Well, it's kind of too late for that, isn't it?"

"I want us to get together, I mean, when you get back. Bren, I just need to think. There're so many things I have to deal with."

"There's no use in talking about it, Barb. There's no 'get back.' There's no dealing with it. The ship doesn't make it any different. It won't be. You made your decision." The bitterness was there, unwished, uncalled-for, and he bit it off, fast. "Which isn't why I called, Barb. I'm not getting anything from Mother. I wondered if you might possibly have been in contact with her."

There was a longer silence than he expected, one of

Barb's mannerisms when she wasn't happy. Then, pure Barb, blithe and light: *"Oh, well, I called her a couple of days ago. She was fine."*

"Could you get through?"

"Yes . . ."

"Toby said she was getting weird calls. I get a phone service recording. I hate to ask this. I know I'm imposing. But would you mind calling her tonight, and if you can't get her, would you just take the bus over and check on her?"

Another prolonged silence. *"I suppose."*

"Barb, level with me. I'm working blind from here. I can't get calls through. Is there any trouble?"

And a third of those small silences. Those silences he knew he was supposed to read, to react to, and then beg her to tell him what was the matter. And dammit, he'd just asked her. He let the silence go on and on, beginning to see it in a different light than he ever had, resenting it more by the second.

"What do you expect there is?" Barb said, then, sharply: phase two, the emotional attack. *"You can do anything you want over there, you can go there where you don't have to have the people who confront you in the grocery store, or stand outside your apartment and ring up on the phones and leave you messages on the system because we're in the public directory and they can't get calls to you."*

"Has that been happening?"

"Yes, it happens," Barb said. He could hear the anger, the accusatory tone. *"It happens, it's always happened. And I'm scared, Bren, I'm really scared."*

"It happens to me, Barb, it happens. I get my mail. I get phone calls when I'm home. What's different?"

"You're over there speaking to the legislature and talking to the ship, and we're here taking calls from people who blame us because we're the only people they can get to, and they're getting scary, Bren. There's this guy that calls me at work, and I changed my home number, but I can't change my work number. There are a lot of people who are real scared, and real mad, and they think you're

*going to betray them, Bren, they don't understand what
you're doing."*

"Betray them." God, how much did Mospheira know?
"What's this, 'Betray them'?"

*"The ship always favored the atevi, they always had
this protect-the-planet argument when we wanted to land,
and now they can deal with the atevi to get what they
want and not even have to deal with us."*

"That's crazy."

"That's what they're saying, Bren."

"Well, screw what they're saying. —Who's saying?
What kind of nonsense is that?"

*"It's people they interview on the news, it's Bruno
Previn, it's—"*

"Bruno Previn, for God's sake, what channel are you
listening to?"

"He's on the regular news, now."

"He's a crackpot."

*"They keep interviewing him. He has an opinion.
Bruno Previn, Dorothy Durer-Dakan, S. Brandt-Topes—"*

One had the idea. "Gaylord Hanks?"

*"He's been on. He's demanding an investigation of why
you were sent back when they threatened his daughter
and why she's not back."*

"Will you call him for me and tell him the family
should have gotten a call from Deana today, and if not,
still, don't worry. She's fine. I had lunch with her and
she's *still* his daughter."

"Bren, I—don't like this."

"Have you talked to my mother?"

"Damn your mother! Bren, listen to me—"

"Have you talked to her, dammit."

*"Not directly, no, but you can call the building man-
ager. That's how I found out what's going on."*

It was one route he hadn't thought of. "Have you got
the building manager's number?"

"Just a second. —It's 1-6587-38-48."

He was writing with the phone stuffed between the cast
and his cheek, and trying to make legible numbers.
"Thanks, Barb."

"Yeah."

"Barb, I hope you're happy, I really do."

"Bren, I—still want to talk to you. I want to see you when you come back. I want—I don't know."

"I don't think so. I don't think so, Barb."

"I think I made a mistake. I think I made a terrible mistake."

"Barb—I'm not coming there. You understand? It's not going back to what we had. It can't. It's not your doing, it's not mine, it's nothing we can fix. The world's changed and Mospheira's changed. Just—that's the way it is."

"I don't think I love him."

"You should have thought of that beforehand. I can't help you. I can't *be* your answer, Barb, I'm sorry. I don't know I can ever be your answer. I never promised to be."

"Dammit, Bren!"

"I know, Barb, I know, but I can't do any more than I've done. It's not my fault, it's not yours, it just is, that's all."

She didn't answer. He didn't find anything else to say. He finally added:

"Barb, I'm sorry. I wish it was better. I wish it could be. But it's not my damn responsibility, Barb. *I* can't fix things for you, I never could. You knew that was the way it would be. And you *married* the man, Barb, be fair to him."

A small silence. Again. *"The hell,"* she said. At least that was the Barb he knew. At least she took care of herself.

Always depend on that. Self-sufficiency—that had been an asset in Barb—took a bent toward self-protection. Against him.

"Good night, Barb."

"Good night," she said. Then: *"Bren, I'll look in on your mother. I'll take the bus. All right?"*

"Thanks, Barb."

He hung up. There was a lonely feeling in the small office, as if somebody who'd been there with him had gone away. Stupid feeling. But he felt drained by the effort, listless as if he'd landed on some foreign beach, no features around him, no landmarks, nothing that said, This way, Bren.

Nothing he'd care to explore.

The thunder rumbled, a constant complaint above the rooftops, and he walked out of the office and ordered the inevitable within-hail servant that the paidhi wanted—

Not tea. A drink. Which the servant hastened to obtain for him, *shibei,* dark and bitter, but safe for him. The servant—her name was Caminidi: he was learning them, one by one, and made a point of asking—was one of the number usually in the offices area, the ones who made spent teapots vanish and whisked wafer crumbs off the tables, as happened when a man blinked. Like the magic castle of fairy tales, it was. Things just were. Things just appeared and vanished. There were doors and halls a little less ornate than the ones the residents used, ways by which the likes of Caminidi arrived in one place and transited to another—but the guest didn't use them, no, hardly proper.

Atevi manners. Atevi ways. Atevi didn't go at you on an emotional pitch. Not—without expecting consequences.

He walked, drink in hand, to the more pleasant venue of the breakfast room—a servant appeared out of nowhere and started to put on the lights, but, deprived of a spare hand to signal, he said, "No, nadi, one enjoys the storm tonight."

He had work to do. He was scheduled to fly tomorrow—ordinarily, he'd pack, but it was a day trip, out and back. He ought to read the Industry Committee report, answering his query about companies currently manufacturing components on a long list he'd bet Jase Graham was going to ask about earliest.

One didn't want to tool up and train workers for a one-shot with no follow-up. It wasn't going to be that, if the paidhi had his way. Their strangers from space weren't going to get a gold-plated vehicle to leap from ground to starflight with beverage and dinner service even if they had one in their plans. They were going to get a reliable, no-frills creature well-integrated into the atevi economy. A workhorse. Lift cargo, lift passengers, and bring it back again with no extravagance of industrial development. If it took space-made exotics, make damn certain that atevi were up there on the station doing the manufacture: no dependencies, no humans at the top of the technological food chain and atevi at the bottom.

Not in this paidhi's administration.

He only wished he had a better background in engineering. He had to cultivate both atevi and humans who did have, and ask the right questions and get honest answers from people with nothing to gain politically, provincially, or parochially.

Meaning people who knew real things about real substances.

Meaning a lot more plane flights, now that the barriers seemed down and the paidhi had, for the first time in history, permission to move around the map instead of sit receiving information in Shejidan, behind the walls of the Bu-javid.

It didn't bid to be a life that would let him go back to Mospheira that often. If he wasn't in Shejidan, he might need to be God knew where, looking at plant output figures and talking to plant managers and line workers.

He'd told Barb, dammit, he'd told her from the outset she couldn't make plans around his comings and goings; and now she expected him to fly in, run around with another man's wife, and flit out again while Barb went back to her suburbs and her husband—if Barb thought it was going to be sequins and satin and nightclubs every few months, if Barb had married dull, computer-fixed Paul, as the high-income guy who'd be so immersed in his little world he just wouldn't notice, or care—

No way in hell, Barb.

The upset came back. Anger crept up on him before he knew what he was feeling, and then decided it wasn't fair to feel it. Barb had given him years of waiting around— he'd not cared—well, not asked—who else she spent her time with; it hadn't been his business. And maybe it had been Paul, but he didn't think so. Maybe he ought rationally to ask, at this point, how long that had been going on.

But he sure as hell wasn't going to drop into town, sleep with Paul's wife, and leave again. Even if there weren't kids involved, there might be, someday; at very least it left Paul having to deal with the gossip, no illusions that people wouldn't find out or that Paul wouldn't, and Paul was a wounded sort, the way a human being got to be from too much intellect and not a soul to talk to on any regular basis—

God, didn't that sound familiar?

But he, thank God, wasn't Paul. Yet.

Maybe he didn't remotely want a real life with Barb. He wasn't sure, wasn't likely to find out—though he was missing the *idea* of Barb enough to have a lump in his throat and evidently a lot—a *lot*—of anger; she'd told him at the outset that marriage and the settled life weren't ever going to be an issue for her, and if that had changed, dammit, the least she could have done was tell him.

Which left him running curious comparisons with what he thought human beings were supposed to feel about a breakup, and the cooler, more analytical emotions he felt when he wasn't actually on the phone with Barb.

Odd how the feelings had just *been* there, on the edge of out-of-control, as long as he was talking to her— emotion had gotten in the way of any sane communication; now that he'd had a moment to calm down, the atevi world closed in again, the sights, the smells, the sounds of his alternate reality. Barb's world grew fainter and farther again, safely fainter and farther.

He supposed part of it was that he'd made an investment in Barb, an investment of energy, and time—and youth. And innocence, in a way. In Malguri, a short week ago, when he'd found himself afraid he'd die, he'd found himself at such a remove from humanity he couldn't reach any regret for the human people he'd leave—

And he couldn't gather it up now. Then it had scared him. Now—now maybe his real fear was not having the free years left to connect with someone else, with all that investment, with no more sense of love, whatever that meant—he wasn't sure, on this interface of atevi and humans, what normal humans felt, who didn't have to analyze what they felt, thought, wanted, did and didn't do. But he did. He had to. He'd become a damn walking laboratory of emotions.

And maybe if you preserved it in acrylic and set it on a shelf, love didn't look quite as colorful or lively or attractive as it did flitting across mountain meadows. Maybe you killed it trying to understand it, attribute it, classify it.

Hell of a way human beings functioned. At least the ones he knew. His mother. Barb. Toby. One could say the paidhiin had generally had trouble with their personal lives. Wilson, God knew, had been a dried-up, tuned-out, turned-off personality, monofocused in his last years on the job. As good as dead when *his* aiji died. Say good morning to the man and the face didn't react, the eyes didn't react. Not just atevi-like. Dead.

So what did you do when the human part of your life started atrophying from want of exercise? Hello, Mother, hello, Toby, sorry about the phone calls, sorry you can't go to the store without the chance of being accosted, sorry about all of that, nothing I can do from here—don't know what it's like to go to the store, buy a loaf of bread, catch the bus to the office. Can't imagine taking kids to school, family bike rides, family vacations.

Wish that Mother would move to the North Shore, to a far smaller, less political environment. But one never got Mother these days to do a damned thing she hadn't done before, and Toby'd moved up there, one suspected, to put a little distance between mom and wife.

The wind shifted, that had been carrying a spatter of rain against the glass. He stood in the dark with his drink, in the new quiet. Curtains billowed out at him, white gauze in the dark, touched him, all but wrapped around him.

Childhood memory. Himself in the living room. The wind from the sea. Mom and Dad in the bedroom. When life was perfect.

He shut the doors, and the draperies deflated.

The air was still. The whole apartment was still, nothing but the soft footsteps of servants—he never needed a thing but that someone was there. Never made a request but that servants hurried to do it. But the silence—the hush about the place tonight oppressed him.

He went back to his room, found his traveling case to put in it what he needed for the run out to the observatory—had servants hovering to see if they could help with that, but he found no need.

It was the first time, the very first time since he'd landed in Shejidan, that he'd had a chance to sit down on the bed and open the medical folder and read it.

"Dammit!" he said. And called, none too moderately, for scissors.

"Nadi?" a servant asked, confused. But he couldn't deal with gentle faces and gentle confusion at the moment.

"Just get me the damn scissors, will you?"

Then he was mad at himself and the world in general, because he'd raised his voice to the servant, and he apologized when she came running back—apologized and worked the point under the thumb-hole in the cast and started working at the layers of bandage.

Gouged his wrist for good and proper.

"Nadi!" Jago said, from the doorway, and clearly meant to stop him; but he didn't mean to be stopped. Didn't want to discuss it. He kept sawing at the bandages, with the blade inserted, his wrist not cut, and with no inclination to give up the angle he'd gotten for Jago's damned well-meaning interference.

But Jago came and caught his hand as the servants hadn't dared do.

And really it ought to be hysterically funny, the misery he'd suffered, when just reading the damn instructions would have set him free—*to protect the fusion during the flight,* the note said, and then *important to maintain good circulation* and *moderate exercise, by flexing and bending and moderate activity.*

Jago tried to take the scissors away, as if she thought

the paidhi had completely lost his mind. And maybe he had; but she didn't apply force enough to disengage his fingers and he couldn't half breathe, and didn't want to explain. The constriction around his ribs afflicted him with temperous, claustrophobic frustration—the paidhi wasn't damned well in possession of his faculties, he wasn't damned logical, he wasn't handling the interface well at all at the moment, and he didn't want Jago's damned reasonable calm trying to tell him wait and consult anybody.

"I know what I'm doing," was all he could get out. "I know what I'm doing, dammit, Jago."

"Is there pain, Bren-ji?"

Damned right there was pain. Every breath he drew. Every move he'd made for days. The tape was cutting in, the shoulder had a fixed angle he'd not been able to relieve in days, and the damned Department shoved him overseas with painkillers too strong to take and a briefing from some damn Department-worshiping fool who hadn't told him to read the damn instructions—

He wasn't winning in his struggle with Jago. He wasn't losing either, Jago risking her fingers, his effort getting nowhere, and Jago, unstoppable in her level-headed, insistent sanity, didn't let go.

"It's supposed to come off," he found the coherency to say.

"That's very good, Bren-ji, but perhaps a doctor should do it."

"I don't need a doctor. I'm supposed to have taken the damn thing off, Jago, I don't want a doctor."

"Are you quite sure, nadi?"

"I'm not stupid, Jago." Which all evidence around him seemed to deny.

"One knows that, Bren-ji, but why now—"

"I just read the damn instructions. In the case. It's all right. It's all *right,* Jago, let me alone to be a fool, all right?"

"You might cut yourself."

"I can handle a damn pair of scissors." He was aware of servants watching from the door and began to be mortally embarrassed. "Just leave me alone, all right, I won't cut myself."

Jago looked in that direction, too. "It's all right, nadiin. I'll manage. Please shut the door."

They might doubt the paidhi was going to be reasonable at all. But they shut the door, then, the first time he'd been that isolated since he'd arrived in Shejidan. It was just him and Jago and the scissors, which was not, at least, a crowd.

"Let me," Jago said, and when he resisted: "Bren-ji, let me. I'll cut it. Just sit still. —You're quite sure."

"I'm quite sure. Jago, dammit, it's all right. I can read!"

"One believes so, nand' paidhi. Please. Sit still. Let me have the scissors."

Small scissors, in Jago's hand. He'd gouged his wrist enough to sting. She set a knee on the bed and worked around where she could get a good, straight cut up the back of his hand, little snips that sliced the bindings of the foam cast as far as the forearm.

"Say if I go too deep," she advised him, and then, "Bren-ji, the shirt must go."

It had to. He unfastened it and Jago laid the scissors on the bedside table and helped him take it off.

"The tape around my ribs," he said. That was the truly maddening stricture.

"Let me do this in good order, Bren-ji. Let's be sure." She'd taken from somewhere about her person a small spring-bladed knife he suspected had more lethal purpose, and delicately sliced along the bindings above the foam cast.

"I'm very sorry," he found the sanity to say, very meekly and very quietly.

"It's no difficulty at all. But are you quite sure? If we take this off—"

"I'm quite sure. I was a fool. I didn't read the things they sent me."

"Then we can do that very easily. I believe I can split the cast right up the top. Let's be sure of the shoulder before we worry about the ribs, nadi."

"Quite all right." He held his breaths to small ones, and held still as Jago sliced delicately along the cast surface, starting with the hand, splitting the foam apart between the knife and the grip of her hand.

It gave. She had to resort to the scissors again, to make the final cut of tape and free his hand from the elastic bandage.

Which ached, freed from confinement; and he could see atevi-sized fingerprints gone purple on his wrist, likewise the marks of cord on his skin, still red, when the marks on the other wrist had begun to fade.

Jago reached the bend of the elbow, and slowly gained ground, up to the chafing spot at the shoulder.

Where she hesitated. "Are you quite certain, nadi?"

"I'm certain. I'm more than certain. I want it *off*."

Jago put a finger under the cast at the neck and carefully cracked the last. The arm began to ache, the more widely the cast split, and then truly to hurt, as Jago kept going all the way down to the elbow, and to the wrist, by which point he was struggling to breathe easily and not to let on it hurt the way it did—he wanted no delays, and took firm resolve as Jago cracked the cast as far as it would go without cutting the tape on his ribs.

"Nadi?" Jago said, having—while his vision was other than concentrated—turned up a curious object from inside the cast, a piece of paper wrinkled and curled and sweated and conforming to his arm. "What is this?"

What is this? indeed. He supported his elbow on his knee and snatched the paper, perhaps too rudely, too forbiddingly, from his own devoted security. It was a printed sheet, with the Foreign Office header, and a simple:

*Do what you can do. I'll stand behind it, long as they leave me here. HD's on my back. I'm using all the credit I've got to get you back to the job. Maintain the Treaty at all costs. Codeword emergency call my line is **Trojan 987 865/UY**.*

HD. Hampton Durant. With Shawn's signature. He had an access code.

Jago clearly understood where it was from and that it didn't belong there. His hand was shaking, but it was only confirmation at this point—only backing what he'd already done: he and Shawn had always been on the same wavelength.

"Silly—silly joke," he said. "Staff. My office. Told me. Do what I've already done. Doesn't do any good now." He let it fall. "Get the damn tape, Jago-ji. I'll regard you highly forever if you cut that damn tape off."

He turned, Jago maneuvered, and got the scissors-point under the edge of the tape on his back, snipping carefully. The split foam cast was still holding the arm braced outward, and Bren took larger and larger breaths, as centimeter by several centimeters he felt the tape give way, Jago peeling it and pulling its mild adhesion away from his ribs.

"Pull," he said, knowing it was going to hurt. "Just pull it, dammit."

Jago pulled. With her greater strength.

Which at once pulled the surface of his skin and jerked the support of the cast from under the arm he had propped on his knee, all that kept the arm from falling—that and his own quick grab at his elbow as the whole god-awful arrangement parted. Muscles frozen for days in an uncomfortable attitude and a joint that hadn't flexed since the bone was fused—all moved. Ribs lately broken—expanded on the reflexive intake of breath.

He thought he said something—he wasn't sure what; he curled over sideways on the mattress while he cradled the elbow, with spots in front of his eyes. His mouth tasted of copper.

"Nadi?" Jago asked, clearly afraid something wasn't according to meticulous plan.

"No, no, it's—quite all right, Jago, just—it's not used to moving."

"One still thinks—"

"No!" he said, surly and short-fused—holding on to his arm as tightly as he could, as if he could curl the pain inward, spread it out, get it out of the sensitive spots. "No damn doctor."

He thought Jago went away. He hadn't meant to snarl. He really hadn't. But after a time still curled into a ball, he thought she was there again, and immediately after, felt the cold of some kind of salve on his arm—which might not be the best idea with a recent incision, especially given the poisonous character of local medications, but he was out of moral fiber to protest anything and, hell, it was, in a moment more, killing the ache—he was aware finally of the servants in the room, and of, quite improbably to his way of thinking, being lifted bodily up off his face. Jago let him go and steadied him sitting, and he sat up long enough for the arm to find a new sore angle and for the servants to take down the bedcovers.

At that point he didn't need Jago's suggestion he lie down. He rested on his face, trying not to move the joint, and trying to protect it, while Jago's smooth, strong hand worked salve across the sore spots. It stung on the new skin of recent incisions, but it diminished the pain, and he gave up his whole arm to Jago's ministrations, burrowed his face in the crook of the other arm, and relaxed completely, finally, eyes shut, just—comfortable, out of pain, out of discomfort for the first time in days, and sinking into a dark, dark pit.

After which the lights were down, some covering was on his shoulders, and something heavy was weighing down the mattress edge. Which was Jago, sitting on the floor asleep against the edge of the bed.

"Nadi," he said, and worked about to reach out a hand, but she waked at the mere movement, and lifted her face and made a grimace, rubbing a doubtless stiff neck. "You should have gone to bed," he said.

"One worried, nadi."

He reached out to pat her shoulder, and bumped her cheek with the back of his hand, instead, being not quite on his aim, which Jago didn't mind, which led to a more intimate gesture than he'd intended, and a more intimate return on her part, her hand on his.

"Jago-ji," he said, attempting humor, "you shouldn't. I'd hate to offend Banichi."

"In what?"

Translation interface. He tried to wake, wary of wrong words, and the situation. And while he was being appre-

hensive, and trying, muzzily, to compose a request to go
to sleep that wouldn't sound like a rebuff, Jago's fingers
laced with his, and in his inaction, wound around his
wrist, and wandered up his arm to his back.

After which Jago got up, and sat down on the edge of
the bed, took off the towel that was covering his skin, and
began to work another dose of salve into his back and
down the injured arm, which was enough to make a
weary human's bones melt, and his recently wary brain
all but disengage.

All but—disengage. After the nagging pain subsided, it
waked up enough to remind that Jago's reactions of recent days hadn't been impersonal. And he remembered,
while Jago's hands were sliding very comfortably along
his backbone, that Banichi had joked about Jago's curiosity from the very start.

The fact that the personal relationship between Banichi
and Jago never had been clear to him, and that he was
alone, and that the temptation more than intellectually
dawning in the forebrain—was already settled and willing
in the hind-brain, and beginning to interfere with his capacity to think at all.

"Jago-ji. Please stop." He feared offending her, and he
rolled over and propped himself on his good elbow to
give an impression, a lie, of a man well awake and sensible, but he was facing a looming shadow against the
night-light, that gave human eyes nothing of her
expression—such as she might show in a moment of rebuff. He tried to touch Jago's arm, but the arm he wasn't
leaning on wouldn't lift all the way, and fell, quite pain-
fully. "Jago, nadi, Banichi might come after me."

"No," Jago said, one of those enigmatic little yes-no's
that maddened human instincts. But it was very clear Jago
knew what she was doing.

"I just— Jago—" He was awake. He didn't know what
reality he'd landed in, but he was aware and awake.

"One need say nothing, Bren-ji. No is sufficient."

"No. It's not. It's *not,* Jago."

"It seems simple. Yes. No."

"Jago—if it's curiosity, then go ahead, I've no objection. But—" Breath came with difficulty. Sore ribs. A fog coming over the brain, that said, Why not? "But," the negotiator got to the fore, "but if it's more than that, Jago, then—give me room. Let me understand what you're asking. And what's right."

Jago had sat back on her heels at the bedside, elbow on the mattress. A frown was on her face—not, it seemed, an angry frown, but a puzzled one, a thoughtful one.

"Unfair," Jago declared finally.

"Unfair?"

"Words, words, words!"

"I've offended you."

"No. You ask me damned questions." Jago gained her feet in one fluid motion, a shadow in the night-light as she turned, stiff and proper, and walked to the door, her braid the usual ruler-line down her back.

But she stopped there and looked back at him. "Nand' paidhi."

"Nadi?" He was struck with anxiety at the formality.

"One asks—is there danger from Mospheira?"

"Why do you ask that?"

No immediate answer. Jago was a darkness. A near-silhouette against the hall light as she opened the door to leave.

"Jago? Why? That paper? It advised me only of how to contact my office. Of persons not to trust."

He had only her profile now. Which became full face, a second glance back.

"Is Hanks-paidhi a danger?" Jago asked.

"Always a danger," he said, but added, in fear for Hanks' life: "but not the sort that would require your action, Jago-ji. The abstract sort of danger. Political rivalry."

"That, too," Jago said, "I can remedy, nand' paidhi."

"No." She frightened him. He'd thought Jago had lost her ability to do that. But coupled with Banichi's absence, the suddenly skewed relationship, and the atevi difficulty in interpreting human wishes— "No, Jago."

Silence. But Jago didn't move from the doorway.

Then: "You look very tired lately, Bren-ji. Very tired.

When you read the letter from Barb-daja, your face showed extreme distress."

He thought of denying it. But it was, from Jago, a probing after honesty. A not-quite professional inquiry.

"We have a proverb," he said. "Burning your bridges behind you. I've done some of that—on Mospheira."

"Cutting one's own rope."

Count on it—mayhem and disaster translated amazingly well.

"Did this woman know you'd do what you've done?"

"Who? Hanks?" Rhetorical question.

"Barb-daja."

Blindsided. Jago'd been upset about Barb, he told himself, now, because Jago didn't understand human relationships, human reactions—didn't above all else understand how a loyalty could fracture. Hers couldn't. Hers came inbuilt. Hardwired. Or almost so.

"Barb's still—" There wasn't a word. "Still an associate of mine. The man she's marrying is an associate. They're good people."

Jago remained unconvinced. He saw it in the stiffness of her back. The lack of body language. And he decided it was good that Barb was on the island, and not here.

She looked back at him, a shadow next to the door. He thought—again—Why not? He was half moved to say so.

But common sense ruled the other half. "Jago. I regard you very highly. Don't be angry at me."

"One isn't angry, Bren-paidhi. Good night."

"Jago. Still—maybe."

A second hesitation, this one with a glance back that caught the night-light, and Jago's eyes reflected gold, one of those little differences that sometimes raised the hairs on a human neck. That and the momentary silence—so much more effective than Barb's. "One hears, Bren-ji."

She was out the door, then, and the door shut.

Damn, he thought. Damn, not knowing what he'd done, or whether he'd upset Jago, or, God, what Banichi might already know—or what a foolish human might have missed, or lost—the brain was sending contrary signals, yes and no, and caution, and the shoulder *hurt,* dammit, he'd be sorry if he had—as he was sorry he hadn't.

He rolled over on his face and tucked the freed arm up close, in possession of both arms at least.

Say that for the situation.

15

Tabini had ordered his private plane, for security's sake, and Tano and Algini were the escort, easier, Jago had said, than seeing to his security in the Bu-javid.

That, he found an odd thing to have to say—

But he was more trying to pick up signals from Jago, whether she was upset or angry, and Jago was all business, seeming perfectly fine.

He worried. Which he couldn't afford. He was still worrying as the plane made its takeoff run. Which he doubly couldn't afford, thinking about Banichi, and trying to puzzle out the situation between the two of them, which he still hadn't done—no more than humans in general understood atevi relationships. The machimi, source of hints about politics and loyalties, steered clear of romantic motivations. Or loyalties lacked such motivations. There was a reticence in the machimi, in the other literature, a silence from tasteful and reputable atevi, except that Tabini maintained a liaison with Damiri years before Damiri acknowledged it in public, and marriage as such seemed to wait years and sometimes after the birth of children. Or never happened. He could think of instances. But you *didn't* ask about something atevi looked past and didn't routinely acknowledge as going on—and his talks with Tabini had been more on the moods of established lovers, not on the proprieties of who could be slipping into one's room at night.

He almost was prompted to ask Tano, who would, he thought, talk; but stopped himself short when he realized it wouldn't take Tano two seconds to conclude he wasn't asking an academic question, that it wasn't Deana Hanks, and that the field of serious choice was relatively narrow, not mentioning the household servants who were acceptable liaisons *if* one was willing to take them into one's permanent household, which he wasn't, didn't have, and couldn't—Tano and, he suspected, Algini weren't slow to perceive things. But he didn't want to put Tano or Algini in a situation.

And he wasn't sure Banichi was the politic person to ask. He decided—decided, as the plane leveled out at altitude—that the sane person to ask might be Tabini.

But that could get Jago in trouble, if things weren't on the up and up.

Which left Jago herself, who wouldn't lie to him in a thing like that. It might be an opening, at least, for a reasonable discussion.

It was certainly against Departmental regulations. It was certainly foolish. It was compromising of the paidhi's impartiality. It was—

—just damned stupid. The paidhi was supposed to be free of biases, influences and emotional decisions. And if Deana Hanks got wind of what had happened last night—

So what *had* happened last night, beyond the fact the paidhi and a good atevi friend—

Friend. Which Jago wasn't. Was a lot of atevi things, but she wasn't a friend. If he got into a relationship with her—he wasn't going to be in human territory at all, with all it meant. A damned emotional minefield that was a lot safer if he wasn't attached to the ateva in question in ways that created an interface he couldn't decipher.

Damn the timing. *Damn* the timing.

Jago at least would give him time. Which she'd agreed to do.

Which didn't give him peace of mind when the paidhi needed it, and dammit, he'd thought he had her on the choice he'd offered: now, with no complications; or later, and then—God help him, he'd ended up saying, Maybe.

The paidhi—whose whole damn *career* was knowing when to keep his mouth shut. And he was upset about Barb. But he was more upset about Jago—he had more regard for Jago, though not in that way.

Which might change the second his feet hit Mospheiran soil—a change he'd begun to find happening to him insidiously for years and critically in the last few weeks, this compartmentalization of his life, his feelings, his thinking. God knew what kind of advice he was qualified to give anyone, and what change it would work in him once the capsule chute spread and he had a regular human presence—Hanks didn't count, he said to himself—to deal with on the mainland.

He didn't think it was going to make a difference. And the moment he said that to himself he knew the situation with Graham wasn't predictable. And he didn't know. From moment to moment any change threatened him, and changes were about to become monumental.

He flipped open his computer and began to compose his specific questions, pull up his specific vocabulary, trying to be as sure of what he was going to imply to scholarly people as he could possibly be.

Universe—*basheigi*—was right at the top of the list. Was there a better word for it? One hoped the venerable astronomer had explanations. One hoped the profession had come up with words that could at least be trimmed down in the minds of nonexpert hearers to stand for certain difficult concepts.

He pulled up a hundred fifty-eight words and spent the next forty-eight minutes being sure of his contextual and finely shaded meanings, before the plane entered final approach and seemed to be aiming itself at a very impressive wall of rock.

"One hopes the airport is coming soon," he said, and Tano, in all seriousness, offered to ask the crew, but he told Tano and Algini to sit down—the plane was suffering the buffeting a mountain range tended to make, and in a moment they indeed made the requisite turn, slipping down toward a wooded, remote area that argued public lands.

It was a fair-sized airport, and there was a hunting village, such as one found in the public lands, all inhabitants employed by the Association, all engaged, the paidhi was informed, in the maintenance and care of the Caruija Forest Reserve.

And one didn't expect there to be too much in the way of public transport, but a narrow-gauge railroad waited for them at the airport, a quaint little thing that had to date back almost to the war.

Cheaper, in the mountains, for small communities. One didn't have to blast out a large roadbed, and the little diesel engine didn't have to haul much in either direction—in this case, one wooden-seated car with glass windows and a green roof with red eaves. A spur led from the airport to the village; another spur led somewhere he had no idea; a third led up to the mountain: Saigiadi Observatory, a small sign informed them, as, with a small stop for a railway manager to throw a switch, they were off on their rattling way.

His hand worked. He could bend the elbow. He was still entranced with that freedom. He exercised the wrist and elbow as he got the chance—hadn't put the salve on it this morning because the salve had a medicinal smell. He sat, suffering just a little discomfort, enjoying the noisy ride up the mountain, enjoying the smell of wilderness and trees and open air that got past the diesel that powered the engine: the Ministry of Transportation was trying to replace diesel in all trains, for air quality . . . but electrics wouldn't make *this* grade; he could report that to the minister, with no doubt at all. The train lurched and a vista of empty space hung outside the window.

Then a beige-furred, white-tailed game herd sprinted along the side of the train, keeping pace until it reached a turn. He turned in his seat to watch them left behind.

Pachiikiin, fat and sleek with the summer. He was in a vastly better mood and didn't care if the shoulder ached.

He'd scared Tano and Algini with his sudden reaction to the animals. They tried to settle unobtrusively, but he knew he'd alarmed them—and they'd looked for some agency that might have spooked them, that was the way their minds worked.

"I miss Malguri," he said to them, by way of explanation. He didn't think they justly should miss the place,

Algini in particular, with his bandages—and he had to ask himself what Algini could do, slow-moving as he still was, if there was a security problem.

Safer than the Bu-javid, Jago had said. Which was probably true.

And a thirty-minute ride, during which he saw no few examples of mountain wildlife, brought them within sight of the Saigiadi Observatory dome. A handful of minutes more brought them to a debarkation at the small depot that verged—inelegantly but efficiently—on a storeroom.

Students met them, bowing and offering to carry anything that wanted carrying—excited students, thrilled, as the student leader said, that the paidhi came to dignify their school, and offering a—God help him—small presentation copy of the observatory's work, which he was relieved to see consisted not of a recitation but a written report, a history of the place, with photographs, put together in that scrapbook way that very small businesses used to promote their craft, their wares, their trade.

"Please keep it, nand' paidhi," they wished him, and he was quite touched by the trouble they'd gone to, and vowed to look through it and see—he was moved to such extravagance—if the observatory could not be recipient of some of the first data that they derived from the ship's presence—

Which he was very willing to do if only he could get through the ceremony to talk to the venerable astronomer emeritus, who was, the students assured him, quite brilliant, and very willing to talk to him, but who—it developed after a quarter-hour of close questioning—was asleep at the present moment, and the students didn't want to waken the venerable, who waked when he wanted to wake and who, it developed in still more questioning, this time of the senior astronomer who put herself forward to explain the astronomer emeritus, became irritable and difficult if waked out of a thinking sleep.

"The paidhi has come all the way from Shejidan," Tano objected, which was the thought going through the paidhi's mind, too. But on Banichi's warning that the man was elderly and noncommunicative . . . the paidhi thought it better to be politic.

"When does he usually wake?"

There was embarrassed silence, on the part of the senior astronomer, her staff, and the students.

"We pleaded with him, nand' paidhi. He said he'd thinking to do, he took to his room, and we—can *try* to wake him, if the paidhi wishes."

"Against your advice."

"Against our experience, nand' paidhi. Assuring the paidhi that the emeritus by no means intends a slight."

"He does it in classes," a student said, "nand' paidhi."

One began to get the idea.

"Perhaps," he said moderately, "the faculty and staff could work on my answers."

"We have," the senior said, bowing again.

"For two days," the second senior said.

"You have my questions, then," he asked, and, oh, yes, the senior said, on receipt of them—no regard to any secrecy of the aiji's seal, oh, no—they'd posed them to the whole class and they had every reference looked up with all propitious calculations—so far as they had data.

"But the shape of the universe," the senior said, "that persistently eludes speculation, as the paidhi may know, since the imprecision of measurements taken from the earth, together with its deviations—which are negligible in the scale of the earth, and considerable in such precise measurement as one makes of the stars—"

"Together with atmospheric flutter and distortion," the second senior said, and dug among his papers while the senior diverted herself to maintain she had taken that into account in her sample figures—

The paidhi was getting a headache, and the head of astronomical philosophy, nand' Lagonaidi, was handing him sheets and sheets of arguments on cosmological theory—while Algini and Tano sat quietly by the door and perhaps understood one word in ten.

"Actually," the head of Philosophy broke in to say, "the Determinists have taken the imprecisions of earthly

measurement as a challenge. But all scientists in astronomical measurement are automatically suspect."

"Because of changing measurement."

"Because, among other things, of eccentricities of
position. —Which can be explained, by modern astronomy. . . ."

"Mostly," the senior astronomer interjected.

"But," Philosophy reprised, "where does one possibly
find smooth transition from the finite to the infinite when
the numbers only grow more and more vague? I confess
I find it disturbing—but I have moral confidence that
such a system will evolve. And necessarily along the way
toward such perfection, atevi will quarrel over the
branchings of the path only to discover that some paths
have woven back together in harmony. There will be gaps
in our understanding, not in the order of the universe."

"They have to be perfect numbers," the senior astronomer said. "Numbers to make more than delusory and
misleading sense need to be perfect numbers."

"I assure you they're perfect numbers," Bren said, feeling out of his depth, but fearing to let the conversation
stray further toward the abstract. "Since stars are definitely there, at a distance and a continual progress of positions relative to our own which is quite specific if one
knew it."

"But the wobble in the earth itself—" Philosophy said,
which launched another argument on divine creation versus numerical existentialism that left the paidhi simply
listening and despairing he could gain anything.

Lunch . . . was a formal affair involving the head of
the village in the valley, the local justice, the chairman of
the Caruija Hunt Association, the Caruija Ridge Wildlife
Management and Research Organization, the regional
head of the Caruija Ridge Rail Association, as well as
spouses, cousins, and the legislative representative's husband, the wife being in the hasdrawad, currently in session.

Not to mention the junior poetry champion, who read
an original composition praising the region, followed by

a local group of children who, with drums, sang a slightly out of unison popular ballad.

The paidhi kept shielding his arm from chance encounters and hoping simply to get through the day. His notes were very little more than he'd arrived knowing, held words the exact meaning of which he was still trying to pin down, and he'd escaped to the academic meeting room where he was due for his next session, with Tano and Algini to hold the door against early arrival.

He had aspirin with him. He dared take nothing stronger. He asked Tano for a cup of water from the nearest source, and sat trying to make his elbow and his shoulder work—his intellectual occupation for the moment.

"I think they're quite mad," Algini confided in him. "I think the faculty has been out in the mountains too long."

"They're a small village," Tano said, bringing him the requested cup of water. "And a truly important visitor and the aiji's personal interest is an event."

"We can only hope," Bren said, "for a felicitous outcome. I do begin to ask myself—"

But the staff was arriving in the room, and the session resumed, with a brief address by the senior astronomer and another by the head of Philosophy, the latter of which was at least contributive of a history of the impact of philosophy on astronomical interpretation, and the formation of major schools of thought. A small and respectful contingent of students sat in on the speech at the back of the room, furiously taking notes; the paidhi took his own, writing, and not recording without formal consultation—he wanted, he made a note to himself, to obtain a copy of the speech. Which he thought might please the elderly gentleman.

"Lately," the gentleman said, "the funding for research into astronomy has sadly declined from the magnificent days of the Foreign Star, in which the science of telescopy was funded by every aiji across the continent, particularly among the Ragi. The estimation that humans have far more exact and secret data, nand' paidhi, has made aijiin and the legislatures certain that such will be handed them on some appropriate day and that funding atevi astronomers is superfluous. Which I do not believe, nand' paidhi. We have dedicated ourselves to the proposition that it is not superfluous to study the heavens in our own way. We hope for the paidhi's consideration of our proposal, for the quick release of human observations of the heavens, and human—"

There was a disturbance at the back of the room. Tano and Algini came to sudden alertness where they stood, at either side of the room, and Bren turned his head, ready to fling himself to the floor.

An elderly ateva had wandered in, in a bathrobe, barefoot, hair in disarray. "The answer," he said, "the answer, to the dilemma of the philosophers: the universe does not consist in straight lines, and therefore the path of light is not economical."

"The emeritus," someone said, and the students rose in respect to the old man. Bren rose more slowly.

"Aha!" the emeritus said, pointing a finger. "The paidhi! Yes, nadi! I have the proof—" The emeritus indeed had a sheaf of papers in his fist and brandished them with enthusiasm. "Proof of the conundrum you pose! Elegant! Most elegant! I thank you, nadi! This is the corroboration I've been searching for—I've written it in notation—"

"Tea and wafers," the senior astronomer ordered, and arrived at Bren's elbow to urge, in a hushed tone: "He's quite old. He will *not* remember to eat!"

"By all means," Bren said, and to the elderly gentleman: "Nand' emeritus, I'm anxious to know your opinions—I fear I'm no mathematician, nor an astronomer, merely the translator—but—"

"It's so simple!" the emeritus declared, and descended on him with his sheaf of papers, which he insisted on giving to Bren, and then, with the students and the astronomers crowding around, began to make huge charcoal notes on the standing lectern pad—

The paidhi sat with notepad in hand and copied furiously. So did the senior astronomer, though, thank God, the charcoaled paper simply flipped over the back, as good as computer storage. And the emeritus began to talk about orders of numbers in terms the paidhi had never quite grasped. There were notations he'd never used. There were symbols he'd never met. But he rendered them as best he could, and rapidly decorated his notes with annotated commentary in as quick a hand as he could manage.

A handful of determined local officials were standing on the tarmac in the plane's lights, a group which faded away into stars as the plane lifted.

Then the paidhi was landing at Malguri Airport, and in the distance his beast wandered over reduced-scale hills, over which other, smaller game fled.

But the subway arrived, a dark figure beckoned and he had to leave his beast; the subway delivered them back to the basement station in the Bu-javid much after supper, and one had to wake the emeritus—to tell him something urgent, and in the dream he said it, but he couldn't himself hear it, or understand the words.

But Banichi was at hand to meet them, with a handful of the Bu-javid officers, and a handful of passes, which lodged the students and nand' Grigiji upstairs, wonder of wonders, in the residence of the dean of the university, who proclaimed himself interested in this theory, and they were holding national meetings on the matter.

He himself couldn't get into the meeting. He'd arrived late, and all the doors were locked. He could see the emeritus standing at the lectern and he could see all the atevi listening, but the paidhi was locked out, able only to see the mathematical notations on the pad, which held symbols that he couldn't make sense of.

Then he tried to go by another stairway to get in by the back entry to the hall—and lost his way. He tried door after door after door in the hall, and they led to more stairs, and other halls, increasingly dark places that he thought were unguessed levels of the Bu-javid. He was supposed to address the assembled scholars, but he couldn't find his way back and he knew that he was the only one that could make the symbols on the notepad make sense to the hasdrawad, which otherwise wouldn't listen to the emeritus.

He wandered into a place with a door that let out into the hall above the lecture hall. But he couldn't find a stairway down. At every turn he found himself isolated.

He found a lift, finally, and pushed the button for 1, or he thought he'd pushed that button. The car's light panel developed numbers and symbols he didn't understand and kept traveling. He knew Banichi and Jago would be angry at him for getting into a car and pushing buttons he didn't understand. But they'd looked fine when he pushed them.

He called on the emergency phone, and Jago answered, but she said she had an appointment this afternoon, would tomorrow be acceptable? And he said, he didn't know why he said, that he couldn't wait, and he was going to get off at the floor where it was going.

Which eventually did come, and let out into a gray and brown haze in which he was totally lost. He called Jago on a phone that turned up, and Jago said, sorry, she would be there tomorrow. He'd have to wait. So he kept walking, certain that sitting still here would never get him to the meeting on time. He came to the turn in the lower hallway.

And became aware that his beast was following him, and that it was the hall outside his bedroom in Malguri. He was out of sandwiches. But the beast was hunting small vermin that ran along the edges of the hallway.

It passed him, snuffling for holes in the masonry, and left him in the dark, looking toward the crack of light that came from under his own bedroom door, beckoning him out of the nightmare and into the warmth of the familiar, if he could only get there. He walked and walked, and there always seemed progress, but he couldn't reach it. The light became the cold light of dawn, and then it was possible, but he had to leave, he had something to do, and couldn't remember what it was. . . .

Thump.
His head jerked up. He blinked, looked about him in confusion.

"We're coming in, nand' paidhi," Tano said.

He looked out the window, at dark, at the lights of Shejidan, unable for a moment to understand how he'd come here. He moved a foot and felt his document case stowed quite safely where he'd put it.

He watched the city lights, the hills and heights and the city spread out like a carpet, all done with numbers. He *had* met such a person as the emeritus and he had a case full of papers—and the lights out there were all numbers.

He drifted off again during landing and was back in that hallway, looking for admittance to what he had to do. It was unjust that no one told him how to get inside. He began to be angry, and he went looking for Tabini to tell him things were badly arranged, and the paidhi needed . . .

But he couldn't remember what he needed. Things were shredding apart very badly. He was just walking down a hall and the doors were very far apart.

Bump. The wheels were on the ground. He saw the field lights ripping past the window. The paidhi traveled at jet speeds. The paidhi's mind didn't.

But he'd had no time. He'd had to get home.

Blink and he was in Malguri. Blink and the plane was slowing for the turn onto the taxiway. Lights going past one another, blue and white and red.

16

It was so troubling a dream he couldn't shake it, not even at the aiji-dowager's breakfast table—he sat in the open summer air, with the dawn coming up over the Bergid, applying preserves to a piece of bread and thinking about beasts and bedrooms, astronomers and city lights and mecheiti, until Ilisidi gave him a curious look, rapped the teacup with her knife, and inquired if he were communing with the ship.

"No," he said quickly. "Your pardon, nand' dowager."

"You're losing weight," Ilisidi said. "Eat. So nice to see you with that clumsy thing off your arm. Get your health back. Exercise. Eat."

He had a bite of the toast. Two. He was hungry this morning. And he *had* had a decent sleep. He had his wits about him, such as they ever served to fend off Ilisidi's razor intellect—even if he had spent the night walking hallways in company with a creature whose whole kind might be extinct. It was a very, very old piece of taxidermy. So he'd assumed in Malguri.

"Young man," Ilisidi said. "Come. Is it business? Or is it another question wandering the paths of intellect?"

"Nand' dowager," he said, "I was wondering last night about the staff's welfare at Malguri. Do you have word on them? Are Djinana and Maigi well?"

"Quite well," Ilisidi said.

"I'm very glad."

"I'll convey your concern to them. Have the fruit. It's quite good."

He remembered Banichi chiding him about salad courses. And Hanks' damn pregnant calendar.

"So why do you ask?" Ilisidi asked him.

"A human concern. A neurotic wish, perhaps, for one's good memories to stay undimmed by future events."

"Or further information?"

"Perhaps."

The dowager always asked more than she answered. He didn't press the matter with her, fearing to lose her interest in him.

"And Nokhada? And Babsidi?"

"Perfectly fine. Why should you ask?"

The gardened and tile-roofed interior of the Bu-javid marched away downhill from the balcony, soft-edged with first light, and there was a muttering of thunder, though the sky was clear as far as the Bergid: it presaged clouds in the west, hidden by the roofs.

He hadn't called Hanks on his return. He wasn't in a charitable mood for Hanks' illusions, or gifted with enough concentration for Hanks' economics report, in any form.

He still couldn't get a call through to his mother. He'd tried, and the notoriously political phone service was having difficulties this morning. Could he possibly wonder that the gremlins manifested only on the link to the mainland?

The note the Foreign Office had slipped him declared nothing helpful, just that his suspicions were correct: nothing was being decided where it had a damn chance to be sane, in the normal course of advisory councils and university personnel who actually knew history and knew atevi; everything *was* being decided behind closed doors and in secret meetings of people who weren't elected, hadn't the will of the people, and were going to, he'd bet his life on it, maneuver to cast everything into the hands of the ship, the station, and those willing to relocate there.

And, worrisome small matter, Jase Graham hadn't called back.

"So?" Ilisidi asked. "You've talked with these ship folk. And now they land."

"Two of them. You've gotten my translations."

"To be sure. But they don't answer questions well, do

they? Who are they? What do they want? Why did they come back? And why should we care?"

"Well, for one most critical thing, aiji-ma, they've been to places the Determinists have staked a great deal can't exist, they want to export labor off the planet, they want atevi to sell them the materials to make them masters of the universe, and they probably think they can get it cheap because humans on Mospheira weren't talking as if atevi have any say in the business."

"Too bad," Ilisidi said, dicing an egg onto her toast. "So? What does the paidhi advise us? Shall we all rush to arms? Perhaps sell vacation homes on Malguri grounds, for visiting humans?"

"The hell with that," he said, and saw Ilisidi's mouth quirk.

"So?" Ilisidi said, not, after all, preoccupied with her breakfast.

"I have some hope in this notion of paidhiin from the ship. I think it's a very good idea. I can have direct influence at least on Graham, and he seems a sensible, safety-concerned individual. If nothing else, maybe I can scare hell out of him—or her—and have more common sense than I'm hearing out of Mospheira."

"Scare hell out of Hanks-paidhi," Ilisidi said. "That's a beginning."

"I wish I could. I've tried. She's new. She's quite possibly competent in economics—"

"And she has powerful backers."

"I have freely admitted to it."

"Amazing." Ilisidi held her cup out for her servant to refill. "Tea, nand' paidhi?"

He took the offering. "Thank you. —Dowager-ma, may a presumptuous human ask your opinion?"

"Mine? Now what should my opinion sway? Affairs of state?"

"Lord Geigi. I'm concerned for him."

"For that melon-headed man?"

"Who—nevertheless occupies a sensitive and conservative position. Whom—a pretender to my office has needlessly upset."

"Melon-heads all. Full of seeds and pulp. The universe of stars is boundless. Or it is not. Certainly it doesn't consult us."

"That sums up the argument."

"Do humans in their wisdom know the universe of stars?"

"I—don't know." He wasn't ready to tread in that territory. Not for any lure. "I know there are humans who study such things. I'd be surprised if anyone definitively knew the universe."

"Oh, but it's simple to Geigi. Things add. They have it all summed and totaled, these Determinists."

"Does the dowager chance to have access to Determinists?" Many of the lords paid mathematicians and counters of every ilk, never to be surprised by controversy.

Certainly Tabini's house had a fair sampling of such experts, and he'd bet his retirement that Ilisidi had.

"Now what would the paidhi want with Determinists? To illumine their darkness? To mend their fallacious ways?"

"Hanks-paidhi made an injudicious comment, relative to numbers exceeding the light constant. I know you must have certain numerological experts on your staff, skilled people—"

More toast arrived at Ilisidi's elbow. And slid onto her plate to an accompaniment of sausages. "Skilled damned nonsense. Limiting the illimitable is folly."

"Skilled people," Bren reprised, refusing diversion, "to explain how a ship can get from one place to another faster than light travels—which classic physics says—"

"Oh, posh, posh, classic folly. Such extraneous things you humans entrain. I could have lived quite content without these ridiculous numbers. Or, I will tell you, lord Geigi's despondent messages."

"Despondent?"

"Desperate, rather. Shall I confide the damage that woman has done? He's trying to borrow money secretly. He's quite terrified, perceiving that he's consulted a person of infelicitous numbers, a person, moreover, who let her proposals and his finances become too public—he's quite, quite exposed. Folly. Absolute folly."

"I'm distressed for him."

"Oh, none more distressed than his creditors, who thought him stable enough to be a long-term risk as aiji of his province; now they perceive him as a short-term and very high risk, with his credit *and* his potential for paying his debts sinking by the hour. The man is up for sale. It's widely known. It's very shameful. Probably I shall help him. But I dislike to trade in loyalties and cash."

"I quite understand that. But I find him a brave man— and possibly trying to protect others in his *man'chi.*"

"Posh, what do you understand? You've no atevi sensibilities."

"I can help him. I think I can help him, dowager-ji. I think I've found a way to explain Hanks' remark . . . if I had very wise mathematicians, *correct* mathematicians from the Determinists' point of view. . . ."

"Are you asking me to find such people?"

"I fear none of that philosophy have cast their lot with your grandson. *You,* on the other hand . . ."

"Tabini asks me to rescue this foolish man."

"I ask you. Personally. Tabini knows nothing about it. Rescue him. Don't buy him. Don't take a public posture. Don't say that I suggested it. Surely he could never accept it."

"Why?" Ilisidi asked. "Is *this* the mysterious trip to the north?"

"I'd be astonished if I ever achieved mystery to you, nand' dowager."

"Impudent rascal. So you were out there rescuing Geigi the melon?"

"Yes."

"Why, in the name of the felicitous gods?"

He couldn't say in terms he knew she couldn't misapprehend. He looked out toward the Bergid, where dawn was turning the sky faintly blue. "There's no value," he discovered himself saying, finally, "in the collapse of any part of the present order of things. The world has achieved a certain harmony. Stability favors atevi interests. Yours, your grandson's. Everyone's. Stability even favors Mospheira, if certain Mospheirans weren't acting like fools."

"This woman is a wonder," Ilisidi said. "She should have sought me out. But she had no notion she should."

"She's harmless on Mospheira. Where I'd like to send her. But in moments of fright, my government freezes solid. This is such a moment. Let me tell you, dowager-ji, one secret truth of humans: we have self-interests, and truly selfish and wicked humans can be far more selfish than atevi psychology can readily comprehend."

"Ah. And are atevi immune?"

"Far more loyal to certain interests. Humans can be thorough rebels, acting alone and in total self-interest."

"So can atevi be great fools. And if Geigi believed this woman, still I wonder why you took this very long, very urgent excursion, and sought advice of such eccentrics."

"A brilliant old man, nand' dowager. I recommend him to your attention."

"An *astronomer,*" Ilisidi said with scorn.

"Possibly a brilliant man, aiji-ma. I'd almost have brought him back to court, aiji-ma, but I feared court was too fierce a place for him. His name is Grigiji. He's spent a long life looking for a reconciliation of human science and atevi numbers. His colleagues at the observatory have devoted themselves to recovering the respectability of atevi astronomers. They want to create an atevi science that uses atevi numerical concepts to look past human approximations . . . approximations which I will assure you humans do use, from time to time . . . to an integration of very vast numbers with the numbers of daily life."

He said what he said with calculation, in hope of catching Ilisidi's interest in things atevi, and in atevi tradition. And he saw the dowager paying more than casual interest for that one instant, the mask of indifference set aside.

"So?" Ilisidi asked. "So what does this Grigiji say to Geigi?"

Ilisidi was intellectual enough to set aside beliefs that didn't gibe with reality, politician enough to accept some for political necessity; and atevi enough, he suddenly thought, to long for some unifying logic in her world, logic which the very traditions she championed declared to exist.

He reached inside his coat and found the small packet he'd made, copies of the emeritus' equations and his own notes such as he'd been able to render them. She didn't reach for it: the wind was blowing.

"What is this?" Ilisidi asked.

"A human's poorly copied notation of what the astronomer emeritus had to say. And his own words, aiji-ma." A servant, young and male —Ilisidi's habit—showed up at his elbow to take the papers into safekeeping.

"Not the astronomer-aiji?"

It was a gibe. Is there some reason, the question meant, that Tabini's own astronomers, high in the court, failed—and a human sought his sources elsewhere? Doubtless this very moment, Cenedi would be sending out inquiries about Grigiji, his provenance, his background, his affiliations. And Ilisidi, who habitually gave the paidhi a great deal of tolerance, but—propositioned—would *not* commit herself to touch such an obviously political gift: clearly the paidhi was being political; so, in turn, was she.

"Nand' dowager," he answered her carefully, "the aiji's own astronomers have other areas of study. And they're not independent. This man, as I understand, and this observatory, have been the principal astronomers engaged on this research. They're not affiliated with any outside agency. This is an exact copy of what I brought your grandson, nothing left out, nothing added. May I ask the dowager—to advise me?"

Ilisidi's hand left the teacup for an insouciant motion. Proceed, she signaled.

"Understand, aiji-ma, I'm not a mathematician. Far from it. But as I understand both what humans have observed and what this man has been attempting to describe in numbers—as I was flying into the city last night, I saw the lights, high places, low places of the city, lights like the stars shining in dark space." He knew Ilisidi had flown at night—very recently—into Shejidan. "I saw— out the airplane window, in those lights in high and low spots, all over Shejidan—what humans have described with their numbers. And what Grigiji's vision also describes, as I faintly understand it. His answer to lord Geigi."

"In the city lights. Writ in luminous equations, perhaps?"

"The paradox of faster-than-light, aiji-ma; say that the universe doesn't stretch out like a flat sheet of black cloth. That it has—features, like mountains, like valleys. Say there's a topology of such places. Stars are so heavy in this sheet they make deep valleys. Therefore the numbers describing the path of light across this sheet are quite, quite true. One doesn't violate the Determinists' universe: light can't go faster, by the paths that light must follow. Light and all things within the sheet that is this universe follow those mountains, and take the time they need to take. So nothing that travels along that sheet violates the speed of light. One can measure the distances across the sheet, and they are valid. Right now the effects of atmosphere diminish the accuracy of atevi observations, but when one observes from the station—as atevi will—the accuracy will be far, far greater."

"You're buying time," Ilisidi said, with another small quirk of the mouth, a flash of golden eyes. "You very rascal, you're setting it on a shelf they can't reach."

"But it is *true,* nand' dowager, and up there they'll prove it. Those papers, as I understand what I'm told, describe that sheet I'm talking about in terms that admit of space not involved in that sheet. What we call folded space."

"Folded space. Space folds."

"A convenience. A way of seeing it for people who aren't as mathematical as atevi, people whose language doesn't express what that paper expresses. It's the way starships travel, aiji-ma. It's the highest of our high technology, and an ateva may have *found* it without human help—if I could read those notations I copied. Which I can't, because I don't have the ability an ateva mathematician has to describe the universe."

"Your madman told you this."

"Aiji-ma, light doesn't travel in a straight line. But because light is how we see, how we define shape, how we measure distance, over huge scale—that makes space act flat."

"Makes space act flat."

"We don't operate on a scale on which the curves normally matter. Like a slow rise of the land. The land still looks flat. But the legs feel the climb. Scale makes the difference to the viewer. Not to the math. Not to the hiker's legs."

Ilisidi regarded him with a shake of her head. "Such a creature you are. Such a creature. And not in touch with your university. Done it all yourself, have you."

"I *know* the essence of things I can't explain by mathematics, 'Sidi-ma." To his dismay he let slip the familiar name, the way he held the dowager in his mind. And didn't know how to cover it. "You show your children far more complex things than they have the mathematics to understand. That's the way I learned. That's what I have to draw on. A child's knowledge of how his ancestors moved between the stars. They didn't teach me to fly starships. I just know why they work."

"Faster-than-light."

"Much faster than light."

"Do you know, paidhi, an old reprobate such as myself could ask to what extent all this celestial mapmaking is new, and how much humans were prepared to give at this juncture. You certainly aren't using Hanks-paidhi for a decoy, are you?"

"Nand' dowager, on my reputation and my goodwill to you, I emphatically did *not* clear Hanks-paidhi to leak that to Geigi. And I didn't clear with my Department what I've just told you."

"*Whence* this astronomer, *whence* Geigi's dilemma, at the very moment this ship beckons in the heavens—when you need the goodwill of such as myself, nand' paidhi? Is this my grandson's planning? Is this one of his adherents?"

He was in, perhaps, the greatest danger he had ever realized in his life, including bombs falling next to him.

The daylight had increased as they sat, and those remarkable eyes, so mapped about with years, were absolutely cold. One didn't betray 'Sidi-ji and live to profit from it. One didn't betray Cenedi and harm Ilisidi's interests—and walk free.

Ilisidi snapped her fingers. A servant, one of Cenedi's, he was sure, brought a teapot and poured for each of them.

He looked Ilisidi in the eyes as he drank, the whole cup, and set the cup aside.

"So?" Ilisidi asked.

"Nand' dowager, if it's Tabini's planning, his means eludes me. This is an old and respected man in his district, no new creation, that I detected."

"Then what is your explanation? Why this coincidence?"

"Simply that the man may be *right,* nand' dowager. The man may have found the truth, for what I know. I'm not a mathematician—but I should never wonder at someone finding what really exists."

"At the convenient moment? At this exactly convenient moment for him to do so? And my grandson had *no* collusion with humans to slip this cataclysm in on us, to destroy a tenet of Determinist belief?"

"It doesn't destroy it! By what I can tell, it doesn't destroy it, it supports it."

"So you've been told. And you just happen to rush out where a man has just happened to find the truth."

"Not 'just happened,' nand' dowager. *Not* 'just happened.' It's the whole progress of our history behind this man. We've not been transferring just *things* into atevi hands. We've transferred our designs and our mathematical knowledge to a people who've proceeded much more slowly in their science than humans did *without* atevi skill at numbers—a speed we managed because we dead-reckon, approximate, and proceed as atevi won't. One can do this—when one builds steam engines and builds things stronger than economical, rather than risk calamity. We were astonished that you took so long to advance. We watched the debates over numbers. We waited."

"For us poor savages."

"We thought so in the beginning. We couldn't figure why you couldn't just accept what we knew as fact, keep quiet, and build by our designs—but the point is, it wasn't fact, it was very close approximation. And atevi demanded to understand. Then, *then,* we began to realize it wasn't just the designs we were transferring: you were extracting our numbers, refining them in an atevi conceptualization that we knew was going to break out someday in a way we didn't foresee. When we gave you the computers that most humans use to figure simple household accounts, you questioned our logical designs. We knew there'd come a day, an insight, a moment, that you'd make a leap of understanding we might not follow. Not in engineering, perhaps. You are such immaculate perfectionists, when our approximations will bear traffic and hold back the waters of a lake; but in the pure application of numbers—no, I'm not in the least shocked that a breakthrough has come at this moment, not even that it's come in astronomy, in which we've had the very *least* direct contact with your scientists. We gave atevi mathematicians computers. We knew study was going on. It never surprised me that the Determinists hold the speed of light as a matter of importance: it is important; it's far from surprising that astronomers seeking precision in their measurements are using it and discovering new truths—"

Air seemed scant. He was walking a ledge far past his own scientific expertise—far beyond his ability to prove—and on a major, dangerous point of atevi belief.

"I don't know these things, aiji-ma. I'd wish the astronomers of the Bergid and the scholars on Mospheira could talk to each other. But I'm the only one who could translate. And the emeritus was using mathematical symbols I don't remotely know how to render—I'm not even sure human mathematics has direct equivalents. I suspect some of them are couched in the Ragi language, and if they rely on me to get them into Mosphei', humans are never going to understand."

"Such delicate modesty."

"No. Reality. Most humans don't speak your language,

aiji-ma, because most humans aren't nearly as good in math as I am. You view it as so important to know those numbers—and we don't, aiji-ma. We can't add that fast in our heads. We *have* to approximate—not that we're disrespectful of atevi concepts; we just can't add that fast. Our language doesn't have your requirements, your expressions, your concepts. At times my brain aches just talking with you—and for a human, I'm not stupid. But I'm working as hard as I can sometimes just talking to you, especially about math—far from conveying folded-space mathematics to anyone whose symbols I can't remotely read, nand' dowager. I'm reduced to asking the man's young students what he said and finding out that *they* don't understand all he says, even with their advantage in processing the language."

There was long silence, once he stopped talking. Long silence. Ilisidi simply sat and stared at him. Wind stirred the edge of the tablecloth, and blew the scent of diossi flowers to the table.

"Cenedi will see you out," Ilisidi said.

"Nand' dowager," he said, feeling both fear—and real sadness in his sense of failure. He rose from the table, bowed, and went to the door and inside the apartment.

Cenedi met him there.

"I've offended her," he said to Cenedi quietly. "Cenedi-ji, she doubts me."

"Justly?" Cenedi did him the courtesy of asking.

"No," he said fervently. "No. But I can't make her understand I'm not smart enough to do what she thinks I've done. I may have given her the ravings of a madman. I hope I haven't. But I can't read his writings to judge. I could only copy them. I can't judge the quality of it. I don't know what I've given her. I hoped it would do some good."

"One heard," Cenedi said as they crossed the room toward the door.

"At least—tell her I wish her well, and hope for her eventual good regard."

"One will pass the message," Cenedi said, "nand' paidhi."

* * *

Banichi picked him up—and asked, since the paidhi wasn't bothering to put on a cheerful face, not how it had gone, but what had happened; and he could only shrug and say, "Nothing good, Banichi. I did something wrong. I can't tell what."

Banichi answered nothing to that. He thought Banichi might try to find out where he'd misstepped—easier for Banichi to ask Cenedi outright, since Banichi had the hardwiring to understand the answer. But it seemed to a human's unatevi senses that he'd simply pushed Ilisidi too far and given her the suspicion she'd very plainly voiced to him: that he was Tabini's, a given; that the whole Hanks business was a setup possibly engineered by Tabini himself; and one could leap from that point to the logical conclusion that if Hanks was a setup designed to push atevi faster than the conservatives wanted to go, it couldn't happen without Bren-paidhi being in on it.

Which meant—perhaps—that in Ilisidi's mind all the relations she had had with him were in question, including how far he'd be willing to go to sweep Ilisidi away from her natural allies. Never mind the broken shoulder: Ilisidi was surrounded by persons of extreme *man'chi*, persons who'd fling themselves between Ilisidi and a bullet without an editing thought: she was *used* to people who took risks. She might not know humans as well as Tabini, but she had expectations of atevi and she had experience of Tabini that might lead her at least to question, and not to risk her dignity or her credibility on someone not within her *man'chi*.

She hadn't poisoned him. He'd not flinched from the possibility. He'd surely scored points in that regard. But he'd trod all over atevi beliefs, atevi pride—which with Ilisidi was very personal: Ilisidi had unbent with him a little and he'd used that, or advantaged himself of it, and asked the dowager to support Tabini—

The wonder was she hadn't poisoned him. And he was attached to Ilisidi—he didn't know exactly how it had happened, but he was as upset at her accusation of him as he'd be if he'd somehow crossed the other atevi he'd grown close to.

Which didn't include, somehow, Tabini. Not in that sense of reliance and intimacy. Not in the sense that—

That he'd damn well regretted Jago had left his room night before last, experimentation untried. And he was mortally glad Jago had stayed out of his close company the last two days.

But he longed to find her alone and find out what she did think, and whether she was upset, or embarrassed, which he didn't want; and didn't want to risk the relationship he had with her and with Banichi, without which—he was completely—

Alone.

And scared stiff.

From moment to moment this morning he dreaded the intrusion of other humans. He didn't know what to do if the interface went bad. He *had* a certain security in his atevi associates and he had to spend, hereafter, the bulk of his free time, such as it was, teaching a foreign human what that foreign human might not ever really understand.

After which, in a number of years, Jase Graham boarded an earth-to-orbit craft and went back to his ship, leaving the paidhi—whatever the paidhi had left.

He was in a major funk, was what had hit him. Two days ago he'd looked forward to Graham's arrival as the panacea for his troubles. But that was when at least his atevi world had been holding together.

And the paidhi always had that image of the clock stopped. The ultimate, shocked surprise of that moment that atevi had reacted in self-preserving attack on the very humans who really, really *liked* atevi.

He had to get his mind back in order, his hurts and his self-will packed back in their little boxes, and, God, most of all he couldn't let himself start brooding over how much atevi didn't *like* him. Ilisidi never had *liked* him. Ilisidi had found him amusing, entertaining, informative, a dozen other things—and now he wasn't. Now things were too serious. Humans were coming down from the sky. Ilisidi had decisions to make and she'd make them for atevi reasons. If he had a duty, it was to inform Tabini of Ilisidi's reaction.

And Ilisidi knew it.

"Banichi-ji, Ilisidi asked me—" One didn't say suspects, didn't say, implied: when the paidhi was deep in the mazes of atevi thought, the paidhi said exactly what *had* happened, not what he interpreted to have happened. "—asked me whether Tabini had set Hanks-paidhi, Geigi, the question, the astronomer happening to come up with a possible answer and all at this crisis."

There was silence for a moment. Banichi drew a long, audible breath as they walked. "Such a tangled suspicion."

"She may have been angry. Under the theory that I may simply have angered her with a social blunder, perhaps you could inquire of Cenedi the cause of her displeasure with me."

"Possible. One might ask. This befell when you gave her the calculations."

"She wouldn't touch them herself. A servant took them before they either blew away or I had to take them back."

"She suspected their content."

"She said she suspected the emeritus as Tabini's creation. I tried to assure her I haven't the fluency or the mathematical knowledge to have understood the reasoning in my own language, let alone to have translated them into this one. The fact that I don't have the concepts is why I went out there in the first place, for God's sake."

"I'll pass that along," Banichi said.

By which Banichi assuredly meant to Tabini. Possibly back again to Cenedi.

"I truly regard the woman highly."

"Oh, so does Tabini," Banichi said. "But one never discounts her."

17

It wasn't an easy thought to chase out of one's mind, Ilisidi's potential animosity, no more than it was easy to avoid comparisons with Tabini's interested reception of the papers. Tabini had sent him a verbal message at the crack of dawn, by Naidiri himself, Tabini's personal bodyguard, stating confidentially that in the aiji's opinion, the emeritus' papers at least presented the numbers-people something to chase for a good long while, it was the craziest proposal Tabini personally had ever seen, and the aiji was sending security to watch over the observatory.

Which he didn't forget in the context of his falling-out with Ilisidi. He didn't like to think of the likes of the Guild moving in on the little village and disturbing the place—because it wouldn't be Guild members like Cenedi and Banichi, who had the polite finesse to make a person truly believe they were off duty when they never were; he didn't like to think of the place destroyed by his brief attention to it, or the astronomers' lives changed irrevocably for the worse.

But security for the observatory was nothing he should or could protest: he'd been chasing the numbers too concentratedly even to think how the importance of the place had suddenly changed, when the old man had come rushing in with his answer: Grigiji had become someone valuable to Tabini, and therefore a target, as everything Tabini touched directly or indirectly was a target. He'd forgotten, in the delusion he could seek an answer for Geigi on his own, and slip it—God, it seemed naive now—into Ilisidi's hands with no untoward result.

The paidhi had been a thoroughgoing fool. The paidhi had not only blown up bridges with Ilisidi, he'd put the observatory and Grigiji at risk, possibly done something completely uncalculated regarding Geigi and Geigi's province and Geigi's relationship to Ilisidi and to Tabini—the paidhi was consequently thoroughly depressed, thoroughly disgusted with his quick and perhaps now very costly feint aside to chase what had looked like a good idea at the time.

The way for the paidhi to do what Wilson-paidhi hadn't been able to and Hanks-paidhi couldn't: get the conservative atevi and Tabini's faction simultaneously behind an idea.

The hero's touch. The heroics he'd accused Hanks of, that Hanks had come back at him with—and by what he saw now, Hanks had had the right of it.

Hanks deserved a phone call, at least to set up a meeting to brief her on the essentials, and on what a hash he might have made of her slip with Geigi. It wasn't going to be easy to explain, it wasn't going to be pleasant, and he wasn't ready to cope with it. Not yet.

He sat down to go through the message stack—the new office was actually settling in to work, and he had a number of appreciations for the cards he'd sent; the table in the foyer was overflowing with the traditional gifts of flowers from the new employees, so many they'd accumulated in a tasteful bow about the table and in other areas of the floor where they wouldn't impede traffic, and he supposed he ought to have been cheered, but his arm ached, his ribs ached, and breakfast wasn't sitting well. He asked Algini for his computer, took his correspondence to the sitting room, and sat and prepared reports, and reports.

Saidin quietly adjusted the windows for ventilation and light, and set a fan to operation. He'd grown less distracted by the comings and goings of the staff. He almost failed to notice, until Saidin crossed between him and the light.

"I need to speak to Banichi, nand' Saidin," he said. He wanted a time for leisurely discussion. "Is he back yet?"

"Not yet, nand' paidhi. Algini is on duty."

"Jago?"

"I believe she went down to the Guild offices, nadi. One could send."

"No," he said. "It's not urgent." His eyes were tired, and among his messages was an advisement Tabini was directing the mathematics faculty to look at Grigiji's notes. And *his* notes, which he hoped he hadn't miscopied. He'd protested that to Tabini and urged him if there were mistakes to attribute them to human copying, not Grigiji's math.

Among his messages was an extensive new transcript from the ship, which contained more document transmissions between Mospheira and the ship, more of Mospheira's very specific questions about origins and direction of travel and findings—which the ship hadn't answered fully. There was a direct question about the supposed other station and its location, and whether—a question that hadn't even occurred seriously to him—the ship might have left the solar system at all, but whether it might in fact have established the long-threatened base at Maudette, the red, desolate further-out planet atevi called Esili—the planet to which, before the Landing, the Pilots' Guild had wanted to move the colony rather than have it land on the atevi world.

No, the ship said. It had visited another star. There was no base at Maudette.

Which star? the President wanted to know, and named several near ones.

The Guild said, logically enough, that they had no such names on file; then asked for star charts with atevi names. And renewed the discussion about landing sites—in regard to which the ship wanted general maps and names.

Which Mospheira, in a sudden reticence, refused to provide until the ship was forthcoming with star charts.

At which point the woman Yolanda Mercheson came on com, wishing to speak to the President.

And the President was quite pleasant. Quite encouraging. The President said he advised a landing on Mos-

pheira as the best way to guarantee human sovereignty—
and Mercheson said she'd present that view.

Then Mercheson presented a shopping list of raw materials and asked pointedly if Mospheira had those goods.

The President didn't know. The President would get
back to her with that information, but he knew they had
some extensive stockpiles of materials.

Stockpiles.

Flash of dark. Terror. Pain. Cold metal and a looming
shadow, asking him . . . accusing him . . .

*Most clearly you're stockpiling metals. You increase
your demands for steel, for gold—you give us industries,
and you trade us microcircuits for graphite, for titanium,
aluminum, palladium, elements we didn't know existed a
hundred years ago, and, thanks to you, now we have a
use for. Now you import them, minerals that don't exist on
Mospheira. For what? For what do you use these things,
if not the same things you've taught us—*

Barrel of a gun against his head. A question he'd taken
at face value at that moment, and pain and fear had wiped
out the context—no, he hadn't *known* the context at that
moment, he hadn't *known* the ship had returned to atevi
skies, he hadn't *known* the situation the interrogator was
implying . . . space-age stockpiles for an event the whole
human population of the planet might have been waiting
to spring on atevi. At that terrorized, dreadful moment
he'd thought only . . . aircraft. Only . . . a hidden launch
program. Only . . . of dying there. And he hadn't half-
remembered the question in the light of what he'd learned
later.

Stockpiles—of goods critical to a space program.

He'd protested he wasn't an engineer, he didn't know
. . . and the interrogator had said . . . *you slip numbers
into the dataflow. You encourage sectarian debates to delay us. . . .*

The argument of Ilisidi's allies. Ilisidi's constituency,
the constituency Ilisidi had ostensibly betrayed—but
never count an ateva to have changed sides completely.
There were always points of stress in an association.

Sectarian debates to delay us. . . .

And he'd said ... *We build test vehicles. Models. We test* what we think we understand before we give advice that will let some ateva blow himself to bits, nadi ...

He'd thought that was all the truth. He'd told that to an interrogator whose identity he still didn't know, a man who might have been Ilisidi's, or a partisan of someone affiliated to Ilisidi.

He'd hadn't known then ... about the ship. He hadn't understood the matter about sectarian debates. Or the significance of stockpiles of materials for a space program. *He'd* talked to them about aircraft. *He'd* maintained human innocence ...

He lost his place in the tape. His fingers were cold as he punched buttons and ran it back, and heard the section through again, and *knew* he'd promised Ilisidi along with Tabini a transcript of all his translations.

Stockpiles ... the atevi held to be extensive. Stockpiles of minerals Mospheira didn't otherwise have. . . .

Stockpiles begun—God knew how long ago. The paidhi, on informed opinion, didn't *believe* they could be that extensive, since the paidhi knew with fair certainty what had generally gone to Mospheira and what Mospheira would use—unless there were Defense Department secrets too deep and too old for the current paidhi to know, or trading—as could sometimes happen—that didn't get reported accurately to Shejidan.

There were bunkers in the high center of Mospheira, places fenced off from hikers and guarded by people with guns, which citizens accepted—you didn't go there. You didn't mess with those perimeters. They were antiquated, increasingly so, in an increasingly peaceful world—at least—the idea of air raid shelters seemed antiquated, in his generation. But there'd been fear of atevi landings on the beaches before there'd been aircraft.

There'd been fear of atevi air attacks, when they'd given atevi aviation, and situated aircraft manufacturing on the mainland. The bunkers were supposed to be nerve centers, critical command posts, things to make sure no attack ever drove humans to the brink of extinction again.

They *said* they were command posts. Nothing about

how deep they were, how extensive they were—or what they contained. And *if* they contained what he'd been asked about, if there were stockpiles the President of Mospheira could use to deal with the ship—

Mospheira *couldn't* call the aiji's bluff. He *couldn't* have set Tabini up to make a threat of boycott and have Mospheira go around the obstacle with some damned antique storage dump.

But it was supply. Even if it existed—it didn't manufacture itself. The manufacturing plants that did exist on Mospheira couldn't be converted at a snap of the fingers to do what they hadn't been designed to do—

But Mospheira didn't educate the paidhiin in what the Defense Department did, or had, or wanted: it was specifically excluded, that area of inquiry. And when the government and State specifically cleared some plastics factory on the East Frontage for ecological impact—you trusted they were making domestic-use articles.

The Department sent the paidhiin into the field not knowing that for an absolute, examined fact. The paidhiin knew there were no death rays. He knew that as an article of faith. There were no nuclear installations. There were no truly exotic sites: the colonists hadn't had those kind of weapons and hadn't given atevi a nuclear capability . . . yet.

But this talk of stockpiles made a chill down his back, and told him the paidhi might for once in a career of mandated consultations before moving truly need to consult—and might now, if his current actions hadn't set the Defense Department on its ear and sent the Secretary of Defense straight to the President's door with a reckoning of exactly how far and with what offer to the spacefarers they could call Tabini's hand and defy a boycott.

Dammit, he couldn't trust his files regarding a history he had no idea whether the censor Seekers had reached, or not reached—he couldn't trust what he'd been told. How did the paidhi even trust that his own education hadn't censored or even lied about vital facts? Once censorship was at issue—how did anyone, any official trust how far it would go, when it would have begun, whose information it would have censored, or what it would have constructed as a substitute for the truth? Humans had come close to annihilation. They *hadn't* had weapons. Atevi in the early days couldn't trade them aluminum or titanium or any space-age material. Mospheirans could get plastics, they could get anything vegetable fiber could produce, anything they could get from limited drilling along the North Shore; they had solar energy and electricity, but they hadn't been set up to realize a need two centuries along and slip enough into storage to hold out against the interlinking of the Mospheiran/atevi economies—

Mospheirans hadn't, all along, been that damn canny, that damn persistent, or that damned concerned about their future—the radicals might wish they'd been, the radicals might have a fantasy they'd been, and maybe something did exist in stockpiles, but it didn't translate to real capacity to hold against an atevi cutoff of supplies—

—or to anticipate some traitorous paidhi cutting a deal with *Phoenix* and trying to exclude Mospheira, all for the planetary good. They *couldn't* have him boxed in. *Never* say to atevi at large that the aiji had made a threat he couldn't back or a promise that made him look foolish. Blood could flow in the streets if that happened. Blood was ready to flow in the streets, if he made such a mistake.

He wrote, *Aiji-ma, regarding the most recent ship conversations with Mospheira, the expected behind the doors negotiations have proposed human stockpiles of materials I have proposed you threaten to withhold. My hope based on experience living on and traveling on the island is that they're small, not containing everything a space program needs, and that they might be used for bargaining and for attempting to attract the ship to their point of view, and that the Mospheiran government might exaggerate their size in an attempt to get a better agreement.*

This, however, does not guarantee I am right about their size. If they should be larger, I have advised you badly, and you must take whatever measures you deem appropriate.

*On the other hand, the ship can determine even buried
reserves from orbit, as well as the character of factories.
It is my hope that factories are not sufficient even if such
stockpiles exist, and that they cannot be built in a timely
enough fashion to satisfy the ship's leaders.*

*Further, we have presented the ship extensive political
reasons to accept your conditions.*

*But I am dismayed to know now that I was asked about
this matter in Malguri and did not at the time realize its
import, nor recall it in preparing my estimates and advisements to you. I am completely to blame for any negative result. I have erred once today in estimating the
dowager's response, as I believe Banichi will have told
you. At the reading of the enclosed transcript you may
judge I have erred repeatedly and egregiously. If this is
so, I urge you not to listen to me further, and to take my
advice as that of an underinformed official to whom his
own government has not confided sufficient truth to rely
upon.*

*I feel I have no recourse now but to write the dowager,
and I have given a firm pledge to do so. But I shall delay
my response and take the disgrace on myself for doing so,
in hopes that events or greater wisdom than mine will
find a means for you to secure your own interests in advance of my fulfilling a rash promise that may have
placed me in a position incompatible with your best interests. If I were placed under arrest, I could not send such
a message, aiji-ma.*

*Please believe, as I have in profound embarrassment
urged upon Ilisidi, that I wished to do good for her and
for you, and that it is not through hostile intent or orders
of my government that I have done what I have done.*

It was not a cheerful message to have to write. He ap-
pended the transcript. He sent the message, via his remote, to the aiji's fax, rather than using courier, if for
nothing else, that propriety mattered less than speed of
getting that message next door.

He sat staring at the blowing curtains and asking himself, with a certain tightness in the throat, how far he
could impose on atevi patience.

Or how far he could even believe in his own increasingly remote attenuation of logic.

He knew what interests he was fighting on Mospheira. He hadn't been utterly sure until Shawn's message turned up—but that confirmed he'd guessed right, that far, once the ship was in the equation, exactly where the pressure would come from and who would apply it. He just—

—had reached the end of his personal credit, his personal ability, his personal strength, and he'd made a couple of mistakes in his sudden downhill rush to get the landing finalized that had cost him, personally, cost Tabini, personally, cost Ilisidi, and might cost political credit and lives across an entire atevi and human world before the shock waves settled.

Where did he *think* he could go setting up an atevi way to see the universe—*knowing*, God help him, that the old, old wisdom in the Department had always held that atevi would make some conceptual break and go spiraling off into a mathematical dark where humans weren't going to understand. And where in human *hell* did he think that point of departure was likeliest going to come if not in the highest, most esoteric math—which he, in his personal brilliance, had gone kiting off to beg of the persons most likely to come up with it—

Good merciful *God*, what did he expect but upset when he tossed the mathematical bombshell into the capital, the court, the touchiest political maneuvering of the last century—and let it lie on the breakfast table of the ateva least likely to benefit?

How in hell did he reconcile that little gift with his emotional appeal for 'Sidi-ji to rise above politics, rise to the good of the Association, sacrifice herself on the altar of her grandson's success?

He'd done that, after what he'd adequately remembered once prompted, and he hadn't seen it? Damned right he hadn't drawn the two threads together, when a faster mind could have anticipated Mospheira would fight back on the boycott issue. He should have asked himself what Mospheira could have stored; most of all he should have *remembered* the stockpile question that atevi themselves

had asked him in what his foundering mind had catalogued as some totally unrelated event.

Damn it to bloody hell, he'd danced into it blindly *sure*
he had a good gift to give in that paper. And it had probably nailed the lid on the coffin, so far as Ilisidi's confidence he wasn't stupidly playing the same game her
associates had accused humans of playing for centuries:
undermining atevi belief, atevi institutions, all at the same
time reserving supplies and fostering an atevi manufacturing program not for atevi's sake but only to get those supplies they needed for themselves.

For a ship maybe some humans had believed more
strongly than others was going to return.

His eyes hurt. He pinched his nose. And the arm hurt,
lying inert in his lap, perhaps objecting to two-handed
keyboard work, perhaps objecting to how he'd slept on
it—he'd no idea, but it ached.

From frenetic, the place had grown too quiet. He
wanted company. But Banichi and Jago were off about
various business, Tabini was probably dealing with the
matter he'd dropped in Tabini's lap. Tabini was probably
too angry to speak to him, or even preparing orders for
his arrest, as he'd invited, who knew?

The very changes he'd taken office to moderate and
conduct slowly and without damage were all let loose
from Pandora's fabled box, without review, without committee approval, without advice—just fling open the lid
and stand back, maybe with one final choice of interven-
ing to try to moderate the effects—

But that choice, even to make it now, entailed human
values, human decisions, human ethics; or, perhaps the
wiser course—to stand back until atevi action made it
clear what was likely to result from atevi values, atevi decisions, atevi ethics—and then decide again whether to
interpose human wisdom, at least as the older of two species experiences, the one of the two species who'd been
down the technological path far enough to see the flex
and flux of their own cultural responses to the dawning of
awareness of the universe. Human beings had surely had
certain investments in their planetary boundaries, once

upon a time. Humans had had to realize the sun was a star among other stars. The paidhi didn't happen to know with any great accuracy how humans had reacted to that knowledge, but he'd a troubled suspicion it could have set certain human beliefs on end.

Though that they couldn't work the numbers out exactly wouldn't have broken up associations, re-sorted personal loyalties, cast into doubt a way of looking at the universe—had it?

For all he knew, the way atevi handled the universe was hardwired into atevi brains, and that was what he was playing games with.

He didn't want to think about that.

He got up and wandered finally as far as the library, and took down delicate watercolored books of horticulture, one after the other, to find whether he knew the names.

Of a book of water plants he was mostly ignorant. It was stupid, in the midst of such desperate events, to go back to his computer and enter words, but he was incapable of more esoteric operations.

Saidin came in to ask whether the paidhi would care for supper in, and whether the paidhi's personal staff would eat at the same time or at some later time.

The paidhi didn't know. The paidhi's staff didn't fill him in. He didn't know whether he'd be here for supper or whether he'd be hauled off to confinement.

But that wasn't Saidin's question.

"I can only hope your surmise is more effective than mine," he said. "Nand' Saidin, I have not been a regular or prompt guest. I apologize for myself and my staff."

"Nandi," Saidin said with a bow, "you are no trouble. Do you admire water gardens?"

The book. Of course. "I find the book beautifully drawn."

"I think so. Have you seen the Terraces?"

"On the Saisuran?" The book held a major number of plates of water plants, delicately rendered in pastel tones. "No, I fear the paidhi has very few chances. Malguri was an unusual excursion."

"If you have the chance, nand' paidhi, I recommend them. They're quite near Isgrai'the. Which is very popular."

He was intrigued—by the idea of the famous water gardens, and the Preservation Reserve at Isgrai'the. By the notion he might someday have such a chance.

But most of all he was intrigued by madam Saidin's unprecedented personal conversation. The book, almost certainly a favorite. One was glad to discover a mutual, noncontroversial interest in a subject; a source of ordinary, mundane conversation.

She'd felt the tension in the house and in the guest— and the protector of the house had followed her inquisitorial duty, perhaps; or just—counting that word of doings in the house *had* once found their way to Ilisidi—

He was too damn critical. Too damn suspicious. Wilson's fate beckoned: the man who never laughed, never smiled.

"Nand' Saidin, thank you. *Thank* you for recommending Saisuran. I'll hope for it, that I will be able to see it. I'd like that. I truly would."

"One hopes for you, also, nand' paidhi," Saidin said, and left the room, with the paidhi wondering where that had come from, or what Saidin had really meant, what she'd heard from what source inside Tabini's apartments—or whether he'd simply presented her a dejected picture, sitting there staring at the curtains, so morose that the provider of hospitality had simply done her duty for the lady who wanted her guest taken care of.

He knew the mental maze he'd wandered into, wild swings between atevi and human feeling, making only half-translations of concepts in that strange doppelgänger language his brain began to contrive in his unprecedented back-and-forth translation, in his real-time listening to one language and rendering it into the other, no time for refinement, no time for precision—leaping desperately from slippery stone to slippery stone, to borrow the image of the book open on the footstool—the water flowers, the stones, half obscured in sun on water—

A visitor would be very foolish to try that pictured

crossing. He knew the treachery of it, from Mospheiran streams—which Saidin, in their crazed, divided world, couldn't visit, either.

There was a place like that once and long ago—a stream set well off the road most took up from a remembered highway, a dirt road he'd hiked up from the ranger station, stones over which water lapped in summertime—

But if one went far, far from that pool, farther up, they'd said in a youngster's hearing, a waterfall poured from high up the side of the mountain. One couldn't hear anything but thundering water from the foot of that waterfall, one just stood there, feeling the mist, enveloped by blowing curtains of it—

Wind-borne, the gray sky above him, and the wind racing off the height: the gale-force winds bent down the trees and swept down deluges on the young and very foolish hiker. He'd been soaked to the skin. He'd had to walk down toward that ranger station to keep from freezing.

There were so, so many half-thought experiences that had brought him to what he was, where he was. He remembered walking long after he thought his knees couldn't stop shaking. He'd known he'd been stupid. He'd known he could freeze to death—at least he'd known that people did, in the mountains; but twelve-year-old boys didn't—he wouldn't, he couldn't, it didn't happen to him.

In fact it hadn't. A ranger had come out looking for him on that trail and brought an insulated poncho. The ranger had said he was a stupid kid and he ought to know better.

Yes, sir, he'd said meekly enough, and he'd known then that even if he might have made it, he'd come close to not making it, and he was aware hiking up there with no glance at the sky hadn't been the smartest act of his life.

But he'd never forgotten, either, the storm sweeping sheets of water off the top of the falls. He'd never forgotten being part of the water, the storm, the sound and the elements up there. He'd felt something he knew he'd never forget. He'd wondered on that shaky-kneed, aching way down if the ranger ever had.

And by the time they'd gotten to the ranger station he'd begun to think, by reason of things the man said, that maybe the ranger had gone up there more than once, but stupid kids up from the tourist camp weren't supposed to have that experience: stupid kids from the tourist camp were what the rangers were up there to protect the wildlife and the falls from. So he'd been embarrassed, then, and understood why the rangers were upset with him, and he'd said he was sorry.

The rangers at the station had phoned his mother, fed him, got him warm, and he'd told the man who drove him down the mountain that he'd like maybe to be a ranger himself someday.

And he'd said that he was sorry they'd had to go out looking for him.

The ranger had confided in him he didn't mind the hike up. That he'd hike up the trail in blizzards and icestorms himself to take photographs.

Then for the rest of the trip the man had told him about what gear you really needed to survive up there, and how if he happened by when he was older, he should come up and see about the summer program the rangers had.

In the way of such things, his mother hadn't let him repeat his escapade. She'd chosen the north slopes of Mt. Allen Thomas the next season, probably to keep him from such hikes, and he and Toby both had taken up skiing, to the further detriment of his knees, Toby's elbow, and the integrity of their adolescent skulls.

Saidin said—he should see this place. Atevi appreciated such sights. Atevi found themselves moved by such things. There was something, *something,* at least, that touched a spot in two species' hearts, or minds, or whatever stimulus it took to take a deep breath and feel— whatever two species felt in such places that transcended—whatever two species found to fight about.

He felt less abraded and confused, at least, in the memory-bath. He regretted lost chances—messages unsent: he wondered what Mospheira would think if he asked the international operators to patch him through to the ranger station above Mt. Allen Thomas Resort.

He imagined what contortions the spies on both sides of the strait would go through trying to figure out that code. It all but tempted him.

But he lived his life nowadays just hoping that things he remembered were intact, unchanged, still viable in a rapidly evolving world. He tried to reckon what the man's age had been. He couldn't remember the man's name. The paidhi—with all his trained memory—couldn't recall the man's name.

More, he was afraid to learn the man might have left, or died. He lived all his life somewhere else—afraid to know something he'd left, if he tried to access it, might have changed—or died.

And that particular cowardice was his defense against all that could get to him.

God, what a morass of reasoning. Sometimes—

Sometimes he was such a construction of his own carefully constructed censorships and restraints he didn't know whether there any longer was a creature named Bren Cameron, or whether what he chose to let bubble to the reflective surface of his past defined the modern man, and the rest of him was safely drowned under that shiny surface that swallowed childhood ambitions, childhood dreams, childhood so-called friends—about whom he didn't like to think—

Was *that* the origin of his capacity to turn off that human function and look for something else?

Strip those pieces away and he guessed there wouldn't be a whole man left. Break down the constructions he'd made of his memories and something essential went— that old business with the ranger station, that was a stone that held up other stones, and it would mean something calamitous to him if the man was dead, he supposed— *that* was why he instinctually tucked it close and wouldn't change it, the way he wouldn't change other things, not the hurts, not the flip down the snowy slope that had provided his first experience with mortality, and crutches, not slipping off a mossy stone on a summer hike on the mountain, either, and squishing back to camp in an experience that gave a portrait of the fabled Terraces textures and temperatures and value in his adult and harried mind.

He didn't know what damn good it did to accumulate more and more experiences like that as you lived, so that you could forget them all when you died—unless somehow what mattered was doing something with them: the older you got, the wiser you grew, the more power you got within your hands.

Maybe that was what it meant. Doing something.

Young, you ran the risks the way he'd gone up on that mountain; fresh from college you ran the risks you knew about because you had life to spare and nothing touched the truly fortunate; experienced in infighting and with more power to screw things up than you ever wanted—you sweated blood, and questioned every damn step of the way, foresaw/remembered the disasters, and kept on the track and kept sweating and trying to do your job only because you knew the young and the educated didn't remotely know where they were going.

The ranger might have his own reasons for climbing up there. But he'd gone up that night after a kid who might have made it on his own, and, who knew? Being a kid all the same: maybe if he'd made it on his own, he might have been the same cocksure disaster as Hanks was.

Or he might have tried hiking up there again in a storm, with less luck, in which case, no Bren, Hanks would have succeeded Wilson, Tabini would have been dealing with her and all history might be different. The ranger who'd trekked up the hill in the driving rain hadn't been interested in returning starships and international crises, and probably wouldn't have stopped to listen to a protestation Bren was going to be somebody vital—he'd have just said, as he had said, "Here, kid, get warm."

That man hadn't counted on knowing the outcome of what he did. He'd done what he did for the reasons that brought him to the mountain. He might have hauled a hundred kids down off the trails. He might not know that he'd saved a life. Or damned the planet to lose what he valued.

There was a step in the hall. It wasn't the aiji's advisement he was under arrest. It was Saidin come personally to say dinner was about to be served.

"Still so thoughtful," Saidin said.

"Still so much to do," he said, thinking to himself that he evidently had to write that letter to Ilisidi—

Saying, what? I'm sorry. Evidently we've been doing exactly what you suspected, and I forgot to wonder about what you asked me?

I'm sorry—the assurances I wanted you to give your associates may not be justified?

Stone to damn stone to damn slippery stone. Tabini hadn't arrested him. Therefore Tabini *wanted* him to do that—he guessed so at least. He'd do so after supper. He'd find diplomatic language. He'd find words to explain himself.

His mind was back in that battering blast of cold spray and rain and sound and wind. Everything was gray and his skin was numb. He should have seen that numbness as a danger signal. To him, at that time, it had been environment, like the sound, like the color of the air. He hadn't known he could die of it. He hadn't known he should question his own reactions.

One was supposed to get smarter than that, over time. At least one told oneself so.

18

Supper was solitary. Algini was on duty, Tano was still
out seeing to something regarding the clerical office,
which had occupied an inordinate amount of Tano's time.
Neither Banichi nor Jago was available yet, and by no
means would Saidin sit down to table in front of the staff.
Everything he wondered about seemed negative. He still
had a difficult letter to phrase to Ilisidi, he hadn't had a
reply to his message to Tabini, he hadn't gotten the anticipated message from Jase, and he told himself that *if* he
hadn't it wasn't Jase's personal decision; no, that level of
responsibility was ultimately by the decision of the ship's
captain, possibly the occupation of ship's communications in hot and heavy conspiracy with Mospheira, and it
wasn't exactly politic to call the ship and ask whether
Jase was available, like some stiffed and forgotten assig-
nation.

Not politic, though an option at this point; but, always
to take into account, he spoke for Tabini, at least until arrested, and if Jase missed appointments it wasn't the
paidhi's job to cajole Jase into keeping them. The paidhi's
job was to report the missed communication to Tabini,
which he had done, translate Tabini's response, which he
hadn't yet received, always supposing Tabini wasn't trying to restrain his temper and weigh the paidhi's value future and present before ordering him dropped into a quiet
place out of the way of trouble.

Harm him—he didn't think so. But he'd given Tabini
one hell of a headache, and reason to think that the human advice he'd had wasn't that reliable.

He *hoped* the Jase Graham matter and the whole agree-

ment with the ship wasn't becoming one more item to
blow up in his face today, unraveled by better bribes from
Mospheira. It would total out his account with no few
skeptics in the hasdrawad and the tashrid, and if he could
guess a reason for the prolonged silence, he'd bet *Phoenix*
was using whatever means it had to discover what
Mospheira did have.

If he had to place an interpretation on Graham's missing two days contacting him, they coincided well with
Mospheira's new proposal, and he didn't expect the diplomatic obstacles at this point to fall like dominoes: things
didn't work that way, not with so many interests to protect.

Which meant, given the initiative toward the ship
might fail, the Mospheiran initiative and his offer of cooperation with the President might fail.

In which case—back to square one, with vastly damaged credibility, even granted Tabini left him in charge of
anything. If they had to go back to negotiations, Tabini
wouldn't budge from what he saw as already his—though
Tabini might sound as if he were budging—and come after the matter from a new vantage, one of those small
privileges of a leader with consensus pre-voted and as yet
unwavering. And he might want to cut off communications for a while. Not what the paidhi would suggest.
But—

Maybe—maybe the ship had found some technical
glitch in the lander. Maybe they found their target date
slipping for safety reasons and they were waiting for reports.

Maybe it just took a long time to analyze the imaging
he was sure they were using.

One certainly had to ask what the captain's motives
were for speaking so frankly with Mospheira, considering
he had to know the mainland picked up the conversations.
They could encode, he was relatively certain, using things
the Defense Department knew and he didn't.

But the ship didn't do that, unless there was something
going through the telemetry.

He could think himself in circles. *Nothing* was worse than sitting in an informational blackout.

He held himself to tea, not liquor, told himself even the quantity of what he'd been pouring down wasn't without effect on the nerves, and he had to stop gulping entire cups of it as the only relief from thought and action—tea that lacked alkaloids was still native to the planet and contained minute amounts of stimulant that could add up.

But, damn, it did keep the mouth from drying. He thought of asking for it iced, which would scandalize the house—and wished the weather would take that pending turn to cooling. The active sea-winds of morning had become a sultry Shejidan night, and good as the concealed ventilation generally was, he longed for autumn, when he could pile blankets on the bed and sleep the night through. *Sleep* was increasingly attractive, even lying abed was—and he still had to draft that letter to Ilisidi.

"Nand' paidhi," a servant came to the tableside to say, "nand' paidhi, the telephone."

Jase, he thought, and left his chair in haste. His glum mood evaporated—he was ready to get on with the business of the ship, the site, the landing, the whole future that otherwise he couldn't deal with.

"Bren?"

Barb.

"Hello? Bren?"

It took a second to catch his breath, switch mental gears, switch languages so he could *think* what Barb wanted. "Yeah," he said.

"Bren, what's the matter?"

"There's nothing the matter."

"You asked me to go over to your mother's."

He remembered. He remembered the conversation with Toby, which didn't rest in the same memory area with Tabini, Ilisidi, and Jase Graham. "Yeah."

"Bren, are we all right to talk?"

"Yeah, yeah, go ahead."

"She's all right. A little spooked. Somebody wrote some letters, somebody kept calling on the phone, leaving messages on the system, got some of her private numbers."

"Private numbers."

"Just things they shouldn't have accessed. She said she was all right. The police are on to it."

Things they shouldn't have accessed. Access numbers. Access to systems. Not random off-the-street trouble, then. That smelled like the Heritage agitators. Connections. Professionals, who'd ring your phone and drive you crazy. "Yeah. Yes. You tell her I'm fine?"

"Sure." A silence followed. *"So how are you?"*

"Fine."

"You sounded a little vague when you picked up."

"I suppose I did. I was expecting a business call. Sorry."

"So how are you?"

"The cast is off. No real problems. Thanks for chasing that down."

"Yeah, thanks, Bren."

"So how are you getting along?"

"Fine." Another small silence. *"I sort of expected you to call me."*

He didn't know what he'd heard for a moment. He replayed it twice in his head and drew a measured breath.

"Bren?"

"Barb, there is no choice. There *is* no choice. I won't be calling you. You did what you had to do, I think you did the right thing—" He found a certainty in his own mind that he wasn't going back to Mospheira again. Not soon. Or not the same.

But he couldn't say it. Not to Barb. Not to Shawn. He couldn't let them draw the conclusion, or Tabini lost his fair broker. "I think you ought to work on it, give it a chance. Paul's a nice guy."

"I love you, Bren."

It wasn't even painful to hear that maneuver, except in the response and comfort-giving it asked of him. And in what it said about her that he'd never wanted to face. That had rung alarm bells the last time they'd talked. And the timing of the phone calls. And her message to him after he'd left. And her not showing up at the hospital. He'd thought in her turning away from him she was giving *him*

the reality dose. He doubted all of a sudden that she had
it to give.

"Bren?"

Tears. He heard the quaver.

"I can't help you," he said. "I can't fix it. You hear
me?"

*"Bren. You don't know what it's like, you don't know,
you've got the whole government around you, and we
protect you from it, everybody protects you from it, because you come home to rest, but we live with it, we live
with it all the time, your mother's scared to answer her
phone, your brother's scared—they're saying you've gone
over, they're saying you're selling us out, and people believe it—people at work believe it, and it's our fault, isn't
it? And we're left here shaking our heads and saying, Oh,
no, Bren's not like that, Bren wouldn't do that, Bren's just
getting what he can get—but I've got reporters ringing
my phone, I've got messages stacked up on the system,
my parents are scared—"*

"All the more reason to keep your distance from me."

"They say you're not coming home."

"Who says that?"

"People. Just people."

"I'm doing my job, Barb. Same as always." He hadn't
been in the habit of lying to Barb. It was one more curtain
falling. It was no worse for his mother or Toby than he'd
already found out. That they hadn't come to the hospital
began to make a certain amount of sense. And maybe it
was a good reason and a good time to say a firm good-
bye. Leave the game to those who had signed on for it.
"You take care, Barb. Don't pay attention to fools. Don't
tolerate them, either. If you're getting those calls, you call
the police."

*"I have. A lot of times you don't know about. I mean,
a long time before this, Bren. A lot of times."*

"Best I can do, Barb. Best I can say. I won't be calling.
Hear? Don't put off the rest of your life. You made a
good decision. Stick by it."

"Don't talk to me like that!"

"You know Wilson. That's my reality. It's not yours."

"Dammit, no—Bren, don't you hang up on me!"

"Don't overdramatize, Barb. It won't work. Good night, see you sometime, get it straightened out."

Her phone slammed down.

Good, he thought, and stood there a moment, aware there were servants near him. Always. Always witnesses. Atevi didn't have a single word for lonely. Just—without *man'chi.*

He laid the handset in the cradle and stood there holding the aching arm against him; stood, with nowhere to go, now that he'd put paid to the account. He was hurt. He was disappointed in Barb. He'd thought Barb had things better put together. He'd thought—he didn't know. He'd thought maybe he was the one who lacked—whatever it took to form relationships. But it was one too many turnabouts, it was one too many richochets from decision to decision—and Barb expecting rescue. Barb expecting praise for living, which in his book, people just—somehow—did.

Maybe that was what he'd been for Barb. The fantasy life. The rescue from mundanity. When the real world piled up—when it rang phones and intruded on her in her life—she'd fled to Paul. When it kept after her and Paul didn't solve it—now she was mad at Paul and she loved him. Angry people on the street wasn't what Barb wanted to confront. That wasn't the fantasy she had. She just wanted the relationship to look forward to. The pie-in-the-sky fix-up . . . *when he got home.* . . . Always when he got home.

Not a charitable analysis. But from hurt, he was back to damned mad, and two totally disparate things fell into place: Paul and his computers. Him and his absences. It came to him that Barb didn't want engagement, didn't want day-to-day reality in a relationship. She wanted to wait. That was what she did. She'd go on waiting. No matter how he wrenched his gut to try to offend her—he couldn't. They'd fought before, and she'd find a reason to forgive him for the way he'd signed off; she'd stop being mad, she'd wait for him. She'd chatter with her friends at work, them with their on-again, off-again relationships.

She'd top all their crises with hers. She'd fantasize about him coming back. What she *had*—was always garbage. What she waited for—was always wonderful.

Far from charitable.

Damn right. But he was madder than he'd ever been in their relationship, and it went back to that not-so-chance-timed message she'd blasted him with. He was a man agencies used; transactions he understood, transactions he was used to tracking and evaluating. And he had a sense when the use had gotten outrageous, he recognized crisis-oriented timing, the phone calls timed to get your attention and leave you with no damn choices—every damn phone call she'd made was right when he damn well knew he was finishing his day and trying to get to sleep. He knew pressuring an opponent down to the limit, and a behavior that twined itself around late-evening emotionally fraught messages instead of level-headed waking-hour phone calls for an ex-lover assumed a pattern that really, really set off alarms in his gut; a pattern that argued that his subconscious had been better informed on the feelings he'd been getting than his waking brain had been for the last several years.

Tabini shoved you to the wall. The Department would.

The Department had. But you didn't have them in your bed, you didn't have them telling you they loved you: atevi didn't have the word, the Department had it flagged under restricted usage, and Barb just used it for what she currently wanted.

God, he'd learned at least some few things in semantics.

And while his mind was still in human-mode, and while he had his head momentarily clear of his own brand of wishful thinking, he picked up the handset again to deal with the other unpleasant and inevitable phone call on his own schedule, before he had to write that damned letter to Ilisidi.

"Nadi," he said to the Bu-javid operator, "ring Hanks-paidhi: this is Bren Cameron."

"Yes, nand' paidhi."

He took a breath while the phone was ringing, leaned

his shoulders against the wall to ease his legs and rest a slightly aching head, waited. *Hoped* Hanks wasn't in a mood. And swore that if she was, and if she crossed him, she was going to run into a meat grinder. He *wanted* a fight on equal terms, near at hand, nothing long-distance. He wanted, dammit, a human conversation, on whatever terms. Hanks at least fought fair and Hanks wasn't a long-distance call.

Obsessive behaviors. Late-evening phone calls. Barb upset his sleep.

Four rings.

"This is Deana Hanks."

In atevi. In polite atevi.

"Good evening, Ms. Hanks. How's the report coming?"

"I'm working on it. Fast as I can. —On my own, Cameron. Using your information."

He dropped into Mosphei'. "A little news I thought you'd like to know. I ran out to a local observatory, talked with the astronomers there on the theory we don't have the full range of concept words we need. I got a report back. I don't know what the whole gist of it is, but I did submit the faster-than-light business to them as a paradox—and there's a gentleman who's been working on something about human origins that at least has the astronomers and the mathematicians talking. I don't know if it has the merit of solving anything—I've a lot of nervousness about it. But it's atevi. And it seems to be on the right track."

A silence. *"I thought that was what you* didn't *want."*

"It's *there*. Slip or not, what you said, you can't stop it being there, not now. The atevi gentleman seems to have struggled up to a notion of a spacetime environment—a glimmer of an answer maybe waiting for the right question. It's the old speculation: atevi theory finally pulling ahead of the engineering."

Another long silence. *"On FTL?"*

"Other sciences, all playing catch-up to what we keep throwing at them—that's filled their time. But astronomers haven't *had* our input on any scale to occupy their whole attention. Their work's all been vindication of what they missed, and why they missed it. *We've* been their focus: where we came from. Why they didn't know. No showy engineering. Just wondering if they could trust their measurements. Asking how to know the real distances."

"That's pretty incredible, Cameron."

"And going from there to the hard questions. How old is the universe? How did a ship get here? Is there substance out there? Is there really an ether?"

"You're setting me up. Right?"

"No setup. I just thought you'd like to know what's going on." The adrenaline had run out. He let himself relax against the wall, let a breath go, actually relieved to have a sane, self-protective reaction on the other end of the line. "We can have our differences, but let's be professionals: nothing to the atevi's detriment. We both make mistakes, that's all. We're bound to. We haven't got a damn lot of Departmental help here. We could blow something up. Major. Let's please try not to."

"What's this about, Cameron? What do you really want?"

"The sound of your voice. It's been a day. The ship's still dealing with the atevi *and* Mospheira, so you know. We still haven't got a landing site—I'm still waiting for a call."

"My sources say a lander is the vehicle. An old lander the station didn't use."

"Your sources are right."

"Graham and Mercheson?"

"Right again. Where *do* you get your information?"

"Exactly where and when your people let me have it, I'm damn sure."

"Not my orders."

"The hell."

"If I could depend on you taking orders, certain atevi could get some sleep, now, couldn't they? So could we both. I'd *like* to, Deana. We've got one job to do, keeping the peace. Neither of us wants it broken. We don't see eye to eye, but at least we agree on what we don't want."

"So what's the news in the great outside?"

"Committee meetings. More committee meetings. Briefings. The mathematicians are holding court." He'd slipped out of Mosphei' and into atevi without thinking, the moment he hit the schedule. "How *is* the report coming, seriously? Have you got everything you need?"

"I have some detailed questions."

"Anything I can answer?"

"I need transport figures. What's the month by month availability on tanker-cars and flatcars, age, type, tonnage, that kind of thing, on the northern lines?"

"God, I can get it. I could tell you, roughly."

"Garbage in, garbage out. But it's a plug-in figure if you want me to play with it and give you for-instances."

He weighed the next offer very carefully. But all the Transport members but Kabisu were solidly Tabini's: that committee was an area of minimal potential damage. "I could set you up with some committee time, if you'd like to have a meeting. I'd do setup with aides first, let them know what you're going to want.

"So what's the catch, chief?"

"None. I see no problem. Fix your vocabulary list in advance. Don't embarrass us."

"Cameron—"

"—Or be an ass."

"I didn't say anything."

Definite improvement in the temperature level. "I'll set it up."

"When?"

"I'll see the minister tomorrow, at least I hope to, barring other glitches. A lot of these committees are running on limited sleep these days. But Commerce, Trade, Transport, any and all of them—they're pretty well staffed, and it's an important piece of work. Just no damn politicking, Deana."

"Don't tell me—"

"—Deana. —All right?"

"All right."

He let go a clenched-up breath. "I want to tell you—"

"Yes?"

"Deana, I appreciate the cooperation. You had a damn

hard landing on the job, I'm realizing that. I just wanted to tell you—"

"*Let's not drown in sentiment, here.*"

"No danger of that. Can we just—"

"*I know—God!—oh, God!—Baighi?* Baighi?"

"Deana?"

Something popped, dim and dull. Baighi was security. He heard the phone fall, he heard Deana's voice, muffled—he had the presence of mind to push Record— and to leave the phone open as he ran out into the hall. "Algini!" he yelled, and ran as far as the center hall, with servants staring in shock.

"Nand' paidhi!" Algini met him halfway to the foyer, gun in hand, servants gathering all around. "What's happened?"

"Hanks-paidhi's in trouble. Something's happened. Get security down there. I think it was gunfire. I was on the phone with her. Hurry!"

Algini didn't ask—Algini ran back for the security station and he turned back from the dining room through a gathering of anxious, frightened servants.

"Just stay inside," he said to them. "Doors locked. Where's Banichi and Jago?"

There was a babble of answers, wide, frightened eyes. No one seemed to know. Tano was out on business. Algini was by himself. Saidin arrived, late and anxious. "Nadi," he said to her as calmly as he could, "an armed attack on Hanks-paidhi. Call the aiji. Warn him. Check all the doors to the hall." He wanted to go back to the phone again and hear what he could—but there was no assurance where the attack was aimed or where it might aim; he ducked into his bedroom, flung open dresser drawers, one after another, desperately searching beneath stacks of clothes for the gun Banichi had told him was there.

Sixth drawer on the left. He pulled it out from under sweaters, checked the clip as Tabini had shown him, his hands starting to shake as he shoved the clip back in. He stood up, tucked it in his coat under the bad arm, and exited his bedroom, headed down the hall to the private rooms, where he'd left the phone open to Hanks' apartment.

Security the aiji could relax at will. Jago had said that. He remembered it as he reached the office and picked up the phone.

The line sounded dead, now. He couldn't tell. He stayed on a moment, thinking of the arrest order he'd courted—looked toward the half-darkened hall. Light stopped where he was, at the office. The rest, toward the lady's personal apartment, was dark.

He laid down the phone, left the recorder going. The apartment around him resounded faintly to doors opened and closed, servants hurrying presumably wherever they had to perform security checks. He went back out into the hall, light to his left, darkness to his right—covering darkness, darkness that didn't cast a shadow. He longed to take a fast look from the balcony down toward the garden courts where Hanks' apartment was to see whether it was a single attack or anything wider going on—wider, meaning an action against the established order. Or failing that—to ask Algini if he'd found out anything. But it was a risk even crossing the wide-windowed rooms in the lighted section of the halls to get back to the foyer where Algini was.

The other direction offered, for someone confident of the furniture and knowing his way in the dark, a chance to look out without silhouetting himself against lights, a chance to spy down from the height at least to see if there were lights below, and where, and if the search was tending higher or lower on the hill.

More—it struck him that none of the servants had come this way. The balcony doors to the rear, the ventilation for the breakfast room, were most probably securely locked—one expected that at this hour—but the servants were all checking the public, more trafficked areas of the apartment, he couldn't call the servants back without risking them passing doors or windows that might make them targets, and it suddenly seemed urgent and incumbent on him to be sure of those balconies. That the doors were shut, granted: he didn't feel a breeze—but whether they were locked was altogether another question, granted also the lady's servants might not have been through two recent attacks—or have any weapon more deadly than carving knives.

He walked briskly down the hall—found the breakfast room as he expected, all dark, the white gauze curtains resting still, in moonlight and the general city nightglow. He took his hand with the gun from under his coat and walked directly and with some dispatch along the wall, taking the lack of draft or movement in the curtains as proof that the doors were closed—the room was almost always drafty and airy otherwise.

He moved them aside, assured of his invisibility there. Light showed, reflected among the lower roofs, not lights that belonged there, he was well sure. One such light even while he watched moved along the roof line, someone carrying a light, he thought—he could see it from the side of the room as he followed the wall.

Then he felt a draft- saw the curtains move, then, and realized to his dismay the farther door was open.

He stopped. He didn't *know* the doors hadn't been open all along. He almost retreated, then thought that was what he'd come for: he had to shut and lock that door.

He went to it, moved to shut it and felt a faint presence on his side of the room—he couldn't see it, he couldn't identify it ... he couldn't swear it was there. Panic sweated his palms.

Don't acknowledge you're awake, Banichi had told him. It was like that. He moved slowly away with the gun in hand, asking himself what now, what next—he didn't know it wasn't his imagination, he didn't know it wasn't one of his own—he didn't know what to do.

The glass doors near him burst in gunfire, curtains billowed, glass fell in shards, and the presence he'd felt hurtled out of the dark, knocked him stunned to the floor, scrambled over him. The gun had left his hand. Weight crushed him to the tiles. A second burst of gunfire punched the curtains back, and lights swept the balcony. An atevi body lay breathing hard atop him as shots flew over their heads, raked the walls, showered them with plaster and porcelain until the shots stopped.

Then the ateva got up to a crouch and went out the shattered doors, leaving him a second to scrabble across a dark and fragment-littered floor after the gun—he found it in the dark, but the floor and his head had collided in that fall, his arm ached with a mindful fury and his knees buckled as he tried to get up.

There was no more gunfire, at least. He found himself sitting on the floor of the breakfast room in the dark, finally got wobbly legs under him and edged in what he trusted was a prudent crouch out toward the threshold of the shattered doors, gun in shaking hand.

"Get down!"

Banichi's voice, clearly. Banichi shoved down hard on his shoulder, the night went red, and he sat down, winded and blind for an interval, while Banichi occupied the doorway onto the balcony and kept him out of line of whatever was going on—watching, Bren thought, but having no such luck as a clear target. There were just too many people, too many windows.

But if attack had come here—

"Tabini," he said to Banichi.

"Safe," Banichi said. "Stay down, nadi!"

"Sorry," he breathed. "I was checking the doors."

"One could tell. I came in that way. Stay down."

He was content for the moment, in the flare-up of pain from the shoulder, to sit exactly as he was, in a fetal tuck, with the arm hurting only vaguely.

"Where—" he thought to ask. "Where's Hanks? Is this set up, or—?"

"Hanks-paidhi is missing from her apartment," Banichi said, "and Baighi is dead."

Then it *wasn't* something Tabini had done. Baighi was Tabini's. Hanks was in someone else's hands. "I was on the phone with her," he said, still having trouble getting breath. "I heard what might have been a shot, I put the phone on Record—"

"This will have been useful," Banichi said. "Is it still running?"

"Unless someone's stopped it. The lady's office. I laid the receiver down."

"I'll see to it," Banichi said. "Are you all right, Bren-ji?"

"I'm fine. Who *was* that out there? Who's done this?"

"I'm not certain. I don't think I hit anyone."

"Ilisidi—" he said. He hadn't thought, until then, of Ilisidi's apartment below his—of the possibility of Ilisidi's danger—or—he suddenly realized—Ilisidi's involvement.

But that was too crazed. An attack like this, lacking all finesse—Cenedi wasn't like that. Cenedi didn't need to blow walls down.

The Atigeini themselves were a possibility. Damiri's outraged relatives might count doors cheap if they could get a human presence out of their ancestral residence, and get their name clear with the conservatives with whom they had more than slight ties—

Two—very good—very alarming—possibilities. And he could hope it was the Atigeini—he could earnestly hope it was the Atigeini—or even the Guisi. The man who'd fired on him in the legislature, the man Jago had killed—his relatives might have planned a retaliation, except—

"The matter against me," he said to Banichi, "didn't pass the Guild. Did it? Or is there another? These— reckless as they are—don't feel like amateurs, Banichi."

"No," Banichi said, to which associated question was uncertain. But it covered the matter. And left him with a chill despite the sultry evening.

"Where's Jago? Is she all right?"

"Roof," Banichi said shortly.

Jago was in condition for that kind of gymnastics. Banichi, with his currently game leg, wasn't. And Banichi wasn't pleased, he picked that up. Jago was the junior in the partnership, Jago wasn't the one Banichi would ordinarily have in that position.

But there was in not too long a time a shadow against the curtains, and an exchange of some kind with a hand signal—Banichi waved to someone he could see from where he sat— and the affair dragged on in nervous silence, maneuvering or scouting going on, but he didn't want to chatter like a fool into Banichi's ear while Banichi needed his attention for business. What it meant was a power struggle going on in the Bu-javid, a quiet, discreet shifting of position among lords' protective security; a matter of fencing, he guessed, arms clenched on a nervous stomach, as various lords tried to figure out exactly who'd moved, where they'd moved, why they'd moved, and what side they were on or who was winning in this unannounced shadow-war.

Ludicrous, on one level. Grimly humorous. And not. Atevi historically didn't engage in vast conflicts, when little ones would do. But important people and ordinary ones could end up quite effectively dead.

Eventually a faint voice spoke from the pocket-com, and whatever the verbal code said, Banichi judged it safe to stand up—hand holding the edge of the door, which Banichi ordinarily didn't need, so the leg was bothering him, considerably; Banichi had taken a heavy jolt himself, in that tackle, and Banichi wasn't in a happy mood.

"Get back," Banichi said to him, no politeness about it, and Bren got up cautiously and moved through the dark room in the direction Banichi pointed him, steps breaking already broken glass where the panes had come in, a shot from outside, Bren judged. There was nothing but empty air out in front of that balcony, until one got a very distant vantage from the ell of the distant roof of the legislative halls: the lower roofs weren't at any useful angle for someone trying to get a shot into the apartment.

The legislative roofs. A very good shot with a very good sight.

Or someone rappeling down from the roof above. Where Jago was. He was worried about her safety up there in what was a very high-above-the-courtyards world of what didn't look like safe tiles. But he had no desire to harass Banichi away from necessary concerns, and he was sure Jago was one of the most urgent.

Banichi shepherded him out into the corridor, out into a darkness farther-reaching than it had been when he'd gone down into the area—more lights were off, and Banichi took him as far as Damiri's dark office before he turned on a very dim penlight, picked up the recording cassette from the phone, and pocketed it.

"This," Banichi said, "was well thought. *This* gives us a chance."

Praise could turn a man's head—and distract him from the other information Banichi gave him by that: that the attack on Hanks might have caught Tabini and the Bujavid staff totally by surprise.

Which left a broad range of the offended and the ambitious for suspects, if Hanks was the principle target.

But it didn't explain what they'd meant by attacking the third floor, which they couldn't remotely reach except from the roof.

And then carry off a human, granted he was the size of an atevi nine-year-old, over the roofs, with Tabini's guard in pursuit?

Maybe carrying him off really hadn't been the objective.

Maybe dead would have satisfied them quite well.

That thought didn't settle his stomach.

He stayed close to Banichi on the way through the equally darkened sitting room and into the brightly lighted center of the apartment where the servants had gathered in an agitated cluster in the protected, windowless area. There Banichi was all business, giving orders to the servants, answering nothing extraneous—he ordered all passages the servants used shut and locked, ordered no one to move in those passages on any excuse until further notice, and the servants listened in solemn attention.

"Damiri," Saidin said, arriving from the foyer, "says no attack came against them. Are you all right, nand' paidhi?"

"I'm fine. I fear the breakfast room isn't."

"Stay here!" Banichi said, and more quietly, "nand' Saidin."

An attack specifically on the paidhiin. An attack— perhaps on the institution, not the personalities: the institution that made negotiation possible between human and atevi. He found himself increasingly shaken, even protected in the flurry of atevi security precautions and communications between various entities that watched over him. Banichi said they should move to the foyer where they could find Algini, and they went that far, with madam Saidin trailing them.

"Nand' paidhi," Algini began—disheveled clothing seemed to tell the tale, and "I'm quite all right," Bren said, then realized he had sparkles of shattered glass on his trousers and coat and couldn't decide where to dust himself off that people wouldn't track it every which way. Meanwhile Banichi went to the desk inside the foyer security office and called Bu-javid headquarters, at least that was what it sounded like: he heard Banichi report the existence of the tape.

Then Banichi put the tape to play at high volume on their own security office phone system, looking for sounds, names, God knew what. Bren drifted in behind Algini, lost behind a solid wall of tall atevi bent over the machine, and heard only bumps and thumps, a sound that could have been Deana's voice, or furniture being moved. Then a closing door.

Then what sounded like muffled gunfire, he wasn't sure. He hoped not. Banichi began to replay the tape, louder.

Tano wasn't available. Jago was somewhere up on the many-angled roofs. Banichi could look for information, and Saidin could give orders to the servants, but the paidhi had no job and no distraction in the crisis: he finally went out to the foyer, cradling an aching arm, worrying helplessly about Tano and Jago and, disturbed, he was forced to admit it, at the memory of Deana's alarm. Banichi and Algini had made another phone call, in the security station, and straying near the door, he overheard with a sinking heart that not one but two of Tabini's agents were dead.

Killed by someone with skill enough to go against the level of Guild members Tabini employed; and not just one, but two of them. No contract was out, Banichi had said so. It surely wasn't amateurs, this time. It wasn't legal, either. That meant Guild-level assassins on private business—which happened, he knew that; but it didn't make the Guild happy.

And whatever Banichi had found, rapid-scanning the audio tape, whatever information Algini was still searching for in his continued phone-calling, Banichi started up a converse now with various posts via the pocket-com and paced the foyer and the security station alike with a predatory glower, *wanting* to be more directly involved, and clearly frustrated in what other searchers had found or hadn't found.

"Nadi," Banichi said at one point, into the com, "don't tell me. *Do* it!"

Someone had just caught the edge of Banichi's exasperation; and the paidhi judged it a good time to stand very quietly against the wall of the foyer and not be in Banichi's way or Algini's, the both of them hampered by injuries and in no pleasant reception of what they were hearing from elsewhere in the Bu-javid.

"There's no sign of Hanks-paidhi," Banichi finally said with a sharp glance in his direction. "This is difficult to achieve in the quarantine of the lower courts."

"Someone who knows the area?" Bren asked. "Inside? Servants' passages?"

"Few such passages, none to that area. Knowledge of the area, yes, and, one suspects, the silence of the victim."

"Dead?"

"Why remove a body?"

"She doesn't weigh much. They could tuck her up in a box, a serving carrier—"

"A possibility. One we're investigating. But so far no one noticed. And that—"

Came a signal at the door of someone wanting entry, and Algini, who had just that instant been on the pocket-com, ordered the door opened, which said, apparently reliably enough for Banichi, that he knew who was there.

Naidiri was wanting entry, Tabini's security—*with* Tabini himself, and Damiri and an accompanying crowd of uniformed security personnel and Bu-javid police.

"Bren-ji," Tabini said, as the visitation flooded into the foyer.

Saidin was quick to welcome Damiri-daja—Tabini was quick to disperse his staff and the police to various points of the foyer, the security office, the apartment and the servant corridors.

Meanwhile Tabini laid a hand on Bren's shoulder, fortunately not the one that ached like very hell.

"You're safe, nadi? One hears there was a window shot through."

"Doors, aiji-ma." He didn't know why now, in all that had gone on, he should suddenly have the wobbles back in his knees or the flutter back in his stomach. He still had the gun in his pocket, and wished, with Tabini's security suddenly everywhere around him, that he had put it back where he'd gotten it, in his bedroom drawer. Tabini knew he had it—or on principle, Tabini knew—but his security might not; and even Tabini might not explain it to the hasdrawad. "I fear there's serious damage to the premises. The breakfast room. I don't know how bad. I'm very sorry. I haven't seen it with the lights on."

"One can hardly hold you responsible," Tabini said.

Not responsible and not entirely useful in the investigation. Did you see anything and did you hear anything? were the obvious questions from Naidiri, and, No, was his lame answer, Nothing except a few words before what's on the tape from the telephone, which Banichi was able with some satisfaction to produce; and graciously attributed its existence to the paidhi's quick thinking.

He quoted Deana's outcry, gave his interpretation of it—and his memory of where Deana would have been standing in that apartment if the furniture was where he'd last seen it.

Then ensued another attempt to hear the background noise—atevi hearing being quite acute, they seemed to pick up something of significance or interest, but they were unclear what. He heard nothing at all, and there wasn't agreement, except to turn the tape over immediately by junior officer courier for Bu-javid security technicians to refine.

Meanwhile the paidhi found it prudent to stay out of the argument of trained security personnel and out of the general traffic: he leaned against the wall, amongst the flowers that had come in earlier that evening, wishing to get out of his glass-impregnated clothing, wishing for a chair, and acutely wishing Banichi had been a little more gentle in falling on him, though he by no means preferred the alternative. He was still trying to think how he could manufacture an excuse to return to his room to rid himself of the incriminating gun, in itself a fracture of Treaty law, a cause of considerable diplomatic flap if even some well-meaning someone happened to notice the weight in his pocket.

And what could he plead then? Tabini gave it to me, when Tabini's position and relation to humans was already being questioned by atevi conservatives *by* this very attack?

Someone else would have to take the blame, and that someone would clearly be Banichi, whose gun it actually was, thanks to a trade they'd made before Malguri, and who was loyal enough to Tabini to take whatever consequences the law or the hasdrawad or Tabini's enemies demanded. If he asked to go back to his room even to change clothes he foresaw some security person going with him for fear of assassins lurking in the shadows, and if not that, at least a handful of servants and maybe Saidin, which had the same result, so it seemed the better part of discretion to stay where he was, to look occasionally interested to excuse his presence underfoot, and to try to remain otherwise as invisible as possible, with the telltale pocket turned to the nearest large vase.

Tabini and Banichi and his senior security began to talk about probable motives: *that* was worth the listening. He strained through the occasional noise from other debates and questionings of the servants to gather where various potential suspects in the Bu-javid had been associating and where certain loyalties were reckoned to lie; who might be exonerated, absolutely, and who might have been tacitly or financially in on the proposal against the paidhi in the Guild, the motion that had failed the vote—a matter in which Banichi and Naidiri knew the specific names and even Tabini, evidently, did not, nor inquire— but there were generalities passed that involved the obvious names, the heads of the conservative clans, not, one noted, studying the floor tiles, the Atigeini, but it wasn't a name to raise with Damiri in the vicinity.

Then notification via pocket-com came in to Tabini and his security chief about the progress of the search through the lower court, where Hanks had disappeared—nothing encouraging so far, and the paidhi, feeling wobblier and wobblier, could, finally, only ask himself whether they were right in suspecting something against the established order and whether it was not instead the paidhiin's doings, placing the atevi universe-concept under attack.

Grigiji's mathematics.

His visit to the observatory.

Ilisidi hadn't read the paper and then gotten angry: Ilisidi had grown colder and colder, once that paper landed on her table and its implications landed in the delicate equation of atevi politics.

Which might mean—another perusal of the floor tiles, which had brown squares and brass inclusions in a floral pattern—the paidhi had stuck his good intentions into atevi affairs and atevi debates Ilisidi was already familiar with, come back with a theory that wasn't as new as he thought, or that was somehow controversial in ways a human didn't easily twig to.

Certainly possible when the math came far too esoteric for the paidhi to unravel, when the search after ultimate rationality that atevi had made over thousands of years was bearing atevi results and things proposed to them were going to break down very, very basic beliefs such as—God knew—might set off psychological, political, sociological earthquakes.

The paidhi could only ask himself in that light how much else could come undone today, and how much of it he might have caused, and what subtleties he should have long since guessed. All well-meaning, he'd brought that theory of Grigiji's to the city, he'd let it loose in blind hope that atevi argument might make sense to atevi, and maybe not known enough—as no human was able to know—what other bombshells might lie buried in the document. Hanks had tossed FTL into the dialogue and he'd called her foolish. *He'd* gone into that meeting to Ilisidi in blind faith in her numerical agnosticism, never once considering that Ilisidi herself might hold some well-concealed articles of faith Grigiji could challenge.

He kept playing and replaying the breakfast meeting in his mind, how strange it had seemed to him then that Ilisidi hadn't looked at the papers, that she hadn't deigned to take them—

Dammit, he didn't yet understand Ilisidi's reaction, except to conclude that she disapproved what he was doing, or distrusted what he was doing—or disapproved unread what he had brought her. He didn't think Ilisidi herself would flinch from intellectual challenge, but she would take offense if she thought he was being a gullible fool or if his actions indicated he took her for one.

All of which still left Ilisidi among the suspects. He hadn't heard Tabini bring up the name, but he suspected she was on Tabini's short list. And failing Ilisidi—

"Show me," Damiri said, "show me where these fools attempted, Saidi-ji. I want to see. I'm tired of waiting. We've chased them, we're surely clear by now."

"Nandi," Naidiri began to say.

"I am *not* going to cower in the foyer, naiin-ji. This is Atigeini territory, this is *my* house, and *my* orders, fact; this is *my* window that was broken, fact; and my security and the paidhi's security has things in hand, fact. —So may we quit discussing theory in my house, please, and have a look at *fact* before we loose the Guild?"

"May we discuss *fact* before we rush into the line of fire?" Tabini retorted. "We have too many willing suspects, not all of whom are outside this house."

"I *suspect* nothing! Look to your own relatives!"

"My relatives? *My* relatives? Give me an heir, woman, and we'll discuss our *relatives*. Meanwhile kindly don't walk in front of windows."

"Heir, heir, heir, of course the heir! Any moment, nai-ji, perhaps tonight, nai-ji, and in the meantime—"

"In the meantime, take *orders* like a lady, nai-ji, and make less of a target, fortunate *gods,* woman!"

At a certain point one decidedly found the floor tiles preoccupying and, as the paidhi reflected that, while it was an honor to be treated as part of the household, along with security and the servants, he had much rather—

"Fortunate gods, inform me why I chose an Atigeini!"

"Intelligence. Resourcefulness. Our distinguished history. *My breakfast room,* nai-ji, if you please, with my servants, with your security if you've such doubts of my relatives."

"Gods least favorable, let's see your damn doors," Tabini muttered, and waved a gesture toward the recesses of the apartment. "Naidiri! Have a care to the windows, the lot of you. Damn!"

Forthwith there began an expedition, Saidin in the lead, along with Algini, a crowd of security and police, even certain of the servants, to let Damiri assess the damage to the doors and the breakfast room.

The paidhi found nothing quite graceful to do but tag along as, at least, a witness to the destruction. He hoped for a chance along the way past his bedroom to duck in and put the gun away; but there was security before and behind, and no lingering invited. Someone at least had closed the inner shutters in the study as they passed, and the servants who lined the way were all very quiet, very subdued and worried, bowing like grass in the storm of Damiri's passage and doubtless staring at their backs after they'd gone.

Lights were on throughout the apartment, now; they passed scattered police, scattered security guards, especially in the area of the breakfast room.

And the damage there proved appallingly worse than Bren had feared: not only shattered glass from the doors, but shattered wall tiles where the shots had raked the walls and splintered antique porcelain reliefs that one only hoped restorers could repair. He felt a physical shock, realizing the small size of the fragments where porcelain had met high-powered bullets—some of it might be the dust on his clothing, and he asked himself if they could possibly recover enough chips of porcelain to reassemble or recreate the bas relief of flowers and vines—

"Gods *damn* them!" Damiri said.

Saidin—Saidin looked absolutely devastated.

"Damiri-daja," Bren felt it incumbent on him to say, perhaps foolishly, seeing the thunderous frown on Damiri's face. "Nand' Saidin—I am inexpressibly sorry. I wish—I wish—if I was the target—I'd stood somewhere far less delicate."

Damiri whirled on him so suddenly he feared she meant to hit him. But all the violence in her scowl and the lock of her arms, one in the other, scarcely reached her voice. "Nand' paidhi," she said, "this affront to my house will have an answer. This attack on my guest and my staff will have a severe answer. This willful destruction will have blood. There are those who will carry that answer with or *without* the Guild, with or *without* other Atigeini approval."

" 'Miri-ji," Tabini said reprovingly.

"Don't caution me! This is intolerable! Our human guest can express his shock—so wherein can civilized atevi accept such goings-on? I do not, I *do* not, aiji-ma! Fire at random into the premises? Shoot the servants wholesale along with the target? Naidiri, Sagimi, is this Guild work or is it not?"

"It is not," a man said, and Naidiri echoed, "Not possibly."

Certainly not Cenedi, Bren thought, then, finally finding a landing place for the doubt that had been buzzing around his brain. Not Cenedi. Not any of the men who worked for Ilisidi. He wanted desperately to believe that that was the truth, and on that thought, he wanted to know for certain that Ilisidi was safe.

Not to mention Jago and Tano and his own household.

He listened to the arrangements for restorationists to come in to assess the damage, without, Damiri said, disturbance to the paidhi.

"I will not," Damiri declared, still hot, "let this insult happen and not retaliate. They have *me* to deal with, if

they trust in your forbearance, nai-ji. They hope to pro-
voke my uncle. They hope to send a signal. Well, they've
certainly sent one." She bent and picked up a shattered
flower, a three-petaled lily. "Look, *look* at this destruction. I want my uncle to see this, aiji-ma. I want the
whole world to see it, I want it sent out to the news ser-
vices, along with the advisement the paidhi is quite well
and undisturbed by this foolishness. He can sleep in my
own bedroom and have breakfast with my staff and with
me in this breakfast room. I tell you I will *not* be intim-
idated."

"No, no, no, 'Miri-ji," Tabini said softly. "I'd rather far
less publicity until we find them and eliminate this problem. *Then* use the television, yes, and all the pictures. On
the other hand—*if* you wish to send the image of this
handiwork to your uncle—"

Damiri cast Tabini a silent, sidelong look.

"Send him a piece of the porcelain," Tabini said. "The
lily . . . would do quite well. One believes possibly someone exceeded orders. On the other hand, perhaps they
wished to signal their contempt of Atigeini claims to
command by using this as a diversion."

There was a positively fierce enjoyment in Damiri's
eyes. "Your plane."

"At your disposal. But I want it back by morning. And
it *doesn't* refuel there. —Bren-ji, you're quite safe, one
assures you, in whatever bedroom you choose tonight.
Don't let 'Miri-daja bully you. It's a damn stiff mattress."

One could well blush. "Tabini-ma." The ache in the
shoulder made his teeth hurt, he had never yet found the
chance to be rid of the gun, and he tried consistently to
keep that side and that pocket away from atevi eyes. Especially those of the Bu-javid police. "I only, earnestly,
regret that I attracted such difficulty to this house, and
I'm quite content with my bedroom."

"The paidhi is very gracious," Damiri said, and offered
her hand, expecting his: he gave it, perforce, compelled to
look up to a straightforwardly curious stare, a very solid
handclasp. "Scandal, scandal, scandal. I think it's a very
nice, a very honest face, myself, and my aunt can swal-

low her salacious and doubtless entirely envious suspicions. —You're so exquisitely polite, nand' paidhi."

"I—hope to be, daja-ma."

"I may never get my staff back. They're quite besotted."

"I—hope I've done nothing improper, daja-ma."

"Bren-paidhi. They *dream* nightly of you doing something improper. I've heard the reports."

"Daja-ma—"

Tabini rescued his arm and his hand and walked him a little distance away. "Atigeini internal politics be damned, the lily porcelains are *not* the question, Hanks-paidhi is. The attack on your residence might have been quite serious, but I doubt they expected to succeed: it was likely intended as a diversion from the real objective, and my prospective wife's relatives will *not* take this lightly, not the attack, certainly not the collateral damage, least of all the slight of such damage being a mere diversion, no matter how they've regarded your tenancy here on other principles. Have you any personal suspects in the kidnaping of Hanks-paidhi, Bren-ji?"

"I—no, aiji-ma, discounting that it was anyone of the Guild, no, all my suspects vanish. Except—someone who wanted revenge. Or someone who—" the thought nudged its way to the center of his apprehensions "—who wanted both: her in their hands and me dead—leaving no paidhi between you and Mospheira at this juncture. For whatever reason."

"If they could achieve that. Which they surely don't expect."

"I would not say," Damiri interjected, having overtaken them, "that this attempt evidences great intellect. Desperation. But not great intellect."

"Or carelessness of Atigeini disposition."

"Stupidity," Damiri said. "Aiji-ma."

"The fact that one doesn't care what your uncle thinks is not necessarily evidence of stupidity. —Daja-ji."

"The fact *I* regard the lilies as *my* holding and the artist however dead as in *my man'chi* should have them sleepless at night. If my uncle demurs, I demand satisfaction!"

"One will have it, lily-daja, but the paidhi's safety is in my own, and you will *not* initiate actions that jeopardize Bren *or* that disagreeable woman whose life I foolishly agreed to protect."

"One has no wish to jeopardize Bren in any way." Damiri laid a hand on Bren's sore shoulder: a very gentle hand, of which he was glad. "Have I ever shown such an inclination?"

What did one do? Flinch from under the aiji's lady's hand? One stood still, aware of the double entendre, and said, solemnly, "By no means, nai-ma."

"Aiji-ma." It was Algini in the doorway, bidding for Tabini's attention, with: "The ship is asking for Bren-paidhi. Forgive the intrusion."

The mind—wasn't ready for one more extraneity, not for Mosphei', Mospheiran politics, or foreign negotiations. The mind was on shattered porcelain, Damiri's not-entirely-joking threats, and the intricacies of atevi association: that, and Ilisidi, and the Guisi, and politics and the disappearance of Hanks-paidhi, which, outside its atevi impact, was going to play very badly in certain Mospheiran circles—let alone aboard a ship contemplating sending personnel down to them.

The ship mustn't find out. The associations within the Association had already absorbed all the strain the bonds of *man'chi* would bear. Tabini could *not* bear any reneging on the landing, no matter the reason for caution.

"If I could guess," Algini said, as he headed for the doorway, "it's a young man, nadi-ma."

"Jase," he said.

"The landing," Tabini said, tagging him close. "Possibly."

"Very possibly," he said, on his double train of thought, trying to gather up the lost threads of the Jase Graham affair: like why the ship hadn't called the mainland for two days, and what Mospheira had been trying to argue with the ship, latest, in the meantime, and what he had to say as a contingency to the ship trying to back out for reasons that might have nothing whatsoever to do with assassination attempts.

At least one answer to matters held in suspension—or news that another deal was collapsing—was waiting for him on the phone.

19

"*H*ello?" Jase's voice was cheerful, perhaps, Bren thought, to put the best face on a change of mind. *"Bren? Is that you?"*

He refused to be seduced. But answered the tone. "It better be, since nobody else here can talk to you. How are things up there?"

"Doing fine, actually. How are things below?"

"Oh, fine." He was taking the call in Damiri's office, standing, because otherwise the crowd overwhelmed him: Tabini, Damiri, Banichi, Naidiri, Saidin and two of Naidiri's aides. Which fairly well accounted for the wall space and all the standing room except the small area by the desk that he maintained, holding the phone. "Just kind of waiting for your call."

"Well, sorry about that. Things just proceeded slower than I thought. I hope I didn't worry anybody, but just getting through the notes you sent up and talking to the captains—meetings, chain-reaction meetings, I suppose it's no different where you are."

"No, no, unfortunately not. One of those things that seems to go with air-breathing biology. —So how's the process running?" He didn't *want* to sound short of breath, he tried to keep his voice cheerful and light, and all of a sudden his hands were shaking so he feared he couldn't keep the tremor out of his voice, either. "Sorry. A little out of breath. Had a bit of rush to get here down the hall. Are we agreeing or disagreeing?"

"Agreeing, actually, pretty well. We've picked Taiben for a landing. What's your assessment?"

He cast a look across at Tabini before it dawned on his

shock-numbed brain that Tabini didn't understand. "Taiben," he echoed, and looked in vain for a reaction. "It's convenient, easy to get to and from. Has a jet-port, wide, wide flat with no trees, no likely complications, at least." He got a sign from Tabini, finally, that told him that Tabini understood the choice and accepted it. "Fine with us."

"I've been practicing. How's Dai ghiyi-ma, aigi'ta amath-aiji, an Jase Graham?"

"Hamatha-aijijin, but that's real good." Ears around him had gone quite attentive, and he hoped Jase tried nothing with infelicitous variants. "I'm impressed. You puzzled that out of notes."

"I'm anxious for this to work. They don't just shoot, do they, if they don't recognize you? The island's been saying there's a chance of attacks. But Taiben is the aiji's estate."

"Public land, actually, in the way atevi reckon. But the people on the land are the aiji's staff. And, no, atevi don't go shooting at the aiji's invited visitors. They're trying to scare you."

"That's not difficult at this point. Tell me again the chute's going to open and this is all going to go without a glitch-up."

"Ninety-nine point nine percent of the pods worked." He'd no idea of the real statistic, but statistical accuracy wasn't the reassurance Jase was asking for. "The second that chute takes hold, you're all right, and I imagine you'll feel it; that's what they say in the old accounts. How's the pod look to your experts? That's the important question."

"They've substituted the heat shield. On your advice and our discussing it in committee, they didn't ever unpack the parachute. They're just providing a second one. If the drop—I really hate that word—doesn't slow after the original chute should have deployed, the second chute's supposed to blow open automatically. If they put the canister together right."

"The first one won't fail. You damn sure won't lose two. You're sure of your coming down where you want.

They've got that figured. Just don't use the old targeting. You'll land on Mospheira for sure."

Another nervous laugh. *"I'll be right on the mark, if the parachute opens. If we go to the backup chute, well, I'll fax you the charts and figures. Can you receive those where you are?"*

"No trouble. Just use the protocols I gave you, and I'll walk down the hall and get it."

"Then we're go for launch. Or drop. Or whatever. Landing's due for thirty-two some hours from now, Taiben's dawn, 0638 hours local. Right? Daybreak after tomorrow?"

Less than two days. He took a breath. "0638, dawn, day after tomorrow. I hear you. —That fast, Jase?"

"They're ready. We're ready. They're going to tow us in close before they drop us, a chance to back out, I guess, down to the point they cut us loose. —At which point we trust to atevi hospitality and the gods of gravity wells."

Atevi hospitality. Taiben. Everything Jase was saying indicated the ship had ignored the President's offer to cut atevi out of the deal. Which was incredible to him.

And in a dizzying two seconds of trying to sort out the implications, he'd bet any amount of money the ship knew it would have the same deal out of Mospheira without giving Mospheira a single one of its requests—

Mospheira being the ally they could always have made it completely unnecessary to risk the ill will of atevi, whose reactions they *didn't* know as well—and, thank God, somebody on the human side had thought down a train of logic. Excitement made it hard to keep his voice calm. "Sounds good," he said, he hoped without missing a beat. "There'll be somebody out there to meet you. *I'll* be there to meet you if I can talk the aiji into ferrying me out to the estate. What do you need from us on landing?"

"Get my partner onto the island as soon as possible. Me—I'm at your disposal, I guess. Next several years."

"Well, it's your partner's choice, a good dinner at Taiben, a personal intro to atevi leadership and a night's sleep—or a quick pickup and no-frills rush to the airport at Taiben, then straight on to Mospheira. *You*, on the other hand, absolutely get the deluxe dinner, the personal intro, and a whole night's sleep before they expect you to be fluent."

Nervous laughter. *"Sounds fine to me. I'll take the fancy deal. I'll put it to the captains and Yolanda about the ace-all treatment. Any requests from space?"*

"Just pack walking boots. Something real comfortable. There are places you can land where there are no roads. You'll get a welcome committee. But even after they meet you, you may have to walk to a road, even to a place where we can get overland vehicles, if you happen to drop in somewhere truly inconvenient. It's kilometers of grass out there, dust and heat with no sanitary stops. At worst case, you come down in some woods and we have to cut you out of the trees first. Please be on target. It's much easier. My mark was in an area where they can drive right in and pick you up in fine style."

"As long as they don't shoot at me and as long as that parachute opens, I'm happy."

"So are we all. If you *should* see wildlife, by the way, don't panic; there's no animal out there in the grassland that's going to attack you, and we'll be tracking you all the way down. We'll be there—hopefully *I* will—but if anything intervenes, trust the atevi, be very polite, bow if they bow, and don't worry about where they're taking you. The aiji will have every ranger on the estate warned to watch out for you and to take good care of you. That's a promise."

"I'll take it. Deal."

"I really hope to be there. With luck, I will."

"I'd really feel better."

"I don't blame you in the least—but with me or without me, you'll make it fine. Keep me posted on progress. If I do go out to Taiben, it may take some moments to get to the phones, but I'm almost never out of reach of radio. You can get to me."

"I appreciate that. —And I'd better sign off, now, and quit tying up the chair. Com's got some people working to link with the pod, I'm just cargo at this point, and I really

don't want to annoy the techs. See you. I really mean see you."

"Yeah. Good luck. Good *luck,* Jase, good wishes from me *and* from Tabini-aiji. *Kaginjai'ma sa Tabini-aijiu, na pros sai shasatu.* All right?"

He was looking at Tabini when he said the latter. And Jase signed off with, gained from the material he'd sent up, a courteous repetition, *kaginjai.*

Tabini lifted a brow. Damiri and Saidin stared in evident amazement as he hung up the receiver. Banichi, arms folded, listening from the side of the room, also lifted an eyebrow as if to say, well, there it was, suns might be stars and stars might be suns, and neither bothered him, but a paidhi falling out of the sky into Tabini's estates was about to become real, and for good or for ill within his *man'chi.*

So now Banichi cared about stars, and suns, and people from them.

"Landing at dawn," he said to Tabini. "Day after tomorrow, at the Taiben site. They want one of them possibly to go immediately to the airport after landing and on to Mospheira, but I proposed a slower schedule and an overnight at Taiben, and they're going to present that idea to their authorities. They could well, referring to the information I sent you, aiji-ma, have agreed to deal with Mospheira. And haven't, so far as what the young man just said."

"This suits very well," Tabini said. "Well done, Bren-ji. This young man—Jase Graham—Jase, is that the name?"

"Yes, aiji-ma."

"A long way from fluency. But comprehensible."

"Aiji-ma. Also—I promised him I'd be there to meet him. Knowing I hadn't your confirmation, I told him it might not be possible, but that it was my hope to be at Taiben when the pod touches down. . . . I want very much to do this, aiji-ma, in spite of events tonight. If security is going there—I'd like to be with them."

It seemed all unreal to him. With the breakfast room in ruins. With Hanks—alive or dead or God knew where, in the proceedings of atevi and human politics. And the lander coming down in a game reserve he'd hunted in not so long ago.

He feared he was, at least in Tabini's reckoning, far too protected a piece, if shooting had begun. But—damn, to see events to change all their lives, and to try to make sure there was no glitch in understanding—

"What does the paidhi's security think?"

"No question," Banichi said. "Nai-ma. One could much easier guarantee security there than here."

"Certainly less breakage," Naidiri said wryly.

"More range of operation," Banichi said.

"Though," Naidiri said, "those who've kidnaped Hanks-paidhi certainly haven't made their last move. Best we secure Taiben tonight. One assumes they've attempted to intercept communications."

"See to it," Tabini said, with a wave of his hand. "Our *man'chi* will already have taken whatever precautions they deem necessary, if they're not deaf and blind tonight. —Miri-ji, Bren and I will spend the next few days in retreat at Taiben—fishing, I think that should be pleasant. I leave it to you to maintain the residence during the interval. Will you appoint suitable staff out of your household, for a gentleman guest?"

"Saidi-ji," Damiri said. "See to it." A wry twist of the mouth. "And arrange for the restorationists to survey the breakfast room. There will be *no* cleaning until they've approved. Have them get at it tomorrow, if the paidhi is determined to leave us; have them get their measurements, collect what they want and get out. If not my bedchamber, I expect the paidhi lodged in suitable comfort at Taiben, if you please. And I expect his return to very quiet, very quick repair."

"Daja-ma," Saidin said, "nand' paidhi. Sixteen staff, I recall, is correct for a guest at Taiben, four more with the paidhi's appropriate numbers of his personal staff—and expecting the paidhi's single guest, would seem to be a fortunate number, even if this additional woman were to stay. But in her interest, three more, which in no event is unharmonious."

On Mospheira no one would have made sense of it. On the mainland, it added five to sixteen to get twenty-one, a three-number of the unbeatably felicitous seven times three union with the three entities correctly represented: the paidhi, the aiji, and the ship; a union which with each participating entity subdivided in twos, as he saw it, let the aggressive Ragi mode of accounting deal with the temporary presence of an additional guest, owed to Mospheira, which made a fourth estate, whose numbers were clearly made transitory in the situation. A transitory influence of less felicitous numbers was acceptable if you could foist them off on an opposition—such as Mospheira. But Saidin gave him the option of shifting the numbers to a five of indivisible fives, likewise fortunate.

And a man could worry about his sanity that he really understood her question.

"One thinks—yes, three more servants to attend the Mospheira-bound paidhi," Bren said, "if one would, nand' Saidin."

"Gods greater and lesser," Tabini said, "just so the armed ones exceed the numbers of the opposition."

Tabini was not a superstitious man.

Nor were those closest associated with him, nor did Saidin seemed shocked at the official irreverence: she was clearly expert in gracefully observant appearances, and would, one could lay odds, never have it reported of her arrangement that things were less than proper.

And with that question of appearances in Saidin's hands, Tabini and Damiri and their security set out to the foyer, declaring they were, for which the paidhi thanked God, going home to Tabini's residence next door, and the police were going to their office after collecting the tape, and the whole commotion was rapidly dying away to a numb, bruised quiet.

"Nand' paidhi?" Saidin asked, when the door had shut on the last formalities. "Will you care to see the list of accompanying servants before I issue it to the staff?"

The tremor that had manifested while he was dealing with Jase on the phone threatened to become thought absorbing. "Nand' Saidin, nadi-ji, I leave everything to your discretion. Please pack what I'll need, for myself and my personal staff. Send only people of discretion, flexibility and good sense. I'd have you along, foremost, except I know the lady needs you here."

"Nadi," Saidin said, with a bow, "please come back safely."

"I promise you I'll try to do that, nadi-ji. Not least to please you."

"You are a scandalous flatterer, nand' paidhi."

"Nadi-ji, never. You're a treasure. Please, rest early. I'll see myself to bed. I've two hands now."

"Nadi," Saidin said, and not least among her virtues, understood when a man was tired enough to fall on his face, and withdrew quietly.

Banichi lingered, speaking with Algini in the small security office—and Bren eavesdropped, wanting most of all to know Jago and Tano were all right. "Any word?" he asked. "Where's Jago and Tano? Do you know, Banichi?"

"We're in contact," Banichi said.

"They're safe."

"Separately. They're safe. —Are you all right, Bren-ji?"

"Tired. Quite tired. That's all right. I can walk."

"Nadi," Banichi said, and left the office and the com to Algini, and took him by the arm.

Which was probably a good idea, considering the wobble in his legs.

He took off the coat. He gave the gun to Banichi, and Banichi said he would take charge of it, which was altogether agreeable to him.

"You know," Banichi said, tucking it in his pocket, "it was very foolish, what you did."

"I didn't know where you were. I thought Algini was alone by the front door. I had a gun. I didn't leave it to the servants to check the back balcony because I stood a better chance to stop someone if there should have been a problem. . . ."

"Then it was, over all, well done. Well you were armed, but I admit to extreme anxiousness when you aimed at me, Bren-ji: you presented a disturbing quandary for your own security."

"I apologize, Banichi."

"Well done, too, that you waited to confirm your target; one hopes you recognized me. But one fears that you simply hesitated, which is not good. Besides, I must teach you about doors, nadi-ji. Due to their size, and the design of the building, those were not, obviously enough, bullet-proof."

"Banichi, as my life's become, I'll pay closest attention to anything you can teach me, and, no, I didn't recognize you. I knew it was a possibility of it being you."

"Far easier for me to tell it's you, paidhi-ji. Anyone can. If you perceive presence, assume they won't fire if you don't seem to see them. Dangerous, but less so to your security."

"I'll remember that."

"Word from Tano. The scene downstairs indicates a likelihood of Guild members operating without Guild sanction. Despite the evidence of the breakfast room, these are professionals, Bren-ji. This is not the sort that assailed you in the legislature."

"Professionals acting under *man'chi.*"

"Evidently so."

"Does every association have such high-level professionals? I assume they are, since Hanks' guards—"

"Not every association has such professionals, and that's a very likely assumption. Such as guarded Hanks-paidhi were not careless."

"Do you then *have* suspicions?"

"Four or five."

"Names known to me?"

"All."

"Then *who,* Banichi?"

Banichi hesitated. "Cenedi is a remote possibility."

"No. Surely not. Not with such lack of finesse."

"A possibility, I say. One believes the breakfast room itself was a target."

"And not me?" He wasn't sure whether to be relieved or insulted.

"Possibly. The other names ... you would not know the Guild members involved, but the second possible instigator is Atigeini: Tatiseigi. Another is lord Geigi. A fourth is Direiso, who, for the Kadigidi, carried the Filing against your name to the Guild. I'm ordinarily restrained from telling you that, but there's been an action which makes it needful for you to know. That the proposed contract was voted down, if she has pursued it, would place her and her *man'chi* in dire opposition to the Guild; but she is constitutionally capable of that, and if the action tonight is on the part of an association of which Ilisidi herself is a part, it would involve Direiso. Likewise another of close association with the Kadigidi—Saigimi of the Marid Tasigin, which is the center of an unwholesome sub-association of suspicious interests. Oil is their unifying interest. Oil. And Talidi province."

He knew the Kadigidi, one of the perpetual annoyances Tabini tolerated both as contentious neighbors and opposition leaders in the tashrid, in the name of, Tabini swore, the value of peaceful opposition—

And though he didn't know Saigimi by direct experience—Saigimi didn't occupy a seat in the tashrid—he knew the Marid Tasigin and most of all he knew the business of Talidi province.

Certainly Banichi did.

"Talidi," he said to Banichi, "is your province."

"Bren-ji. Don't doubt *me*."

"Banichi," he began to say, and then knew salads didn't remotely cover it, and the language didn't really have a word for lonely. You could substitute. But it didn't communicate. And neither could the paidhi, on what the paidhi felt Banichi's loyalty to be.

"Bren-ji," Banichi said, "I am *not* the one."

"I know that, Banichi. I'm capable of being deceived, of course. But if I were—" A knot had arrived in his throat, and he flashed on that painful darkness as Banichi carried him to the floor. "—if I were, Banichi-ji, it's hardly necessary for you to go to such trouble. I've no association outside Tabini's but to you and Jago."

He'd disturbed Banichi. Clearly. "Not to *us,* paidhi-ji."

He was in a dark, self-destructive humor all of a sudden—emotional, and not knowing why. "To Tabini, oh, yes. And to you. I stick like glue. You'd have to kill me to get rid of me, you know. We're like that."

He'd never seen Banichi show such a troubled expression. "Nand' paidhi, one has no such intention. I assure you. But you have *no man'chi* to me *or* to Jago. Which I'm assured you don't feel, anyway, nadi. So this is nonsense. Is it not?"

"Who knows what we feel? Maybe I do feel it, Banichi. If I'd shot you, I'd have been very upset."

"One is certainly glad to know you'd wish otherwise, nand' paidhi. And I would have been professionally embarrassed. You scared me."

That, from Banichi, of the Guild he was from, was an intimate confidence.

"But you are *not*," Banichi insisted, as if it still troubled him, "of my *man'chi*. Nor, I hope, physically attracted to me—which is your other choice. Jago, on the other hand—does not entail necessary loyalty to me. —Or does it, among humans?"

They were entering far too deep a subject for a man as tired as he was, as emotionally frayed as he was—and as guilty as he was, on that touchy private ground between Banichi and his partner. He was getting in well over his head, and suddenly Banichi, whom few secrets eluded, seemed to be implying a suspicion and questioning an event he couldn't forget, couldn't altogether ignore, and had no wish ever to admit had happened.

So he ignored the question at least, in favor of what he most wanted to know. "Where *is* Jago right now?"

Ordinarily neither Banichi nor Jago answered such questions of whereabouts, except obliquely. He realized by now that it might be the policy of their Guild or of Tabini's service, to say nothing about business in progress, and that therefore Banichi would never give him a straight answer. But Banichi seemed to consider a moment, perhaps noting the sidestep he'd done on Banichi's question.

"At the airport, at the moment. No planes got away. No rail left the Bu-javid underground."

"Then Hanks can't have left the premises."

"One wishes that were the only conclusion. It's almost impossible to move fast enough to guarantee about rail on the perimeters, unless one is at least anticipating a movement or a direction. The damned hotels down below are a security sieve with connections to the rail."

"Hard to conceal a human."

"Less so a willing one."

"You do strongly think she knew them."

"One suspects so."

"Banichi, in my hearing, Hanks called out to her own security. She was distressed and concerned for their danger as well as her own. I heard it in her voice."

"That's a very great deal to hear in a voice."

One couldn't overgeneralize with Banichi. "Say—I know the woman personally, and I know my species and my culture. I recognized her concern and by the tone of her voice the concern was for them—she was warning them. Hardly logical for a conspirator—though humans have certainly been known to fail in logic."

"This one more than most."

"But not unwilling to fight for them, Banichi. That was in the voice. Take my word it was there."

"She may well have been startled. She may even have been opposed to the attack. Then either overpowered or simply pragmatic, if their *man'chi* lies with the trouble-makers. I suspect they went right down among the hotels, they went directly onto the public rail, and to a safe place somewhere in Shejidan, after which, with some less notice, they'll attempt to leave the city. Willing, she could pass as a child quite easily. A little large for a sleeping child. That's why I say, willing. A family group on holiday. What police would question them?"

"The Bu-javid could equally well have swallowed her. Some apartment, some lord sympathetic—"

"True. But less likely. Very few of the dissident lords would act openly against the aiji's declared interest, unless something happened that seemed to undermine the present order. It's a short list of those who would dare under other circumstances. It's even remotely possible someone seeking favor with Tabini misapprehended and thought disposing of the woman would quiet the waters. Certainly the list of those she's annoyed would be a much longer list."

He sat down on his bed, exhausted, to pull off his boots—and remembered, suddenly, and now that they were alone, the most critical question he had to account for. "Hanks' computer. Where is it? Do you know?"

"It apparently went with her. They've searched the apartment."

"Damn. *Damn,* Banichi."

"Indeed."

And one wished, earnestly wished, that one could exclude the searchers or even Banichi and Jago from those with a motive to take the computer and claim otherwise.

But one didn't ask. Instead, exhausted, he unfastened his shirt and peeled it off, with nothing to do with it, but Banichi took it and hung it on a chair.

"You'll make the trip with me to Taiben. Won't you? Won't Jago?"

"We certainly intend so."

He felt a little less shaky in that knowledge. Perhaps even willing to sleep once his head hit the bed—except the computer business told him he didn't have that luxury. He had to think what to do. What to report.

Or not.

"Tano and Algini are coming, too?"

"We purpose so."

Things on the mainland were as well handled as they could be, given the situation. As for Mospheira, he'd no notion what was happening there or what might be going on when the news of the landing and his treasonous assistance to Tabini spread across Mospheira—but coupling that with a warning that Hanks' computer was in foreign hands ... God, how would *that* look? And what could they think?

Please believe me, Mr. Secretary, but it was some *other* atevi group that snatched her?

Sorry about cutting you out of the landing, but I was preserving my credibility with the aiji?

Sorry about Hanks. Sorry *for* Hanks. I wish I could help her. I wish I knew where she is.

He unfastened his pants, peeled out of the rest of his clothes while Banichi lingered—but he wasn't focused on Banichi: his brain was beginning to sort wildly through other matters he couldn't lay hands on—like Barb, like his mother and Toby and his family.

He personally couldn't protect them, if somebody reacting to his treason decided to break through a less than enthusiastic security and attack his relatives, but he had friends in the State Department all through Foreign Affairs, friends well enough in the information flow and maybe—sometimes he thought so—well enough organized against administrative actions that some of them, some who had security clearances and some who even had covert operations skills might see a problem developing for his family beyond the usual nuisance groups and quietly try to handle it for him, if for no other reason than to to prevent him receiving a piece of news that might make him unstable in the field.

But, God, what could they really do? How fast could they realize it for a problem—and how thin could they stretch their confidence in him, when he'd gone step by step past the limits of their interests—at least, their interests as essentially supportive of the government.

His mother's letter the censors had reduced to lace. And his mother not returning phone calls. But Barb had talked to her. Barb said she was fine. Barb wouldn't lie to him about that. And his mother was as self-protective as Barb was. Took care of herself. First. Centrally.

Rely on her for that much. On friends in low places for the rest.

He lay down and pulled the covers over him, to look, at least, as if he were going to sleep.

Banichi, strange action, pulled the second coverlet up and lingered with a touch on his covered shoulder.

"Bren-ji," Banichi said, "over all, it was well done."

"I wasn't too stupid?"

"You did quite well, considering. Just—please leave things to your security personnel."

"If security personnel would keep me briefed in future where they are and what they're doing—it would relieve my anxieties, Banichi-ji. And make my targets much easier to identify."

"Not a bad notion."

"Please," he said, and let his head sink into the pillow, let his eyes drift shut to what he wished were a totally numb and night-lasting dark.

"In respect of security," Banichi said, "you should bear in mind that a chief suspect in the attack is Damiri herself."

The eyes came open. He couldn't prevent it.

"The aiji," Banichi said, "favors Damiri of the Atigeini. This doesn't mean he can rely on her."

The eyes still wanted to slide shut, as if he'd been slipped a tranquilizer he couldn't fight. On one level, Banichi could have said the building was afire, and he would have asked himself if he could possibly wait till the next alarm.

But the thinking brain said, Ask. There won't be another chance. Banichi wants to talk.

"So? Where does Tabini stand?"

"He doesn't rely on Damiri. In my own estimation, perhaps in his, Damiri-daja is testing the currents and trying to decide for her own association how powerful Tabini is and what an alliance with him is worth—pragmatically and historically. The Atigeini official position is against him."

"I know that—but this business of shooting in among your own servants—"

"The uncle she named, Tatiseigi, happens to be senior in the family and officially opposes her alliance to him. She, we *think*, favors it, being quite strongly attracted to Tabini, who is—" Banichi seemed to search for a word "—a man of some natural favor with various women."

"One understands."

"Tatiseigi might have decided that Damiri's gone much

too far, and Damiri might be in extreme danger from within her own staff."

"And mine."

"Just so. In moving to Tabini's apartment she's abandoned her own security as a sign of affiliation with Tabini. On one level her personal security may back what she's doing. And certain ones might be offended. If she has offended her security—they'd immediately fall under Tatiseigi's *man'chi,* to her great danger. If they're not there already."

"Are they here?"

"At least one."

"An assassin? Of the Guild?"

"Saidin."

"Good—God." He was waking up faster and faster.

"One would have thought you'd suspect so."

In a lordly house. In the Bu-javid. In an apartment clearly under potential threat conspicuously lacking in Guild presence, except those Tabini provided. It *was* a reasonable question to have asked, Banichi was right, and he—had no excuse.

"But you," he asked Banichi, "personally think Damiri to be telling the truth to Tabini?"

"What I think is little relevant. One doesn't know. I do believe someone exceeded orders in the destruction of the antiquities of that room. I believe Damiri's anger is real. I suspect Tatiseigi won't be pleased—whoever ordered the attack. The aiji's jet leaves within the hour, taking security to Taiben—and a lily porcelain on a side trip, to the Atigeini estates not so far distant."

"I appreciate the nature of speculation. And how little you dare do it, Banichi-ji. But what of Ilisidi's involvement?"

"One doesn't know. One frankly doesn't know whether you've persuaded her. That's a major point at issue. Clearly she leaned to your side once. Now one has to ask you where Ilisidi stands."

"I might have failed. I might well have failed."

"Even Tabini, who knows her very well, does not think he penetrates the dowager's reserve."

A clear enough warning—for a human astute enough to take it. "Emotionally speaking, Banichi, I confess I'd rather it not be Ilisidi behind this."

"Certainly a formidable individual."

"More than that, I think her a pleasant conversationalist. An antidote to my isolation. This is perhaps foolish on my part."

"Perhaps a human who flings himself down mountains for recreation could think her a challenge. But one cautions you, most earnestly, nadi, this is not without risk, this flirtation with the aiji-dowager."

"Oh—damn."

"Bren-ji?"

"I need to send her word about the attack and the landing. I promised her, Banichi, to keep her briefed. No matter what. This isn't a time to break promises to her. And I have."

"The dowager has left, nand' paidhi."

"Left?"

"An hour before the attack."

He felt mildly sick at his stomach. Mildly, numbly—chilled to the core. "Damn," he said again.

"It could be prudence," Banichi said. "But one can't rely on such gracious supposition."

"The ones who took Hanks—what do they likely want with her? Stupid question, Banichi, I know. But do you see something I might not?"

"Certainly no suitors for marriage," Banichi said dryly. "I'd say—the obvious things. Her skills. —Her computer."

"She's not a bad woman," he found himself saying—never would have credited he'd be pleading Hanks' case. But it wasn't Deana as a hostage: atevi didn't quite understand hostages in the human sense of personal value; the conservatives she most appealed to for reasons of opposition to Tabini were the very atevi not long on patience with human manners—some of them not long on patience with human existence.

If it was those, as best he could think, it wasn't a live

human they wanted. It was information on human activities and on secrets Tabini might hold.

Or they wanted words from Deana that might inflame popular feeling against Tabini. God, he knew the position Hanks had gotten herself into. He felt it, personally, in the pain that nagged at his shoulder and his ribs.

Behind his eyes, another pain, a stinging, angry pain, that a man in his job shouldn't feel, shouldn't entertain— not—not regret for Ilisidi's behavior. Attaching affections to atevi was a foolish, personally and professionally dangerous mistake.

One could be like Wilson. One could forget how to love anyone. One could stop doing it.

Or one could take the pain, and try to stand it, and steadfastly, professionally, refuse to be surprised or self-accusatory when atevi answered to their own urges and ran roughshod over human sentiment.

"Thank you," he said to Banichi. "Did I say thank you? I meant to."

"My—"

"—job. Yes, dammit. I know that. But prefer me just adequately, Banichi-ji, to Hanks-paidhi."

"Fervently so, Bren-ji."

"Still too little," he said. "Still too little, Banichi. I'd have let you shoot me before I took a chance it wasn't you tonight. Does that reassure you?"

"Far from it."

"Then you worry about it, Banichi-ji. I'm far too tired to."

"It's my job," Banichi said, infallibly, reliably numb to human feelings, missing the point. "You're quite right. We should keep you better informed."

The knot in his throat didn't go down. But there wasn't a solution. There wasn't a translation. Not in the paidhi's vocabulary. Not in the dictionary.

Banichi turned out the lights with, "If there are alarms tonight, trust I'll answer them, Bren-ji. And stay in bed."

Atevi asked what *he* couldn't feel, either. He supposed it might bother them just as much. Atevi hadn't a word for lonely.

There was something like orphan.

There was something like renegade.

Otherwise they couldn't *be* alone—and knew, better than humans, he supposed, why they did things. Psychiatry was a science they hadn't practiced, and still didn't, possibly because no atevi would confide outside his *man'chi,* possibly because, among them, there was just pathology.

And, ever popular, solving all possible mental health problems—bloodfeud.

Or whatever atevi actually felt that answered to that ancient human word.

Possibly he'd troubled Banichi's sleep tonight. Possibly he'd made Banichi ask himself questions for which Banichi had fewer words than he did. If there was indeed some secret atevi dictionary of human language, Banichi might be consulting it tonight and asking himself what the paidhi had meant.

He'd kept after Banichi until he knew not only that everyone he cared for was safe—but as far as he could, until he knew to his satisfaction, *where* they were; which possibly wasn't love, just a neurotic desire to have them all in a predictable place for the night so he could shut his eyes.

But he couldn't shake the punched-in-the-gut feeling he'd felt when he and Banichi started talking about loyalties, and he'd seen how far he'd gone from safety in his dealings, how much, God help him, he *needed,* and kept telling himself wasn't—ever—going to be there for him. He'd known it when he'd gone into the job, and he'd known in the unscarred, unmuddied wisdom of youth that he'd one day meet the emotional wall, of whatever nature, in whatever remote time of his career, and remember where he'd been heading and why.

Need was such a seductive, dangerous word. *Need* was the vacancies. *Need* wasn't, dammit, love, not in any sense. If love was giving, it was the opposite of love, it drank love dry, it sucked logic after it, and it didn't ever output. Barb was need. She'd tried to become *his* need, and he'd seen that shipwreck coming.

Then he'd gotten himself the possibility of a backup in Graham, if Graham made it down safely. And the shaky character of his dealings with Banichi, who knew how to forgive him, at least, told him he *had* to pull himself together or hand Jase Graham the keys to his soul, which Jase might not be good enough or benign enough not to use. Jago touched him, not in an unknowing way, and he hadn't, in small idle seconds, forgotten the feeling of her hands, the sensation that shivered through his nerves and said ... he needed. He wanted not to have been responsible. He wanted Jago to have ignored warnings and gone ahead with ... whatever atevi did with their lovers, which had become in his thoughts a burning curiosity.

Jago ... and Ilisidi. He'd made a place in his human affections for the woman with all her edges and all her secrets—he'd ignored all the rules, even given her a piece of human loyalty that must have, in some intrusive way, taken Ilisidi herself by surprise and sent her judgment of him skittering off at angles no ateva could figure, as if he'd touched on *man'chi* and given a chivalrously honorable—aristocratically possessive?—old ateva a real quandary of the spirit. Like Tabini, he suspected, she'd tried to figure him, adjusted her behavior to fit her conceptions of *his* action, and gone off into that same unmapped territory of mutually altered behavior that he and Tabini wandered.

His fault and not hers. Ilisidi was angry with him. Jago, thanks only to Jago, could take care of herself. Jago *had* taken care of herself and walked out when he warned her. And Banichi knew. Banichi found everything out.

Or Jago had outright told him. Whatever that meant, in a relationship Bren had never puzzled out.

Damned fool, he said to himself. He heard people move about in the apartment, up and down the hall outside his bedroom. But he knew that Banichi knew who they were, and that no one moved there who Banichi didn't approve. So that was all right.

He heard the door open and close, very distantly. But, again, he expected comings and goings. He hoped it was good news. Or at least that bad news of whatever nature was being handled as well as it could be.

He had the damn code. Shawn or somebody had risked a great deal to get him a code that he didn't, on sober reflection, believe he'd gathered in his computer when he'd plugged in and sent out his Seeker.

He had a sure knowledge that Hanks' computer was in unauthorized hands, on Tabini's side or the opposition's. And that code Shawn had gone to great lengths to give him could, if it was what it seemed, blast through Mospheira's electronic obstructions and get at least one message to the right channels in the Foreign Office.

He had the remote unit plugged in. He could send that warning here, from his bedroom, without any need for lines, without tipping off more than the massive security he was sure Tabini mounted on his phone lines, that he had been in direct communication with Mospheira after the attack. But Tabini gave him all the latitude he wanted—an enviable position for a potential spy.

If that spy wanted to act, tipping off Mospheira that violence had happened in the Bu-javid, that Hanks was in foreign hands, possibly being interrogated, possibly being coerced to breach Mospheira's electronic defenses.

The aforesaid spy could also expect that Mospheira would lose no time relaying the information to the ship, who might delay the landing, or change the landing site, just the same as if he'd admitted on the phone that he was standing in the aftermath of a double murder and the kidnaping of a human representative.

In which light—he didn't send the warning to Mospheira. The aforesaid potential spy and employee of the Mospheiran government had to lie abed and not make a move more than he had, letting whatever happened to Deana happen, because Mospheira couldn't do a damned thing. His own security and Tabini's was the only chance Deana had for rescue, and if he made that call, as Shawn and other people pinning their careers on him might not understand in its emotional or logical context, Tabini could lose his gambit with the ship and Deana—

If they let her live, Deana could find herself in the position of paidhi to the opposition to Tabini, dammit.

Exactly the position she'd courted, if she lived to have the honor, if her bones held out—atevi didn't always exercise due caution—and if she could use her head.

God, she might *call* Mospheira and say she'd been kidnaped with precisely the idea of aborting the landing. She might, in fact, work for the opposition. It might serve Mospheira very well.

On that thought his eyes came open again, staring into an answerless dark. He asked himself how he'd gotten into this position, except one good intention at a time; asked himself, too, how he'd gotten so much invested in betraying his president, his government and every democratic process on Mospheira that said one man didn't make decisions like this.

Step by step and on understandings of the situation Mospheira's government didn't have: it wasn't the kind of answer a good government servant gave to his government—

But, dammit, the officials *of* his government backed Hanks, who might still be able to reach Mospheira, with the conspirators' full permission, for all he knew—and blow everything.

He wasn't thinking clearly. He wasn't reasoning in a way that came up with answers—just—the arrangement he'd worked out led to atevi being dealt in on the development; Shawn might stand by him, a handful of the FO might stand by him, even in *not* using that code, and letting the landing go ahead—at least Deana couldn't use the big dish. Not without relay to Mospheira.

Which might tell the ship folk something, too.

That was the only thought that let him finally settle toward sleep.

20

The plane's engines were running as they boarded, not surprising since the plane had flown two trips during the night before their own, at dawn, and refueled. Of baggage, there was a mysterious lot already going on board that had Tabini's red-and-black seals on the bags, nothing to do with his own small bags, all for cabin storage, which were simply clothes enough to last until the lander came down, to last until they came back to the Bu-javid.

There were at least thirty cases out there on the baggage ramp.

There were—persistent since he'd waked with a bowlful of urgent personal messages in the foyer and, as he left, bouquets standing in the hall outside—well-wishes from officials and others to whom the event was not as secret as he wished.

Now as he looked out the window a van pulled up, the driver argued with security, there was waving and pointing toward his window, the driver peered up at him, and understanding his presence was in question, Bren gave a tentative wave.

After which the driver and an assistant set more bouquets out in view of his window, in the vicinity of the plane, that being as close as his nervous security would let the deliveries come.

It wasn't the last van. Two more pulled up, with more flowers, until it looked like a funeral or a wedding. And the cards at least reached him, carried up by boarding crew, and security, even by the crew who carried the carefully inspected galley load aboard. The bouquets were from committee heads. They were from the serving staff.

They were from the clericals, lately begun in their jobs, one of which said,

Nand' paidhi, this is my first job. I am rereading all the mail I did in hopes that the threat against you was nothing I missed.

And another:

Nand' paidhi, please be very careful. Don't let there be a war.

And one in elaborate court calligraphy from the gentleman of Tano's acquaintance, the manager who'd come out of retirement, who said, more expansively, *Nand' paidhi, I have all confidence in your security. Please accept my wishes for your long life and the wishes of all my house for the continued benefit of your good counsel to the aiji and his house, long may he direct the Association.*

The latest delivery people understood their restrictions and simply laid the bouquets within sight of his window, a mass of pastel color in the grayed and cloudy dawn. He felt walled off from his well-wishers, lonely, seeing the bouquets abandoned to the weather and the wind from the engines, comforted by the gesture, though, and also appalled, thinking how expensive some of those bouquets were, from clericals who didn't make all that lot of money. He tucked the cards one and all into his document case, the ones with plain citizen ribbons, the ones with heavy noble seals, to answer when he could. He vowed to send at least a small floral recognition along with each one of them to the clericals, who, he was confident, hadn't missed any warning. No, dammit, not a blossom or two—real bouquets, and put it on the paidhi's florist bill, which went right to the State Department, with notations to bounce it back to him if State balked.

Another van. Another bouquet arrived, a huge, extravagant one. The delivery agency wished vehemently to board with it. He watched the argument through the window. But his security was adamant, called Banichi, and Banichi himself brought the card aboard and gave it to him, clearly the price of the agreement.

"An importunate well-wisher," Banichi said, and the

first glance determined that it and the bouquet were lord Geigi's.

Nand' paidhi, it said, *wiser heads than I are studying the answer which you have returned in regard to my question, at unanticipated personal effort. I deeply regret that your absence in pursuit of this answer may have given opportunity or motive to some person or persons to attack the paidhiin, an action in which I realize that I am necessarily suspect, but which I personally deplore. I have written under separate seal to Tabini-aiji, and hope that you will also confirm my good wishes to your associates of whatever degree. I also hope for the safety of Hanks-paidhi and will bend whatever efforts I and my staff can make to assure that no harm comes to her.*

"Do you believe this gesture?" he asked Banichi.

Banichi took the card, read it, lifted a brow. "One would never question." And added: "Nor accept the bouquet from this source under one's roof."

"Surely it doesn't contain bombs. They've been fueling out there. The truck—"

"One doesn't know what it doesn't contain. Gambling is not a passion with me. I'll convey your politic appreciation. I've already suggested they move the fuel truck, and pull us away from the area ahead of schedule."

"Jago isn't aboard."

"Jago is coming," Banichi said, "at all possible speed. If she should miss us, she'll come out this afternoon with Tano and Algini. I agree with you. I increasingly dislike this accumulation of good wishes near our fuel tanks. Especially the latest."

"Have you any word yet on Hanks?"

"They're still looking."

"Jago—" He could see, past Banichi's shoulder, the aiji's other security preparing to shut the door.

And a running figure coming from the building and headed for the steps.

The men inside evidently saw her, too. They waited. In a moment more Jago was through the door, the door shut, and the crew outside was pulling the ramp back.

"Have they found anything?" he asked as Jago,

smoothing her uniform to its usual impeccable state, came down the aisle to join them.

"One doubts. Would you care for a snack after take-off?"

"Just word on Hanks."

"None. Are you sure? I'll be having fruit juice, my-self."

"The same, then. Thank you." He cast a look at Banichi as Jago passed him down the aisle. "I thought the new policy was to tell the paidhi the truth."

"No. One resolved to brief the paidhi on matters re-garding his safety. Not on operations."

"Dammit, Banichi!"

"Information which might tempt him to assist. Or make impossible his innocent reaction to other information. You have such an expressive face, Bren-ji."

The engines grew louder. The flowers and the fueling truck passed out of view as the plane turned and moved out toward the runway.

Banichi and Jago sat down with him and belted in. Other security moved from the door to the cluster of six other security agents at the rear, men and women who talked together in voices that didn't carry above the en-gines and held no humor at all. The servants had gone on the last flight, before daylight; servants in the number that Saidin had determined as fortunate.

Saidin. Damiri's security. Tabini had directly suggested Saidin do the picking, knowing, as the paidhi hadn't known at the time, Saidin's nature. It had been a direct in-vitation to Saidin, a challenge to Saidin, to put one of her people on the Taiben staff—for good or for ill.

The paidhi had been so stupidly blind on that point, *knowing,* intellectually, that security necessarily went in such places—but he'd come in drug-fogged, had formed his subconscious, subsequently unquestioned opinions on the staff, catalogued Saidin as an elder matron, and never, dammit, asked himself the obvious. He'd gotten fond of Saidin—and Saidin might have assumed he knew what she was; which might, Banichi was right, have changed his reactions, his expressions, his levels of caution, if he'd known what he should have known, what any atevi would have known—

He must have perplexed Saidin no end. And, dammit, he still liked the woman.

There seemed a quality to people the Assassins' Guild let in and licensed. He didn't know why. He didn't know what they had in common, except perhaps an integrity that touched chords in his shades-of-gray soul, a feeling, maybe, that one could do things that rattled one's conscience to the walls and foundations and still—still own a sense of equilibrium.

Banichi was going to teach him about doors. It wasn't what he wanted to learn from Banichi. What he wanted to understand was something far more basic.

When he and Jago had almost—almost—gone over the line, and he'd panicked, maybe it was that integrity he'd felt shaken. That very inhuman integrity. That more than human sense of morality.

That Jago hadn't given a damn about.

Which didn't fit with her character.

If one took her as human. And Mospheiran, at that. Which she wasn't.

She was—whatever atevi were in that department. In that sense he *trusted* Jago not to have put him in a difficult position.

And, dammit, he was thinking about it again. Which had absolutely no place in considerations that ought to be occupying his mind.

They swung around for the runway. The wheels thumped down the pavement and cleared the ground. The familiar roofs slipped under the wings and the noise of one more outgoing jet probably disturbed sleep across Shejidan, making ordinary atevi ask themselves what in hell was going on that took so many doubtless official and unscheduled flights to and from the capital—

They might well ask. And—in the light of recent crises—guess that it involved the paidhi, the foreigner ship, the aiji, and a great deal of security and government interest.

Atevi added very well.

* * *

The plane climbed above that altitude regularly jeopardized by atevi small aircraft and into a magnificent view of sunrise above the cloud deck—doubtless the better view was from the other set of windows, where the Bergid would thrust above those clouds, but the paidhi hadn't the energy or the heart to get out of his seat to take a look. He wasn't in the mood for beautiful sunrises. The one he did see jarred his sense of reality. The gray below the clouds had better suited his mood. The unseemly sheen of pink and gold made hope far too easy when so much was uncertain.

But the security personnel began to stir about at the rear of the aircraft, and Jago went back, she said, after fruit juice.

"Biscuits," Bren said, before she escaped. Maybe it was the sunrise, but he began to decide he wanted them—having rushed off before breakfast, into a chancy situation.

And in not too long Jago was back with biscuits, a hot and fragrant pile of them, adequate for healthy atevi appetites, *one* of which was sufficient for a human stomach, along with tea and juice he knew was safe.

"Thanks," Bren pronounced, on diplomatic autopilot. He took his biscuit, he took the tea, he took the fruit juice, and reflected that he finally had what he'd wanted all along: *his* people safely gathered for breakfast, well, except Tano and Algini, who were still chasing about the local investigation. They proposed, Banichi had said, to take another cycle of the same aircraft out to Taiben this afternoon.

But he couldn't get Hanks out of his head, and couldn't convince himself yet that things were in hand. One didn't attack the aiji's guest in the Bu-javid and carry her off as of minor consequence to the welfare of the Association. A lot of firepower had gone out to Taiben. Tabini's arrival out there was still to come—if it came. Tabini was stationing security out there in numbers that could repel real force.

And in the excess of feeling that had suddenly, after

this assassination attempt but not the other, prompted a deluge of flowers and well-wishes from associates, one had the notion that ordinary atevi took this attempt far more seriously than they took the actions of a single irate man in the legislature.

This attempt smelled to them like serious business.

It smelled that way to the paidhi, too.

"Have you heard?" he asked. "Have you any current notion whether the troublemakers will make an attempt on the landing itself?"

"No doubt they'd like any means to make the aiji look weak," Jago said. "An attack on Taiben is fully possible."

"Aimed at Tabini? Or at the whole idea of human contact?"

"One certainly wishes the ship had chosen some other site than that near and convenient to the city," Jago said. "It makes logistics for the conspirators far easier. Direiso *and* Tatiseigi are both in the region."

"Meaning anywhere but Taiben would have been preferable. Then why for God's sake was it on the list?"

"It has its advantages. Access is equally easy for us. And we sit close to the neighbors' operations, which means more readily knowing what they're doing."

"But there're more than nonspecific reasons to worry?"

"There's a suspect association," Jago said. "Local. But powerful."

"Localized geographically?" One *never* knew the full reach and complexity of atevi association. Atevi themselves didn't admit the extent or the nature of them, God help the university on Mospheira trying to track them.

"Understand, nand' paidhi, Taiben is one estate of a very ancient area, of very old, very noble habitation—very old households, adjacent, of longstanding uneasiness of relations."

"Meaning historic feud." It was the Padi Valley. It *was* an old area. Historic.

"No, not feud," Banichi said, "but along this ancestral division of lands—the paidhi may be aware—one has thousands of years of history, among very ancient houses each of whom have powerful modern associations."

Not to say borders. Division of lands. There was a difference.

"An easy neighborhood in good times," Jago said. "But many unsettled issues. In chancy times, very easily upset."

"Meaning," Bren said quietly, "if there was a conspiracy a thousand leagues away, it would most easily nest here, next to Taiben, because of these houses."

"Five households," Jago said. "Before there were humans in the world, there were five principle landholders in the Padi Valley. Historically, all the aijiin of the Ragi have come from these five. The Association at large would hardly be able to settle on any aiji who *didn't* come from this small association. They're all the Ragi families who have *ever* held power."

"But Tabini's house settled the Treaty. By donating its lands to the refugees, from the war." That was answer number one anytime the primer students heard the question. Unquestionably there was more involved. There was the intricacy of the atevi election process. "They brokered the Treaty."

"Keeping only the estate at Taiben—not alone for its nearness to Shejidan, on the Alujis. Clearly association by residence. But also by nobility. The hunting association. And, very clearly, the association of ancestral wealth."

"And the Atigeini have holdings fairly close to Taiben."

"Thirty minutes by air," Banichi said.

"You think there'll be trouble from them? Is that what you're saying?"

"The relationship with the Atigeini may become clear before sundown. Old Tatiseigi is still the chief question."

"And Ilisidi," Jago said.

"What about Ilisidi? Where *is* she? Does anyone know where she went?"

"Oh, Taiben. But Tabini moved her out last night. Now—we think she's guesting upland at Masiri, with the Atigeini. With Tatiseigi himself."

"Damn," he said quietly. But what he felt gathering about him was disaster.

"Tabini, of course, knew where she would go," Banichi said.

"And proceeded," Jago said. "He will not be pushed, at Taiben. *That* small association is historically sensitive."

"Challenging his enemies?"

"Collecting them, perhaps, under one roof."

He had an increasingly uneasy feeling. But it was empty air outside the window. He was wrapped about by atevi purpose, atevi direction, atevi mission. A trap—a conspiracy, a—God knew what. He'd called down a landing from the ship into the thick of atevi politics, arguing them out of trusting Mospheira.

And the atevi he most trusted—one of those words any paidhi should, of course, flag immediately in his thinking—had let him propose Taiben among the other sites he'd offered to the ship, and hadn't mentioned until now the web of associational relationships around Taiben, which—God, was it only a couple of weeks ago?—hadn't mattered once upon a time in his tenure. He'd no more wondered about local associations before the arrival of the human ship threw everything into uncertainty than he'd asked himself with daily urgency about the geography of the sea bottom.

Atevi associations in the microcosm, which atevi tracked in all their complexities back hundreds of years, weren't something the paidhi could politely ask about, weren't something the paidhi was well enough informed on to involve himself in, and he didn't. The larger Association was stable. He'd not questioned it. He wasn't even supposed to question it. It had been ironclad Foreign Affairs policy that the paidhiin dealt only with the central Association and kept their noses out of the smaller ones. Reports the paidhiin could get were laced with misinformation and gossip, recrimination, feud histories and threats—

But ask how Taiben's neighboring estates had stood with each other in prehuman times—and, damn, of *course* the Padi Valley associations must be among the oldest: take it for that if only because archaeologists—a new science, a contagion from humans—had established several digs there, looking for truths earlier aijiin might not have tolerated finding.

"There were many wars there," Jago said, "many wars. Not of fortresses like Malguri. The Ragi always prided themselves that they needed no walls."

"Association would always happen among those leaders, though," Banichi said. "And Taiben belonged to Tabini's father-line. The mother-line, two generations ago, was from the Eastern Provinces."

"Hence Malguri," Jago said.

"Which," Banichi said, "to condense a great deal of bloody history, then united with the Padi Valley to marry Tabini's grandfather. Which had one effect: Tabini's line is the only Padi Valley line not wholly concentrated in the Padi Valley—or wholly dependent on Padi Valley families. An advantage."

"So if a new leader tried to come out of the Padi Valley now, he or she couldn't hold the East. Is that what you're saying?"

"There's obviously one who could," Banichi said.

"Ilisidi."

"She failed election in the hasdrawad because the commons don't trust her," Banichi said. "The tashrid would be altogether another story. Unfortunately for Ilisidi, the tashrid isn't where the successor is named—a profound reform, Bren-ji, the most profound reform. The commons choose. The fire and thunder of the debate was over the Treaty and the refugee settlement, all the lords struggling for advantage—but that one change was the knife in the dark. The commons always took orders how to vote."

"Until," Jago said, "the Treaty brought economic changes, and the commons became very independent. And will not vote against the interests of the commons. The Padi lords used to be the source of aijiin. Now they can't get a private rail line built—without the favor of the hasdrawad *and* Tabini-aiji."

"It's certainly," Banichi said, "been a bitter swallow for them. But productive of circumspection and political modesty—and quiet, most of the time. The commons simply won't elect anyone with that old baggage on his back."

"The Atigeini?" he asked. It wasn't a conversation, it was a rapid-fire briefing, leading to something Tabini wanted him to know—or that his security thought he'd better know—fast. "Does Damiri tie him back to them? The paidhi, nadiin-ji, wishes he had information that helped him be more astute. I suddenly don't follow what Tabini intends in this alliance."

"An heir."

"And an alliance with someone from these families? These very old families? I don't know what you're trying to tell me."

"No other aiji has the history with the commons that Tabini's line has," Jago said, "Tabini-aiji was elected by it; naturally the aiji whose line it favors wishes to keep the democratic system. Certain of the other lords, of course, might wish to change it back. But they'll never secure election. A coup, on the other hand—"

"Overthrow of the hasdrawad itself?" Suddenly he *didn't* like the train of logic. "Change back to the tashrid as electors?"

"Such are the stresses in the government," Banichi said. "One certainly hopes it hasn't a chance of happening. But that Damiri-daja, of the Padi Valley Atigeini, suddenly came into the open as Tabini's lover—was directly related to the appearance of the ship, and to *your* safe return from Malguri."

Stars and galaxies might not be in Banichi's venue. But Banichi was a Guild assassin and very far up the ranks of such people: depend on it, Banichi knew the intricacies of systems and motives that caused people to file Intent.

"*My* return."

"It meant," Banichi said, "ostensibly that she felt Tabini-aiji was likely to be strengthened by this event in the heavens—not overthrown. That the longtime Atigeini ambition to rule in the Bu-javid was best achieved in the bedchamber, not the battlefield."

"Is that *your* assessment of her thinking?"

"The paidhi is not a fool." Banichi had a half-amused

look on his face. "Say I ask myself that question often in a day. Exactly. The affair between them—I doubt is sham. They've shown—" Banichi made a small motion of the fingers "—singularly foolish moments of attraction. That, I judge, is real; and staff in a better position than I to judge say the same. That doesn't mean they've taken leave of higher senses; Naidiri has standing orders that propriety is *not* to keep him out—while Damiri has relinquished her security staff, at least so far as her residence in the aiji's apartment: the necessary concession of the inferior partner in such an arrangement, and a very difficult position for her security to be in. Your presence—has been an incidental salve to Damiri's pride, and a test."

"In case I were murdered in my bed."

"It would be a very expensive gesture for the lady—who's made, by both gestures, a very strong statement of disaffection from the Atigeini policies. You should know that Tatiseigi has made a career of disagreement with Tabini and Tabini's father and his father with Tabini's grandfather, for that matter. And Damiri offers the possibility of formal alliance. Not only her most potent self as mother of an heir, but a chance to break the cabal in the Padi Valley—and possibly, *with* Tatiseigi's knowledge . . . to double-cross the aiji. Or possibly to overthrow Tatiseigi's policies and his grasp of family authority."

"I take it this is not general knowledge."

"Common gossip. Not common knowledge, if the paidhi takes the difference in expressions."

"I do take it."

"This is a very dangerous time," Banichi said, "within the Association. Quite natural that stresses would tend to manifest. In Mospheiran affairs . . . likewise a time of change. As we understand." Banichi reached inside his jacket and pulled out a silver message cylinder. "Tabini asked us to brief you at least on the essentials of the neighbors. —And to destroy this *and* the accompanying tape after you've read it."

Tabini's seal.

Damn, Bren thought, and took it with no little trepidation. He unrolled it, read, very simply put, after Tabini's heading,

Please observe great caution, do nothing to elude your security even for a moment. We expect a great deal of trouble, on very good advisement from very good sources.

The whereabouts of Hanks remains, specifically, a question. But we would not be surprised to find that she has been moved near Taiben, since the conspirators are few, their connections are strong in that vicinity, and they wish to bring as few as possible others of their fringes into public knowledge should matters go wrong for them. Certainly their more cautious supporters will not want to commit until and unless they demonstrate success.

I will not at all be surprised if individuals frequent in Hanks' association initiated the matter. She seems to be operating in some freedom. Banichi has a tape copy of a communication we intercepted on the mainland. Listen to it and see if you can make sense of it.

He expected, dammit, before Banichi gave him the tape and Jago got up and brought him a recorder to play it on, that the tape involved not ship-to-ground communications but very terrestrial connections indeed.

And that the front of the tape would be a great deal of computer chatter—as Deana's access code went through Mospheira's electronic barriers like a knife through butter.

Damn right her authorizations weren't pulled. Completely live. Completely credited, where they were going. He jacked in, captured-and-isolated, read-only, as scared of those codes near his computer as he would have been of a ticking bomb.

The text was, again foreseeably, scrambled. He tried three code sets with his computer before one clicked.

After that, text flowed on his screen.

Cameron has turned coat and threatened the ship with unspecified atevi hostilities in order to have them land under the aiji's control. He has meanwhile participated with the aiji's authority to place me under communications blackout and, I am warned by reliable sources, to have me assassinated. The motive is complex, resting in the aiji's ambitions to make the precedent of central control of dams, power grids, and rail apply to all natural resources, which will strip the provincial aijiin and the landholders of financial resources and centralize all international trade, with monopoly to the aiji in Shejidan, and consequently price controls which will considerably enrich the central government at the expense of local governments and rightful landholders.

Cameron has cooperated in this plan, whether wittingly or unwittingly, has actively backed the nationalization of resources, has suggested boycott as a tactic, has gone on a remarkable excursion to a remote observatory supported by the aiji of Shejidan and brought back a warped space theory that I strongly believe is not based on atevi research, but on unauthorized translation of classified human mathematical concepts. This is calculated to disturb certain atevi conservative religious beliefs which are in stark contrast and political opposition to the aiji, who is not a believer in any philosophy, most particularly to throw certain provinces into religious upheaval and certain philosophical leaders into disrepute and disregard.

I am making this transmission from a secure base afforded me by the persons who have placed their lives in jeopardy by opposing this power grab on the part of the central government. In my judgment, we will do well to make this situation extremely clear to the representative from the ship if she in fact reaches Mospheira alive, which my informants suggest may not happen. The aiji may assassinate this individual and put the blame on his opposition. Since he clearly controls the Assassins' Guild, getting a filing against his political enemies at that point would be possible. This would also, I am informed, serve as a purge of the Guild, as all Guild members opposing his aims would very quickly find themselves targeted by the aiji's very extensive network.

I urge under the strongest terms that the government recall Cameron, revoke his authority and his codes, and demand an explanation of his actions, which are by no means in the interest of Mospheira, of the human population in general, or of atevi citizens. I do not know and

*cannot ascertain whether he is aware what he is aiding or
to what purpose his advice and ability is being used, but
I consider that my life is in present danger from agencies
with whom he is working. Therefore I will move from
place to place and attempt to preserve my usefulness in
my job.*

*Please pass a message to my family that I am at the
moment safe and well and protected by persons who have
acted in behalf of their freedom and rights of self-
determination.*

He didn't swear. He didn't want expression to cross his
face—he wasn't sure he was going to translate this message exactly, at this time, or in the foreseeable future. He
rested his elbow on the armrest and his knuckle against
his lip, thinking. He'd defined the beginning of the section; he defined the end; he captured, reran it, rereading
to determine that, no, there was no hint of it being taken
under duress, there were none of the words to signal that
such was the case—and he'd hope, in a piece like that, to
see words like *discorrespondance, decorrelationary,* or
contrarecidivistic, that to a human eye didn't quite belong
in typical text in the worst diplomatese—the standard
freehand signal that the whole piece was under duress, always a worry when a note that explosive came in on
computer-to-computer transmission.

But there was no such clue. He read it a third time simply to absorb the tenor and content, to try to strip out
emotional reactions, and to ask himself honestly whether
there was any remote, even astronomically remote or con-
ceivable likelihood that Deana was actually right and he
was wrong.

That Tabini's true aim in the current crisis was elimina-
tion of dissent.

No, dammit, it was *not* the purpose of Tabini's actions.
It was not the action of the aiji whose answer to rebels in
Malguri had generally been understated, as witness
Ilisidi's corroboration that things were settled; the aiji
whose punitive use of the Guild had been, if at all during
his administration, so covert as to be undetected. It was
not the action of the aiji who, if reports were true, having

perhaps assassinated his own father, at least declined to assassinate his grandmother, who was still in all accounts a very reasonable culprit in the demise of her son.

One added sideways and up and down and power grab didn't describe Tabini in the least.

It didn't describe Tabini's overenthusiastic (by Ilisidi's lights) embrace of things human; or his willingness, in personal argument with common citizens, constantly to push court suit and trial as an enlightened substitute for registered feud; his insistence to push air traffic control as the system countrywide in spite of lordly objections *because* it made sense, even if it sequenced five and six commoner pilots in line ahead of provincial aijiin and their precious purchased numbers in the landing sequence—it also kept aircraft from crashing into each other and raining destruction on urban Shejidan.

It didn't, as Banichi had pointed out, describe the aiji's support among the commons. Elected by the hasdrawad. It was a very enlightening view of *why* the Western Association was stable. Human scholars called it economic interdependency, and believed the public good and public content propped Tabini's line in power—which might be the same information; but the economic changes Jago mentioned, bringing real economic power to the trades and the commons—yes, it was the same thing, but it was the atevi side of the looking-glass. And in the concept of *man'chi,* and atevi electorates—it was an atevi explanation for the peace lasting.

Because the hasdrawad wasn't about to vote against the interests of the commons. Which the hasdrawad hadn't seen as congruent with Ilisidi's passionate opposition to things the hasdrawad wanted, like more gadgets, more trade, more commerce, roads if they could push them, rail if that would move the freight, and to hell with the lords' game reserves: wildlife didn't rank with trains as long as wildlife, the only atevi meat supply, was in good supply in general. He'd heard the arguments in Transportation, in Commerce, in Trade . . . always the push for the big programs. Which no lord wanted if it wasn't in *his* district or his interest—or, contrarily, if it infringed his public lands, meaning the estate he used, and on which he hunted, during his seasons of residency.

He was aware of Banichi and Jago sitting opposite him, across the small service table. He was aware of them watching his face for reactions—and he shot Banichi a sudden, invasive stare.

"You *can't* have broken the code in this document," he said to Banichi.

Banichi's face was completely guarded, not completely expressionless. A brow lifted, and the appraising stare came back at him.

One didn't pursue the likes of Banichi through thickets of guesswork and try to pin him down. Banichi wouldn't cooperate with such petty games.

One went, instead, straight ahead.

"You know this is from Hanks to Mospheira. And you know who she's with and what they'll have told her."

"One can certainly make a fair surmise."

"Hence what you just told me. About the election. About the hasdrawad."

"Bren-paidhi, what Tabini-aiji asked us to tell you. Yes."

"Meaning a handful of lords want to restore *their* rights at the expense of the commons."

"One could hold that, yes. And, yes, if that is Hanks reporting to Mospheira, and the persons who have her have let her do this, *and* she's done it willingly, one does rather well believe that she's at least convinced them she believes them. I take it the report she's made supports their view."

"You take it correctly. She has the opportunity, I'll be frank, to use words that would negate everything she says even if they did have a translator standing over her shoulder. There's no linguistic evidence an atevi dictated it word by word, and I'm not pleased with the content."

"I should have shot this woman," Jago muttered, "on the subway platform. I would have saved the aiji and the Association a great deal of bother."

"I've a question," Bren said, and with their attention: "Ilisidi—has always—to me—supported preservation of the environment, preservation of the culture. Not preservation of privilege."

"But," Jago said, "one must *be* a lord to assure the preservation of the fortresses, the land holdings, the reserves. A lord on his own can knock down ancient fortifications, rip up forest—it belongs to him. No association of mere citizens can stop him. And no decree of the hasdrawad can dispossess the lords. The tashrid can veto, with a sufficient majority."

The airport at Wigairiin, he thought. The fourteenth-century fortifications. Knocked down for a runway.

For a lord's private plane. The lord's ancestors built the fortress. The lord inheriting it knocked the wall down, the tourists and posterity be damned.

"Do brickmasons and clericals on holiday . . . ever tour Wigairiin?" he asked—clearly perplexing Banichi and Jago.

"One doesn't think so," Jago said. "But I could find out this information, if there's some urgency to it."

"Nothing so urgent. One just notes—that such ordinary people do tour Malguri. With the dowager in residence. Whose doing is that?"

"Ultimately," Banichi said, "Tabini's."

"But Ilisidi has made no move to prevent it."

"Hardly prudent," Jago said.

"Nevertheless," he said.

"If some human reason prompts you to justify the dowager," Banichi said, "I would urge you, paidhi-ji, to accept atevi reasons to reserve judgment."

Things were at a bad pass when his atevi security had to remind him where things atevi began and things human ended.

"One respects the advice," he said. "Thank you. Thank you both—for your protection. For your good sense, in the face of my . . . occasional lapses in judgment—and security."

"Please," Jago said, "stay within our guard at Taiben. Take no chances."

He looked straight at Jago, and imagined, the way he'd imagined Jago avoiding him for the number of hours, that she intended the meeting of the eyes, that she looked at him in a very direct, very intimate way. Which made him flinch and duck.

"Considering all this," he said, trying to recover his train of thought, "in atevi ways the paidhi may be too foreign to reckon—*how* did Ilisidi know about Barb the morning after I'd gotten the news? How do you think she knew that fast, if not directly from Damiri's staff? And why should Damiri and Ilisidi associate?"

There was a sober look on both opposing faces.

"Tabini has asked himself that very serious question," Banichi said. "And one does recall where Ilisidi is guesting today."

"Has he asked Damiri about it?" a human couldn't refrain from asking.

"Far too direct," Jago said. "We do lie, nadi-ji. Some of us do it very well. Certain of us even take public offense."

"Do *you* believe Damiri to be honest?"

"One can believe that Damiri-daja is quite honest," Banichi said, "and still know that she might be closer to her uncle's wishes than Tabini would wish. That is honest, paidhi-ji."

The only thing showing under the wings at Taiben was the endless prospect of trees, and at the very last the rail that ran between the airport and the township at Taiben, and the estate of Taiben, at opposite ends of the small rail line, two spurs.

And one was aware, watching that perspective unfold, that other short lines ran up to various townships, villages, hunting lodges and ancestral estates—including those of the Atigeini, and the other three lords of the valley.

The paidhi did have the rash and foolish thought that if, after collecting their luggage, they asked for a train not to Taiben but up to the Atigeini holding, in the north of the valley, they might actually have a civilized reception, a fair luncheon with Ilisidi, an exchange of civilized greetings, and a train ride back again to meet Tabini for supper at Taiben.

That was the way things went when lords met.

When the Guild met—other things resulted, and he wouldn't throw Banichi and Jago up against Cenedi and others of Ilisidi's household, not for any urging and not for any cause that he could prevent. Not that he lacked confidence Banichi and Jago would deal with the situation. And Cenedi. Who would be equally determined, at Ilisidi's order, though they'd fought together, cooperated, shared all the struggle at Malguri. In some ways, he suspected, humans who thought they had a monopoly on sensitivity couldn't imagine the feelings atevi had when some damned fool or some lord's ambition threw them into a conflict they didn't want and weren't going to win—in any personal sense.

So he was quite glad *not* to find any delegation from Cenedi waiting for them once they were on the ground; he was exceedingly glad that a quick security mate-up with personnel Tabini had had the foresight to send in last night in the dark had already ascertained that there was no bomb, no ambush and no accidental derailment to worry about on their route to Taiben. Everyone worried, at least aloud, about the paidhi's physical comfort, and asked how the flight had been, and the paidhi smiled and said it had been very pleasant.

More pleasant than security, who'd had to dislodge Ilisidi from the premises last night, damned sure; security who'd gotten no sleep whatsoever last night and, looking a little less crisp than the wont of Tabini's personal guard, undoubtedly hoped that they could get some rest very soon, now. So he asked no questions whatsoever of his own and boarded the rail for a rattling, slightly antiquated train ride to the south.

It took a winding long time getting there—no one who came to Taiben was supposed to be in a hurry—

Thinking about the lander, and the drop out of space; and the fact that the trip to push the lander into the atmosphere was actually underway by now, if he remotely understood the distance the station sat from the world, or the speed of the craft shoving the lander into final descent.

Thinking about Deana Hanks, and his having listened to her explanations, and halfway believing her—that was what made him angry: he'd *asked* for her help, given her the looseness in contacting atevi sources which she'd probably used to get two good men killed—

He was mad, he was damned mad. And feeling betrayed, in a very personal sense, in his own judgment of another human being—he'd have thought instinct was worth something; and he'd argued with Banichi that she'd been upset at the attack, she'd tried to warn her guards—

One of them was a fool. Again. He'd fallen for her line about searching for him because it was noble, because it was what he'd have done—the search for him was *her* damn excuse for contacting what Tabini called unacceptable persons, for going outside the lines; God, she'd had a field day in the atevi opposition, and not a theoretical opposition. She'd dropped FTL into the mix, all right, and maybe that had been a mistake, but she'd also damned near fractured a province and damned near taken out Geigi's influence—Geigi was one of the most scientifically literate lords in the tashrid *and* in the scientific committees. Geigi had fallen into her arguments, and so had he—refused to maintain his intellectual conviction that she could possibly be the ideologue he'd thought and still do a credible job—he'd held out in the contact they'd had, because at the back of his mind had been the fear of being alone, the need for somebody human to check with, to *have* her contrary but human train of thought to consider. He'd needed her.

But right now, if something happened in the landing and the ship concluded atevi weren't civilized enough to deal with directly, that would suit her and her friends on Mospheira *and* her friends in the tashrid. They wanted something to go wrong. The radicals of both nations had found common cause. And he'd seen it possible—but he'd not seen it coming from the angle it had. He'd counted on Deana slowly gaining an understanding of atevi—God, how did you work that closely with them and still maintain humans had to have absolute dominance?

And how did atevi lords not see what she espoused—if not that it was so damned uniquely human?

He thought about aijiin, and antiquity, and how, yes, humans had studied the Padi Valley origins of the Western Association, but in the way of humans not hardwired for such understandings, humans hadn't known instinctively, as would have been obvious to atevi, that that formerly powerful association would never turn the participants loose, not so long as they retained any territorial holdings here, not so long as they remotely had interests here— The hierarchies would still operate and the rivalries would still exist.

(Mecheiti on the hillside, shoving each other dangerously for position, because there was just one mecheit'aiji, one leader, and there was a rival, and there were almost-rivals—and those far enough down the order of things they didn't contend.)

Humans concentrated on the competitions of economics and never saw the opposition of the tashrid to Tabini as significant. They saw atevi adopting a human pattern, democratization following a rise in the middle class.

Wrong.

Very damn wrong. Democratization had happened *before* the economic rise of the middle class, democratization in order to secure the rise of a middle class, maybe because the first paidhi, in his need to communicate about human decision process, had let slip something to his aiji as disturbing in its day as FTL to Geigi's philosophy.

There wasn't such a thing as a solitary creature in all the world. The wi'itkitiin perhaps came closest. But even they nested in associations. If there was one—there'd be others. Crawling their way uphill from their brief flights, doggedly, determined in their courses, they got back to their cliffs, those that survived the predators. Damned stubborn. As atevi were. As mecheiti were. They didn't give up on a project. They didn't give up on an effort. Lords didn't give up. It could go thousands of years; they didn't give up, the way, perhaps, wi'itikiin didn't give up their ancestral nests on ancestral relative heights on ancestral cliffs. Atevi wrote *down* their purposes, and told them to their children, so they never damned well forgot.

Very bad enemies, he thought, watching the valley unwind in front of them, watching the distant brown tile roofs of Taiben appear in the distance above the trees.

Humans who didn't know that, didn't know the atevi. Not their good points nor their bad. Deana didn't know what she'd tied into. Deana was still operating—he was willing, in the face of all other misjudgments he'd made, to bet on this one as truth—on the theory that what one saw in atevi now had always been true; that the opposition to Tabini was a political and not a biological impulse; that economics drove atevi to the same extent and in the same way as it drove Mospheiran humans.

Naturally. It was her specialty. What was her paper? Economic determinism?

It wasn't his field, but he knew the premise: that industrial society ultimately produced like social institutions.

No need for Deana to struggle with nuances of the language—atevi would grow more and more like humans. She'd just deal with the atevi that agreed with her position. Her friends in the Heritage Party didn't want to understand atevi—just deal with them. Just the way it was when Wilson was in office.

Right, Deana. No arguing with success.

21

The servants were waiting on the rustic back porch of the lodge as the train pulled in to the platform. They insisted on snatching his bags and they chattered at him about the accommodations.

And perhaps it was the sight of familiar ground, where, at every visit, only pleasant things had happened; perhaps it was, despite the crowd of female servants, the comfortable recognition of an odd stone in the porch wall, the sight of its unshaped wood, its muted browns and stone grays, the plain character of its timber-and-stone halls—he felt as if he'd shed the Bu-javid at the door, as if, here, the landing itself was finally real, and he could actually do something about the problems it brought with it. He walked from the train depot door, down the hall with its hunting memorabilia and the leather couches and wooden benches, let his baggage find its way to the other wing while he lingered in the formal reception hall with the benches and the fireplace. To his pleasure, the servants or, more likely, Gaimi and Seraso, chief of the permanent, year-round ranger staff, who used Taiben when the family wasn't in residence, had a small fire going to welcome him, mostly of aromatics, the sort of thing the rangers laid by after clearing brush. The room smelled of evergreen and oilwood.

Beyond that was his room. *His* room, when he stayed at Taiben, a very comfortable room, with country quilts as well as the furs, a bedstead that could have stood in an earthquake, a trio of tables, and a wood-carving of a stand of seven trees that wasn't grand art or anything, but elegantly executed and pleasant.

His bed. A mattress he knew. A bathroom with a propane heater for winter. Shower tiles with wildflowers hand-painted on them. He realized he'd drawn a deep, deep breath, and that something in his chest had unknotted the minute he'd stepped off the train.

Then Tabini's security staff arrived to say they had chosen two rooms next to his for the foreigner paidhiin, if he would care to inspect them, and his mind snapped back to the business of descending landers, terrified spacefarers probably enroute at the very moment.

He viewed the rooms, one after the other; rooms like his own, one with a sling chair made of marvelously shaped driftwood and red leather, one with a human-high carved screen showing a hunting party, and asked himself what they'd think, surrounded by stone and wood and live flame, which was, he was sure, very unlike the station or the ship. But he assured Naidiri's two assistants and the servants that they were magnificent rooms fully proper for foreigner paidhiin—they didn't, he was thinking to himself, have trophy heads on the walls, which was probably just as well.

A senior servant came in with a bouquet of wildflowers of, she assured him, felicitous color and number, and said that such rooms and such a place would surely help assure harmony, as the servant said, "The numbers of the earth run through this house. They can't be infelicitous with the numbers of the heavens."

"One certainly agrees, nadi," he murmured, finding a comfort in the reckoning that wasn't humanly rational— just that atevi thought it worked, atevi arranged things with good will in mind, very simply conceived good will that said they should all be harmonious and fortunate. "I think it's very well done. Very well thought, nadiin. They should feel well taken care of."

He *could* relax, then, at least enough to leave the servants to install his small amount of clothing in the drawers and the closet and to press what wanted pressing. He went outside to stand on the porch and breathe the free air, looking out over the hillside.

Taiben sat on a gentle slope, its rearmost sections camouflaged in the edge of a hillside forest, its porch shaded by trees. In this season, in the nightly chill of the hills, grasses were just turning from green to gold: a hundred meters on, trees and brush began to give way to meadowlands which ran on and on, interspersed with trees, to what they called the south range—and the landing site, a good drive distant.

He'd hiked a lot of the grassland. And the south range. Tabini had dragged him here and there around the reserve—an easy matter for Tabini, whose long legs never felt the strain. Which wasn't fair—in a man who spent his life in the Bu-javid and came out here to wear the paidhi to a state of exhaustion.

A lot of dusty hiking about, and firing guns, which the paidhi wasn't supposed to do, and which, not so long ago, the paidhi would have been just as glad to skip in favor of sitting about the fire all day and resting—when he'd come here, he'd usually been on the end of a long, long work schedule. He was now.

But if he'd the choice, he'd like to leave the porch and take a long walk off into the meadow. Which would be about the stupidest thing the paidhi could think of. When atevi security said, Stay in sight, they meant, Stay in sight. They were understandably short-fused, and being very efficient, very polite. He'd no desire to make their job harder.

So he trudged back inside, called for a pot of tea and watched—rare sight—the play of flames in the fireplace for the better part of an hour while servants hurried about their business and security crawled about in places atevi didn't fit, installing security devices, some of which might be lethal: he didn't ask.

Banichi came back with traces of dust and gravel on his knees and said he'd appreciate a pot of tea himself. Which meant, he was sure, Banichi had overtaxed his recent injury and was feeling it.

"Game of darts?" Banichi said when he'd had a chance to catch his breath and sip half a cup of tea. It was one human game atevi had taken to with a passion approaching that for television. He suspected he was going to lose.

Worse, as happened. Banichi offered him a handicap. He refused to take it. Banichi shrugged and still backed up a couple of meters—"Longer arm," Banichi said. "Let's be fair."

It was a slaughter, all the same. Four rounds of it.

"I don't think you *can* miss," Bren said.

Banichi laughed, and put one in the margin. "There. What do you say? No one's perfect?"

Bren made his best try to put one dead center. Which got him a finger's breadth out. "Well," he said, "some of us miss better than others."

Banichi thought that was funny, and sat down and stretched his legs out on a footstool.

"Sit down," Banichi said. "Enjoy the rest."

He did. He sat down, and without clearly realizing how tired he was, nodded off in the chair. And finally gave way to sleep altogether, a comfortable nap, with Banichi close by him.

"He's quite tired," Banichi said to someone quietly. "Keep the noise down."

People were walking nearby, a lot of people, and the paidhi finally had to pay attention to it. He heard Banichi talking to someone, and rubbed the soreness in his neck, blinked the room into focus and realized by the preparations and the conversations that Tabini was coming in, and with him, he was sure, Tano and Algini. Commotion preceded the aiji like a storm front: running through the sitting room and the kitchens, armed security headed through back halls of Taiben where the discreetly camouflaged rail station had its outlet on the side of the building, a station blasted out of the living stone of the hillside. Tano and Algini in fact came in, carrying their own baggage and a couple of heavy canvas cases that looked to hold electronics.

And if the place had felt homelike in his arrival, it felt far other than that now, with weapons in plain sight, Tabini's personal security with armored vests and heavy rifles—Tano and Algini in similar dress and no longer occupied with the ordinary business of clericals and offices:

that was surveillance or communications equipment, he was certain.

If Saidin had—and he was sure that she had—put an Atigeini Guild member in the staff—it wasn't such an obvious presence; it was one of the quietly efficient women in soft, expensive fabrics and soundless soles, who whispered when they spoke among themselves and who had such a hair's breadth sensitivity to a design out of adjustment.

Damiri's. Or even Tatiseigi's.

While Damiri was, he recalled with a jolt, still in the Bu-javid—wasn't she?

In the Bu-javid, where *her* life might not be secure if an Atigeini moved against Tabini at Taiben. Atevi didn't take hostages, as such. But you damned well knew when you were in reach, and Damiri was—evidently voluntarily—staying in reach.

So very much went on tacit and unspoken—and the paidhiin one and all had had so little idea until he'd had the crash course at Malguri, and finally, rammed through a stupid human head on the plane, the implications he'd missed by not knowing well enough where the associational lines lay, the sub-associations the paidhiin had always known were there, the potency of which the paidhiin had completely underestimated.

The paidhiin had learned to appreciate atevi television, and machimi plays, in which, so often as to be cliché, the stinger in the situation was atevi not knowing an ally had a more complicated hierarchy of *man'chi* than even the lord had thought he had. Or the lord, who theoretically lacked *man'chi* by reason of being a lord, turning out to have *man'chi* to someone no one accounted for.

God, it was right out there in front of the paidhi; it had been right there in front of the State Department and the FO and the university, if anybody had known remotely how to trace it: the university kept meticulous records of genealogies, the provable indications of *man'chi*—and he knew who was related to whom; more or less. But that didn't say a thing about what Banichi had talked about, the *man'chi* of where mates came from—or why.

Or the *man'chi* of servants; or the *man'chi* one atevi awarded another—Cenedi had found it necessary to tell him, perhaps as a point of honor he'd pay any deserving person, perhaps just a warning for the dim-witted human, that he couldn't regard any debt of life and limb ahead of his *man'chi* to Ilisidi. Cenedi hadn't needed to say that: he'd understood when he'd put Cenedi in a position humans would call debt that Cenedi would owe him no favors.

Banichi had protested vehemently his announcement he'd attached *man'chi* to him and Jago. He didn't know why they should object—unless—

—of course. He felt his face go hot. Banichi had said, with some bewilderment and force—you're not physically attracted to *me,* and then added that about Jago. *Man'chi* was hierarchical. Except the exception Banichi had hinted at. He'd declared *man'chi* either reversing the order of hierarchy, the paidhi toward his security—

—or he'd said something exceptionally embarrassing to Banichi, who couldn't even, in what Banichi might know about the incident between him and Jago, entirely swear that that wasn't exactly what a crazy human *was* feeling at the moment—

And the university didn't, couldn't, without more shrewd observations from the paidhiin than they'd ever gotten, trace the hidden lines of obligation, the not-so-obvious lines that evidently came down through generations that *could* be inherited, but that weren't, universally; or that could be acquired through physical or psychological attraction; or that could be forged behind closed doors by alliance of two leaders way up in the ranks of the nobility, and bind or not bind their kinsmen, their followers, their political adherents, according to rules he *still* didn't understand and atevi didn't acknowledge, at least out loud, maybe even in the privacy of their own self-realizations. There might be atevi who really, just like humans, didn't wholly understand the psychological entanglements they'd landed in. For a human, he thought, he was doing remarkably well at figuring out the entanglements of *man'chi* after the fact; he'd yet to get ahead of atevi maneuvering—and he'd no assurance even now he was looking in the right direction. He'd asked Jago once where her *man'chi* lay—and Jago'd taken at least nominal offense and told him in so many words to mind his own business: it wasn't something polite people ever asked each other. Banichi likewise.

He wondered if even the recipients of such *man'chi* always knew what was due them, or if that was, among the other logical and perhaps embarrassing causes, also why Banichi had turned his declaration away with, Not to *us,* nand' paidhi—in, for Banichi, quite an expression of dismay.

Servants made a last frantic pass about the sitting room, whisking the suspicion of dust off the fireplace stones, tidying the position of a vase so the largest flowers were foremost.

None of which Tabini gave a glance to when he came in—just a brightening of expression, and, "Ah, Bren-ji, I thought you might be resting. Any difficulties?"

"No, aiji-ma, none, absolutely an easy flight."

"Sit down, sit down—" Tabini sat, flung his feet onto a footstool, and glancing at Naidiri said, not so happily, "See to it, Naidi."

One thought it might be time to get out of Tabini's way and retreat to one's room. But Tabini seemed to have disposed of the matter and proposed a round of dice, which, unlike darts, at least evened the odds for a human participant; and named low stakes, pennies on the point, *and* a glass of something safely potable for the paidhi, on peril of the purveyor's life.

The purveyor being Banichi, the paidhi had no concern at all. And after that it was himself and Tabini and elderly Eidi, and two of the servants, on order of the aiji, the ladies protesting they couldn't, daren't sit with the aiji, and Tabini saying they'd damn well—they needed a five and security was busy.

So they sat, two gentlemen and a pair of nervous young ladies afraid they'd be beyond their betting limit—they sipped appropriate fruit liqueurs, the ladies as well—they bet pennies, and Tabini and he both lost to one of the maids; Tabini because he was distracted in other thoughts, Bren judged, himself because math counted at least a little in the game of revenge they were playing.

"We're up against a counter," Tabini said, to him and to Eidi. "And these ladies have made common cause."

"And you have a human for a handicap. We should rearrange the alliances."

"Never," Tabini said.

Which lost them, collectively, for an hour and a half, twenty and seven, and a bottle of fruit wine.

And he had a fair idea, by the looks that passed between Tabini and the truly lucky gambler of the pair, that Tabini very well knew Saidin's proxy on the staff, and perhaps more than one of them.

It didn't help the paidhi's anxiety about the peace of the evening at all. But the serving staff was on notice, Tabini, who was very prone to notice the ladies in any gathering, was an absolute gentleman, possibly because it *was* Damiri's staff, and there was no hint that anything at all was different from previous, all-male visits to Taiben—Tabini might have done as in the past, and had only his own security about them; and didn't—which had Damiri's name all over the situation.

Possibly the aiji didn't want to signal distrust of Damiri. Perhaps the aiji wanted to use the paidhi and himself for bait to draw some action from Tatiseigi, who was, as Banichi and Jago had advised him, an easy train ride away.

Not mentioning overland transport, which the rangers certainly had, and which one could well assume the Atigeini estate had.

Tabini at last leaned comfortably in his chair, one arm draped over the chairback, and waved a hand at the table. "The playing field is yours, dajiin. The bottle. The coin. —The honors. Kindly report us well to your house."

"Aiji-ma." There was a profound bow, profound confusion from one as she rose from the table. A smile from the other that could be challenge, could be acknowledgment—the young woman was surrounded by Guild seniors, against which she wouldn't have a chance for her own survival if she even looked like making a move, and she had to know that.

There was no Filing. Which meant blame and consequences flying straight to the Atigeini head of house, which she had to know also.

Bren drew in his breath and found immediate preoccupation with the position of his glass on the table.

"Pretty," was Tabini's comment after they'd withdrawn with the prizes. "Very sharp. The one on the left is Guild. Did you know?"

He looked up. It wasn't the one he'd thought. "I guessed wrong," he said, chagrined.

"I'm not sure of the other one, either," Tabini said. "Certain things even Naidiri won't say. Damiri herself professes not to be sure. But one suspects it's a pair. I understand you'd no idea of Saidin's position."

He didn't breathe but what Tabini had a report of it.

"I'm completely embarrassed. No, aiji-ma. I hadn't."

"Retired, actually," Tabini said, "but an estimable force. If I can trust Naidiri's estimate—and I wouldn't be living with the lovely lady sharing my bed if I hadn't certain assurances passed through the Guild—she answers primarily to Damiri. Only to Damiri, in point of fact."

There were cliffs and precipices in such topics. He drew a breath and went ahead. "What of Damiri? Are you *safe,* personally *safe,* aiji-ma? I'm worried for your welfare."

"I take good care," Tabini said, and turned altogether sideways, one long leg folded against the chair arm, booted ankle on the other knee. "Concerned on behalf of the Association, Bren-ji? Or your directives from Mospheira?"

"To hell with Mospheira," he muttered, and got Tabini's attention. "Aiji-ma, I've quite well damned myself, so far as certain elements of my government are concerned."

"I take it that the message was Hanks, that it said unpleasant things, and that it was not under duress."

"It was accusatory of me, of you, as instituting a seizure of others' rights—" He was aware, as he said it, that

he placed Hanks in direct danger, if Tabini were even remotely inclined to retaliatory strikes—and that, in atevi
politics, Tabini might no longer have the luxury of toler-
ating Hanks' actions. "I apologize profoundly, aiji-ma—
they're my mistakes. I spend my life trying to figure what
atevi will do; I misread her. Of my own species. I have no
excuse to offer. I'll give you a transcript."

Tabini waved a hand. "At your leisure. Knowing the
company she's keeping enables one rather well to know
the content."

"Banichi and Jago seemed to have a very good idea of
the content."

"She accuses you to your government."

"Yes.

"Will this be taken seriously?"

"It—will be raised officially, I'm fairly sure. Depending on what goes on *in* the government, I will or won't be
able to go back to Mospheira."

"Without being arrested?"

"Possibly. That Hanks hasn't gotten a recall order—I
fear indicates she still has backing."

Tabini said, "May I speak personally?"

"Yes," he said—one could hardly refuse the aiji whatever he wanted to say, and he hoped it entailed no worse
mistake than Hanks.

"I hear that your fiancée," Tabini said, "has reneged on
her agreement."

"With me?"

"With you. I know of no other."

"There wasn't—actually a clear understanding." He'd
talked about Barb with Tabini before. They'd discussed
physical attractiveness and the concept of romantic love
versus—*mainaigi,* which rather well answered to a young
ateva's hormonal foolishness. "No fault on her part.
She'd tried, evidently, to discuss it with me. Couldn't
catch me on Mospheira long enough."

"Political pressure?" Tabini asked, frowning.

"Personal pressure, perhaps."

"One suggested before . . . this woman had more vir-
tue."

He'd made claims for Barb, once upon a while. Praised her good sense, her loyalty. A lot of things he'd said to Tabini, when he'd thought better of Barb.

And if he were honest, probably that weeks-ago judgment was more rational and more on target than the one he'd used last night.

"She's stayed by me through a lot," he said. "I suppose—"

Tabini was quiet, waiting. And sometimes translation between the languages required more honesty than he found comfortable: without it, one could wander deep into definitional traps—sound like a fool . . . or a scoundrel.

"Did political enemies affect this decision?" Tabini asked.

"Certainly my job did. The absences. The—likelihood of further absences. Just the uncertainty."

"Of safety?"

He hesitated to get into that. Finally nodded. "There've been phone calls."

"She has, as you've said, no security?"

"No. It's not—not ordinary."

"Nor prospect of obtaining it."

"No, aiji-ma. Ordinary citizens just—don't. There's the police. But these people are hard to catch."

"A problem also for your relatives."

He had a suspicion about the integrity of his messages. And the pretense that no atevi understood the language well enough, a pretense which was wearing thinner and thinner.

"There is—" Tabini moved his foot, swung his leg over the arm of the chair. "There is the Treaty provision. We've broken it to keep Hanks here. Would Barb-daja consent to break with this new marriage and join you in residence on the mainland?"

He didn't know what to say for a moment—thought of *having* Barb with him, and couldn't imagine—

"It seems," Tabini said, "that there is difficulty for your whole household, on Mospheira, which has perhaps inspired this defection. In her lack of official support, one can, perhaps, see Barb-daja's difficulty."

Or perhaps Banichi or Jago had told him a certain amount. It proved nothing absolutely. He *had* talked to Jago. He'd even talked to Ilisidi.

"This is a security risk," Tabini said. "You should not have to abide threats to your household, if a visa or two would relieve their anxiety—and yours. They would be safe here, your relatives, your wife—if you chose to have this."

His heart had gone thump, and seemed to skip a beat, and picked up again while the brain was trying to work and tell him they'd been talking about Hanks, and accusations, and Hanks' fate, and it could signal a decided chill in atevi-human relations—which he had to prevent. Somehow. "Aiji-ma, it's—a very generous gesture." But to save his life—or theirs—he couldn't see it happening—couldn't imagine his mother and Toby and Jill and the—

No. Not them. Barb. Barb might think she wanted to. Barb might even try—there was a side to Barb that wasn't afraid of mountains. He could remember that now: Barb in the snow, Barb in the sunglare . . . Barb outside the reality of her job, his job, the Department, the independence she had fought out for herself that didn't need a steady presence, just not some damned lunatic isolationist agitator ringing her phone in the dead of night.

"My relatives—wouldn't—couldn't—adapt here. They'd be more tolerant of the threats. —Barb . . ."

He couldn't say no for her. She had no special protection, no more than his family. But she *could* adapt. It was—in a society she'd not feel at home in—a constant taste of the life she'd seemed to love: the parties, the fancy clothes, the glittering halls. Barb would, give her that, try to speak the language. Barb would break her neck to learn it if it got her farther up the social scale, not just the paidhi's woman, but Barb-daja; God—she'd grab it on a bet. Until she figured out it was real, and had demands and limitations of behavior.

Stay with at that point was another question. Adapt to

it, was a very serious question. He didn't think so, not in the long term.

More, he didn't want to sleep with her again. It had become a settled issue, Barb's self-interest, Barb's steel-edged self-protection: the very quality that had made her his safe refuge raised very serious questions, with Barb brought into the diplomatic interface, under the stress the life necessarily imposed—

And the constant security. And the fact—they needed each other more than they loved each other. Or loved anyone at all, any longer. They'd damaged each other. Badly.

"So?" Tabini asked him.

"Barb is a question," he said. "Let me think about it, aiji-ma, with my profound gratitude."

"And your houschold, not?"

"My mother—" He'd spoken to Tabini only in respectful terms of his mother. Of Toby. "She's very human. She's very temperous."

"Ill-omened gods, Bren, I have grandmother. They could amuse each other for hours!"

He had to laugh. "A disaster, aiji-ma. I fear—a disaster. And my brother—if he couldn't have his Friday golf game, I think he'd pine and die."

"Golf." Tabini made a circular motion of the hand. "The game with the little ball."

"Exactly so."

"This is a passion?"

"One *gambles* on it."

"Ah." To an atevi that explained everything—and restored Tabini's estimate of Toby's sanity.

"My relatives are as they are. Barb—I'll have to think. I fear my mind right now is on the ship. And the business last night. And Hanks-paidhi."

"Forget Hanks-paidhi."

That was ominous. And he resolutely shut his mouth. Protest had already cost two lives.

"I trust," Tabini said then—but Naidiri came in, bowed despite Tabini's casual attitude, and presented a small message roll, at which Tabini groaned.

"It came with a cylinder," Naidiri said. "Considering

the source, we decided security was better than formality."

"I certainly prefer it." Tabini opened it and read it. "Ah. Nand' paidhi. Geigi sends his profound respect of your person and assures you his mathematicians find great interest in the proposed solution to the paradox, which they believe to have far-reaching significance. He is distraught and dismayed that his flowers were rejected at the airport, which he believes was due to your justified offense at his doubt. He wishes to travel to Taiben in person to present his respect and regret. The man is determined, nadi."

"What shall I answer this man?" Bren asked. "This is beyond my experience, aiji-ma."

"Say that you take his well-wishes as a desirable foundation for good relations and that you look forward personally to hearing his interpretation of the formulae and the science as soon as you've returned to the capital. Naidi-ji, phrase some such thing. Answer in the paidhi's name before this man buys up all the florists in Shejidan. —You've quite terrified the man, Bren-ji. And quite— quite uncharacteristically so. Geigi is not a timorous man. He's sent me very passionate letters opposing my intentions. What in all reason did you say to him?"

"I don't know, aiji-ma. I never, never wished to alarm him."

"Power. Like it or not." Tabini gave back the message roll, and Naidiri went back, one presumed, to the little staff office Taiben had in the back hall. "On my guess, the man doesn't understand why you went personally to the observatory. He doesn't understand the signal you sent—*we* know your impulsive character. But lord Geigi—is completely at a loss."

"I couldn't rely on someone to translate mathematics to me when so much was riding on it. Third-hand never helps on something I can hardly understand myself. —Besides, it was nand' Grigiji's work. Banichi said he baffles his own students."

"That he does," Tabini said. "I've asked what we should

do for this man. He professed himself content, and took a nap."

"Did he?"

"The emeritus' students, however, begged the paidhi to give them a chance to write to the university on Mospheira."

Bren drew in a breath and let it go slowly. "Very deep water."

"One believes so."

"Access to atevi computer theory discussions? The university would be interested. It might move the cursed committee."

"Possibly."

He couldn't help it, then. He gave a quiet, rueful laugh. "If Mospheira's speaking to me. I've yet to prove that. And the ship—will change a lot of things."

"Ah. No challenge even for my 'possibly.' So sad."

"I will challenge it. But I won't tell you how in advance, aiji-ma. Leave me my maneuvering room."

Tabini laughed silently. "So. You and I were to go fishing. But I fear there's a business afoot—"

He didn't know how he could drag himself out of the chair. Or, in fact, sleep at night. "One understood back in Shejidan, aiji-ma, that the fish might have to wait."

"You look very tired."

"I can look more enthusiastic. Tell me where and when. Otherwise I'll save it for the landing."

"I think we should have a quiet supper, the two of us. We should talk about the character of our women, share a game of darts, and drink by the fire."

"That sounds like a very good program, aiji-ma."

"The fish can sleep safely this evening, then. Possibly the paidhi will get some rest."

"The paidhi certainly intends to try."

It was, as Tabini promised, a quiet supper. Other people were very busy—Banichi and Jago had gone off duty for the last quarter of the afternoon and, one assumed, fallen facedown and slept like stones, Bren told himself: it had to be rare that they could sleep in the sure knowledge they were absolutely safe, absolutely surrounded by security, and the primary job wasn't theirs.

He certainly didn't begrudge them that.

And after supper, Tabini defeated him soundly at darts—but he won three games of ten, whether by skill or the aiji's courtesy, and they sat, as Tabini had promised, by the fire.

"I'd imagine our visitors are well away by now," Bren said in the contemplation the moment offered. "I'd imagine they'll board the lander at the very last—ride out in whatever craft will take them to the brink, and perform their last-minute checks tomorrow. Everything has to be on schedule, or I'm sure they'd have called."

"These are very brave people," Tabini said.

"Very scared people. It's a very old lander." He took a sip of liquor and stared into the endless patterns of the wood fire. "The world's changing, aiji-ma. Mine is, the mainland will." Tabini had never yet mentioned Ilisidi's presence in the house. "I have a request, aiji-ma, that regard for me should never prompt you to grant against your better judgment. They tell me the dowager was here last night. That she's with the Atigeini. —Which I do not understand. But I would urge—"

Tabini was utterly quiet for the moment. Not looking at him. And he looked back toward the fire.

"In my perhaps mistaken judgment, aiji-ma—the dowager, if she is involved, seems more the partisan of the Preservation Commission than of any political faction. At least regarding ideas expressed to me. Perhaps she was behind the events last night. But I don't think so."

"You don't think so."

"I think if Cenedi had meant to do me harm, he had far subtler means. And they wouldn't guest with the Atigeini if they'd shot up the breakfast room. That's all I'll say this evening on politics. But I want to speak for the dowager, if I have any credit at all."

"Your last candidate for favor was Hanks-paidhi."

"True."

"Well, trust grandmother to find a landing spot. *I* offered her a plane. Which she declined."

"It's, as I said, Tabini-ma, the limit of my knowledge. I only wish to communicate my impression that she viewed the experience of atevi before humans came as an important legacy to guide the aiji in an age of change and foreign ways. I realize I'm a very poor spokesman for that viewpoint. But even against your displeasure I advance it, as my minimal debt to what I believe to be a wise and farseeing woman."

"Gods inferior and blasphemed, you're so much more collected than Brominandi. That wretch had the effrontery to send me a telegram in support of the rebels, do you know?"

"I hadn't known."

"He should take lessons from you. At telegraph rates he's spent his annual budget."

"But I believe it, aiji-ma. I'd never urge you against what I believe is to the benefit of atevi."

"Grandmother will take no harm of me."

"But Malguri."

"Nor will there be public markets at Malguri. —Which some would urge, you understand. Some see the old places as superfluous, an emblem of opprobrious privilege."

"I see it," he said, "as something atevi can never obtain from human books."

Tabini said nothing in reply to that. Only recrossed his ankles on the footstool, and the two of them stared at the fire a moment.

"Where is *man'chi*," Tabini asked him, "paidhi-ji?"

"Mine? One thought atevi didn't ask one another such questions."

"An aiji may ask. —Of course—"

A hurried group of security went through the room, and the seniormost, it seemed, stopped. "Aiji-ma, pardon." The man gave Tabini a piece of paper, which Tabini read.

Tabini's leg came down off the chair arm. Tabini sat up, frowning.

"Is it distributed?" Tabini asked.

"Unfortunately so."

"No action against the paper. Do inquire their connections. One wonders if this is accidental."

"Aiji-ma." The security officer left.

And Tabini scowled.

"Trouble?" Superfluous question.

"Oh, a small matter. Merely a notice in the resort society paper that we're here *for* the landing."

"Lake society?"

"The lake resort. A thousand tourists. At least. Passed out free to every campsite at the supply store."

"God."

"Invite the whole damned resort, why don't we? They'll be here, with camping gear and cameras *and* children! We've a chance of heavy arms fire! Of bombs, from small aircraft! We've a thousand damned *tourists,* gods unfortunate!"

Public land. There was no border, no boundary. One thing ran into the other.

"*Damned* if this is a mistake," Tabini said. "The publisher knows it's stupid, the publisher knows it won't make a landing easier or safer. Dammit, dammit, dammit!"

Tabini flung himself to his feet. Bren gathered himself up more cautiously, as Tabini drew his coat closed and showed every sign of taking off.

"We can't be butchering tourists in mantraps," Tabini said. "Bren, put yourself to bed. Get some rest. It's clear I won't."

"If I could help in any way—"

"Since none of our problems of tonight speak Mosphei', I fear not. Stay by the phone. Be here in case we receive calls from the heavens that something's gone amiss. Don't wait up."

Property where private was sacrosanct and even tourists respected a security line—but a landing was a world-shattering event. The Landing was the end of the old world as the Treaty was the beginning of the new. Atevi were attracted to momentous events, and believed, in the way of numbers, that having been in the harmony of the moment gave them a special importance in the universe.

There couldn't be an ateva in the whole world, once the news got beyond Taiben and once it hit the lake resort and the airport, who wouldn't phone a relative to say that humans were falling out of the sky again, and they were doing it here, at dawn tomorrow.

It wasn't a prescription for early sleep. Tano and Algini came in briefly to say they'd indeed contacted the rangers, who took the rail over to the lake and personally, on the loudspeakers, advised tourists that it was a dangerous area, that and that they risked the aiji's extreme displeasure.

"One wonders how many have already left," Bren said.

"The rangers are all advised," Algini said.

"But one couldn't tell tourists from Guild members looking for trouble."

"Many of us know each other," Tano said. "Especially in the central region."

"But true," Algini said, "that one has to approach closer than one would like to tell the difference. It's very clever, what they've done."

"Who's done? Does anybody know who's behind this?"

"There's a fairly long list, including neighboring estates."

"But the message. Was it the dowager's doing?"

"One doesn't know. If—"

"Nand' paidhi," a member of Tabini's staff was in the doorway. "A human is calling."

"I'm coming." He was instantly out of the chair, and with Tano and Algini who had come from that wing, which they'd devoted to operations, he followed the man to the nearest phone.

"This is Bren Cameron. Hello?"

"Jase Graham. Got a real small window here. Closer we get ..." There was breakup. *"Everything on schedule?"*

"We're fine. How are you?"

"I lost that. Where are you?"

"Fifty kilometers from the landing site. I'll *be* there, do you hear?"

"We're ... board the lander. Systems ... can you ... ?"

"Repeat, please.

There was just static. Then: *"See you. You copy?"*

"Yes! I get that! I'll be there!"

The communication faded out in static, tantalizing in what he didn't know, reassuring in what he could hear.

And what could they say? Watch out for hikers? We hope nobody shoots at the lander?

"They're on schedule," he said. "When are we going out there?"

"One hasn't heard that you were going, nand' paidhi," Tano said.

That was a possibility he hadn't even considered. If he was at Taiben, he'd damn sure be at the landing in the morning. He wasn't leaving two humans to be scared out of their minds or to make some risky misassumption before they reached the lodge.

"Where's Tabini?" he asked. "I need to talk to him."

"Nand' paidhi," Algini said, "we'll make that request."

"No talking through relays. I want to talk to him."

He was being, perhaps, unreasonable. But if the tourist emergency had hauled Tabini off where he couldn't get to Tabini before they arranged details that left him out, he was damned mad, *and* surprised, *and* frustrated.

"Yes, nand' paidhi," Algini said, and a certain part of Taiben's whole communications diverted itself, probably not operationally wise, probably an obstruction of operations and possibly a dangerous betrayal of the fact Tabini wasn't under Taiben's roof at the moment.

"Don't make noise about it," he said. "Just—I need this straightened out. They could come down in need of medical help. They could need a translator. Or first aid. Which I can give—at least have a good guess. There's a chance of a rough landing. And I don't want a mistake."

"I'll find the aiji," Tano said.

"Thank you, nadi."

Which meant Tano hiking out through the dark himself.

He was sorry about it. But the reasons that came to him were real reasons.

Dammit.

So he went back to the central hall and paced and repositioned bric-a-brac, and waited, in general, until, short of breath, Tano came in with, "Paidhi-ma. Banichi confirms you're to be picked up with the rest, two hours before dawn."

"*Thank* you, Tano-ji," he said, and felt foolish, having had Tano run all over the estate, in the dark, but it eased his mind enough he at least lost his urge to pace the floor.

And after that, he decided it might be wise at least to go to bed, get what rest he could without sleeping—he refused to sleep, for fear something would happen and they *would* leave him behind—and be ready to go in the morning.

So he went down the hall into the guest wing, dismissed the servants who were determined to be of help, and began, alone, to lay out the clothes he wanted for what might end up being a hike.

But the jacket he regularly wore for hiking had the brilliant red stripe down the sleeve that warned hunters he wasn't a target—and he wasn't sure, counting the problems with the neighbors, that he wanted to be that conspicuous an object in the brush.

He laid down the plain brown one he was wearing, instead—leather, and comfortable for Taiben's hall, seeing that end-of-season evenings often turned cold, and human bones chilled faster than atevi's.

"Bren-ji? One heard you were questioning arrangements?"

Jago's voice. He turned, stood there with the jacket in his hands—Jago—was different to him. He wasn't seeing her the way he'd always seen her, not a hair different, not a hint of impropriety in her being here, or in her appearance, or his, but suddenly the room was too close, the air was too warm, and a human brain with too much to do was all of a sudden trying to think about details in the circuits left over from a very stupid whiteout in the forebrain.

"I—uh, I wanted to know what time we were leaving. In the morning." The paidhi, the source of international communications, wasn't doing well. "Tano found my answer."

"There was a phone call?"

"I—uh, yes. There was."

"Bren-ji—is something wrong?"

"I—no. No. Everything's on schedule."

Jago stood there a moment. Then shut the door, shutting them both in.

He felt a sense of panic. And knew it showed. He wasn't about to throw Jago out. Or to request a good friend to leave.

Which *wasn't* what she was, dammit, he wasn't thinking.

"I've made you uneasy," Jago said. "Bren-paidhi, I was stupidly mistaken. I apologize. I most sincerely apologize."

He didn't know what to say. He stood there. And Jago said, with great correctness, "Excuse the intrusion, nand' paidhi," and turned quietly to go.

"I—" he said, in all the fluency he had. "Jago."

"Nand' paidhi?" She had her hand on the latch. He wanted and didn't want. He relied on Banichi and Jago for life and death. But Jago had touched off something—so tangled in his psyche he didn't know what to do with it, didn't know where to take hold of it, even what to call it.

"Jago—"

She was still waiting. He didn't know how many I's he'd started with, but he knew it was far too many for anyone's patience.

"Nothing," he said desperately, "nothing could make me distrust you, in any way. You—" Breath was not coming easily. "You affected me very profoundly—that's all I know how to say. I'm not sure what you think. I'm not sure what I think. I *can't* think at the moment, there's just too much, too much going on. There will be for a while. —Do I make any sense at all? It's not you. It's me. I'm not—just not at my most stable, Jago."

He ran out of words. Jago didn't seem to find any immediately, and the silence went on, so deep he could all but hear his heart beat.

"Have I angered you?" Jago asked then.

"No." A vehement shake of his head. But it wasn't an atevi gesture. "In no way. Most emphatically not."

"Disturbed you?"

"Yes."

Jago bowed her head and seemed to take that for dismissal.

"Jago." He was floundering. Clinical was all he knew how to be, to save them both. "It's the *friend* business. It's that word. We say we *love*. Even when we need. When we need, it's something not very productive. It's a lot of human damn wiring, Jago-ji. Expectations. —Like *man'chi*. How do you stop it logically? —And I can't know—maybe you're just curious. Maybe just—nothing more than that. Maybe a lot more serious than that. I don't know."

"One meant well," Jago said, still with that unbreakable control. "Evidently one was very wrong."

"No. I just—Jago, God, I'm embarrassed as hell. I just want you back. The way things were. For a while. Just that—if that doesn't offend you."

"No," she said.

"No, it can't be the same? Or no, it doesn't offend you?"

"No, nand' paidhi. I am not offended. I find no possible way to be offended."

"Can I say—at least—I'm very attracted?"

She laughed, a jolt, a startlement. "You can say so," she said. "One takes no offense, paidhi-ji."

"Is it always No, from this point? Or maybe someday?"

"What does the paidhi think?"

The paidhi was shaky in the knees. It wasn't his habit. It wasn't his style, not with Barb, not with anybody else. He felt like a total fool. And stood there with the coat in his hands. "The paidhi knows when he can't translate. When he hasn't got a hope of translating. The paidhi thinks he's extremely damn fortunate you're not mad at him."

A shy look he'd rarely seen from Jago. A nervous laugh he never had. "By no means. If you—"

But the damn pocket-com went off at that very moment. Jago pulled it from her belt, held it to her ear, and frowned.

"Fourteen," she said, probably—he'd grown wiser in the ways security communicated—her station number, acknowledging hearing a message.

Then: "If you wish to change clothes," she said, "hurry. We're moving out. Now."

"To the landing site? To there? Or where?"

"We've just been asked to go to the front of the building at moderate speed. This isn't a run, but it doesn't leave you any time, nand' paidhi."

"Damn," he said, and unbuttoned his shirt without a second's further question, was pulling on his sweater when Jago left, which only put him in more hurry to switch trousers and change to heavier socks and heavier-soled boots. He exited the room, still struggling with his coat, to find Jago waiting for him.

"What *is* the hurry?"

"Perhaps," she said, "that someone is on the way here. That's a guess, nand' paidhi."

"I'll take your guesses over some people's information." He had gloves. He'd put them in the coat pocket. They reached the main hall and joined a small number of the house security moving out toward the doors. The Atigeini servants gathered in alarm and dismay.

"Not everyone is leaving," Banichi was telling them. "There's a shelter in the cellar. House permanent staff has the keys. Extinguish the fire, pull the fuses. That will shut down everything to emergency power. Go below in good order, wait for authorized signals to open the door. You'll be safe." Banichi fell in with them as they went out the open front doors, onto the porch—an open car came around the corner of the east wing, running lights on, no headlights, and Bren's heart jumped, but Banichi and

Jago didn't react to the appearance, just hustled him along the length of the porch.

Something heavy was shoved into his coat pocket on Banichi's side, jammed down—he put a hand over the weight to stabilize it, no second guess needed what it was, no guess why Banichi picked now to give it to him and had no time to waste in the paidhi's questions, just—

"Do we have a radio? Do we have communications? We need—"

"No difficulty," Banichi said and, atevi having better night-vision on the average, seized his arm, the weak one, and made sure his feet found the steps downward. The car had pulled up and security opened the door for him, atevi eyes glowing pale gold in the faint light, there, floating disembodied the other side of the car. He had qualms about getting in, he feared that they might send him off somewhere and they might stay behind in defense of Taiben, but that wasn't the indication about the situation. Jago got in ahead of him and Banichi took the seat beside the driver, one more climbed into the back and shut the door—that was Tano, he realized all of a sudden.

"Where's Algini?"

"The car behind, nand' paidhi. With the radio." The car took off with a spin of its tires, then lumbered over tree roots and took the downhill by a series of tilts and bounces—they were on what the estate charitably called the branch road, which had far more of branches than road about it. It went around trees rather than have one cut down, it relied on four-wheel drive and a good suspension, which the staff cars had—along with the bar along the back of the front seat that became a good idea as they veered with the road along the side of the lodge and down again, toward the junction of service roads which the staff used getting equipment to and from the various wells and stations—he knew this road, Tabini'd been easy on his slight-of-stature guest, in the first visit he'd made to Taiben.

Not afterward. Not now.

"What's happening?" he asked, clinging to the safety bar. "Where's Tabini?"

Maybe Tano and Jago didn't know. Banichi turned around, arm on the seat back, head down because of the branches that raked over the windshield. "Somebody leaked the event to the local news—we've got intruders in the woods and we can't tell who're tourists from the lake district and who's not, which is not a tolerable situation for security. We've very good reason to believe this release of information was not a prank."

"Meaning the same people who have Hanks are out there."

"Most likely they are." Banichi turned his head back to the short view of tree trunks and underlit branches as the car jolted its way into a turn.

The driver—probably a ranger—had his hands full: it wasn't every atevi who knew how to drive, and nobody could avoid collision who didn't know this road, not from where he sat—the wheel went this way and that, in furious efforts that exerted atevi strength to keep the wheels on track at all, bouncing over roots and jolting over low spots, the low running lights bouncing wildly, amber lights from a car behind them casting their shadows on the seat backs in front of them and reflecting in the windshield.

"Are they likeliest to move on Taiben itself?" he asked. "Or the landing site? Do they *know* exactly where?"

"They may," Tano said. "It wasn't in the news report, but no knowing the other information that's passed."

"They won't waste time on Taiben when they know we've left. They've come in afoot. So far. Now that we've moved—they'll probably have transport come in."

"We're a one-point target," Jago said. "They're diffuse. This is by the nature of a wide border with uncertain neighbors."

The road took a series of jolts that made the handhold a necessity, even for atevi, then smoothed out, and Banichi turned around again, eyes shimmering momentarily in the following running lights. "We've a secure place if we need it," Banichi said, "nadi-ji. We're not in trouble. Yet."

"That lander's going to come down slowly tomorrow,"

Bren said. "If they've got any kind of weapons—if they were willing to attack it—"

"We think rather their target is Tabini himself," Banichi said. "Possibly you. We've tried to persuade Tabini to fly back to Shejidan. But the aiji says not. And he extends that decision to you."

Banichi wasn't pleased by that. And the reason for the confused, abrupt exit became more clear: scatter vehicles through the woods, keep the opposition guessing where Tabini was and with what group, or at Taiben—and where the paidhi was. Tabini thumbed his nose at the opposition. Tabini's staff *and* the paidhi did, that was the message Tabini was sending, and he understood that, but they had a very vulnerable capsule coming down in a place that wasn't exactly neatly defined—they couldn't set up a specific watch over a specific ten-meter area and trust the capsule might not be a kilometer or so away, exposed to God-knew-what. Bren sat holding the elbow of his sore arm, in the interval he wasn't clutching the bounce-bar, feeling the jolts in his joints and in muscles gone cold and tense.

He wasn't scared, he wasn't scared, this wasn't like Malguri, with the chance of bombs falling on them. They were playing tag through the woods, but keeping ahead of the people trying to shoot at them; they'd dodge and switch through ranger tracks the opposition might have maps of, but it wasn't the same as their driver's evident experience of the roads. They'd out-drive them, out-maneuver them . . .

They were in open cars, that being what the rangers used for these narrow trails, and probably the only vehicles with a wheelbase that could take them—but they were visible targets, and the landing wasn't in a meadow interspersed with trees, or hillside forest, it was down on the flat, in a grassland split by a couple of rocky patches—profoundly eroded and wooded escarpments that ran eighty, ninety kilometers northwest to southeast, with stands of scrub that gave ambushers plenty of cover.

You could see wheel tracks in the grass. They couldn't get there without leaving a trace that small aircraft could spot well enough. Neither they nor the opposition could maneuver in a sea of grass without a trail someone else could track.

"They won't chase us here," he muttered to Jago and Tano. "They don't need to. They know where we're going. At least—close enough."

"Diffuse versus specific," Jago said. She'd said that. He'd not arrived at the same conclusion until then. But that told him at least his security had thought of it.

Then he had a cold and terrible thought.

"Oh, my God. My computer."

Banichi turned around in his seat. Flashed a shimmer of yellow eyes. And a grin. "Right between my feet, paidhi-ji. We didn't forget."

Hormones, he said to himself, his heart settling back to steady work. Damned hormones. Brain fog. A schoolboy mistake. He found himself shivering as the car found a reasonable stretch of meadow grass and ripped along at a reckless bounce. He tried not to nudge against the atevi on either side of him. He didn't want them to feel it.

But he had the hard weight of the gun in his pocket, too, and finally had the wit to ask, "Has anybody got a spare clip of shells?"

He got three, one from Banichi, one from Jago, one from Tano. The driver had his hands occupied, and the paidhi was out of convenient pockets and carrying enough weight.

The rebels had Hanks. "Is there any way—" Figuring to himself that with all of an aiji's resources to draw from, there might be personnel to spare. "—any way—" A pothole. "—Hanks has to be somewhere close." Pothole. "With them. Get into *their* territory. Go get Hanks." Bounce. "Let them worry."

Jago laughed, silent in the growl of the motor and the slap of branches. Grinned, holding on to the side of the car. "Good idea, nand' paidhi."

"You thought of that."

"So will they, unfortunately. I fear they'll move her out."

Damn, he thought. They would. As a strategist he wasn't

in the game. "Can't use the airport. Ranger trails, more likely."

"Good, nai-ji."

"A peaceful man hasn't a chance with you," he said, and Tano patted his leg from the other side.

"Paidhi-ji, we listen because you have good ideas. They'd do these things. So are we doing them."

"Then where are we going? Around in circles, to make them crazy?"

"If we can," Jago said. And after a fierce series of bumps and a turn, "There's a classified number of storm shelters, where we can rest about an hour or so, move around again. Tabini's plane's left, or will, very soon now. Just keep them wondering. We hope so, at least."

22

It was a scary business waiting for two men to find or not find a bomb. Especially when the two were Tano and Algini, who, one came to understand, were good at what they did and had state-of-the-art equipment, at least as good as the potential bomb-placers might have, if someone, however unlikely, had been fast enough to penetrate deep into Taiben Reserve and booby-trap the shelters.

Which no one had, apparently, since Tano and Algini signaled with a double flash of their hand-torch that the way was clear.

So they left the cars, hiked through the brush of the little copse that hid the excavation.

Storm shelters.

Classified storm shelters, with, as they could see when they opened the door, a well-kept interior, electric lights, at least enough to see by, which didn't depend on generators; and some which did.

For legitimate storms, Bren said to himself, not the political ones for which he suspected the aijiin of Shejidan had built such strong concrete bunkers. There were in fact fairly considerable storms, occasionally tornadic, not infrequently with hail, occasionally deep snow, and there were reasons the rangers who served the estate might want to pull in and take shelter, reach medical kits, even take a shower—the place could shelter twenty atevi, had no trouble at all tucking a stray human in. Bren found a quiet corner, pillowed his aching shoulder against a wad of folded blankets, and discovered a degree of comfort that let him shut his eyes and actually sleep a minute or two, to his own mild surprise, perhaps because things *were* finally moving in a direction he couldn't do a damned thing about, and people around him *were* alert, and knew there was harm aimed at them, and were doing everything in their considerable professional skill to stop it.

He'd felt like the only warning and the only fix in the system for so—damned—long. Now everybody knew what he knew, did what they knew how to do, nobody he cared about was going to get caught by surprise, and nothing was going to be his fault if a bomb dropped on them and blew them to hell—he could sleep on that understanding.

But in not long enough there was an alarm, at least enough stir to rouse him out of sleep. He waked with a thump of his heart and an awareness everyone was coming on guard, but Jago patted his arm, saying it was the aiji coming in, go back to sleep.

The eyelids were willing. But nobody slept through Tabini's arrival anywhere. There was a general stirring about, discussion among the Guild, who should go where, and then a decision they should go on, but they should leave the paidhi.

"The paidhi doesn't want to be left," he protested. "Jago?"

"We stay with you," Jago said quietly. "We don't split up."

He felt reassured in that—as the door opened and Tabini and Naidiri and his group came in, and all of their group but his own security and the man working communications with Algini went out.

He sat still, wished Tabini a good evening, or morning, or whatever it was in this dim place, and held his shoulder against the ache, wishing he had had the foresight to bring his own first-aid kit.

"Bren-ji," Tabini said, patted him on the ankle in passing his perch on a raised bench.

And then he grew a little uneasy, since Tabini was not as cheerful nor as outgoing as one might look to have him. Tabini was preoccupied and spoke quietly with

Naidiri and Banichi, after which Banichi and Naidiri talked with him for some little time, and then went and talked to each other.

"What's wrong?" he asked Jago quietly. "Can you tell?"

Jago got up, apparently wanting that answer herself, squatted down with Banichi and Naidiri, listening, arms on knees, talking with them for no little while.

Then she came back and said, in a low voice, "There's a breakthrough we're relatively sure isn't tourists. We think we have them identified there, but we're betting it's a feint, and that they might have created all this incursion area including the tourists to mask a move more to the south. We're trying to get information from several sources, but we have some feeling that either they weren't totally surprised by a landing at Taiben—or a move against the government has been in preparation for far longer than the Hanks matter."

"How serious?"

"Very. They didn't move after the ship sighting. They had a chance then. Tabini was at Taiben. But they likely expected tight security."

"They can't think it's lighter now!"

"The tourist move was very good. When we first sighted the ship, there was nothing at Taiben to draw citizen interest. But a landing—that's attracted the innocent public. That's drawn ordinary folk to lose their good sense about the proprieties. One *doesn't* drop in on the aiji for tea, Bren-ji, one can't think of it."

"Unless there's a spaceship on the aiji's front porch. With death rays and disintegrator beams. Jago-ji, they're out of their minds!"

"This is the public, nai-ji. You've made them confident of human good will. Here they are."

"My God."

"One could wish we had more time to scour the hills to the south. Banichi asks, as an option, if there's a way to delay the landing a few hours."

He looked at his watch, needed the display light in the faint light. "It's too close. I don't know. I could try right now. Not later. —But if we advise them what's going on—Jago-ji, they'll land on Mospheira. They won't proceed against hazard, I very much fear they won't, and that has its own problems."

Jago's lips pressed to a thin line. "We're not prepared to urge a delay yet. It may not be a good idea to delay. The search just has to move faster."

"We're talking about very little time, Jago. Once they go point-of-no-return, they're falling, and they have no choice."

Jago went back and talked to Banichi and Naidiri, who went and talked to Tabini.

Tabini came back to him, again put a hand on his ankle and said quietly, "Bren-ji. A group is coming in, within a very few moments. They're stopping. We're going on to the site immediately. We're going to make a certain amount of radio noise, in hopes they'll think us one of the patrols. I've a squad or two in the hills that's going to clear an area that has nothing to do with the drop, which we hope will attract attention to that area, and we're going on. We've a bulletproof vest. It's a little large. Please wear it."

"No argument, Tabini-ma. None from me. You're aware, I hope, that that capsule drops quite slowly as it nears the ground. It's not armored. It's tough—but I don't think it can take being shot at."

"We are aware. We're going to have air cover, at a respectful distance, of course. We'll be tracking it." A second pat at his leg. "We believe we know where Hanks is. They've been indiscreet with the phone lines. And the aiji has one advantage. *I* run the phone company."

He got up, he put on the vest Tano held for him and, worse, the helmet Tabini presented him, which had its advantages, he supposed, if someone were shooting at his head, but disadvantages if he didn't pad it with a folded small towel until he could see where he was going.

But other helmets were going on, and vests under jackets that probably had their own protection. It gave him the advantage, he thought, of looking a little less like a human and more like an atevi kid playing army.

He put his gloves on. There was nothing to do with his face, except, as Jago advised him, keep his head down, which sounded like a good idea to him.

"They're coming," Algini said, listening to his head-set, over in the corner, and went on listening.

Banichi passed a woman a cassette. "The aiji's voice. Mine. Naidiri's. Dole that out and it's several hours' worth of our presence here."

"Yes," the woman said cheerfully. "Thank you, 'Nichi-ji."

'Nichi-ji? Bren thought with a second glance, but it didn't seem politic to ask. He gathered up his computer from where Banichi had set it when they came in and he held himself ready as the signals passed at the door.

They were going. Himself, Tabini, their respective security forces—the old gambling game, move the cups that held the stone, fast as they could; or pretend to move—meanwhile both sides were doing the same. For the second time in two weeks he was headed for a situation with atevi shooting at each other, he had his pockets weighted with ammunition clips, the bulletproof vest made his shoulder and ribs sore already, and the helmet kept obscuring half his vision—he wasn't a particularly martial specimen, he thought with a lump in his throat; he'd been shot at enough lately he'd decided he really didn't like it, and right now he wanted to strangle Deana Hanks barehanded for a situation she'd precipitated, if not directly caused.

FTL and stockpiles, hell.

It was dodge and turn in the dark through a confusing maze of small service roads, over hills, through meadows and down and across bridgeless streams in wooded areas—trees grew quite successfully wherever there was water and, increasingly so as they entered the wide south range, only where there was water.

They weren't in the lead: two other cars were in front, and Tabini rode with Naidiri in a car two back from them in the six-vehicle column, security clearly taking care to have them protected in the middle, but not together in the middle. The road ripped along a wooded streamside and out across open grassland for a space and back again into trees. They parked twice, each time in such wooded areas, at places where other roads diverged, and waited for what event wasn't clear, for maybe five minutes. Everyone sat in total silence, listening into the dark, the motors cut off, nothing but the night sounds of the range and the mild whisper of a breeze moving through the branches overhead. Tano relayed Banichi's messages to someone on his pocket-com—Banichi didn't talk, neither did Jago: voices that might be too well-known, Bren thought, especially to the neighbors. Tano said something about section eleven and some incursion and taking the number twenty-one. "Easy," the driver said, and motors were starting ahead and behind them. The lead driver backed a little and nosed off onto the divergence, leading the way onto a rougher, less-traveled road. Brush scraped the undercarriage and escaped out the rear, branches already broken by the first and second vehicle scraped along their sides.

Change of plans, Bren thought and, sandwiched between Jago and Tano in the backseat, cradled his elbow to protect his arm from the weight and irritation of the vest.

But taking it off didn't tempt him in the least.

"Are we still going toward the site?" he asked once, as quietly as he could, after Banichi and the driver had exchanged a couple of casual words.

Then a branch hit their windshield and scraped over their heads, so atevi had to duck and the human in the middle suffered a rain of pungent and bruised leaves.

Three violent bounces over roots, a sharp turn, and they made an uphill climb over a ridge in which the view from the backseat was black sky and then the lumpish, weathered granite that told him for the first time they were on the cross-range ridge. He checked his watch, risking knocking into Jago and Tano.

"Hour before dawn," he said with a nervous flutter of his stomach. "They'll be underway, the lander will—" A fierce bounce, then a break out of the woods: the faintly lit detail of branches gave way to total black interspersed with trees, as the driver made furious efforts with the wheel to keep them up to the speed they'd carried.

Going as fast as they possibly could, he thought.

"We're not far from the junction east, then access to the—"

He heard a thump. Jago and Tano folded over him, shoving him down as a shock of air blossomed all around them in a sound, a pressure, a force that heaved up the road, shoved them and the whole car over, spilled them in a heavy tangle of limbs and stickery brush and lastly pelting earth and stone and wood.

He couldn't get his breath for a moment. He braced himself as somebody leaned on him trying to move, then—then the car exploded in a ball of flame, somebody grabbed his vest by the bottom edge and dragged him downhill, shots were going off. He'd lost the helmet, he'd every awareness his most essential job right now was to keep his head down and keep out of the way—he knew Jago and Tano were alive, they'd fallen tangled with him, they'd hauled him back. In a flurry of small-arms fire, he heard car engines whining—in what sounded like fast reverse, cars from behind them getting out the only direction they could; but his ears were ringing from the explosion, and in the glare of fire he couldn't make out anything but the burning vehicle they'd been in, black in the center of the fireball, uphill in front of them. Trees were catching, going up like matches. The whole area was lit in fire.

Then he heard someone shouting, and Banichi—thank God, Banichi—shouting back they couldn't maneuver where they were, don't try to come after them, they'd hold here.

"Stay down!" Banichi yelled, then, and a strong atevi hand shoved him flat as fire spattered chips off the rocks and thumped into the other side of the burning car.

"My computer!" he protested.

"Your head, nadi." Jago kept up the pressure on his back. There was another thump from up the hill, then an explosion that hit beyond them and rained rock and dirt.

Tano said, while his ears were recovering from the shock, "Firetube. I can go up after it."

"No!" Banichi said. "Too damn much light out—"

Another shell hit beyond them, starting a minor landslide. Jago hauled him into a hollow of rocks and Tano joined them, as Banichi fired a rapid series of shots toward the height.

He had his own gun. He pulled it out of his pocket, aware when he rested his weight on the other elbow that he'd strained the shoulder enough to make his eyes water. He wasn't sure what the target was, he wasn't even sure where the attack was coming from, but the blowing smoke was headed down the road and the fire had skipped to brush in that area.

Tano and Jago stretched out in the scant cover they had and began laying down fire at the uphill as well. He tried to find a way to do the same, but he had a rock in his way and tried to get a vantage above it, but Tano jerked him down, none too gently.

"I've extra clips," he said, trying to be useful at something.

Another shell hit. Banichi and another man he thought was the ranger took shelter with them as a tree came down in a welter of branches, right on the front of the car, and caught fire, making a screen of light between them and anything they could possibly aim at.

"Steady firing," Banichi said. "All we can do. We're a roadblock. They're trying to go behind. Keep their heads down. Bren, watch our backs. Hear?"

"Yes," he said, and edged around to do that. Go behind what, he wasn't sure, but he suspected Banichi meant Tabini's group was going behind the hill: they'd backed the cars out of the area, headed in reverse back around the curve of the ridge, the way the car in front of them seemed to have gotten away down the road. He didn't know if there was a plan, if some of them were going to go up and others were going to get Tabini out of there, or if Tabini and his security were going to try the hill; but Banichi and Jago and Tano and the ranger-driver were all firing as if they could see what they were shooting at—

and as if they had more ammunition than he thought they had. He had a branch gouging his arm as he'd faced about to the downhill: he took a hitch on one hand to shift to a more long-term position—and saw a movement in the firelit dark downhill.

"Man!" was all that came out of his mouth—he fired, and a blow knocked him back into the rock, his head hit stone, and guns fired on either side of him.

"Bren-ji!" Jago's voice.

"Vest," he managed to say, bruised in the ribs, winded, realizing there'd just been justification for the body armor. He had his gun still in hand; he braced it on his knee, his arm and leg both shaking. "I'm watching! It's all right!"

Guns were going off next to his ears, Banichi and the ranger were still shooting. Tano and Jago turned their attention back toward the hill and he sat there and shook—which tightened the muscles in his ribs, which didn't help him get his breath. Heat was rolling down the slope on gusts of wind, bringing stinging smoke.

At least they weren't landing more of the heavy shells. Their attackers might not have any more. The fire they were sending upslope might be keeping the enemy's heads down.

But they couldn't have that much ammunition left to keep up their own fire, and the attackers on the ridge had sent at least one man below them—surely not just one. His eyes weren't as good as atevi eyes in the dark: he didn't know how they were against the fire-glare, but the pitch of the slope made deep shadows interspersed with firelit branches of trees and rocks, and out beyond, grass, just—grass forever, past this stony hump of a ridge that ran a diagonal across the south range, the one exception in a flat that went on clear to the ocean bluffs—

And that antiquated space capsule was already on its way, committed beyond return: a fast push of a button on his watch and a steadying of his wrist said it wasn't the eternity he'd thought, but it wasn't that much time left, either, and they weren't where they were supposed to be, even if Tabini's people got them clear; they weren't going to make it out of here in any good order; and the question was whether they were *going* to make it out, or whether, if Tabini was being his stubborn self up there, they were going to have a government left in another hour to care at all whether there was a paidhi to translate for humans. He felt sick at his stomach, partly the heat, partly the shock of the hit he'd taken, and partly the knowledge this wasn't going to work. . . .

"Clip, nadi," Jago said with complete calm, and he dug in his pockets with the other hand, gun still braced generally downslope, and reached around to hand her two of the three. "I've got one more, no, two, counting what's in my gun." His voice wasn't entirely reliable. He tried to keep watching where he was supposed to watch.

"Go easy, go easy," Banichi said, and the shots kept coming—Banichi's, Jago's—keeping his ears ringing. "We can't have that damn firetube back in action."

"The grass is catching fire," the ranger said, and Bren threw a glance to the ranger's side: fire *had* spread downslope, not directly below them, but where the burning line of brush had caught down the hill to their left.

It was end of season. The grass was drying. Green-gold in the view from the porch—

All that grass. All that grass, clear to the sea. The capsule coming down in a sea of flame. The heat shield was mostly on the bottom, mostly there—how hot did a grass fire get, when the flames rolled ten meters high and scoured the land black?

Gunfire broke out on the slope above them, a sudden lot of it. He felt a rush of hope and terror, resisting the temptation to turn and look toward what he couldn't hope to see anyway. Gunfire rattled above them, and suddenly a nasal, angry squeal.

That didn't belong at Taiben—he heard a scream cut short, and that godawful squalling snort that, God, anyone hearing a mecheita attack a man would never, ever forget—

Mecheiti were on the ridge. Riders.

He did turn on his hip, striving to try to see through the spreading fire. Leaves on trees just over their heads were catching, a thin flicker of fire, a rain of burning ash, carried on a gust of firestorm wind. Heat was building. The trees near them could go up the way the first had.

"Trees are catching fire!" he said. "We've got to get to the clear—we're going to get caught—"

But the rattle of gunfire that came to them through the roar of the fire had stopped; atevi voices upslope were shouting at each other.

He didn't know what to think. He crouched on his knees with the gun in his good hand and everyone around him equally confused, for the instant. A sapling burst into flame, all the leaves involved at once. He felt a heart-pounding panic, no better excuse. And faintest of all was a thread of a voice from an active pocket-com.

"Hold fire, hold fire, blue, below."

"They've got it," Banichi said. "Stay down!"

"Stay down yourself!" Jago said, the only time Bren had ever seen Jago defy an order. Her arm shot past him to grab Banichi's sleeve. "Your leg, dammit, stay here!"

"The hell," Banichi said, and broke his arm free, but he stayed down.

There was just the roar of the fire, now, no rattle of weapons fire. Nothing seemed to move. There was a reek of gunpowder, of burnt plastic, through the stinging woodsmoke, and Tano edged over, finding cover further away from the fire. They crept over sidelong across the slope, below the edge of the road, while a thin conversation over the pocket-coms continued, directing movement, directing roundup of surrendering rebels.

Then he heard Jago say, "The dowager. Yes, aiji-ma—we're fine. All of us. We're holding fire."

He hoped there hadn't been a carnage up there, that people he cared about were still alive, that there was some means of reaching a peace. He heard names like Dereiso, whom Banichi had named to him as a problem in the region. He heard orders to say they should stay still, and he heard the sound of a small plane overhead, which he didn't like, but Tano said it was theirs.

A motor started up, from around the bend of the ridge, and a second one—in a moment more, cars came down the road, Tabini's end of the convoy coming up behind and around their burning vehicle: ahead, nothing but fire—the downed tree that had buried the front end of their own car in its branches was a burning log, and the wind had carried sparks all over the ridge in that direction.

The third car didn't show, but down from the firelit hill came a ghostly soundless darkness: mecheita and rider. Others followed. *Not* under guard. Rangers, Bren thought. He hadn't known there were mecheiti at Taiben. He'd never heard of any. But there they were, fifteen or so riders, coming off the sparsely wooded ridge beyond where the cars were stopped. Riders in metal-studded black, the brief glimpse of one who wasn't—no intimation of threat to the cars or hostility to them: people were out of the cars, Tabini among that body-armored, helmeted group, he hoped.

Banichi stood up, and Tano and Jago did. Bren reached out for a careful grip on a branch, hauled himself up to his feet as he recognized the smallish, plainclothes rider among the others.

Ilisidi.

Cenedi—Ilisidi's bodyguard—and at least fifteen of what she called "her young men," on towering, long-legged shapes with the flash of war-brass about their jaws, short rooting-tusks capped with deadly metal, armed for trouble, the ridden and the unridden—fully ten, eleven more mecheiti shadowing through the brush and rock of the area, catching up with their herd, high-tempered with the fighting and the fire crackling away from already burnt ground.

And definitely Ilisidi, Ilisidi on the redoubtable Babsidi, leaning on Babsidi's withers and surveying their resources as another rider came up—leading—

God, it was—

"Hanks!" he said, and in the same instant recognized the slightly portly ateva leading that rider, an ateva also in plain riding clothes.

Lord Geigi looked straight at him. "Nand' paidhi! One is *very* glad to find you in good health."

"Indeed, I—received your messages, lord Geigi. With great appreciation. Hanks?"

"Get me away from these people," Hanks said, in Mosphei'. "Bren, get me loose!"

Hanks' hands were tied. To the pad-rings. "Hanks," he said, "shut up."

"We've the whole damn ridge going up," Tabini said. "We can't get the cars through the fire. We're going to have the whole south range going up if the fire units don't get ahead of it fast. Grandmother's graciously agreed to furnish transportation. Haven't you, 'Sidi-ji?"

"I don't know," she said over the constant quiet give of leather and the clash of harness rings. "Throwing me off the estate. Having your *staff* throw me off the estate. . . ."

"Grandmother." Tabini had a rifle in his hands. He rested its butt on his hip and kept the barrel aimed skyward. "One apologizes. One *needed* the estate. For business. One knew *you'd* know exactly who of the neighbors to go to."

"And your security couldn't figure it out?"

"Not with your persuasive charms involved, *no,* light of my day. Can we get moving?"

"Lovely morning for a ride. The smell of gunpowder and morning dew."

"Please," Bren said, foreseeing more quarrels, and more delay. "Nandiin. Please. It's descending by now. The fire's spreading—"

An explosive snort from one of the mecheiti, a squalling exchange and a scattering of armed security as a mecheita nosed through an unwilling barrier of its fellows and riders grabbed reins.

He knew when the incomer singled him out—he was sure when a perilously sharp pair of tusks nudged into his protesting hands, but he *didn't* shove down on the nose; he let the sensitive lip taste, smell, wander over his gloved fingers—

Nokhada remembered him. Nokhada had reestablished herself, *his* mecheita. It wasn't love, it was ambition, it was *man'chi,* it was a fight looking to happen, and a warm gust of mecheita breath and a slightly prehensile lip trying for his ear while he tried to get the single rein off the saddle-rings where it stayed secured, when a mecheita had no rider.

He clipped the rein to the jaw-loop of the bridle, *not* the slowest rider to get sorted out. He whacked Nokhada hard and, despite the ache and a breathtaking pain when he hauled, got her to go down, and got himself aboard for the neck-snapping rise back to her feet.

Not the last. Far from the last. Far from the most fuss. He surveyed a burning landscape from a height at which a rider was lord of most everything around him and a threat to the rest, and looked out at a sea of grass below the ridge.

A line of fire was eating away at the edge of that sea. He heard Hanks talking to him, demanding he get her loose.

He said, quietly, to lord Geigi, "Nand' Geigi, would you possibly have an idea where Hanks-paidhi's computer is?"

Geigi patted the case slung from the pad-rings on the left side. "One thought this machine might have some importance."

"Thank you," he said fervently. He saw Algini from his vantage. He'd been searching for him since he'd gotten up, and that was the last of his little household at risk— they were all safe, they'd come through without no more than the smell of smoke.

Ilisidi was vastly pleased with herself. Babsidi was fidgeting about, anxious in the fire, and the last of their party, two of Tabini's security, were still trying to get aboard when Ilisidi set Babsidi at the downward slope, straight out for the threatened grassland.

He looked back, not sure the last two were going to get up at all, but they'd made it, scarcely—drivers were getting back in the cars to pull them out, so far as he could tell, safe from the fires.

But he had the slope in front of him and his hands full—cut off abruptly as Cenedi's mecheita insisted on maintaining second-rank position with Ilisidi's, that being the established order, and Nokhada fought with one thought in her mecheita brain: getting up there and taking a piece out of any mecheita in her way to Babsidi, which he wasn't going to allow, dammit. He thumped her on the shoulder with his foot, held on with a sore arm, and held her back to give precedence to Tabini's beast as they moved out.

It wasn't the way the mecheiti understood the precedence to be, and it necessitated fits of temper, nips, squalls, kicks and threats as they reached a place to spread out.

It wasn't the way Hanks would have had it, either—she yelled after him, until someone must have told her her life was in danger.

Himself, he kept Nokhada back from Ilisidi and Tabini as they rode, Nokhada having ideas of fighting her way up there.

But Cenedi dropped back and rode beside him a moment.

"These were members of an opposition," Cenedi found it incumbent on him to say. "Those that surrendered go home. Tabini's men will see to it. We were aware 'Sidi-ji was under suspicion."

"I knew it wasn't you," he said. "Cenedi-ji, you have far more finesse. You wouldn't have shot up the porcelains."

"The lily," Cenedi said, "the lily that Damiri-daja sent. That was a dire mistake on their part. Not to say we hadn't almost persuaded Tatiseigi." Cenedi's mecheita was starting to fret, wanting to move forward in the column, and Nokhada gave a dangerously close toss of her head, nose much too near the other mecheita's shoulder, but Cenedi was looking back at the moment. "Fire's spreading. Damn, where are those planes?"

"They're sending firefighting equipment?"

"Too much is diverted because of the trouble," Cenedi said. "Which does us no service now. Hope the wind holds to the west."

One devoutly did hope so. Cenedi moved back up with Ilisidi and Tabini, and Bren cast a look back—the stench of smoke was in his nostrils, but that was only what he carried on his clothes. The wind was still in their faces, retarding the fire so far.

But he became aware he could see the leaders—the light had grown that much. The grassland stretched out in front of them, a pale, colorless color, like mist or empty air, through which the foremost mecheiti struck their staying pace. When he looked back, the same no-color was there, too, with the shadows of riders following, but the east was a contrast of dark and a fiery seam across the night that would obscure any dawn behind the ridge.

Banichi overtook him. Jago also did, from the other side, company Nokhada tolerated.

"Algini's all right," was the first thing he thought to tell them. "I saw him."

"We were talking to him, nadi," Banichi said. "Tano was."

He couldn't always tell voices on the pocket-coms. He was relieved, all the same. Hanks had settled down, damned unhappy—his computer was a melted mess, he was sure of it.

Until Jago passed it across to him.

"It took one bullet," Jago said. "I don't know if it works."

It might, at least, be made to. He slung its strap over his head, under his good arm.

He said, "Geigi's got Hanks'. I need it. I'll try just asking."

"One believes the man wants your good will," Banichi said. "A partisan of Geigi's knew where she was. Geigi's security simply walked in last night and took her—having credence with the opposition. And a very good Guild member also on his side."

"Who?" he asked.

"Cenedi," Jago said. "Of course."

"But Ilisidi wasn't responsible." What they said upset his sense of who stood where. "She was on Tabini's side. She *is,* isn't she?"

"Lords have no *man'chi,*" Jago reminded him—the great 'of course' in any atevi dealing. "The dowager is for her own interests. And fools threatened them. Fools went much too far."

"Fools attacked you," Banichi said, "elevated Hanks, broke Tatiseigi's porcelains and threatened what could be a very advantageous move for Tatiseigi, granted Tabini's desire actually to have an Atigeini in the line. Fools doubted Tatiseigi's commitment and thought, I believe, they might scare him."

"I don't think they did."

"One doesn't think so." Banichi set his knees against the riding-pad and rose up slightly, taking a look behind and skyward.

"Not quite yet," Bren said. "By the time the light is full. Then we can look. These things are very precise."

"I was looking for planes," Banichi said. Then: "The wind's changing. Do you feel it?"

It was. He saw the stillness in the grass around them, which had been bending toward the fire.

"It's not just when the lander comes down," he said, with a rising sense of anxiety. "It's where and when, in the firefront."

"Naidiri's carrying the chart," Banichi said, and put his mecheita to a faster pace, leaving the two of them.

"How fast can it burn?" he asked. He'd seen the grass-lands fires on the news. They happened. A front of fire, making its own weather as it went, creating its own wind.

"Not as fast as mecheiti can run," Jago said. "But longer. They try to stop them."

Dumping chemicals from the air.

The planes that hadn't shown up. The cars that had left them had radio. The rangers had to be doing something.

God, they had hikers out. Tourists, out to see the lander parachute down.

The rangers already had their hands full. Picnic parties. Overland trekkers.

The light was growing more and more. The wind was decidedly out of the southeast, now, the grass starting to bend.

The smell of smoke came with it, distinct from that about his clothing. The mecheiti were growing anxious, and the ranks closed up. The seam of fire was very, very evident behind them.

But Ilisidi, astride Babs, held the lead and kept the pace. No mecheita would pass Babs—pull even, maybe, but not pass.

And the talk up there was . . .

"You could have said," Tabini was saying. "You could have left a message."

"Pish," Ilisidi said. "Anyone would leave a message. I made no secret where I was going."

"The place I least wanted you, nai-ji. Unfortunate *gods,* you have a knack for worst places!"

"I could have been aiji, grandson. All it wanted was a little encouragement. And you, damn your impudence, toss me from Taiben in my nightclothes—"

"You could have been *dead,* grandmother-ji! These are fools! Have you *no* taste?"

"Well, I certainly was not going to be your stand-in for a target, nadi. I assure you. You sent me Bren-paidhi. Was I not to assume this very handsome gift had meaning?"

"A foot in every damn province!"

"As I should! Who knows when you'll stumble?"

"They regard you no more than they do me. They want the office under their hand. And you'd never do that, grandmother-ji. They'd turn on you as fast as not."

"I'm not so forgiving as you, grandson of mine. *My* enemies don't get such chances."

"Oh? And how *is* Tatiseigi?"

"Oh, sitting in Taiben, having breakfast, I imagine—waiting for a civil phone call from a prospective relative."

"I proposed an honorable union in the first place!"

"This is not a man to rush to judgment."

As the wind gusted up their backs. As the light grew in the sky.

"I tell you," Ilisidi said, "this hacking up the land with roads is a pest, and they're never where you want them. I *told* you I was against it. No, follow the precious, nasty roads, won't they, Babs? Scare all the game in the countryside, rattle and clatter, clatter and rattle—game managment, do you call it? Look, look there across the

land. *There* are herds. I'll warrant you saw none in your
clanking about last night."

"Unfortunate gods," Tabini muttered. "Demons and my
grandmother. *Naidiri! Where are the damned planes?
Call again!*"

"They say they're loading," Naidiri said.

The herds in question were in general movement, traveling away from the fire, like themselves. Once in recorded history fire had swept clear to the sea, jumped the
South Iron River and kept going until all the south range
was burned.

The paidhi didn't want to remember that detail.

"Look!" one of the hindmost said. "What's that?"

Pointing up.

Atevi eyes *were* sharp. He could scarcely see it. He had
to bring Nokhada to a stop, and others stopped.

"That's it!" he said. It had a feeling of unreality to him.
"That's it! It's coming in!"

Far, far up, and far in the distance and to the south. It
wasn't where, on the charts, they'd said.

"It loses us time," Banichi said, "southward, in front of
the fire."

It was true.

But it was in sight. They could do it. They could make
it—please God it came down soft.

23

There was one stream in kilometers all about, maybe within a day's ride, and the lander found it—landed up to its hatch in water.

Draped all over in blue and red parachute.

And not a sign of life.

"Damn quiet," Tabini said as they rode up on it. "Are they able to open the hatch, Bren-ji?"

"One would think," he said. There was, unremitting, the smell of smoke on the wind. A glance to the side revealed the fires: a long, long line of black darkening the dawn.

They rode up on it, as far as the stream edge. It was pitted and scarred. And quiet. He urged Nokhada with his foot, and Nokhada laid back her ears and didn't want to go until he started to get down—then she moved, waded down into the water.

Atevi weapons came out. All around him.

"Tabini-ma," he said. "Banichi—"

"In case," Tabini said, and Banichi urged his mecheita out, too, into chest-deep, silty water. They reached the side of the lander, mecheiti wading through an entangling billow of parachute.

Not just one chute.

Two.

Banichi leaned down and pounded with his fist on the hatch, the bottom edge of which was underwater.

Something inside thumped back. Twice.

And very slowly the hatch began to loosen its seal.

"Can you hear me?" Bren shouted. He didn't think they

could. And where the seal gave, water was surely going in.

A further gap. A flood. And the hatch folded back, dropped to the inside, in a small waterfall of incoming brown water—giving him two sweaty, scared, and very human faces.

Nokhada stuck her nose toward them and he reined her over with a wrench that half-killed his shoulder.

"Hello, there," he said. "Better vacate."

"Don't believe him!" Hanks yelled from the shore.

"That's Hanks," he said. "I'm Bren. This is Banichi." He suddenly realized he was smudged, sooted, and there was smoke on the wind.

The visitors to the world, with water risen over their couches, their stowed gear, and up to their waists, took a fearful look outside—at a dark sky, rolling smoke, and a batch of armed and suspicious riders on brass-tusked mecheiti.

Two mecheiti were still riderless.

"It's perfectly all right," Bren said. "They've got planes coming. They're beginning to put the fire out. They swear to us." He held out his hand, sooty, slightly bloodied, and shaking as it was, and put on his friendliest smile. "Welcome to the world. For the rest, you've got to trust me."

Pronunciation

A=ah after most sounds; =ay after j; e=eh or =ay; i varies between ee(hh) (nearly a hiss) if final, and ee if not; o=oh and u=oo. Choose what sounds best.

-J is a sound between ch and zh; -ch=tch as in itch; -t should be almost indistinguishable from -d and vice versa. G as in go. -H after a consonant is a palatal (tongue on roof of mouth) as: paidhi=pait'-(h)ee.

The symbol ' indicates a stop: a'e is thus two separate syllables, ah-ay; but ai is not; ai=English long i; ei=ay.

The word accent falls on the second syllable from the last if the vowel in that syllable is long or is followed by two consonants; third from end if otherwise: Ba'nichi (ch is a single letter in atevi script and does not count as two consonants); Tabi'ni (long by nature)--all words ending in -ini are -i'ni; Brominan'di (-nd=two consonants); mechei'ti because two vowels sounded as one vowel count as a long vowel. If confused, do what sounds best: you have a better than fifty percent chance of being right by that method, and the difference between an accented and unaccented syllable should be very slight, anyway.

Also, a foreign accent if at least intelligible can sound quite sexy.

Plurality: There are pluralities more specific than simply singular and more-than-one, such as a set of three, a thing taken by tens, and so on, which are indicated by endings on a word. The imprecise more-than-one is particularly chosen when dealing in diplomacy, speaking to children, or, for whichever reason, to the paidhi. In the nonspecific plural, words ending in -a usually go to -i; words ending in -i usually go to -iin. Ateva is, for instance, the singular, atevi the plural, and the adjectival or descriptive form.

Suffixes: -ji indicates intimacy when added to a name

or goodwill when added to a title; -mai or -ma is far more reverential, with the same distinctions.

Terms of respect: nadi (sir/madam) attaches to a statement or request to be sure politeness is understood at all moments; nandi is added to a title to show respect for the dignity of the office. Respectful terms such as nadi or the title or personal name with -ji should be inserted at each separate address or request of a person unless there is an established intimacy or unless continued respect is clear within the conversation. Nadi or its equivalent should always be injected in any but the mildest objection; otherwise the statement should be taken as, at the least, brusque or abrupt, and possibly insulting. Pronunciation varies between nah'-dee (statement) and nah-dee'? (as the final word in a question).

There are pronouns that show gender. They are used for nouns which show gender, such as mother, father; or in situations of intimacy. The paidhi is advised to use the genderless pronouns as a general precaution.

Declension of sample noun

Singular	Nonspecific plural
aiji Nominative	aijiin Nom pl. Subject The aiji
aijiia Genitive	aijiian Gen pl. Possession's, The aiji's
aiji Accusative	aijiin Acc. Pl. Object of action (to/against) the aiji
aijiu Ablative	aijiiu Abl. Pl. From, origins, specific preposition often omitted: (emanating from, by) the aiji

Glossary

Adjaiwaio	a remote atevi population
Algini	glum servant's name, security agent
Alujis	river Brominandi disputes re water rights
agoi'ingai	felicitous numerical harmony
aiji	lord of central association
aijiia	aiji's
Aishi'ditat	Western Association
ateva, pl. atevi	name of species
Babsidi	"Lethal"; a mecheita
Banichi	security agent
Barjida	aiji of Shejidan during the War
basheigi	universe, world, earth, environment, ecosystem
Bergid	mountain range visible from Shejidan
Brominandi	provincial governor, long-winded
baji	Fortune
bihawa	impulse to test newcomers
biichi-gi	finesse in removing obstacles
bloodfeud	principal means of social adjustment
bowing	if done deeply, with hands on knees
chimati sida'ta	fait accommpli; lit. the beast (is) cooked
daja	lady
dajdi	an alkaloid stimulant
Dajoshu	township of Banichi's origin
dahemidei	a believer in the midei heresy
Didaini	a province visible from Malguri
Dimagi	an intoxicant

haronniin	systems under stress, needing adjustment
hasdrawad	lower house of atevi legislature
hata-mai	it's all right
hei	of course
Ilisidi	grandmother of Tabini
insheibi	indiscreet, provoking attention
Intent, filing of	legal notification to the victim of Feud
Jago	security agent
kabiu	"in the spirit of good traditional example"
Maidingi	Lake Maidingi
Malguri	estate at Lake Maidingi
mainaigi	hormonally induced foolishness
Matiawa	breed of Ilisidi's horse
Moni	servant of Bren
Mospheira	human enclave on island; also name of island
Mosphei'	human language
machimi	historical drama with humor and revenge
man'chi	primary loyalty to association or leader
man'china	grammatical form of man'chi
man'chini	grammatical form of man'chi
mecheita	riding animal
midarga	an alkaloid stimulant, noxious to humans
midedeni	a supporter of the midei heresy
midei	a heresy regarding association
mishidi	awkward, regarding others' position
Nisebi	province that allows processed meat
nadi	mister
nadi-ji	honored mister
nai'aijiin	provincial lords, pl. form
nai'am	I am
nai'danei	you two are

na'itada	refusing to be shaken
nai-ji	respected person
naji	Chance
nand', nandi	honorable
Nokhada	"Feisty"; a mecheita
o'oi-ana	nocturnal quasi-lizard, likes vines
pachiikiin	game animals
paidhi	interpreter
paidhi-ji	sir interpreter
Ragi	culture to which Tabini belongs; eats game only
Ragi Associa-tion	Tabini's area, also known as the Western Association
ribbons, docu-ment	important in culture, on braids, documents
ribbons, braid	status, class
ribbon, color	says who's in what class
rings, finger	ornamental and official: used as seals
Shejidan	City of the Ragi Association
shibei	dark, bitter alcoholic drink, safe for humans
Shigi	township in weather report
sigils, docu-ment	marks on documents, seals
somai	together
Tabini	aiji of the Ragi
Tachi	herding community once on Mospheira
tadiiri	sister
Tadiiri	The Sister, fortress near Malguri
Taigi	previous servant of Bren
Taimani	province visible from Malguri
Talidi	Province of Banichi
Tano	more cheerful partner of Algini
tekikin	techs
Toby	Bren's brother
Transmontane	crossmountain Highway
tashrid	upper house of the legislature
Valasi	Tabini's father

Weinathi Bridge	bridge in the city, site of air crash
wi'itkiti	dragonette
Wilson	Bren's predecessor
Wingin	city mentioned in weather report
-ji	sir; miss; ma'am
-ma	honored sir, honored lady

C.J. CHERRYH
THE ALLIANCE-UNION UNIVERSE

More Top-Flight Science Fiction and Fantasy from
C.J. CHERRYH

SCIENCE FICTION